David Gray

Letters, Poems and Selected Prose Writings

David Gray

Letters, Poems and Selected Prose Writings

ISBN/EAN: 9783744771160

Printed in Europe, USA, Canada, Australia, Japan

Cover: Foto ©Andreas Hilbeck / pixelio.de

More available books at **www.hansebooks.com**

LETTERS, POEMS AND SELECTED PROSE WRITINGS

OF

DAVID GRAY.

EDINBURGH, SCOTLAND, 1836.   BUFFALO, NEW YORK, 1888.

EDITED, WITH A BIOGRAPHICAL MEMOIR, BY J. N. LARNED.

---

*

LIFE, LETTERS, POEMS, ETC.

BUFFALO:
THE COURIER COMPANY, PRINTERS.
1888.

PREFACE.

A DESIRE for some collection of the writings of David Gray, and for some adequate account of his life, was expressed at the time of his death, last March, very generally in his own city and by many voices elsewhere. Several friends, who felt moved thereby, came together and formed what may rightly be called a self-constituted committee of publication. They were: The Hon. James O. Putnam, the Hon. Henry A. Richmond, Mr. James N. Johnston, Mr. John G. Milburn, Miss Annie R. Annan, and the present writer. In the editorship of the work, which the latter undertook at the request of his associates, he has had their help in many ways and their counsel throughout.

The labor of collecting the scattered poems of Mr. Gray, from scrap-books and portfolios, from the files of newspapers and magazines, and from other places of obscure burial, was performed by Miss Annan and Mr. Johnston. The exertions of Mr. Johnston, Mrs. David Gray and Mr. John S. Gray brought together a rich mass of private correspondence, for the

use of the editor in preparing the biographical memoir.
If the life of David Gray and the development of his
mind and character are represented satisfactorily, it is
by the self-delineation which his letters afford. Thanks
are due to the friends who preserved them and who
have permitted them to be used.

The editor must likewise acknowledge, very thankfully, the great assistance he has had, in the proof-
reading of the work, from Mr. Walter S. Bigelow,
who has contributed to it his time, his labor and his
knowledge, without stint. The same labor has been
shared by others.

There seems to be nothing to add to these just
explanations. The work is offered, primarily, to those
who knew David Gray and who loved him; and it
needs no introduction to them. So far as it reaches
others, it will speak best for itself.

BUFFALO LIBRARY, *December*, 1888.

CONTENTS.

BIOGRAPHICAL MEMOIR.

PAGE.

I. CHILDHOOD AT EDINBURGH. 1836–1849, ... 1

II. BOYHOOD IN WISCONSIN. 1849–1856, ... 13

III. FIRST YEARS IN BUFFALO. 1856–1859, ... 35

IV. APPRENTICESHIP IN JOURNALISM. 1859–1865, ... 67

V. YEARS OF TRAVEL. 1865–1868, ... 100

VI. THE PRIME OF LIFE. 1868–1882, ... 128

VII. RELIGIOUS EXPERIENCE, ... 153

VIII. LAST YEARS AND DEATH. 1882–1888, ... 170

IX. ESTIMATES, ... 196

POEMS.

THE FOG-BELL AT NIGHT, ... 209

SIR JOHN FRANKLIN AND HIS CREW, ... 210

THE CREW OF THE ADVANCE, ... 211

TO GLEN IRIS, ... 213

OUTRIVALLED, ... 214

THE LAKE, ... 216

ELIHU BURRITT, ... 217

JEANNIE LORIMER, ... 219

COMING, ... 224

	Page.
A March Scene,	225
The Bark of Life,	227
From the German of Bodenstedt,	229
On Lebanon,	229
A Golden Wedding Poem,	231
The Soul's Failure,	232
From the German of Bodenstedt,	233
Dedication in a Lady's Album,	234
To Miss Clara Louise Kellogg,	235
Murillo's ' Immaculate Conception,'	235
New Year Greetings,	236
The Cross of Gold,	245
To J. H.,	247
Divided,	247
The Last Indian Council on the Genesee,	248
Communion,	250
A Fragment,	252
Soft Falls the Gentlest of the Hours,	254
Poem read at the Celebration of the Twenty-fifth Anniversary of the Young Men's Association of Buffalo, March 22, 1861,	256
A Nineteenth Century Saint,	263
The Chimes,	265
Poem read at the Annual Meeting of the Young Men's Association of Buffalo, February 17, 1862,	266
Poem read at the Opening of the New Library Building of the Young Men's Association of Buffalo, January 10, 1865,	272
How the Young Colonel Died,	277
The Last of the Kah-Kwahs,	281

	PAGE.
THE MINISTRY OF ART,	287
HUSHED IS THE LONG ROLL'S ANGRY THREAT,	291
THE TENTH MUSE,	294
MARY LENOX: A NEW YEAR'S ITEM IN VERSE,	299
THANKSGIVING IN WAR-TIME,	307
THANKSGIVING DAY,	308
REST,	310

LECTURES AND MISCELLANY.

ROBERT BURNS AND HIS POETRY,	311
SCIENCE AND POETRY,	323
NIAGARA FALLS BY WINTER MOONLIGHT,	347
THE GREAT STORM,	350

DAVID GRAY.

CHAPTER I.

CHILDHOOD AT EDINBURGH. 1836–1849.

DAVID GRAY,—the David Gray of this memoir,—
was born in Edinburgh, Scotland, on the 8th day of
November, 1836.* His father, Philip Cadell Gray,
was then a stationer in the Scottish capital, living and
doing business in Broughton street, at No. 68. This
is not far from the Zoölogical Gardens, in that part of
Edinburgh called the New Town. Some eight years
later, the stationer's shop was given up, and the father
made a new business venture, in the crockery trade,
establishing it in Candlemaker Row; while the family
home was removed, first to Clerk street, in the old
town, and then to No. 9 East Sciennes street, a little
farther south.

For three generations, at least, David's family had
lived in Edinburgh, or so near to it that they dwelt
continually, as it were, within the shadow of its acropo-
lis and the atmosphere of its traditions. His grand-
father, whose name he bore, had lived at the ancient
village of Cramond, six miles west of the city. His

---

* He was not akin in any known degree to the young poet of 'The
Luggie,' David Gray, whose birth, near Glasgow, was two years later,
and who died in 1861.

great-grandfather—also David Gray by name—had
been an Edinburgh tradesman, in the grocer line;
while the father of the latter, described as 'merchant,
teacher, session-clerk and land-surveyor,' passed his
days in the near village of Currie, where he married a
farmer's daughter whose name was, likewise, Gray.

David's mother, Amelia Tasker, was the daughter
of a farmer, who, during her childhood, removed from
the neighborhood of Perth to a farm known as 'Maw-
hill,' a few miles west of Loch Leven, in Kinrosshire.
This was her home until 1829, when she went to
Edinburgh, to live with an uncle, Charles Alison,—a
well-known builder, and a man conspicuous for noble
qualities. Four years afterwards, she married Mr.
Gray.

The stock from which David Gray came was thus
deep-rooted at the historic center of Scottish life; and
deep-rooted, likewise, in the fine and refining simplici-
ties and sincerities,—the thrift, the plainness, the honesty of personal and social habit,—which seem to condition life for the Scottish middle class in a nobler way
than is known to any class among other English-speak-
ing peoples of the world. Those who knew David Gray
in after-life, and in a new land, could never fail to find
in his character and in his genius a certain subtile,
distinguishing flavor—aroma—tone,—how shall we de-
fine it?—which seemed unmistakably to be the quin-
tessence of his Scottishness,—a final distillation from
those naturalizing and wholesome influences which his
ancestry, for generations, had absorbed. He was the
product, in fact, of a kind of hereditary culture very
different from the garden-tilth of conventional socie-

ties, but like the slow soil-ripening of an old vineyard, which yields after some generations an incomparable wine.

David's school-education began early, but ended too soon, perhaps, for the best training of a mind like his. His first school was one kept by his 'Aunt Ann,' in Buccleuch street, facing 'the Meadows,' and quite near to his home in Sciennes street. Among his school-fellows and playmates at that time was John Pettie, now a Royal Academician at London and one of the foremost British painters of the day. The artist-lad and the poet-lad were drawn together by a sure affinity, and the latter is said to have caught, for a time, the passion of his companion for the pencil, showing no little aptitude; but it cannot have been the true bent of his mind. From the child-school in Buccleuch street he passed, soon, to what was known as 'Brown's School,' at No. 1 Nicholson Square—just a square south from the Edinburgh College, and a short distance from the 'Heart of Mid-Lothian.' Finally, before the family quitted Edinburgh, he was a pupil, for a couple of years, at Forester's Newington Academy, situated at the corner of Newington and Salisbury Place, on the road from his home in Sciennes street to the Queen's Park. He made a mark in both schools, by quickness of learning and brilliancy of power, which never lessened his faithfulness to study, but kept him always in advance of his appointed work. He thirsted for every kind of knowledge and drank from every source that became open to him, his mind growing by what it fed on, with a healthy vigor. The fine, clear quality of his understanding was notable from those earliest days, and, for all that he knew and all that he felt, the inborn faculty of expression was ready-gifted to him. An essay on the then recondite subject of Electricity, which he wrote at that period, when scarcely eleven years old, owes its preservation to the fact that the principal of the Newington school had it put into print, as a surprising production from a pupil so young. 'Strange to say,' writes one who read the piece not long ago, 'it does not even mention the electric telegraph.'

But, while David at school was first in all forms and winner of all prizes, he was none the less a hearty school-boy, as eager for play as the rest,—as full of healthy animal life and a boy's natural lust for sport and frolic. His brother, five years younger, writing his recollections of those days, says:

David was as eager for sport as any boy could be, and, once outside the schoolroom, was continually at play. The Meadows and Links,—large parks near to our old house,—afforded ample room for the indulgence in games of ball known as 'goff,' and in many running games which he was fond of. In marbles, he was the terror of the neighborhood. No boy could win from him, but, if reckless enough to undertake it, was almost sure to come off minus his stock in trade; so that David's pockets were nearly always loaded with the plunder of the game. Indeed, the tendency to win might have taken possession of him, had not his conscientious nature asserted itself very early in life. . . . Our Saturdays were spent in taking many long walks about Edinburgh, climbing Arthur's Seat, wandering round Duddingston Loch, or making a pilgrimage to some of the suburban towns, so beautifully situated on all sides of the 'Modern Athens.' He was the enthu-

siastic observer of every object in these youthful travels,
and the love begotten in him for the old places continued through life, as his letters of later years from
there so plainly show. . . .

Our home, on East Sciennes street, was within half a
block of 'the Meadows' (a large open park and play-
ground) on one side, and five minutes walk, on the
other, of Queen's Park, in which are Salisbury Craigs
and Arthur's Seat. From our front windows, loomed
up the Lion's Head,—the crowning peak of Arthur's
Seat,—the veritable figure of a crouching lion. Up
the side of Salisbury Craigs runs the 'Radical Road,'
made famous by Walter Scott. Such places for climbing and frolicking cannot be found so near any other
city. On our way to the Queen's Park we often passed
the old house known as Jeannie Dean's house.

For a boy such as David Gray must have been,
emotionally stringed like a musical instrument, and
in tune with all the harmonies of the world, both sen-
suous and spiritual, there could not well have been
given a life more fitly and happily surrounded than
that which he lived in Edinburgh. There were the
stimulating activities of a great metropolis to play
upon the intellectual side of him, and to produce for
him, by their frictions, some tempering and quickening
of faculty, which a country lad is apt to lack; and, yet,
he had that gain of city life without the grievous losses
that fall usually on town-bred boys. For Nature is
not banished out of Edinburgh, nor made forlorn in
captivity, there, as happens to her at most places where
the human throng grows thick. She keeps her sover-
eignty, and the city is subject to her. She tolerates it,
—condescends to it,—smiles on it,—frowns on it,—
dominates it,—from her Arthur's Seat and her Castle

Rock. With Time and History for her architects, and
with Romance for her colorist, she has made it a town
to her liking, in the spirit and the image of herself,—
the town of all towns in the world for the soul of a
young poet to be nourished in.

How David's heart was held to Edinburgh through
his after-life, by the always fresh memory of his short
thirteen years of Scottish childhood and youth, appears
in the letters which he wrote, on his first visit to the
old home, returning from America in 1865,—sixteen
years after the migration of the family and himself.
They are the letters referred to by his brother in the
notes which have been quoted above. Some passages
from them will be read with more interest at this point
in the story of the life of David Gray than if left to
appear in their chronological place. Dating from
Edinburgh, August 10, 1865, he wrote to his sister:

It was on the afternoon of Saturday, the 29th ult.,
that our somewhat long and meandering and very
delightful journey through England, from London, ter-
minated at the Tweed. I was on the lookout, of course,
for the first glimpse of Scotland, and, in due time, I
had it, through a truly national shower of rain. I got
off at Berwick, just for the fun of the thing, and felt
my feet tingle strangely. Round by the sea-coast we
drove, and, soon, the names of the stations became oddly
familiar. At last, Arthur's Seat loomed up, unmistakably, and a few minutes more landed us at Prince's
street, down-stairs, on a level with the gardens. O,
but the old town looked glorious, at that first sight!
It did not seem changed in a single detail, but only
gave me an impression of its having, at one or two
points, shrunk in its proportions.

We put up at the Royal Hotel, nearly opposite the

Scott monument, and, as soon as I could go, we were off, up the Bridges for the South Side. South Bridge and Nicholson street were the same, except that 'Hutton' stood for 'Brown' on the Square Academy. I saw old 'Hooky Walker's' grocery sign, 'Pie Davy', even, survived, and half-a-dozen other old names met me from the shop doors. St. Patrick's square, Gifford Park, Clerk street,—all unchanged. I easily identified our stair, and saw the name 'Benton,' which, I think, belonged to the vicinity of old. Along Clerk street, toward Preston, there is a deal of new building. I looked over and saw that more than half of father's old garden-ground is built upon; but our corner still holds its ancient green, . . . and No. 9 East Sciennes street, barring a *little* added out-at-elbows look, is just as ever. Imagine my feelings, as I walked along the old street and turned into Bertram's yard, to see a lot of youngsters playing, one of whom at the moment proclaimed 'a scatter o' papes.'

Then he tells of a visit made to old family friends, where he found a warm welcome, and from the pleasant story of it goes on:

After tea, the three young folks of us took a long daunder over the old ground. We went to No. 9, and up the stair, and rang the bell of the old house. It is a '——— ———' who shines on the door-plate and the bell, formerly P. C. Gray's; but he didn't happen to be in,—so I only saw the door. I looked over the stair-windows, however, and saw the back green, which smells of clipshears and clockers, as of yore. Then we walked round by the Sciennes, past Eden Cottage, and away by Lover's Loan to the Grange. The place is terribly built up, and only at points here and there, with L.———'s help, could I recognize it. We went round by the cemetery, too, and past Sir Thomas

Dick Lauder's, and almost to Pow Burn, in that direction. Returning, we passed the old convent, with its carved rope of stone over the door, near Morning Side, and came down through the Links to the Meadows. There are great changes all about that locality, now; but we easily identified the trees behind which we often had played 'Hospy' and 'Tig.' All the way, as we walked, old memories came thronging up. . . .

In the same letter he gave a charming account of a visit which is explained by the following remark in his brother's notes: 'Our school vacations were spent at our cousins' in Kinrosshire, across the Firth of Forth, and the delightful theme of *Middleton* was one often recurred to among us when we met in after-life.' It was to that 'Middleton' of his summer play-days, in boyhood, and to the aunt and cousins there, that the following,—written to his sister,—refers:

Only yesterday afternoon, I went down to Granton, loitered on the pier, awhile, with the wind blowing salt about me and savoring of tangle and buckies, and took the boat thence for Burntisland. Although it was half after five P. M. when I landed, I chose to eschew the railway. I easily found my way up to the top of the Kilaly Braes, where I stood, full of queer emotions, and with you and mother uppermost in my mind. The road has been changed somewhat; so, except at Moss Mevin and Cowdenbeath, I could not, with all my trying, recover my old impression of it. Two hours of brisk walking, however, brought me full in front of Benarty, and then, of course, I was at home. I passed the Blair Adam postoffice, and there was the Lodge and the Lodge-gate,—all unchanged, except that Benarty seemed to have moved close down to the back of the postoffice buildings. O, it was a strange thing for me to turn my feet up that sweet little road, that I had trodden, last, nigh twenty years before! I followed the hedge up, close, and, soon, there was Maryborough glistening through the trees, and the old thorn standing sentry at the turn, as of yore. Then I stood on the little bridge and looked sair at the dell it crosses, which used to seem so deep and shady. A few steps more and I touched the big gate at Middleton, and peered curiously in, at a score of objects dear and familiar. I passed to the little gate and entered,—all was as it used to be. I went up, before going to the door, and examined the places where our gardens used to be, and saw that the bushes and the walks and the porch and the dial,—all—all were there, as if I had only been dreaming a score of years and had waked up among them, a little child again. I rapped at the front door, but nobody heard me; so I stole through the little gate to the back of the house, and rapped there. A little fatter than of old, but rosy-cheeked, hale, and not much older-looking than I remembered her, the dear old body met me at the door of the kitchen. I couldn't say much, but kind o' mumbled out 'didn't she know me?' and 'wouldn't she let me kiss her?' 'Na, na,—I'm no' ane o' the kissin' kind. Wha are ye? Tell me wha ye are, before ye come in here?'—something like this greeting I got; but I crowded past her, and in to the fireside; for I heard a voice that was very familiar, thereabout. 'Let me see him,' said Teenie. She was sitting at her tea, dressed in deep black, when I kissed her and vacantly asked if she didn't know me. For about a minute she looked at me, with a very hunger of eagerness in her eyes, and then, starting up, she cried: 'It's David Gray!' So Teenie knew me,—the only living being in Europe who has, or will. How she did so is a mystery to me,— for I was as unexpected as the Sultan of Turkey. . . .

Before closing the long letter from which these bits are taken, he broke into a kind of exclamation that was not usual in his writing:

Scotland! Ah, how beautiful she is! How my pen would run on if I should begin to speak her praise! Strange,—isn't it?—from the day I set foot on her soil, my tongue has lapsed into its olden forms of speech, and I am scarcely distinguishable from the braidest of the talkers I meet. 'You're no a Yankee, ony wa,' is the constant exclamation.

In a later letter, written from London, he finished the tale of his stay at Edinburgh and his report of familiar places and people; then he tells of his final visit to the dear Middleton; and of a long walk which he took, with a couple of bright lads, his cousin's children, 'away up the burn through the glen':

As I sauntered along the ancient foot-paths, and looked and listened, I could not but think that these old plantin's still hold, in their hushed and shadowy hearts, some sort of sympathy for us who loved them so well;—some sort of dim consciousness that they are dear with the memory of days that can be but once in life. It was very queer to me to be walking there, with my old and unrestful heart, while my companions bounded along with me, now picking a flower, now catching a butterfly, and full of just the same exultant, joyous sense of youth which used to fill me. Alas! I cannot say it made me feel young again.

When this was written, sixteen years had slipped between David and his Edinburgh childhood, and they had been years very full of changes and experiences for him. He had been transplanted, in the most literal sense, from an old world to a new world. The contrast between the two could not possibly have been made greater than it was; and the effects, on a spirit like his, of the shock of his readjustment, were profounder, perhaps, than he ever measured in his own thought.

At thirteen, he had welcomed the project of removal by his family to America with extravagant delight. His imagination had been set aflame by the idea of a life in the western wilderness, with all the possibilities of adventure that it seemed to hold in store. He was too full of happy visions, as his brother relates, to be saddened much, even when the time that was sore to his elders came, for parting with old scenes and friends. And, so, he turned his young face, in a fever of gladness, away from the venerable country of his birth, and voyaged westward, with as much eagerness for discovery as Columbus, and going quite as much as he into the shadowy unknown. His brother, whose recollections supply most of the materials for this earlier narrative, has written the following brief account of the family migration:

Early one morning in April, 1849, our party of something over a score was surrounded by several scores of old friends, gathered at the station to see us off; and the hurrahs for America were heartily joined in by David, as our train pulled out and sped away towards Liverpool. It was April 9th when we boarded the sailing-vessel *Constitution* at her wharf in the Mersey. Our first night was one never to be forgotten. The bunks were filled with every imaginable article needed for a sea-voyage, and scarcely room enough was left for us to huddle together. Sleep was impossible, and even David's ardor was dampened that memorable night; but, once out on the broad Atlantic, all his love of the sea, so often manifested in after-life, kept him in continual delight.

Twenty-one days brought us to New York; so that on the 1st of May we were driving up Broadway to the residence of relatives on Murray Hill,—at that time a country suburb of New York. We sojourned a week in New York, and then came the trip up the Hudson by steamer to Troy, thence by rail to Buffalo.

CHAPTER II.

BOYHOOD IN WISCONSIN. 1849–1856.

AT Buffalo, the family were welcomed and entertained by relatives who had preceded them from Scotland, and there was much endeavor to persuade them to go no farther into the west. The inducements seemed strong, but they did not prevail. David was among the loudest in protestation against a thought of drawing back from the original intent. It was the pioneer life of the Far West,—the Great West—the Wild West,—that he had set his heart upon living, and nothing less could satisfy him. How much his eager wishes had to do with the carrying of the decision, we cannot tell; but it was decided, in the end, as he urged, and the family journey was resumed. They took passage, May 22, on the screw-propeller *St. Joseph*, and were landed five days later at Sheboygan, Wisconsin. David was the historian of the voyage, and there is still preserved a letter which he wrote to his uncle, on the 29th, chronicling its few incidents. The handwriting of the letter is like a piece of copper-plate engraving, for neatness and elegant regularity.

According to Mr. John S. Gray's account, the state in which the party was dropped on the shores of Wisconsin had no encouraging aspect. He writes:

We were landed at Sheboygan, Wis., one dreary, rainy night. Why we did not all throw ourselves into

the lake, as we were left in sorry plight on that long
wharf, may have been largely due to David's hopeful
disposition.   Scarcely a place could be found in the
miserable town for protection; but we did find rooms,
while father and Walter Sanderson (our large party
from Edinburgh scattered at New York) went through
the woods to Waupun to seek a farm.   It was during
our week's sojourn there that we first saw the lovely
wild-flowers of the west, and David's admiration of
them was unbounded.

Three days teaming was required to take us to
Waupun, a distance of only sixty miles.   A short distance out, we met a man of whom we inquired if it
was very muddy on the road to Waupun.   He replied
that there was only one mud-hole, but that extended
all the way,—and so we found it.   David, trying once
to walk, sank into the mud so deep that a friendly
woodsman's aid was needed to pull him out.   Our
second night was spent at Fond du Lac, then a
miserable collection of log-huts and a long, low building
of a hotel.   It was near there that we got our first view
of the prairie, covered with spring flowers.

Several years afterwards, David began on one
occasion to write his recollections of that epoch, and of
the impression which the western wilderness made on
his feelings at the first sight.   He seems to have
planned a series of 'Chapters from a Boy's Diary',—
which would now be an invaluable piece of autobiogra-
phy to possess.   But nothing that fulfills the design has
been found, except a few introductory sentences, which
it will be proper to quote in this place: 'I come to
the true beginning of these chapters,' he wrote, 'on a
cold, dull morning in April,* which broke very dully
and slowly, some ten years ago, over a prairie in Wis-

* It must have been early June, according to the dates given above.

consin. In the person of a small twelve-year-old boy, I looked over that prairie, early that morning, in no very exuberant state of mind. The belt of trees, the brook and the farm-house where I had spent the night, appeared to be, as indeed they were, the outskirts of life and civilization. Far to the westward, nothing was visible but the waving line of prairie-horizon, as smooth and unbroken as the ocean, which, if geologists say truly, once rolled there, and which has left for all time a likeness of itself, as nearly as one could be made from solid earth.' There his pen paused, in the middle of a sheet of paper, which came to light, among other scraps and fragments, thirty years later, after his death.

The notes furnished by David's brother continue, as follows:

Our farm was two miles from Waupun village. There we spent the summer; but we were not pleased with it, and a move to a new farm was proposed. The fall was dry, and soon we had our first fight with prairie fires. One eventful Sunday morning, when ready to shut up the house and go to the village, to church, the approaching fiend was seen. All hands able to fight fire turned out. I was left by the well, to keep the cattle from drinking the water that had been drawn for the putting out of the fire. The others went out as far as possible, to keep it from getting to our hay-stacks and buildings. They were, at first, unable to check the fire, and they came running towards the house, crying that all was lost;—but a foot-path near our buildings made a second place of defense, and there, much owing to David's courage and hard labor, the flames were subdued. What a weary, begrimed-looking family we were, after that fight!

The winter of 1849–50 was spent by the family in Kingston, a little town 20 miles to the west of Waupun; but David and Walter Sanderson (afterwards our brother-in-law) were left on the old farm to care for the stock, our feed being there. Their experience that winter in keeping bachelor's hall has furnished many an amusing anecdote. It was then, as he has often told us, that he succeeded in cooking something that not even the dogs or pigs would eat. But the novelty of the situation kept it from being too tiresome. Besides, a few miles distant, a Scotch family named Lindsay lived, and the boys from there often came to enliven the time, while David went as often to stay with them for a day or two. So, the winter was not without much jollity and enjoyment.

With early spring, came the time for driving the stock to the new farm, which had been purchased from the government, on the banks of the Fox River and 30 miles west. It took David and Walter three days to drive the short distance. The family was now reunited, on this new farm, in an unsettled neighborhood, far from civilization, and its log-house was the best protection we had for several years. Indians were, at first, our only neighbors, and David's love for them was not increased by acquaintance. I remember that a large encampment of them was established, once, on the bank of the river, only a few hundred yards from our house. One night, after all was quiet, David and I stole quietly down to their wigwams and picked our way amongst many sleeping natives. Their mode of living, as seen at that time, was certainly not what inspired 'The Last Council.' They were a thieving set, and we often had articles taken by them. On one occasion, David went on horseback to the little village of Packwaukee. He had to tie his horse at the end of the corduroy bridge which spanned the river, and walk across to the town. When he came back, he found his horse gone; but he saw the tracks of the animal and followed them, and came on a party of red-skins deliberately leading his horse away. Quick as a flash he snatched the bridle, mounted, and was off at full speed, before they realized what he was doing. In those days he was quick and nimble in his movements.

The work of clearing the farm began, now, in earnest; and David, from that time, never did less than a man's work, cutting down trees, splitting rails, laying fence, or breaking up the wild land.

Although there was all a sportsman could ask for in the way of game, David was never a success in that rôle. Not long after our first coming to the Fox River, he and I went out on it and paddled our way into a bayou, overgrown with weeds and bottomless in its depth of mud. Ducks were packed in on all sides of us, and David stood up in the boat to give a broadside amongst them. The gun had been heavily loaded for several days, and the rebound sent him, head over heels, down amongst the slimy weeds. He had not learned to swim at that time, and, even if he had, it would have made him no better off; for the weeds kept him from helping himself. It was with difficulty that I got hold of him and helped him into the boat, and, for a time, the chances for both of us seemed strongly in favor of the ending of our careers there and then. A pair of badly frightened boys, in a boat half filled with water, and minus our gun,—we did not stop to see how many ducks had suffered, but made our way to shore as best we could.

Our winters were employed in clearing new fields for cultivation, and, for three years, David had no chance to attend school. It was not till the winter of 1853–4, when we had sufficient land under cultivation, that he was able to advance his education, so long neglected, by going back to Waupun to attend the High School. He was joined by several of our old friends,—the Lindsays. They took rooms in an old store, belonging to father, and how they got on may be

2

judged from their first day's experience. On setting
up their stove, they put the pipe through an opening in
the ceiling, and thought very little of what was to
become of the smoke, but started their fire without
solving that question. For a minute or two, the fire
went well enough; then, suddenly, the smoke began to
pour out of every opening, in volumes. They cast lots
to see who should investigate the cause of this trouble,
and it fell to David. Going up-stairs, he found they
had run the pipe into the room of another tenant, who
had quietly covered over the end with a plate. The
boys had many adventures that winter and were very
happy together; but their time was well spent in
earnest study.

At the end of this term of school in Waupun,
David, with one of his companions, returned to his
home at Roslin, on foot, doing what he called 'a valiant
trudge,' in which 'we had a chance' (he wrote a few
days after) 'to become intimately acquainted with our
bundles; for my part I felt, for a long time, as if some
vast responsibility had been sustained by my shoulders.'
This was said in a letter dated April 8, 1854, which
was the first of a long correspondence that he carried
on with one of the Lindsays above mentioned, who had
been his school-mates and room-mates at Waupun.
The friend to whom he wrote, now a prominent business man at Milwaukee, has preserved all these letters
with affectionate care, and they are the earliest which
have been found for use in the preparation of this
memoir. 'I am now,' continued David, 'fairly into the
working system, again. Occasionally, I take a lazy fit,
and sigh for the happy days we spent in the old room.
. . . Alas! I am afraid neither you nor I will see such
a good time again in a hurry.' That he did not drop

his studies when he came home, even though the work of the farm was hard, appears in this: 'I am now studying algebra in all my leisure time (which is not very much). I have got as far on as the binomial theorem (which see), and find it very interesting. I am determined, if I can make it out, to prosecute my studies and amass something like a respectable education. What is the use of spending our lives in this world without having our minds ever lifted above the muck or sand which we cultivate? To be sure, there is little leisure time, but it will increase; the winter, at least, with some calculating, can be ours, and, certes, there's good long ones in this country.'

Some months later, writing again to the same friend, he said: 'I think I will be better able to push my studies this winter; at least I am anxious to do so. I think of adding land-surveying, geometry and, perhaps, Greek grammar. I am sure you will not fail to make great advancement this winter under J——'s tuition. I would advise you to devote considerable attention to English composition, than which there is nothing more essential and available for the cultivation and refinement of the mind.'

At about this period, some time in the year 1854, David formed an acquaintance which proved to be one of the important occurrences of his life. His brother tells of the beginning of it, in this wise:

Our neighborhood had now become well settled, and, in one of the new families, not far from us, was a young man of David's age whose name was also David, —David Taylor. During the summer of 1854, or about that time, they began to find in one another a

common sentiment which drew them together. This
was a wakening love of literature. They were together
as constantly and as often as if they had been the most
ardent lovers,—closeted in their rooms beyond midnight,—and no one was admitted to the secrets of their
conclave. This devotion to each other was continued
till David went, in August, 1856, to Buffalo. Not long
since, talking with Mr. John Muir,—who was then a
neighbor, and who is now the well-known naturalist of
California,—he said that he remembered working, one
day, on the roads—as was the custom in those days—
with the two Davids, and their conversation filled him
with envious delight. They had been reading some of
Dickens' works, and their comments on the characters
were such as he had never heard before. Their talk
gave him the first spurring to read and learn from
books that he had ever had.

David's knowledge of books and authors had been
greatly extended by constant association with Walter
Sanderson, who was a walking encyclopedia on these
matters; and, now, the poetical part of his nature was
stirred by contact with David Taylor. We found
ways and means, sometimes, to discover what was going
on behind the locked door. Often, the one was reading
to the other an attempt at verse. It took a long time
for them to muster up courage enough to send a poem
from each to *Graham's Magazine*, and then with what
disgust did they find an acknowledgment of 'two pretty
poems'! The word '*pretty*' was an offense beyond
forgiveness.

It was a rare, strange fortune—if we dare name it
so—which brought these two lads, David Gray and
David Taylor, out of different parts of Scotland, across
the ocean, into one lonely neighborhood of that sparsely
peopled region of the earth where they found themselves together. They seem to have fitted one another

as if it had been in the decree of their lives that they should meet. There were obviously great differences of character between them, but only such as piqued and stimulated their strong affinities of feeling. They were alike in poetical temperament, and so equally sensitive to the intoxicants of the imagination that they found a common ideal world, into which they were rapt, and where they lived together, feeling themselves mostly apart from other men. The result was a kind of twinship, closer than friendship, which is sometimes seen in the world, but not very often. David Taylor appears to have been, in some respects, the more strenuous spirit of the two, and the poetic fire had been kindled in him at an earlier time. The inflammable imagination of David Gray, which flashed at the contact with this fiery soul, had scarcely discovered itself before. He, always, in after-life, spoke with a kind of awe of the wonderful awakening in him which occurred through his intercourse with David Taylor, and never stinted his acknowledgment of the debt he was under to the latter, for influences that lasted as long as his life. That the influences of that singular and passionate communion were not altogether healthful, intellectually, but that they tended toward a certain fantastic exaltation of mind, looks probable, and it may be well that the intercourse of the two friends was interrupted; but, for so long a time as it continued, one cannot doubt its great importance to the development of the genius of David Gray.

David Taylor, who has never quitted the scenes of his companionship with the former, still cherishes the memory of it, with a fondness which time does not wear

out, and has told some interesting incidents of it in
recent letters to a common friend. Gray had often
spoken, in later life, of a memorable day in the field,
when the two Davids, sitting together at the plowman's
dinner which they brought with them, read something
in the scrap of newspaper that wrapped it,—something
by Gerald Massey, or about him (those who remembered the story were not distinct in their recollection
of this point)—which stirred them very deeply and
marked a notable date in their experience. It is in
allusion to this that David Taylor writes the opening
passages of the following:

I remember the circumstance, for I was the companion. Gray brought his dinner in that paper; but it
was the spinning of Massey nigh to death, in the silk-
mill, that was talked about. Gray was very indignant
about his usage, and so was I. Some of his lines may
have been read,—I do not remember; but I do remember repeating better poetry,—which was the pretty
stanza of Moore, beginning with—'Let fate do her
worst, there are moments of joy,' and ending with—
'But the scent of the roses will hang round it still,'
together with other scraps I had upon my memory.
Gray was greatly taken with the matter and the manner, and, from that day forth, we were bound together
like a team of wild horses which no impediment or
barrier could stop.

Byron was my poet in those days. I had read *Lara*,
but I had not the book. After a great deal of manœu-
vering, for there was scarcity of capital, I bought
Byron complete for a dollar and a half. Then, the
opening lines of *The Bride of Abydos*, and the grand
cadences scattered through *The Corsair*, etc., had to
take it. Then Gray got Moore—a splendid book; but,

as I had told the bookseller to send for it, on that ground I claimed it. I have both the books, yet.

We lived little more than a mile apart, and visited one another *in the night*. Had that mile been water, and that water the Hellespont, I have no doubt it would have been crossed, or a brand-new tragedy given to history. At our meetings, we passed through wonderful states of excitement, which I can hardly understand at the present day. Gray complained, once, that my eyes frightened him; fire from them, he said, being actually seen. The light in his own eyes, no doubt, contributed to the illusion. Every night that we met, our pockets, of course, contained original compositions in prose and verse, to be commented upon, approved or condemned. Poe, I remember, was a great gain. We ran across *The Raven* in a magazine. We had never seen nor heard of Poe, before; but all earthly cares were set aside till the three volumes of his poems and tales were got.

Of all our lucubrations I can remember little. One couplet of his struck me very forcibly. It was before a battle, fought at night, both sides for the most part invisible. The enemy's bugles are heard, challenging, but faintly and from afar, and

> Then shrieking echoes through the glen,
> For ours are answering back again—

prelude to the onset. The whole yet lingers in my mind like a picture of Rembrandt's.

Night after night we had it,—not in succession, but at uncertain intervals; each giving the other always the old-country ' convoy,'—that is, going nearly home with him. One night, I remember, we were greatly delighted with the northern lights,—a most unusual display,—but, as we remarked, more to the east than was common; and, indeed, they were,—for before I got home it was broad day.

Before he left for Buffalo I thought it a pity he

should go unprovided; so I bought another Byron for
him (Gray did not like Byron very well; his private
character being in the way), and, in return, he gave
me Coleridge. . . .

He had the one quality that might be blazoned on
all the ensigns of his nation, as their own transcendent,
embodied word—*courage ;* although that was not his
own opinion, either, and he used to complain to me of
his lack of it. I remember distinctly of his writing
to me of the great fear that possessed him on the train,
when he first went to Buffalo.

In a subsequent letter, David Taylor tells more sig-
nificantly the story of the purchase of Moore's poems,
which he had mentioned above:

That time he got 'Moore,' I remember, he came over
with it, not caring to keep it, seeing I had a sort of
claim on it, although he had really bought the book.
I recollect he had his good clothes on. Now, neither
of us cared a pin for what we wore, and why he was,
in a manner, *dressed* on that occasion, I know not; but
I noticed it in the middle of the excitement. After
mentioning the way he had got the book, and signifying
his wish to keep it, if I was so minded, he undid it
from its wrappings and gently handed the splendid
volume over to me. I seized it, greedily, ran rapidly
through the engravings,—paused at one, in which the
view was carried to the sea-line: 'The light above the
ocean,' I cried;—' see the light along the far horizon !
Is n't that beautifully done ? '. Selfishness got the better of me; the book must be mine. Gray, a little
sorrowful at seeing me thus giving way to temptation,
and doing by him what he would not have done to me,
was pleased, too, on the whole, turning his face toward
me, patiently bearing with me and forgiving me. The
memory of that transaction haunts me, ever since I

have recalled it. It is all in Gray's favor; but, at the same time, not altogether against me,—seeing he could *borrow* the book as long and as often as he pleased.

The following is related in still another letter by the same writer:

One day I found him rather quiet and thoughtful, and expected something of moment; for whoever is quiet and thoughtful has generally something to make him so. I was not disappointed when he began, very softly, by asking me if my folks ever bothered me about the poetry business and our carryings-on. I said, no, they never did; that they rather inclined to curtail the storing-in of so many books, all of the same kind, it was true,—but, continued I, 'they have found out that that's no go.'
'Well,' said he, 'you are well off'; and proceeded to inform me of what he had to undergo with his papers,—his sister generally pilfering and irreverently reading and deriding our 'best efforts.' 'But,' said he, 'I have put a stop to it; I have been to Portage, and—look here!' He then showed me a large leather folio, with a little lock and key attached. 'I can put our things in there, now,' said he, 'and lock them up.' 'How much did you give for it?' said I. 'Ten wretched shillings.' 'Oh!' said I,—'Campbell might have been got for that.' 'Well, but what could I do?' 'You could have made a box,' said I, 'and I have a little brass padlock,—just the thing.' 'Well, well,' said he, 'it's done, now, and we are safe, anyway.' But, alas, it appeared that the safety proved as fanciful as our wares; for his sister informed me, long afterwards, that, by squeezing in the edges of the folio, it opened at the ends, where the female hand could be deftly introduced and the whole precious documents of Apollo taken out and read without difficulty.

Returning now to the notes furnished by Mr. John S. Gray, we take up the thread of David's life on the Wisconsin farm, as it is traced in them:

One of the duties of backwoods life was going to mill, and, for several years, our nearest grist-mill was Kingston, eighteen miles away. An early start in the morning was necessary, and David was the one often chosen to go on the long, lonely drive. The return home was delayed by waiting for the grist, and it was always far into the night before we would hear the welcome sound of his return. The drive was a lonely one, but David had always so much 'communing with nature' to do that he never seemed to mind it. It was in the summer of 1854 that, coming home very late one night from Kingston, he was caught in a terrific storm. The lightning flashed continuously, and the thunder kept up a deafening cannonade, while wind and lightning together tore up trees in the woods, as he passed along; but, beyond the wetting, he enjoyed it all, and gave a most graphic description of it, many years after.

Early in the summer of 1854 we began to build our new farm-house on the hill. A raftsman, taking his lumber up the Fox River, was induced to make an exchange of lumber for a gold watch and some money; so that the materials were landed at our door. David was helping to excavate for the cellar, one day, when he struck what had the appearance of a round, smooth stone, but which proved to be an Indian's skull; and, soon, the whole skeleton, with Indian ornaments, was exhumed. Some of the latter were given to a museum in Portage City, and the former was laid in another resting-place.

We remember that fourth of July well, when we all went to a grand celebration at Packwaukee. A band was advertised to furnish music. There were to be volunteer toasts and minute-guns, and a free dinner to all. David was greatly amused at the band, which was composed of two drums and one fife. The minute-guns were fired from a blacksmith's anvil.

Through all our years on the farm, the *New York Tribune* was a constant visitor. When *Uncle Tom's Cabin* was published, the two were enough to work us up to fever-heat on the subject of slavery, and largely to that is due the fact that David became a radical abolitionist. The fall of 1854 was a time of great importance, for it was then we moved into our new house.

In the autumn of 1854, David had planned going to Portage, for a term at the academy, there, and was hopeful of securing, again, the companionship of his friend Lindsay, who had been one of his mates at Waupun the previous winter; but circumstances caused a change of plan, and he became school-teacher instead of pupil. In a letter to Lindsay the following January he wrote:

You will be rather astonished when I tell you that I have, instead of going to Portage, as I talked of, taken upon myself the duties and responsibilities of dominie *in veritas*. I got a pretty good chance, there being a small school and easy duties, with $15.50 per month; and, as we were none too plentifully supplied with the sinews of war, I concluded it was best to take it. I get on first-rate, have no difficulty at all, and consequently like it pretty well. I have taught just half of my term (three months), and have not wearied, scarcely. The location is about ten miles north of Roslin, near Montello, and on the banks of that classic stream, the Fox. Isabella [his sister] is also teaching, about four miles from here, on the same road; she gets ten dollars per month and board at one place, close to

the school-house.   So, you see, there is quite a learned
circle of dominies assembled at Roslin every week.

Another passage found in this letter seems to indicate that there were thoughts, that winter, in the family
at Roslin, of a fresh migration, Kansas-wards.

The public mind [of Roslin] appears, with regard
to the subject of emigration, to have a hankering a
little farther south, instead of north, as Minnesota is.
From comparing the temperature with that of Green
Bay, the winters average four degrees colder at Fort
Snelling, and a corresponding shortness of summer
season is observable, also.   So, I think, if we take a
trip this fall, we should try it somewhere in the Kansas
direction.

But, however much it may have been talked of, the
projected reconnoissance beyond the Mississippi was
never undertaken.   Another spring and summer found
David hard-bound to farm-work, deeply interested in
the ravages of the potato disease and quoting the
prices of potatoes and oats in letters to his friends.
At the same time, he was making diligent use of all
his scant leisure hours in reading and study, and was
preparing, more determinedly than before, for a term
in the fall at the Portage academy.   Towards the end
of October, that year, he wrote to his friend Lindsay
that he hoped to be able to go in about a month, and
expected 'to get board for two dollars per week.' Again,
striving to persuade his former school-chum to go with
him, he adds: 'I think we could do better for ourselves than we did at Waupun.   We might take
monastic vows for the winter, and eschew wrestling
and evening parties, which things are a snare.'

This time, the ambitious hope was realized, and David entered the school in Portage (Brittain's School, his brother calls it); but it can have been for a few weeks, only. He left it, even before the end of December, to engage once more in teaching, 'tempted,' as he writes, 'by lust of gold,' to earn twenty dollars per month for three months. He had greatly enjoyed his little taste of student-life at Portage, as he wrote to Lindsay, who had failed to accompany him:

There was a number of good scholars, evidently bent on improvement, and I had a most excellent boarding-place; so that, if there was less of 'game a-foot,' there certainly was a proportionally less degree of rowdyism than at Waupun, during our ever-to-be-remembered, never-to-be-forgotten campaign of 1854. The young men have a lyceum, at which your humble servitor, of course, cut a figure; and the scholars make up a paper regularly, the editorial chair of which, during a fleeting season, was occupied by the afore-mentioned servitor. Besides my old studies, of algebra, etc., I have commenced geometry, and—and—Latin and Greek, to what end deponent saith not—yet. By the by, I have two 'right smart' scholars in algebra and geometry; so I have some encouragement to study, just now, to keep ahead of them.

This letter was written January 20, 1856, and he had then been, he says, teaching for a month, with two months more of his engagement to fill. 'I get along very easily,' he adds; 'have fifteen scholars, and board at one place,—which circumstances, combined, tend greatly to the amelioration of my social state.' His school was four miles east from his home at Roslin.

There is nothing in his letters at this period—the

few which have been found—to show that David was depressed in spirits or lacked ambition in his work; but his brother states that some disheartening had happened to him. During the summer of 1855, his uncle William, from Buffalo,—an uncle much loved and admired by David, always,—had visited the household at Roslin, and the visit had been a great delight. It was the wish of this uncle that David should quit the farm and quit the west, to try his fortunes at Buffalo. The idea of such a change in his scheme of life, being once lodged in his mind, produced an inevitable unrest. As his brother writes:

Hard labor had begun to tell on him. The enthusiasm of the first years was giving way to a sober conviction that nothing but a life of toil could be looked for on the farm, and, instead of the once happy boy, he was sadly silent and abstracted, nearly all the time. The exception was when the two Davids got together, to consult on literary subjects, and that was as often as circumstances would permit. Their separation during the winters was generally followed by a several days session, to make up for lost time.

More than ever, during this interval of anxiety and unrest, he found solace in books and in his pen. By good fortune, some moderate fund for a town library had come into existence, and the expenditure of it was wisely entrusted to David and his brother-in-law. He enjoyed a feast beyond description in the selecting and the reading of the books got together for this little library, which remained, for the time, in his custody, at his father's house. Meanwhile, he and David Taylor were writing a deal of verse, more or less overstrained in motive and more or less rough in workmanship, no doubt, but full of lyric promise. His first published poem, *Outrivalled*, which appears elsewhere in this volume, was written during some of these last months of Gray's life in Wisconsin. It was contributed to a magazine issued by students at Carrol College, on the solicitation of a young gentleman whose acquaintance David had made at Portage, and who is now an eminent clergyman at Chicago—the Rev. Charles Thompson.

In August, 1856, the new path in life which he had longed for was opened suddenly before him. There came to him, from his uncle at Buffalo, the offer of a place which seemed to have been niched for him by the kindest of all kindly fates. It was the post of secretary and librarian to the Young Men's Christian Union of Buffalo,—an institution in its prosperous youth. He accepted the proffered office with glad eagerness; but, when the time came for quitting his home, his parents, his sister, his brother, his friends, he suffered as only a warm nature can. His heart was, most of all, wrenched by the parting with his mother, for whom his love exceeded the common bounds.

So ended David Gray's *Lehrjahre*—apprentice years —in the then far west. The life and the labors of a pioneer family in middle Wisconsin, thirty years ago, among neighbors dispersed at mile-wide intervals, with the chances of intellectual companionship that such a neighborhood would offer, with two brief terms of schooling at the high school or academy of a small western town,—these are not quite the training and education that one would plan for a boy of genius, between his thirteenth and his twentieth years. But

who can say that they were not better for David Gray
than Harvard, or Oxford, or Heidelberg might have
been? His natural genius was never warped, as might
possibly have happened to it from a more artificial cultivation. The unique, indescribably charming native
quality that was so marked in it, may have owed no
little development to the long brooding-time of that
isolated, worldless, primitive life. He kept his orig-
inality of imagination and speech, his independence of
thought and of act. He did not stay uncultured,—for
he was of those who cannot be uncultured;—of those
who will find the means of culture in all situations,
under all circumstances. On Fox River, the circumstances were more difficult than they might have been
at Oxford; but the boy on Fox River found more in
his *Weekly Tribune*, his half-dozen books, his one intimate intellectual companion, and the wilderness around
him, than another would find in the Bodleian Library.
It is possible that he had the rare fortune to be full-
fed, without being over-fed. If he did come to manhood with some leanness of knowledge, there seems no
certainty that even that was ill to him, in after-life.
He made himself a scholar whom any college might
have had pride in producing, and he carried no burden
of learning which he could not use.

CHAPTER III.

On his coming to Buffalo, in the summer of 1856, David found a home among his relatives which replaced, as far as could be, the hearth he had left; and the new life into which he settled himself was, undoubtedly, pleasant to him, from the first. He seems to have looked at Buffalo with expectant eyes, that were ready to grow fond; while the good city turned a kindly face to him, as though promising that she would take him to her heart. His employment was to his liking, and the surroundings of it were delightful. The Young Men's Christian Union—it was styled so at that period —was then in the fourth year of its existence, and fairly well sustained. It had collected a well-chosen, small library of miscellaneous literature, and most of its books were still invitingly new. Its rooms, on the third floor of the Kremlin Hall building, at the corner of Eagle and Pearl streets, were extremely attractive, and the prospect from their windows, looking westward, toward the river and lake, was one which lives in the memory of the people who used to enjoy it. In those days, there was no city hall, nor other tall building,—nor many buildings of any description, in fact, —to shut in the view. In Gray's first letter, after settling himself in Buffalo, to his friend David Taylor, he gave this description of the place:

3

The Kremlin Hall, in which I am at present sitting,
is a large four-story building, on a rising ground, about
half a mile from the shore of Lake Erie. A little to
the right, I look and see the mouth [the head] of the
Niagara River,—the spot where the accumulated waters
of the great lakes first get the hint about Niagara.
The very Fox River sends its dribble right past
my nose. And, then, away in front, the great lake
stretches, full in sight, without a break, into the dim
distance. In storm and calm it is splendid. At night,
I see the long sea-line dimly illuminated, like the ocean
in the picture in Moore; and, sometimes, in a storm of
wind, the waves come down upon the long breakwater
like a thousand regiments of Scotch Greys. It takes
no great stretch of imagination to make it into the
ocean. . . . If you had n't written 'Beyond the Ocean'
I would have penned it, myself. Something must come
out of that, and shortly, too.

These last words intimate a stir of impulse which
he felt little of, on the whole, during those first weeks
or months in Buffalo. He was not quite himself in
his new environment. He experienced a certain distraction from the life of the city. After a month of
it, he wrote to his school-friend, Lindsay: 'It is a
great change—so great that I am almost inclined to
think that I have not fully realized it, yet; but, on
the whole (it is a dull, wet day, to-day, and my spirits
are tolerably sober), and on the whole, I say, I think
the change, whatever the ultimate upshot may be, is
for the better. It is rather a comfortable thing to
keep your hands clean and your back dry in all
weathers, and never to feel the oppression of labor,
dragging at your boots and making you an inch shorter
at night than at morn.' He possessed, as he knew, a

wonderful protean quality of talent and temperament. 'I can adapt myself,' he wrote to David Taylor, 'to everybody and take everything as a matter of course. I am always wondering that I don't wonder. I've never been surprised at anything.' So, it amuses him to find himself 'spinning along the broad streets of Buffalo, jostling beaux and belles,' and he 'laughs in his sleeve,' he says, 'at passing for one of them.' He is forced, nevertheless, to confess, that he has not yet found new inspirations to replace the old ones. 'There is a great temptation,' he writes, 'to smother the flame.' 'Not that the city can furnish,' he goes on to explain, 'any purer or keener pleasures; but the bustle and confusion, the brick walls and paved streets and lamp-posts, form a scene for dreaming not quite so favorable as sunset from the end of your house, or moon-set from John Mahaffy's fence.'

But, if the new surroundings are a little distracting, he would not have it supposed for a moment that he is discontented with them, or unhappy in them. It is true that he looks forward with strong hopes to a possible visit home, the next spring; and he notes it as very strange that he has 'lost all idea of going to visit Scotland,' because 'thinking of Wisconsin has fairly scorched Scotia out of my head; but do n't think,' he makes haste to protest, 'that I am homesick and rue coming here. No, sir! I do n't intend to do that, by any possibility. The fact is, as far as the world goes, I am a hundred per cent. better off, here. But, if I had been transported into the Mussulman's heaven of houris' eyes, I should have occasionally fallen asleep in their full blaze, and taken a quiet doze and dream of home.'

Then, 'talking of eyes,'—and valiantly dashing, perhaps, a homesick tear or two out of his own,—he runs off into a slightly rattling discourse about the 'stunningly bright kipples' he has seen since he came to Buffalo. He finds it 'a perfect study to walk down Main street and draw blanks and prizes out of the lottery of passers-by. All sorts and sizes are exhibited.'

The half-understood confusion of mixed feelings which he found in himself, at that transition-time of his life, is revealed in the outpouring letters which he wrote to his supreme friend, 'Davie,' during his first months in Buffalo. There is a medley of topics and a medley of moods in every one of them. Somewhat slowly, David worked himself back into occasional states of mind fit for verse-making, and began to exchange bits, outlines, and sometimes complete poems, with his correspondent, for reciprocal criticism. His first venture was an attempt at the 'something' which 'must come out,' as he had said, of that inspiring view of Lake Erie from his windows. Unhappily, it was only a fragment—a few lines of melodious, fanciful verse—which he seems to have never finished. He wrote to his friend that it 'had birth from Lake Erie one fine summer-like day, and would have been *The Vision of the Lake* if it had lived.' The lines were these:

Oh, never breaks the sound of oars
Along these misty mantled shores !
Oh, never stirs among the trees
The spirit of the slumbering breeze !
But, like a freighted bark with golden sails,
The sunset fails and fails,
Without a breath, into the blest
Enchanted regions of the West.

Oh, never on these changeless shores
Pale winter blights and spring restores ;
But, gathering glory year on year,
The flowers their living faces rear,
While over all forever streams
A summer rich and dim with mist and dreams.

Oh, silence, silence ! Not a breath
Troubles the calm—the calm of Death.
And never, never, as I wist,
Stand dimly pictured on the mist,
The ships, or phantom-ship-like things,
With spectral light upon their wings.

This is in the spirit of Poe; and Poe was, at that time, very nearly, if not quite, Gray's first favorite among the poets. His tastes were rather catholic,—he had a hungry appetite for everything that was really poetry; but the music and the mysticism—the weird dream-haze in Poe's poems—were peculiarly fascinating to his imagination and his ear.

The two Davids, in their correspondence, exchanged opinions on many poets, and on many poems besides their own, and the frank criticisms of the one whose letters we are permitted by his friend to read are extremely interesting. Some passages may be quoted with justification:

BUFFALO, *September* 23, 1856.

. . . That . . . brings me back to a favorite topic—Poe. Almost the first thing I did when I got into this library, was to lay violent hands on an old volume of the *Southern Literary Messenger*, wherein, you know, our spink figured as editor. I found nothing new, except some critiques which we have not seen. No new poems,—but a good many of the old ones, in dif-

ferent stages of progression towards the state in which
they are booked. I tell you, Poe was an awful fellow
to revise and alter. You could hardly tell some of
his pieces in their primal form. Partly to give you an
idea of this, and partly because there is little that is
new, I will copy *The Valley Nis:*

. . . .

No wind in Heaven, and lo ! the trees
Do roll like seas in Northern breeze
Around the misty Hebrides.

. . . .

Don't you think he should have left that as it is,
which commences 'No wind in Heaven'? That 'Do
roll like seas' is first-rate. You've seen, in a storm of
wind, the trees roll and sway, and, especially if you are
looking down on them from a hill, the white backs of
the leaves turned up, the pitch and turmoil of the
whole, give it the very look of a sea in a storm.

. . . I have never made out to see an edition of
Chatterton, yet, although I have tried several times;
neither have I seen Tenny* in his last coat and trow-
sers; but I shall make it out soon and report faithfully.

BUFFALO, *October* 28, 1856.

. . . Now for general remarks: You have written,
this time, too wildly, too savagely. You must calm
yourself down, or you won't fulfill printing requisites,
which are, care, perfect guardedness at all points—not
a rib exposed nor a useless feather flying. . . . In
writing about love, great caution is required, for it's a
risky business. There's no fear of your writing *silly*
things in this line; your error is, galloping splash-
dash, and drawing in things out of place. You would
always need carefully to review, and if you could, in
some kind of way, have your steed well bitted when
you start out with her, it would be well. Do you write

* Tennyson.

with printing in view? That should help you greatly. For I do believe that you have in you what the favored few only possess,—namely, imagination. Again, before you can stand up in print, you will have to undergo a world of labor and study. Your powers are the most undisciplined I ever knew. If I had half your brain I could make Buffalo vocal. As it is, a dry meal-pock occupies the region of my caput, and whatever is shaken out is unmistakably dry.

BUFFALO, *November* 17, 1856.

. . . I'm bursting to divulge. Tenny is yours, and with the morrow's sun will be speeding to your embrace. I am afraid you will be disappointed; and yet, if you have any bowels, I don't see how you can. The fact is, I am aware that you like a large book, and the book is a small book; but oh! gem! pearl! chucky! what a book. The portrait, I cannot pick a flaw in; it far transcends the one in my copy. There are numerous pieces not to be found in mine, and all that are in mine or elsewhere are here. The type and arrangement, according to my ideas, are beautiful, and the gilt—Finis.* . . .

I am glad you are coming to your senses at the eleventh hour. I have long known *The Lotos-eaters* as a poem which swayed me mightily. I don't see how the idea of dreamful calm and repose could be better conveyed. . . . The fact is, Tenny does a thing invariably after a way of his own—as nobody else would think of doing it. He is silly on his own model, and his namby-pamby (an abominable word—a word of my father's) is nobody else's namby-pamby. Enough. My sentiments on Tenny are well defined. . . . Altho' his powers are none of the mightiest, they are unquestionably of the finest kind. The piece you quoted in

* It was undoubtedly a copy of Ticknor & Field's 'blue and gold' edition.

your letter has long been a favorite passage. I knew
a kiplet of it and used to operate on it, long before I
saw Moore between boards. . . .

Having botched a sea-piece, I turned my energies to
the construction of a ' Love-song;' but I was so thoroughly heart-whole that not a whine could I emit. I
endeavored repeatedly to tear up some old gashes, failing the infliction of any new ones; but the whole was
such an entire failure that I immediately conceived and
mentally executed a device, with motto. (The thing
is not entirely original, but never mind.) Heraldically
described the thing is this:—a heart gules, on a field
azure; Cupids twain kicking and otherwise maltreat-
ing the heart, in which they have vainly endeavored
to stand a good article of the harpoon description.
Motto (foreign): ' *Devi lishto ughw ork.*'

BUFFALO, *December* 13, 1856.

. . . You must know that the strange, migratory
tribe of strolling lecturers, musicians, men with pano-
ramas, etc., are brought into immediate connection with
your servant, he being guardian of a public hall.
Well, a couple of this tribe hove in sight one day, pro-
posing to hire the hall for a lecture on ' The Spiritualism of Poetry, to be illustrated by copious recitations
from the poets, English and American.' One of the
coves I soon discovered to be the operator himself,—a
short, broad man, who carried his breadth to a climax
in the regions of alimentativeness and ideality. An
enormous red beard and whiskers only added breadth.
He was yclept Edward A. Z. Judson, and has, doubtless,
been familiar to you as ' Ned Buntline,' a New York
editor, romance- and tale-writer. . . . My lad came
betimes, with a bundle of books under his arm; among
Scott, Shelley, etc., I was swift to perceive the second
tome of the *despised Edgar.* ' Hillo!' says I; ' you
have one of my men there, I see.' ' Which?' quoth
Ned. He then opened and told off, in pithy sentences,

how Poe and he had been bosom friends; how, amid all the caprices and misfortunes of both, the friendship had been warm and close to the last; and how, among all the men that America was proud to call her sons, none was fit to be compared with the unmourned one she had lost. I fairly leaped and yelled. Enough of Poe; he's sure enough to

> Win futurity's plaudit note,
> And rise like the dead from the river's bed,
> But deaf to the cannon that bid them float.

BUFFALO, *January* 10, 1857.

. . . I am beginning to detest letters as a medium of intercourse. That part of me which is my share of the currency between us defies me to nail it in a letter. I get prosing away on something else, or, if held to the subject, it is the mere body that is put on paper,—the soul all the while skimming out of arm's reach and daring me to touch a feather of her. Davie, my boy, it takes actual contact to strike fire, like what was wont to blaze o' nights. . . . Does n't it have a strange appearance to you, looking back, now? To be sure, you are not so fairly out of it as I am, and may not feel as I do; but, here, plucked up by the roots, so to speak, and without a single outlet for the old stuff, except these paltry letters, the recollection of some of those fiery nights comes over me like an experience got in some other planet. I do n't think our case is often paralleled, nowadays. Just think! Two minds, to all appearance in mortal slumber, suddenly burst into volcanic action of an extraordinary character. For I maintain, without intending to insinuate that our powers—mine, at any rate—are anything more than common,—I maintain, I say, that seldom is the human imagination, the ideal and supernatural of the mind, so wildly excited, so unnaturally distended, as were ours at intervals during the years of our 'treck.' Of course, drugs, fevers, etc., I do n't put in the count.

You remember the era of tales grotesque and hor-
resque? You remember the two nights—the first
especially—in which the act of Fascination was practiced on me? Enough. I am sure, if I should present
myself for your inspection, now, you would find that
vast alterations have passed over me and over the spirit
of my dreams. What they are, I have not the slightest
idea; so, of course, I can't be expected to describe
them. Since leaving you, I have sort of lost track of
my *inner self.*

> ' O'er many a wild and magic waste,
> Thy footsteps, Psyche, I have traced.'
> But now the shadows fall so thickly
> Above me, round me, and so fickly
> Do thy pinions gleam before,
> I shall see thee nevermore.
>
> I would that we might take again
> The backward path by glade and glen ;
> That thou would'st clasp my hand in thine,
> And thrill me with thine eyes divine,
> And breathe low in mine ear the themes
> That angels sing to thee in dreams.
>
> Oh·! once, before me, far and clear,
> I heard thy singing, ' Here ! 'tis here ! '
> But all so loudly jarred the strife,
> The clangor and the battle of life,
> Alas ! the affrighted echoes bore
> The voice away—I hear no more.

Pretty fair, that. What do you think? Positively
an off-hand shot. . . .

I have got Mrs. Browning's new book, *Aurora Leigh,*
and partly read it. It is a perfect pyramid of poetical
accretions. Inexhaustible imagination—mines of words
—new ideas in myriads, and piercing eye-sight for
human nature in all its forms, done up in blank; and
after all—what? I admit it all: Shakspere is good;
so is Mrs. B.; but give me Tammy's *Canadian Boat-
song,*—let me doze over Poe's *Sleeper,* or thrill with
his *Raven,* or grow weirdly happy in *The Lotos-eaters,*
—and, rising from my carouse, I will maintain, with

all my might and mind, that I have imbibed more *poetry* than can be squeezed or *bittled* out of Shakspere, with *Aurora Leigh* thrown in. . . .

Don't, for love's sake, Davie, ever hunt for something to praise in anything I write,—to break the stroke of the correcting rod, as it were. Let it come. At least do as well by me as I do by you. I am honest. Every abominable thing I've sent you has been only fit to be scouted into annihilation, and you should have said so. I would have felt better, when telling the truth about you. But I'll send you something soon, my boy, that will gar ye jump.

BUFFALO, *February* 16, 1857.

. . . I occasionally take an opportunity to *sing* a few verses of a favorite poet, after your own style and tune, and with all the rhetorical tremor I learned at your feet. I heard my uncle say, the other day, that I was a good reader of poetry—he liked to hear me read poetry—or something of that sort. Very good. I'll give him *Across the Lake** some day. The fact is, Davie, I have sounded a good few youths since I came here, and, in various ways, gathered a good deal of observation. I know of no one in whom poetry is the same article it is in us, at all. Many *like* poetry; but I have yet to meet *one* who has trod on the lonely shores we were wont to haunt. Here's for you:

I.

It is a thing that few have ever gained,
  Or (being ignorant) have cared to gain—
The key, whereby our souls step forth unchained—
  The power that launches worlds within a brain.
Few, few, can follow when the viewless train
  Of Poesy sweeps by ; when, face unveiled,
Wild Wonder leads ; when space and years are slain,
  And seas whereo'er the wing of Dreams had failed
  Spread backward, till undreamed-of shores are hailed.

* One of David Taylor's poems, which had just reached him.

II.

The scenery of Earth hath might to dart
  Angelic longing thro' the sluggish vein ;
But quicker, wildlier thrills and throbs the heart
  Who steers his bark forth on the mighty main
Of mind : O ! wanderer, why seek Earth again ?
  Dew-giving stars do guard these regions. Moons
Above the valleys circle ever, nor wane.
  There dwell in dance and dream a thousand Junes,
And Dawn, star-chained in the east, forever upward swoons.

BUFFALO, *March* —, 1857.

. . . No, Davie,—I am not the man to slur Shelley,
or take an inch from the measure of his mighty genius,
because he utters sentiment utterly repugnant to my
soul and mind.   I will enjoy him in the face of all the
world, and no one shall decry Shelley in my hearing
without hearing something from me direct.   But try
to put yourself in my position, for a moment; try and
realize the relation which I believe (to use no stronger
word) to exist between Almighty God and myself ;
and then you will see that, in doing what I have said
above, I strain endurance and charity to the utmost.
I am not, like some you have probably seen, pretending
to the same name that I myself appropriate, who can
listen coolly, and even smile wanly, when they hear the
Being they believe to be their Creator reviled.   I can't
stand it, and my emotions towards you are what they
are because you never asked me to stand it.   Now I
have done on this subject.

Of all the glorious things that ever I read, I think
The Spirit of Solitude cows the gowan.   Have you
ever read it?   If not, don't delay a day.   I can't
understand that jargon of Poe's, about Shelley's poetry
requiring to be improved on in Tennyson's person, in
order to reach the ideal of what poetry should be.   It
appears to me that Shelley's poetry is as perfect, as
regards style and diction, as ever poetry will be, or
need to be.   Do you know that piece in *Prometheus*,

where Asia (or Panthea) sees the Hours chasing Eternity thro' Space? What a picture! Talk of grouping and effect on canvas! There never was anything put on by brush to approach that, for terrific power; every word gives the idea of speed, speed—fearful! When I read it and hold the book away, so that I can scarcely distinguish the words, I seem to see *speed* in the very arrangement of the sentences. . . .

I am weary, I am dead-tired and heart-broke to see how blind and more than brainless, with regard to poetry, the bulk of mankind are. . . .

There is nothing to be seen, here, but the eternal swing of women's dresses and men's legs on the street. I don't think I study faces as much as I used to do, when I saw fewer. I am often driven, when I do, to the conviction that they are a miserable, mysteriously restless, hurrying set of beings that swarm upon this earthly ball. Nothing in their faces but uneasy hurry, as a general thing. I sometimes think that my own phiz ought to be a matter for exhibition, in regard to serenity and apparent peace among the wretches.

BUFFALO, *April* 19, 1857.

. . . I trudged contentedly with you, the other day, to the moon and Venus; so bear with me if I jaunt you a little, where I have been sojourning a good deal of late, myself. Expect nothing wonderful, or beautiful; but, if you feel as I feel, you will be full of glorious sadness while we tarry in the far away Valleys of Childhood. Childhood is a mystic thing—a scroll if you will—with strange lettering and characters, committed for a little while to every member of the human family. For a *little while*, only; for, before he is able to know the writing,—before he even knows that it is secret and mysterious,—the scroll is drawn out of his reach, rolled up and sealed. He may philosophize as much as he pleases on it, afterward,—he can never experiment. I do n't know whether it was you who struck me with a love of sunsettings; I rather think it is born, always, with any share of the poetic temperament; at any rate, I always go ' jaunting ' in a country of sunsets. It was in a broad, breezy meadow, with slopes in it, where the boys could lie down and roll horizontally to the bottom, and towards the end of the afternoon, that I struck into the Land of Childhood, lately. It seems to me that the scene is a memory, not a fancy, and, if so, very, very far distant. At any rate, when I went into the meadow, there were a great number of boys and girls playing; some of them seemed big, like; but I know it was only because I was very little, myself, and *very* young, that they seemed so. They were all really young and small, and could not, most of them, speak other than childishly. The noise of play was boisterous, while the sun kept moderately high; but by and by the shadows began to lengthen, and the children gathered into little knots and talked to each other, and the sound of voices was the only sound;—whereas, before, the sport was deafening and indistinguishable as to speech. The wind had blown pleasantly, thro' the afternoon, and kites were high, high up. As sunset came on, everything fell motionless, and the kites stood away off, serene and far, with their strings tight and visible, the whole length up. The children, I say, had gathered into knots. They were mostly little girls,—I rather think I was the only boy; but that could n't be, for there were kites,—and some of the lassies had curly hair and had their bonnets swinging behind them by the ribbon round their necks. Presently, they began a quiet kind of game. In it they had to sing. They made strange motions and actions to one another, and their song came every little while to me (I was walking away by this time):

Water, water, wall-flower, growing up so high,
We are all maidens, and we must all die.

Everything was done soberly and without mirth. The sun set, and the whole air was an ocean of amber light, that colored the faces of the children, and gave all the landscape an air of unreality. It stayed a long time so; they played the same game over and over again, and their voices got sadder and sweeter, as if they were mourning for something. But, at last, the whole meadow with the amber light upon it took the aspect of a shore, which grew slowly into distance, as if I had been sailing away. All the children kept playing on, solemnly, taking no notice of me; and away they faded, with the song floating behind them:

Water, water, wall-flower growing up so high,
We are all maidens, and we must all die.

And so the shore remained, with them playing on it, while I was wafted backwards, towards the evening star. *Finis.*

I astonish youngsters, here, sometimes, by my actions. I make numerous acquaintances in my daily peregrinations. I ask sometimes for a 'hudd' of a fine, steady-flying kite, and I feel her tugging (*tueging*— much better, is n't it?) with all my old pride. I tell you, sir! a kite is good play for boys, but it is also good enough for men. There must be delicious agony in pulling the thing out of the clouds.

BUFFALO, *April* 30, 1857.

. . . I have been, just now, as near having the crystal fountains unsealed as is often my lot in this drying, scorching world. Over what, do you think? Nothing less than old Wordswords! There 's a quality in some of his things which melts you down into a little child. You lose all manliness and weep like a wean; *i. e.*, going in that course, such is the result.

> A simple child, dear brother Jem,*
> That lightly draws its breath,
> And feels its life in every limb,
> What should *it* know of death?
>
> I met a little cottage girl,
> She was eight years old, she said,
> *Her hair was thick with many a curl*
> *That clustered round her head.*

Wordsworth has a kind of weanly way of giving a life and speech to humble animals, and even plants, and especially children, which, if not poetry, is yet unclassed in literature. . . .

I often feel, about nightfall, a sort of wanting something. I strive to recollect what it is lacking, and then it flashes: I would just jump over the fence and thro' the pasture-lot, and ower the swamp, and be on you in a crack! Alas! alas! 'Tears, idle tears—I know not what they mean.' (Read it). . . .

Let me give you some pickings from my readings lately. Wordsworth has the finest description of a cataract at a distance from the beholder! He describes it as 'frozen in distance.' Does that not hit the thing? There is a fine line, speaking of a flower in a lonely place, and giving it a sort of woman or spirit life in the solitude. It is like so and so, or

> lady of the mere,
> Sole-sitting by the shores of old romance!

De Quincey thinks this, perhaps, the finest line in the poetry of earth. I don't. But is n't it rather a startling idea,—to be called on to point out the highest line that ever formed beneath a mortal pen? Where would you go? Certainly not to Shakspere. Shelley, perhaps.

I am too late of beginning, now, but I had it in my head, last week, to give you a kind of recantation of

---

* Coleridge, who improvised the first stanza of the poem *We are Seven*, gave this form to the first line of it. Wordsworth cancelled the 'dear brother Jem,' and it has usually been published with the line incomplete.

my former poetic belief. I abjure Tennyson, in a certain sense, and cling to Shelley and Robert Burns. Tennyson, in this sense: He is a poet—a true poet—but not a model, as Poe would have us believe. He has made no advance in the riddle of poetic diction. It is as much a riddle as it ever was. What, in your idea, is the true language of poetry? It is n't the language of carters and idiots, as Wordsworth would have us believe. It is n't full of dictionary words ending *osity* and *ation*, as Barrett says it is. It is n't drawing-room clack, as Tammy Moore has it. What in thunder is it?

BUFFALO, *June* 17, 1857.

. . . I am taking lessons from a tall, officer-like Tenton, in the mysteries of the German tongue. Already, I begin to have the veil lifted a little, and, of course, it is to the poetic quarter in the new language that I first resort. My feelings are not so strong as yours. It is a rare occasion that makes my voice falter and my eyes feel in the least like tears. I never remember of crying for anything, short of a whipping or a severe scolding. Stumbling across an extract from Goethe, though, the other day, I was powerfully moved, again and again. I do n't expect you will care anything about it; for, of two coves who ever covenanted together, you and I, in most things, are the most unspeakably different; but I will tell it, at all events : ' Mignon,' says a foot-note, in the coolest possible voice, ' Mignon is one of the most interesting characters in Goethe's *Wilhelm Meister.* In her earliest childhood she was secretly carried off from her home in Italy by a company of strolling jugglers and trained to perform feats on the rope, etc. Meister, who one day happened to witness the performance of this troupe, during which the child was unmercifully abused, obtained possession of her and became her protector. One morning, he

4

was surprised to find her before his door singing this
song [I will append it]* to a cithern which had acci-
dentally fallen into her hands. On finishing her song
for the second time, she stood silent for a moment,
looked keenly at Wilhelm, and asked him, *Knowest
thou the land? It must be Italy*, said Wilhelm (the
history of the child was yet a mystery to him); *where
did'st thou get the little song? Italy!* said Mignon,
with an earnest air,—*if thou go to Italy take me along
with thee, for I am too cold here. Hast thou been
there already, little dear?* said Wilhelm. But the child
was silent, and nothing more could be got out of her.'
Oh, Davie! I think that is the most pathetic, the most
tenderly touching thing I ever read. . . . '*Italy*, said
Mignon, with an earnest air; *if thou go to Italy take
me along with thee, for I am too cold here*'! Oh,
man! I tell you that touches me in a tender spot, somehow or other.

BUFFALO, July 10, 1857.

Behold me a hulk, from which the lowest ebb of the
tide has drawn away the water, so far that only a distant sound of the sea comes where there once was the
fresh lash of waves. Whether there ever will come a
time which shall set me afloat, anew, is a question. I
think—floating being understood to mean the motion
of the pure poetic temperament in which, with you, I
once gloried—not. Can it be possible that I shall
subside into the miserable, contented, evenly-balanced
wretch my present dispositions indicate? When I have
any stirrings of the old kind in me, now, they never
amount to anything above the merest commonplace.
I am totally out of the land of visions. . . . I think,
now, it must have been your influence upon my sus-
ceptible (*no more*) mind that made me, for a time,
what I was. I have no power within myself,—none.
I could almost throw up everything, now, and come

* Kennst du das Land wo die Citronen blühn ?

back and sojourn with you, away on the hills, up from your high field, as far as Wilson's and the Observatory. I think if I was there it would be all right.

BUFFALO, *September* 22, 1857.

Yours of the fifth September has lain, a thorn in my side, till now. I have not felt able for the effort. . . . Of all my experiences, down among the dry, dark, rocky barrens of the 'valley,' I think none are so thorough and far-reaching as my late ones. Poetry— fled. Not a rag of her raiment left; nothing but a vague, gnawing regret, at best, and a dull, aching vacancy, at worst, where she used to reign. If I could fall in love; if I could meet somebody who could raise me; if I could get letters from you every day,—I might feel like my old self again. But, alas! none of these turn up, and I am in the very depths of soulless-ness. . . . The fact is, the old Davie Gray had better be declared defunct, at once. I do n't feel as if one of my old powers was left me,—those which I counted so much on improving. . . . O, I wish you had me a day, the now, Davie—ony a day—up there somewhere between your field and the old Observatory! It would be worth millions to me. . . .

The weather has lived out the summer, now; the air to-night is clear and cold, with a brisk breeze. I can fancy you in the old howff, as vividly as possible, and almost persuaded myself, a minute ago, that I was threading my way among the trees, between Willie's and Davie Mair's. If I am—

The stars are out, and eastward fly
Some scattered clouds along the sky ;
The night is clear, but sharp and shrill,
The wind is whistling o'er the hill,
And with a dreary autumn sound
The trees are stirred, above, around.
Oh ! with a sweet and strange surprise
Each sigh o'erfloods me, soul and eyes,
And every sound—

Bless me! I'm far on the road to tool-ool,—which is an exercise unworthy manhood; so avaunt, such lugubrious imaginings! . . .

What do you ever read now? Are you still among the old books? I haven't read a book this summer.

BUFFALO, October 28, 1857.

Since I have had yours by my side, my mind, to quote from some fair authoress or other, has been 'a tumult of conflicting emotions.' One thing only is clear in my mind: poetry must go up, now. The star is clear and in the ascendant. All my old literary fire is aglow, again, and Davie, my boy, I will stick by you in this till *something* gives. . . . Let me tell you of a scheme now in motion among myself and one or two others. It is, to start a weekly paper, or magazine, to be devoted purely to literature and art,—something after the model of *Chambers' Journal*, although not, perhaps, so large and ambitious, at first. It would be designed to subsist for a while solely on a city circulation; but might and would undoubtedly thence expand, as *Chambers'* did. Now, if this goes off, you are nailed as a constant contributor. It is with my eye on you that I mostly feel so sanguine.

Before the close of his first year in Buffalo, Gray had gathered around him a considerable circle of young men, more or less congenial in character and tastes. He had exercised a kind of selective attraction on the bookish and thoughtful-minded youth of the city, drawing them together, as to a place of rendezvous, at the pleasant library-rooms of the Christian Union. One and another had found him out there; had discovered that the quiet charm of the place gained another charm when they got speech with the young Scot who reigned

in it. Making acquaintance with him, they were led
to acquaintance with one another, and thus was formed
a considerable group, which became cemented by strong
friendships, lasting far into the years that were then
to come, even down to the present day. The first-
comers of this group, which had David Gray for its
nucleus and the Christian Union Library for its rally-
ing-point, presently organized themselves into a modest
and small literary club, which held formal weekly
meetings, for the reading, discussion and criticism of
original papers, and for self-improvement in other
modes. Four countries—Ireland, Scotland, America
and England—were represented in the membership of
the young club; and so they framed an odd name for
it out of the initials I, S, A, E. It was called the
'Isac Club.' But the weekly club meetings of this
'Isac' group were the mere formalities of their intercourse. They came together, additionally, on all opportunities. It was an understood principle of conduct
among them that, whenever one had the smallest half-
hour of time at his command, he should carry it
straight for expenditure to that certain southwestern
corner of the Christian Union Library which was the
appointed trysting-place. There were not many after-
noons and evenings that did not witness a gathering of
David's confederates, there, in full force or partly, for
high talk, about many things. Sometimes they sus-
pended their own talk for an evening, to take part in
the public debates which the Christian Union had
instituted, and which took place, for a time, in an
adjoining committee-room. From among the visitors
to those debates they drew occasionally a new recruit

into their ranks, and the group gradually increased to a dozen or more in number. One who was really the first to be joined with David Gray, in gathering up the other friends into that most natural growth of comradeship, wrote about it some years afterwards, as follows :

Whether debates were held or not,—let the weather be foul or fair,—let amusements be many or few,—in the afternoon and evening of each day, more or less young men could be found in that library-room. Serious, earnest and profitable conversations were held there ; strong and vigorous discussions of varied and endless character, on science, history, philosophy, political economy, politics and poetry. All subjects and all matter were themes for those hours. Art, too, was studied, from Ruskin, whose fine, rhetorical sentences carried the young mind captive. Then, in the quiet evening, those wonderful sunsets, away over Lake Erie, down by the Canadian woods, (surely there have been no such sunsets since, or the Kremlin is the only place to see them!) when the purple and crimson and filmy white shot up the deep azure, and, with other gorgeous tints and hues, painted lake and island, tower and pinnacle, away above the western horizon! Never poet expressed such beauty ; never painter caught on the canvas the resemblance of it! You may think this language extravagant ; but every one who watched, night after night, those summer and autumn sunsets, will bear witness to their inexpressible glory.

Perhaps the glory of the sunsets and the fine fury of the talk which we enjoyed, on those long-ago nights, borrowed some effect from the exalted glow of feeling which Gray could so easily kindle in himself and communicate to others, around him. It is certain that the

scenes and the feelings of those nights are burned as
with fire in the memory of all who shared them.

The organized club of the ' Isac ' had no long existence. It was drowned out, as it were, by the freer
and larger association that followed it and went on
around it. But, after a little time, it was succeeded by
another organization, which enveloped the companions
of the Kremlin in an ampler way and acquired a more
permanent character. This was a club which, in sheer
despair of finding a satisfactory name, called itself 'The
Nameless.' Its objects were those common to its kind.
It debated all sorts of questions and practiced all sorts
of literary composition, in verse and prose; but its
chief end, after all, was to cultivate good-fellowship
among its members,—and it did so with excellent success, for many years.

As factors in the life of David Gray, these clubs,
and the more spontaneous rallyings in the Kremlin
Hall library-rooms, out of which they came, were unquestionably of great importance. They gave him some
of the enduring friendships of his life. They stimulated him when few other stimulations were acting on
him; they stirred his interest in a greater variety of
things, among the subjects of thought and knowledge,
than he was naturally disposed to give attention to;
and so they contributed some breadth to his development.

Meantime, he was becoming considerably known in
larger circles, outside of these more intimate comrades.
He had given several short poems to print, in one of
the newspapers of the city, which discriminating eyes
quickly recognized as being poetry, in very truth. The

first of them was *The Fog-bell at Night*, which appeared in the *Buffalo Express* one day in October, 1856. It was followed by *Elihu Burritt*, *The Crew of the Advance*, and other modest ventures, all of which will be found among the poems printed elsewhere in this volume. The reputation they gained for the writer was, so far, slight and very limited, of course; but they were helping to open his way in life —the way that he was appointed to tread. A little later, he began to make himself known as a prose-writer to the reading public of Buffalo, by a series of charming essays, on such simple topics as *Houses*, *A Winter Night and its Visitors*, *A Word about Grave-yards*, and the like, which he contributed to *The Home*,—a literary monthly then published in Buffalo, by Mrs. H. E. G. Arey and Mrs. C. H. Gildersleeve.

During the year 1858, and most of 1859, David's life is traced sufficiently in a few passages taken out of his letters to his friends. His father and family had lately quitted the Wisconsin farm, at Roslin, and settled in a new residence, at Detroit. The first letters from which we quote were written during a visit to them, and were addressed to one of his Buffalo friends:

TO JAMES N. JOHNSTON.

DETROIT, *January* 21, 1858.

. . . Day before yesterday night, I was at a friend's house, where a lively, friendly party prevailed. My friend has two of the most prettily beautiful little girls! You have often heard me express myself on this portion of created things, and I will only say, again, that, notwithstanding my fervid appreciation of

female humanity in a more advanced stage, I would be
content to forego all, if I might but be permitted to
dwell in the perfect purity and quaint delicious happiness of little girls' society. There is something in it
that satisfies me almost to tears. Ye shades of Parnassus!—all the glory of the rose is in the rosebud,
and the veiled mystery of the bud is dearer to me
than the flaunting openness of the full blossom! I
discovered, here, at my friend's house, a new power,—
namely, for faery tales. I addressed myself to the
little girls, and I speedily had them touching me with
their delicate, feathery-soft hands and coaxing me to
tell a story. And, at once, the flood-gates of faery
romance opened and the stream flowed. I took them
up to the top of a high hill, lush with flowers and
crowned with a brake of bells—bluebells—and built a
little bower for a fairy in a moccasin flower, furnished
faery fashion; and I filled them with longing for the
sweet shadow and ecstacy of the flower-land. Then, I
took one of themselves to be a little kilmeny—and so
forth, and so forth, and so forth. At any rate, they
hung around me for the rest of the story, and took my
heart away, up-stairs, with them to bed, and only left
the sweet press of their soft faces on mine, to keep me
happy forever. . . .

There's an industrial school here, which, mentally
viewed, in connection with the region of the Canal
Street Sunday-school, stirs strange desires and designs
in my mind. I am more and more convinced that, if
a fellow does not make himself useful, he is *losing* his
time in this world, whatever may be the result in
another. I believe this is a conclusion demonstrable
on strict principles of logic. Don't you feel as if an
unlimited field is discerned through the scarcely open
portals of Canal Street Mission?

Did you ever see such a winter? Of course not,
nobody ever did. The sun is monarch of an untainted
realm of pure ether. Winter! perish the thought!

Take it out into the sunshine,—melt it,—dry it,—scatter it, upwards, in the immeasurable heights of light and heat. I put for the nearest point of woods, this morning, and again realized the truth that the city is not universal, but rather a dot, or blot, surrounded by an expanse of unpolluted country, inhabited only (or for the most part) by things of God's own instituting, and traversed by the wandering winds.

TO EDMOND LINDSAY.

BUFFALO, *March* 5, 1858.

. . . Your account of John L——'s death fills me with sorrowful thoughts. I mind not only of him, though his quiet face and modest demeanor are vivid enough with me, but of a time when it seemed to me death came very near and grew familiar with me. I mean, when Robert P—— died, when his sister's death was still fresh in our minds, and when the thrill of your sickness and possible death were all so terribly close upon me. Oh! I tell you I was better and wiser then than I am now, with forgetfulness and the presence of the new all but smothering the old out of my mind. Just think of it! Robert's life and mine were parallels. Since his stopped, what a rugged and straining line mine has drawn, and by how many rough, winding stages will it draw itself, till the long line of the parallel be, also, cut off by a grave? Then the prayer of that old impracticable anomaly of a father of his comes audibly into my mind: 'Fit us a' for leevin', faither! but, above a', prepare us for deein'!'

TO THE SAME.

BUFFALO, *May* 9, 1858.

Your very acceptable letter, long and most interesting, awaited me on my return home, two weeks ago. 'Return home' implies absence, and I may as well tell you, now, the delightful journey I took. I went as delegate from the Y. M. C. Union, here, to a national convention of similar bodies, held April 22, at Charleston, S. C.; so that, when you were writing the sheet now at my side, I was pacing, in delicious mood, the almost tropical vicinities of Charleston. I went to New York, thence by steamboat to C. The voyage was glorious,—perfect halcyon days, three in number, —calm, sunny, and in the face of a gentle wind that softened to absolute balm as we sailed south. Then, Charleston! Just think of leaving ice in the harbor, here, and, at the first sight of land, seeing the luxuriance of the tropics—almost (again); for, what with palmettos, figs and a hundred other trees and products strange to my eyes, I seemed floated into a new world, altogether. I can only think of Columbus at San Salvador. My time in the city and the convention was spent in a continual festival of enjoyment. I returned to New York again by sea.

TO JAMES N. JOHNSTON.

CHARLESTON, S. C., *April* 18, 1858.

I should have written you sooner, had I not, in the first place, been made somewhat lazy by the glorious tropical weather, and, in the second, been fain to indulge. mine eyes, ears, soul and sense in the torrent of surrounding novelty. . . . My host is a Mr. N——, anciently of Scotland,—a retired and very wealthy merchant, keeping a regal establishment. A carriage and an immense crowd of darkies are at my command. Verily, this is seeing life! My room-mate (O, such a room!) is Richard C. McCormick, editor of the *Young Men's Magazine*,—the man of all others whom I wished to come across. Singularly enough, all has come out in a peculiarly favorable manner. . . . If I were n't too lazy, I should laugh incessantly at the darkies. They are amusing, numerous and perfectly opaque. Slavery, in my mind, however, does not change its position the one-hundreth of a hair's breadth.

TO DAVID TAYLOR.

BUFFALO, August 2, 1858.

. . . The other night it rained, in brief showers, and, in the pauses, the moon came out brightly upon the wet leaves. The fresh smell, the stillness, the light, —everything, brought up to my mind you piece of yours, *The Thunder-King*, and I would have given my purse to have had it by me.

> Every leaf of the *soundless* oak
> Lent its voice as the melody broke.

Oh, bliss! What a rapture came over me with these lines! I thought they portrayed a sort of hidden inner life in nature, which only revealed itself in such rare seasons, and I was happy,—happy almost to tears. If it isn't too much trouble, hunt up that piece and copy it off for me; or, better, take a copy and send me down the old original. I remember every flourish. Do this last without fail, next letter. . . . I am sure, nobody but you or I can see anything very meritorious in that poem; and yet I know it gets deeper into a certain ecstatic vein of poetic passion than any lines extant in any language. Or, rather, it touches a vein untouched,—totally untouched,—elsewhere. Either that, or it must be by association with ideas originated and in play in our minds about that time. It is an indubitable fact, that lines of your poems have a firmer hold upon me, and stir me up to the true, delicious thrill, more, far more, than *any* lines of any poem in print.

TO EDMOND LINDSAY.

BUFFALO, September 3, 1858.

. . . I am sorry to hear such poor accounts of your crops, this year. . . . I am beginning to be in the wheat trade, myself, a little now. I act as clerk, half my

time, for my uncle, who is engaged in milling, again.
. . . I am already considerably initiated into the mysteries of book-keeping, etc.

TO DAVID TAYLOR.

BUFFALO, *March* 11, 1859.

. . . When I wrote you last, I was in a somewhat uncertain state as to my occupation for the year to come. I have now got that matter settled, thank Heaven! It gave me a great deal of worry. I stay as book-keeper with my uncle's firm—engaged in the milling business; so I expect, though I shall have harder work than ever, hitherto, that my pecuniary matters will be in a convalescent condition. Well, about six weeks ago, I took a sudden notion in my head and threw up my situation in the library. It was a nominal one, as regards salary, and I felt myself becoming too much of a fixture; so I bolted. Then, in the interim, before my uncle's folks decided that they wanted me, I had a queer time, walking about the streets with all the strange feelings of an isolated, independent mortal; independent to roam the world and seek adventure; independent to lie down in some quiet corner and die; free to get rich or to starve. I tell you, I had some funny times. All the while, I had a vague vision at the back of the whole, of me, coming some night—one of those warm moonlight nights in which we used to walk and talk half-way into morning —and wakening you up and telling you that I was coming to stay with you; and then of us, working together, up on the hill, and sitting at the side of the field, having long confabs, and taking journeys off, when it suited us, and being able between us to make an easy living out of the land. . . . If you were to take a new location, in some new place, I think I would join you, to-morrow. . . . I am likely to do well; my friends tell me that my prospects are good, and I suppose they are. I suppose this means that, as far as eye can reach or imagine it reaches, ahead, there is unlimited worldly work, and that all the old joys and toys are left forever behind. Oh, I can hardly bear it —this change—this pushing off into the desert!

> I sit on this last oasis of youth ;
> Before me stretches the dim desert-sand ;—
> No more—no more,—I feel it now, in sooth,—
> Shall gushing streams refresh and glad the land.
> Around me, rising slow, the phantom-band
> Of hopes and joys, that all my way beguiled,
> Fade backward from me—wave the parting hand,
> And leave me lonely in this desert's wild,
> With no more heart or hope than a forsaken child.
>   [Exit funeral.]

TO DAVID TAYLOR.

BUFFALO, *April* 19, 1859.

. . . I was up at Detroit in the beginning of the month, and I may as well tell you a thing or two about that. . . . Next night, after everybody was in bed, I called Walter to account, in a matter which he had undertaken under oath to do for me—to wit, the keeping of my documents, gathered in Wisconsin. He produced them, all safe, under seal. Did I ever tell you the agonized attempt I made, the morning I got up to go away from Roslin, to put them (the papers) in a bottle? I couldn't get one big enough in the neck, and so was obliged to give them up to Walter. I meant to bury the bottle, over about the big hollow.

I was very much surprised to see many things so good as they are, of that early period; and very much amused at many of them, too,—especially the ones I thought, once, were least amusing. With scarce an exception, the pieces I thought were hits, beyond controversy—these are perfect trash. It was like taking off my grave-clothes—as if I had been a mummy—undoing the wrappages, one by one. Some pencilings of yours are on some of the papers, which brought to mind many queer things.

TO DAVID TAYLOR.

BUFFALO, *May* 5, 1859.

. . . I am going about, these days, in a kind of
referee, as Mr. Weller phrased it, consequent on the
complete change of the weather prospects and the
accompanying results. With May, began a period,
unbroken till now, of weather absolutely awful in
beauty. Unclouded skies, the warmth and softness of
air of the South Sea Islands,—perfect, regal Summer
on her throne, already. Slowly, as the days advance, a
sort of filmy haze gathers over her features, making the
stars, at night, and the sharp semi-circle of the new
moon, as they approach the horizon, assume a bright
red appearance, as of ship-lamps hung up in unseen
shrouds, and, in the day-time, taking the sharp azure
from the lake and from the sky and welding them in
one sheet of burnished whiteness. High up in this
magic element, ships pass, dreamily, to and fro, or
mysteriously float upon extended wings, where, a moment before, you saw nothing. The leaves of the trees,
the flowers and grass of the fields, all stand in their
accustomed places, but with an odd sort of astonished
look upon them, as if they had wakened out of some
queer dream, and had not yet found their speech. I
know this is the way things are going on, altho', as far
as material vision goes, I have seen little but glimpses
of the soft sky over tall brick walls.

TO DAVID TAYLOR.

BUFFALO, *June* 24, 1859.

. . . She holds herself inscrutable. Not a ray, not
a hair of light will she suffer to drop through her words
to me. She sent me, however, a little bunch of flowers
—a common present among young folks, here—and
before them, as before a shrine, I have been sitting,
solus, for the past two days, at the office. . . . You

know, I never cared a great deal for flowers. In humble coincidence with, if not in imitation of, a better man, I always prefer trees, vastly, to flowers. But, as I have been sitting here, hour after hour, I vow, sir, a strange affection has sprung up in me for them. I find the word applied to them sometimes in poetry, '*breathing*' fragrance, etc., etc., is a true one. They seem to pulse delicate gusts of perfume, that fleet over my nerves, making them thrill with sweet pleasure. These little currents of scent are never mixed in the same proportions. Sometimes, it is the rose that colors all; anon, that delicious breath of the lily's waxen lips is predominant; and, again, from the bouquet before me, there is a sweeter than either—a plainer odor, of green leaves, dashed with the shadow of a scent from some little meadow-flower, that brings the blood into my face, it speaks so plainly of some forgotten glory in the past. . . . When I wrote you before, I wrote nothing but what was true at the time. I did not write for the future, but for the present,—and so I do now. I believe, at the last,—unless a certain presentiment I once had,—a strange glimpse into futurity that, for the time, carried absolute conviction with it, as if I saw what was going to be, with my bodily eyes—unless that presentiment, that I am a bachelor booked to the end of the chapter, prove true,—I say, I believe, at the last, when I do go off, it will be in a perfect unguarded hurry. . . . And yet—and yet—I have an awful notion that I am going to meet somebody about whom there will be no uncertainty,—upon seeing whom some voice will speak in my soul in unmistakable tones, '*This is she.*'

TO DAVID TAYLOR.

BUFFALO, *August* 5, 1859.

. . . I do admire and love *Maud Muller;* she has long been a favorite. I agree with you, too, that the moral tacked on to the end would easily break off, if

the whole thing were cracked like a whip, and no loss
would be sustained, either. Tennyson grows more and
more into my blood. I can't help it; he is the man
for me. I have just read his new book, *Idyls of the
King*,—four stories in the style of *Morte d'Arthur*,
on the same general subject, viz.: King Arthur and
his Knights,—all full of the same wild, tender romance. . . .

I went to the theater the other night, for the first
time in my life, and saw *Hamlet*. The actor was
Barry Sullivan, the greatest British tragedian now
living. Everything else, the other actors, the audience
—all disgusted me; but that one man—I was fairly
riveted, eyes and ears, to him. From the first moment
he stepped on the stage you saw Shakspere's *Prince*.
I could not help thinking that Shakspere must have
studied *him*, instead of its being the other way. I
remembered all you said, 'once, about the depth and
mystery of the play, and realized it for the first time.

TO DAVID TAYLOR.

BUFFALO, *August* 18, 1859.

I am infinitely weary of the city, its business, its
clatter—all, to-day. It seems as if I would almost
sell my birthright to be out of it for a day, away in
the impenetrable stillness of some darkened valley,—
yea, or even away out, sitting at some quiet roadside,
beside a dyke, where the bees come, where tansy grows,
where there is the city with its accursed ways behind,
and unlimited scope for wandering on and on, before.

The perfection of business habits and ability is to
create, of the man you are dealing with, the complete
ideal of a thief, and then guard and prepare for him
at every point. If you trust anything to his honesty,
you are soft and unbusiness-like; and, ten to one, you
are also 'done brown.' This, disgusting at first, grows
funny after a while, and, finally, intensely wearisome.

5

I am living in hope of being a pilgrim in some of the countries of the old world before this time next year. A regular foot-tramp, I propose making. Would n't you like to go along?

TO DAVID TAYLOR.

BUFFALO, *October* 31, 1859.

. . . I feel a perfect fire in my bones to travel, and have determined, by hook or crook [to carry out the scheme]. My plan is purposely left very undefined. I intend to travel in Europe, on foot, in the cheapest and humblest manner, and begin my wandering in Spain, crossing the Atlantic to Gibralter. As a circumstance which may assist me some, financially as well as otherwise, I have an arrangement made by which I shall write letters for the *New York Times*. Now you know all about it.

CHAPTER IV.

SOMETIME during the summer of 1859, David entered, rather curiously, into a connection with the *Buffalo Daily Courier* which was decisive of his vocation in life. Rather curiously, because it was the work of a commercial reporter—a reporter of the local markets—that he was first engaged to do. He was employed that year as a clerk in the office of his uncle's firm, Messrs. Kennedy, Gray & Co., and his time was not fully occupied. Their office was on Central Wharf,—the mart in those days of nearly all the greater commerce of Buffalo. These circumstances were favorable for his using a few hours of every day in gathering notes of the market, and there happened to be a want of that service at the publishing-house of the *Courier*. So, it came about, oddly enough, that the most uncommercial young man in Buffalo (it is hardly too much to say so) was engaged for several months in counting the pulses of the produce-exchange, and recording them in the jargon of a newspaper commercial reporter. But this arrangement was undoubtedly made with the understanding, on both sides, that it should lead to something else, and with a distinct perception on the part of the editor and chief proprietor of the *Courier*, the late Joseph Warren, that he had enlisted

a pen which he could not afford to waste, very long, on
the writing of market reports.

As a matter of fact, the market work seems to have
come to an end before the close of the year, and David
had quitted the mill-office to make a complete plunge
into journalism, as associate editor of the *Courier*,
having charge of its city department, especially, but
prepared for a service of general utility, according to
the demands of the day and of the press. The provin-
cial newspapers of that time had nothing of the ' staff '
that is busy about them at the present day. A chief
editor and his associate, with a reporter of markets,
were quite commonly the entire editorial corps. A
news-reporter, as a distinctly added functionary, had
not yet made his appearance among the few servitors
of the press in Buffalo,—though the date of his advent
was not much later than the time here referred to.
The journalism of the city was in that primitive stage
when David Gray entered it. Then, and several years
afterwards, the large, strong figure of Joseph Warren
was often to be seen on the platform at public meetings, taking notes of speeches for next day's print.
He shared that kind of labor with his younger assist-
ant, and claimed from the latter more or less of aid in
the leader-writing and paragraphing of the editorial
page. The two were colleagues, to a considerable extent, in all departments of the newspaper work; and
much the same arrangement prevailed in the ' staff ' of
the other city journals. Those were days of hard work
in Buffalo journalism, and, generally speaking, of good
work. There was an all-round capability demanded
and exercised, which the present specializing of tasks

is not so well calculated to produce. The newspapers gave less to their readers than they now do; but possibly the readers may have suffered no loss. It is certain that much news was neglected advantageously,—with great conservatism of dignity to the newspapers, themselves, and with a benevolent sparing of those who read them.

Gray's introduction to journalism, therefore, was one which opened all its fields to him at the outset—except the political field. It is not likely that he had aught to do or say in connection with the politics of the paper, for a long time after joining it. There is no touch of his pen in any of its political writing,—and his touch was always unmistakable. He cared nothing, at that period, about politics,—knew nothing about political questions,—except as concerned the one intolerable thing, Slavery, about which his feelings were very strong. He was an Abolitionist, of the radical school of Garrison and Phillips. He condemned both political parties of the day, alike, scorning the assent to existing slavery which Republicans conceded, as much as he abhorred the friendlier attitude of Democrats towards it. Hence, he could not have assumed political relations with any partisan newspaper; but, being alien to both sides, could undertake the neutral and peaceable labors of journalism under either flag. The *Courier* was then, as it is now, a pronounced organ of the Democratic party, and David Gray came ultimately to agreement with it, and with its party, in political views; but that was not until after the slavery question had been burned out of American politics.

The exact time at which David became associated with Mr. Warren, in the *Courier*, is not known; but it seems to have been near the close of the year 1859. It is certain that he wrote the Christmas article that year, and there is no recognizable mark of his pen at an earlier date. Nobody who knew his work can doubt that he wrote such passages as these :

For one night and day in the year, we feel disposed to quarrel with the reverend shades of our Puritan grandsires, and to look with loving leniency on that other faith which has given us Christmas. . . . Nor would we undertake a chronological argument with any who might endeavor to prove that the twenty-fifth of December was not the day when Bethlehem became the center of the world's desire, and its manger the cradle of the world's hope. The air is vibrant with the music of chime and carol; the welkin rings with the joyful sound of Christmas bells; and to us, all this is none other than the echo of that first wonderful chorus sounded over the Judean hills. Passing from year to year,—from century to century,—it is the prolongation of that new song of humanity, begun by angels. . . . Ah! it is not the schoolboy, only, who looks forward to the day of evergreens, when trees bear such funny fruitage of toys and candy, and to the week of weeks so snugly tucked in between two holidays, and to all the pleasant things which make old Winter's harsh visage soften into the most lovable of faces. Thank God that we all, old and young, have these days left us! Mammon must close his temple-gates, rusty on their hinges with standing open so long, to-day.

This was, probably, his first work on the paper beyond itemizing and paragraphing, if not actually his first writing in its columns. A few days later, on the

5th of January, 1860, he wrote to his friend David Taylor: 'I still hold to my purpose of going to Europe next season. Meantime, I have had an opportunity to step entirely over from commercial matters to the newspaper business, and, at present, I am sitting at the editorial desk, where, from day to day, I spread my brains on paper. Although the work is hard, yet I like it better than anything I ever got into, and it is quite likely this may be the deciding point of my life, leading me henceforth into this paper business, for good and all.'

After two months of added experience, he wrote to the same friend, in March: 'The drudgery of a daily paper, writing from morning till night, and far into the night, nobody knows who has not tried it. Yet, judging from the degree in which I find my inclinations follow the work of my hands, this profession, before any other that I know anything of, is the one for me. If so, I am content. "There's a divinity that shapes our ends, rough-hew them how we will"; this I firmly believe, and I am content in great measure to submit, like passive clay in the potter's hand. Yet, if I am not much mistaken, I shall not for a great while occupy a subordinate position, in this or anything else. It's a queer, not to say egotistically-appearing thought, —but you will understand me when I express it. I say I think, frequently, that I am bound to *succeed*, sometime or other in life.'

Of the incidents of his life and of his feeling and thinking during that important year, 1860, and the succeeding year, we have scanty records. He was burdened with much work, and it is probable that he

wrote few letters to his friends. At all events, there
are few that can now be found. One who looks through
the files of the *Courier* may trace his hand, by the
marks of its fine workmanship; but mostly, from day
to day, it was employed on very common tasks. Sometimes it found the subject and the opportunity for a
bit of vignette-writing, like this (*Buffalo Courier*,
March 21, 1860):

A FUNERAL SCENE.

Last Sunday, there were balmy influences afloat in
the cloudless blue sky; there was a hint of the resurrection of summer, and all beautiful things; there was
more, we think, to make the heart thrill and yearn, in
its nameless and indefinable sympathies with nature,
than a day in the prime of May or the flush of hot
July affords. It was a day, last Sunday, with such a
heaven brooding over it as makes it most difficult for
us—most trying to the flesh—to reconcile the presence
of death and shadow with the new-springing life of all
nature. Those who have read De Quincey, remember
his theory on this subject. Sunday was surely a day
when Death ought to have removed himself afar off, to
the outer boundary of the world.

But, walking one of the long, European-looking
streets that stretch through the little Germany of our
city, we saw what seemed as the dark shadow of the
day's light. A funeral came wending its way towards
the outskirts,—Death riding out, in the glad exuber-
ance of the afternoon's sunshine. It carried a little
child to the church-yard—a little *fraulein*, perhaps, of
the poorer class of Germans. The train had no hearse
—there was but one carriage, followed by several common conveyances. The little coffin, soon to lie so lonely
and so far from home, lay, as yet, on the knees of the

father and mother, in the carriage. *They* carried the child to its burial. The custom may have looked cold and uncouth to some. To us, it was full of a beautiful propriety. Not yet away from the lap, where it was her wont to nestle; not yet removed from the clasping affection which death only could break; not yet compelled,—poor little one!—to journey in darkness and solitude, in dreary hearse, to the hillock where she *must* be left alone with God and the angels; not while it was possible to feel the pressure of their child's form, did they give her up,—albeit, that gentle burden lay on their knees with the coffin's strange pressure, when, of old, it was the yielding feel of soft, warm limbs! So, at any rate, whether it were seemly or unseemly, they carried the little one to its earth-bed, in Buffalonian Germany, last Sunday.

In early April, he found the advent of kites a matter of news which no right-feeling reporter could neglect to make note of. The kite, in fact, was one of the lasting objects of enthusiasm with him, as his letters have indicated to us, already. 'The kite,' he wrote, 'is a sort of aerial plummet, sunk into the deeps of the upper ocean; and we were fain to think, yesterday, as we watched them, high and motionless above the city, that they had reached, beyond the troubled and chilly currents of lower air, a kind of gulf-stream of warmer atmosphere, setting in heavily and steadily from the south.' And, again: 'It may be blowing cold and cheerless down below, but when you see a kite sitting steadily aloft, among the light passing drifts of vapor, with the sun upon its face, it is impossible not to believe that it has got up to a point where Spring is visible, as she comes, scattering blossoms in her path, from the sunny, southern side of the world.'

But, after a few months on the treadmill of the daily press, the young journalist had little spirit left for themes like these. His busy and tired eye could not catch the suggestion of them so easily, and, when it did, he found, probably, that the springs of eloquence and poetry in his brain were well-nigh dried up. There seems to be a time in the experience of almost every young newspaper writer,—and the measure of it is proportioned, pretty nearly, to the original freshness of his powers,—when that half-paralysis by sheer drudgery is suffered. It fell upon Gray, and there are long months during which the columns that he filled betray scarcely a gleam of the characteristic qualities of his writing.

During the summer of 1860, he made his long-coveted visit to the old home-scenes in Wisconsin, and to the friends there; but it was too short for satisfaction, —a mere flashing vision to him. He passed a single night with David Taylor—one night, only, to answer the longings of four years, and to unpack the hearts of the two friends of all that they had laid up for talk. Unhappily, there is no report of that memorable fore-gathering extant.

A few months later, David was constrained to make a test of himself once more in poetry, and to re-open, as it were, the abandoned shafts and chambers of a mine which he had nearly persuaded himself to be worked out, or to have had no existence. 'The Young Men's Association of Buffalo,' the library and lyceum society which afterwards named itself more simply 'The Buffalo Library,' was preparing to celebrate its twenty-fifth anniversary, with notable commemorative

exercises.   David had become an active member of the
Association, warmly interested in its growing library,
and he was solicited to write a poem for the occasion.
He found it hard to consent, but he did so, and the
result was a poem (printed elsewhere in this volume)
which gave a real distinction to the event.   This was
the first of a trilogy of poems which he wrote on different occasions, as tasks of love, for the Young Men's
Association, and they represent the greater part of his
poetical productiveness during half-a-dozen years.   The
second of these was read at the annual meeting of the
Association, February 17, 1862,—the evening of the
day on which news came of the taking of Fort Donelson.   It was a very noble piece of verse, and one that
will hold its place among the most finely-inspired poems
of the war.   The third and last was written for the
celebration (January 10, 1865) of the opening of the
library in the building, then just purchased and fitted
for it, which it occupied for the succeeding twenty-two
years.   This, too, was a glorious war-song, of triumph
and of wailing,—an ode and an elegy in one.   It contained the story of *How the Young Colonel Died*,
which has often been separately printed and is one of
the best-known of David Gray's poems.   The 'young
colonel' whose memory is embalmed in it was Colonel
James P. McMahon, of the One Hundred and Sixty-
fourth Regiment, New York Volunteers, who fell at
Cold Harbor.

Before his first year in journalism closed, David had
found reason to abandon, definitely, for the time, his
projected foot-tramp in Spain.   His relations with the
Courier were made so advantageous in promise that it

looked unwise to break or interrupt them. He was given the opportunity to purchase one-fourth of the establishment and business, on terms that were as liberal and favorable as they could be made by his generous colleague and friend, Mr. Warren. Writing on the subject, October 19, 1860, to another good friend, William P. Letchworth (since known as the President, for many years, of the New York State Board of Charities), while the latter was at his beautiful country place, 'Glen Iris,' near Portage, at the middle falls of the Genesee River, he said:

It is not to be wondered, that we, poor dingy souls, here, should think of you, yonder, in your glorious seclusion—in your Happy Valley, where the earth runs to flowers and the air to rainbows; but that you, in 'Glen Iris,' should patiently and lovingly think of me and my affairs, is a marvel only to be explained by the fact that you are—William P. Letchworth. Since you have done so, I will even make so bold as to pursue the theme. Well, then, I may consider myself as identified, for some time to come, with the *Courier* establishment,—stereotyped as a Buffalo editor, in fact. I had a good deal of time to deliberate before I made my choice,—a good many talks with my friend Warren. . . . I feel that this opening is much better than I had any right to expect, and is one, moreover, by which I may expect to struggle through to a legitimate independence and a modest position, quicker than most young men are privileged to do. Therefore I am thankful. . . .

Alas, for my 'castles in Spain,'—untenanted, desolate, emptied of light and beauty,—I fear me they will be Spanish dust before I, their prince and proprietor, may come to occupy! I am painfully conscious that one bubble has burst which never can be re-blown:

> We are stronger and are better
> Under manhood's sterner reign ;
> Yet we feel that something sweet
> Followed youth, with flying feet,
> And it never comes again !

Forgive this sophomorical gust of sentiment. Yet, when the poor corpse of that European project gets stretched out before me, I think her worthy of an epitaph.

When shall I get out to Portage? That is a question I often ask D. G. Not now, *not now* (if you comprehend the emphasis), seems the inevitable answer. I think of Thanksgiving, and two or three more of the antique 'Nameless' with me, in 'Glen Iris,' what time the trees are skeletons and the torrents awful in their giant nakedness. If that were to coincide exactly with your plans, perhaps it might be carried out; but it is only a perhaps. As for me, I have laid myself on the altar!! I've got to work and attend to that first. Pardon this (as Stillson would say) *hideously* big sheet of paper. It's the only piece I could lay my hands on when I came home to the wigwam after midnight, this blessed date. I have read half a novel and written this, since then, and it must now be three A. M., at least.

So the yoke of a hard calling was bound finally to his neck. He bore it with little relief and little incident during the troubled first year of the civil war. His feelings, that year, were deeply stirred, and none born under the flag were bound to the cause of the Union by a truer patriotism than his. As the war went on, he found much in the conduct of it that made him impatient and critical; much of what he thought to be a criminal carefulness of slavery, and much of political intrigue and gross self-seeking; so that he was alienated even farther than before from the party in

power. But his allegiance to the great cause at stake
—the cause of the American Union and of the principles of self-government and freedom bound up in it
—raised his mind above considerations of party.

His first considerable respite from the grinding
labors of the daily press came in February, 1862, when
he made a trip to Cuba, which was one of the delightful passages of his life. His companion in the excursion was Mr. Henry A. Richmond, whose acquaintance
he had recently made, and who was counted from that
time, for life, among the nearest of all his friends.
A few passages from the letters which he wrote to the
Courier while on this brief 'outing' deserve to be
quoted :

IN THE BAY OF HAVANA, Feb. 25, 1862.

. . . On the afternoon of the twentieth, this good
ship (all voyaging letter-writers' ships are 'good')
steamed down the bay, past gloomy Fort Lafayette,
and into the open Atlantic. It is a grand sensation
for one whose stomach, like your correspondent's, defies
the sea-fiend,—this being rushed, by steam, away into
the embrace of old Ocean. A fresh, bracing breeze,
and a sea which had the long-remembered rapture in
its motion, waited outside Sandy Hook to welcome us.
Who that has been for years away from the salt sea
air, which was native to him, once, could choose but
give, with all his soul, the cordial greeting back? . . .
All the inevitable cases of sea-sickness were observable:
The malignant type, as illustrated in those who capitu-
lated immediately after the first dinner, and were not
afterwards seen, but abode down-stairs, like spirits in
purgatory, dolefully bewailing their state, till, perhaps,
the last day of the voyage, when they were laid like
wet rags on the deck, limp and bleached,—their cheeks

the color of the pickled oysters they abhorred. Type No. 2, as shown in those who struggled valiantly with the demon, alternately victors and vanquished. They had a way of quitting the table abruptly, without being excused; and, indeed, for the most part, they were fed atmospherically, the odor of dinner escaping from the cook's caboose having a very satisfying effect on their stomachs. A still milder variety of the malady haunted a portion of the passengers. Like my friend, X. Y. Z., they were given to fits of abstraction, but were ready at all times to prove that they were not by any means sea-sick. . . .

We had one or two celebrities on board. Mr. Rarey, whose exhibitions [in the taming of horses] at Buffalo are well remembered, was the first face I identified on deck. His nephew, Mr. Fairrington, the successful professor of Mr. R.'s science, was also with us. . . .

So, we wended our way, the perfect circle of the sea-horizon moving with us as we went, under skies of the softest azure by day, and of deep, starry violet by night. The blight of secession has fallen, also, upon the sea; for there were no passers-by on that once busy highway of ocean. We were out of sight of land, but still near enough to fancy, in the lulls of wind and sea, that we heard the thunder of battle along the coast, so strangely and suddenly become that of an enemy's country. On Sunday afternoon, we seemed to pass through a grand archway of cloud into the realm of perpetual summer. That night, standing on deck, with the luxurious wind sweeping upon us from the land, and the long wake of the vessel stretching behind us, a trail of phosphorescent silver, I could distinctly perceive odors of the tropical vegetation which gave the name of Florida to the coast. The breath of strange fruits and flowers, lifted from some land of gardens in the west, filled all the air and made it rife with dreams and fantasy. Next day—yesterday—at daylight, we came alongside the shore, and, till night, when the reefs of Cape Florida sank into the sea, we kept close company with the long, singular shore of Florida. It seemed to be a low, wild, barren ridge of sand, in which only the stunted mangrove has a precarious footing. But twice in the whole length of the peninsula was there a sign of human habitation visible,—nothing but the desolate monotony of the ridges, and the mangrove foliage. A glass revealed, in the distance, beyond, flocks of wild fowl darkening the air, far over the eternal solitudes of the everglades.

Early this morning, we were steering away from the continent—across the Gulf Stream, which sweeps outward, with the warmth and balm of the tropics in its current,—and away toward the islands of the Gulf,— the Hesperides of the older world. Blue and bluer grew the water, till the ship's wheels seemed ploughing a channel through deeps of darkest indigo. A soft and silent dream of rain, in which the morning had been wrapped, melted into softer sunshine, and, at last, suddenly, above the sea-line of the south, a visionary range of high, precipitous mountains formed itself out of the hazy distance, and a shout from a group of eager, homesick Creoles drew our eyes to their first sight of Cuba, the Beautiful.

HAVANA, *March* 6, 1862.

. . . It was a veritable sensation, to move slowly up the magnificent Bay of Havana, in which the flags of a dozen nations languidly floated above a forest of shipping. A despicable little secession schooner entered before us, just in time to escape our guns. She had run the blockade, with a few bales of cotton, and slunk up the bay with her rag drooping astern like the tail of a scolded cur. Then, the landing, the custom-house, and the first glimpse of an Havana street. What a population, to be sure! Spaniards, Creoles or Cubans, Chinamen or Coolies, and the all-pervading negro, jostle each other in every street of the city. One of the latter, riding postillion-fashion in front of a *volante*, 'snakes' us from the wharf, and, before we are done wondering at the funny vehicle in which we dangle, with its motive power half a block ahead of us, Havana stores and houses are passing in rapid panorama, and, in a few minutes, our stock of interjections is exhausted. Through streets fifteen or twenty feet wide, with sidewalks which amount to a prohibition of crinoline,—under one of the antique gateways of the city wall, at which a guard of soldiers stands sentinel, —and we are at the hotel.

Havana is built of white stone and whiter plaster, is one story high, has tiled roofs, no steeples, three or four plazas or squares, any quantity of paseos or drives, very beautiful, and 180,000 inhabitants. Besides these, first to be mentioned, are its forts. The Spanish government, in its proclamations, addresses Cuba as '*siempre fiel*,' the ever-faithful ; but Cuba is watched, nevertheless, with the carefulness of a cat keeping vigil over a lame mouse. An army of Spaniards on the island and a navy on its shores eat up one-third of the twenty to thirty millions of Cuban revenue. These soldiers must be employed, and they build forts. . . .

Cuba has churches, about in the proportion of one to every thirty or forty thousand inhabitants, and the supply is vastly in excess of the demand. One of the first I saw, a little, quaint old chapel, against the city wall, had an inscription on its front, telling that on this spot, three centuries and a half ago, mass was celebrated for the first time in the new-found hemisphere. That would be a scene for the historical painter. Rembrandt might have wrought that effect of *chiar-oscuro*, where the single primal ray from the star that rose in the far east fell and glistened, amid the darkness of the west, on the palm-bordered shore of Cuba.

. . . But there is even more to strike the foreigner with a sense of strangeness in the dwellings of the

6

Cubans.   What would a Buffalo lady think of having
the front door of her house open plump into the stable;
or, worse, to have one side of her parlor occupied by
the family carriage?   The former circumstance is inevitable, the latter occasional, in Havana; and it is the
boast of some senoritas that their feet never touch the
soil.   They ride out, or do not go out at all.

MATANZAS, March 10, 1862.

. . . The first week of our stay in Cuba, we saw
only the city life of the islanders.   Nature looked in
upon us from far-away hills, dotted with the strange
foliage of palms.   The plaza was brilliant with the
bloom of tropical flowers, gorgeous and large.   The
fruit-stands, with a score of fruits whose very names
and existence had been unknown to us before; the
orangemen, with diminutive horses and exaggerated
panniers, trudging in, dust-begrimed, from the country,
with magnificent oranges for sale at half-a-cent apiece;
Regla, a suburb of the city, with its forty or fifty acres
of sugar warehouses,—these and a thousand other
intimations we had of the wealth and wonders we had
not yet seen.   A week ago, we came to this place—
Matanzas—a city of forty-five thousand inhabitants,
on the sea-coast, fifty or sixty miles east from Havana.
Every mile of the road hither, tropical Nature met us
with new surprises.   There were winding streams whose
courses we marked, far up and down the rich valleys,
by the tortuous rows of regal palms which stood with
their white feet washed in the limpid wave.   There
were fields of plantain, or banana, waving in the sunlight like young forests.   Orange trees, golden with
their fruit, grew by the houses and way-side as apples
in New England.   Groves of bamboo; avenues of
palm, stretching away in mathematical straightness, to
unseen plantations; waving oceans of sugar-cane, whose
shores were hills of timber unknown to the axe of the

northern woodman,—all these the locomotive, guided by American engineers, whirled past, till we arrived at Matanzas, built between the two rivers, Yumari and San Juan.

The valley of the former river is celebrated as, perhaps, the loveliest spot of Cuba. We saw it, first, from the heights of a range of hills overlooking, at once, the valley and the ocean. The morning sun was breaking through clouds, transmuting the mists of the valley to gold, and the dusk of the ocean to brightest blue. Perfectly circumvallated by mountains, the radiant region lay far beneath us, like another Eden, into whose lap was gathered the opulence of a continent. If some pencil, such as sketched the *Heart of the Andes*, should sometime immortalize itself by a picture, here, those who see the copy of nature will agree with us that it were idle to attempt to paint in words the beauty of the valley of the Yumari.

TO HIS BROTHER.

BUFFALO, *April* 7, 1862.

You will see by this superscription that I am again in 'ken'd ground,' and I may add that fifteen additional pounds of bone and muscle accompanied me home;— that, in short, I am very well indeed. . . . I got here yesterday P. M., after having had forty-seven days of the tallest kind of a time. It seems frightful to have to sit down to the desk again. Never did I ride the winged horse to such an extent before. I have come back, not only heavier in flesh, but with my mental stock in trade largely increased. It certainly paid me, richly; but, as I said before, it is awful to go to work again.

TO THE SAME.

BUFFALO, *April* 25, 1862.

. . . It has been very hard work to knuckle down to the desk again, after such a jubilant stampede and a rampage of jollity as I have been on; and, what with trying to attend to my business and nourish a stupendous article of the blues at the same time, I have not felt much like letter-writing, I assure you. Blues, did I say? Why, John, really, as you're a man of honor, did you ever see such splendid weather for the blues as we have had? The idea of suicide actually seemed to gather about it a halo of comparative cheerfulness, on some of these days. Oh, Cuba!—bright skies, palmy valleys, balmy airs, dark-eyed, bewitching senoritas, rides on the paseos, flirtations by moonlight,—how I have yearned after you, as one might yearn after the fragments of a golden dream, when he has risen, with the thermometer below zero, and the water frozen in his pitcher to a boulder!

The gloomy summer of 1862, after the calamitous Seven Days of the Army of the Potomac and its retreat from the Peninsula, brought to Gray, as to many others, the feeling that he must not be any more a looker-on at the grim battle in the South. He resolved, seriously, to join the army, and began to make his preparations, accordingly; but was persuaded to abandon the patriotic intent by entreaties of his mother, whom he loved with an exceeding tenderness. Writing afterwards to a friend, he gave this account of his undertaking and its frustration:

I have been for some time past the most unsettled wretch in all Christendom, as a brief chronicle of my recent career will explain. A few days after I wrote you, I actually went and obtained a permit to raise a company, and, with good backers, started as captain. I was comparatively happy, until, after I had begun to get things going swimmingly, down came a letter from my father and mother, so full of agony and despair that I was struck 'of a heap.' I went up home to try and reason with them; but they were inexorable. It seemed that I should have to step over my mother's grave, in the first place. So I just had to back out disgracefully. If you had known how I felt, then, you would have expected me at Groveport by next train. I thought I could not stay another hour in Buffalo. But some of my conservative friends got hold of me, and I did, and am here, yet, still scribbling editorials and, again, the slave of my 'prospects.'

This was told in a letter, written Sept. 21, 1862, to Mr. Charles W. Fairrington, whom he met, first, on the voyage to Havana, and with whom, at that time, he entered into relations of warm friendship and intimate correspondence, which continued until his death.

At the period in Gray's life which has now been reached, he was drawn deep into that feverish way of living which is called 'being in society.' From the moment he entered those whirling circles in which acquaintanceship becomes a vocation and gaiety an art, he charmed them and was temporarily charmed by them. He could so harmonize himself with all places, all people, all situations—so put himself on terms with everybody—that he helped in a rare way to produce the pleasant feeling of social harmony, wherever he went. His temperament was one of the most delightfully sympathetic that ever sweetened human intercourse, and his manner was the naive expression of a gracious feeling. His courtesy was in his nature, —his politeness was one of the gifts with which he was born. When he talked with people, all the faculties of his genius rallied to make the talk

pleasant to them. He never gave the cold-shoulders
of conversation to anybody. He met all people as
though he and they, for the time being, were the only
inhabitants of the world, and had nothing to interest
them but their present speech with one another.
This hospitality of intellectual disposition will make
even a dull man agreeable. Given to one who had
humor and imagination, a fine mind and a full one, for
the service of it, he was made supremely charming as a
companion for women or men, for young or old, for the
thoughtful or the gay. It used to be often said among
his friends, that no one else could say pretty things so
prettily, nor witty things so wittily, as David Gray.
But that did not half describe the exquisite quality of
his conversation. There was no such glitter of brilliancy about it as this characterizing might seem to
intimate. It was too quiet for that. It shone lumin-
ously, rather than brilliantly, with a peculiar glow of
warm color in it, one would choose to say, if any meta-
phor can be used.

It was to be expected, therefore, that 'society'—in
the limited and misappropriated sense of the word—
would be delighted with Gray when it made his
acquaintance, and would catch him with a thousand
hands, to drag him into its unceasing festivities. It
did so, not only in his own city, but wherever it encoun-
tered him. And he, for some years, was a yielding
though unwilling victim to its seductive blandishments.
There was one side of his nature which enjoyed the
living for gregarious entertainment immensely. There
was another and better side which revolted; but the
revolt had no success for several years, during which he

was bitterly in conflict with himself. His more confidential letters, through that period, reveal a profound unhappiness of mind, while, on the surface, he was appearing to be intoxicated with the laborious pleasures of the world. He felt that he had been false to his ideals, unfaithful to his most cherished beliefs. He knew that he was living a more than half wasted life, unworthy of his powers and forgetful of his responsibilities. He was stricken, moreover, with a sense of his moral deterioration. The grave principles and the simple habits in which he had been reared were both being sadly relaxed. Before the stop came, in fact, he had slipped down the flowery decline quite too far for one of his character, and the horror of that smooth sinking was continually in his consciousness. This suffices to explain the bitterness of the tone of some of the letters which follow:

TO CHARLES W. FAIRRINGTON.

BUFFALO, *September* 21, 1802.

. . . Write me again of your South American yearnings. Is it only a day-dream, or is it a proposition? Certain it is, I must and shall travel; but I am twenty-six years old, now, and I feel that I stand at the turning-point of my life. I have to choose, whether I shall turn a rover, ending up a sort of misanthropic, solitary old bachelor, if I live so long, or whether I shall absolutely refuse to roll,—gather moss, make a nest of it, and become a domestic animal. . . .

You speak of my having a good influence over you, my boy. It cannot be so, I doubt. Never did I, myself, so feel the need of good influences. I am running down, morally and intellectually, I think. I have been humiliated to despair, to think how utterly the creature of circumstances I am. . . . I wake up at times, only to see how far down I am, and then to go asleep again and slide. In a multitude of counselors there is safety; but, among hosts of acquaintances, here, I find myself, now, almost without friends. My artist boy has gone to this wild war,* the sword I gave him slung at his side, and the love I had for him, I find, was greater than I knew. Stillson,† also, has plunged in, and so with many of my friends.

TO DAVID TAYLOR.

BUFFALO, *November* —, 1862.

My Dear and Ever-beloved Old Friend David: It is with sensations altogether indescribable that I now turn my face to speak to you, after a silence of— God knows how long! I should be doing myself injustice if I came before you with apologies. I have none to make. If ever a man has been in the hands of a fate, hurrying him on, and controlling his action, so that he is left utterly irresponsible for non-compliance with the forms and conventionalities of life, that man is myself. Why have I not written to you? I scarcely know. If you were with me, now, and had an opportunity to know me as I am, now, you would not ask. Perhaps you will be satisfied on this point before you read this letter.

When your letter, with the old familiar superscription, came into my hands, to-day, I dared not open it. It lay before me for an hour; while I busied my hands with fifty other duties, my head and heart thought of it, alone; and yet I dared not open it. The reason was, that I feared this, to me, terrible calamity: that you had lost faith in me, and my old friendship. I

---

* Charles Caryl Coleman.

† Jerome B. Stillson, one of Gray's early companions in Buffalo, of "The Nameless"; at this period just entering the field as a war correspondent of the *New York World.*

do n't know, now, whether you have or not, and the thought tortures me, as it has often before. . . . My God! what a strange life I have led since I saw you last! How utterly the elements of my being have changed! I am almost driven mad when I contem-plate myself,—the identity almost obliterated. Yet I know that my feeling for you has not changed, and never has changed, for an hour. I have thought of you every day; but it has seemed as if you belonged to some pre-existence, with which communication was impossible. . . .

I have no ambition, now, as I once had. The fiend comes back and haunts me, occasionally, but it is easily quieted. All I want, now, is quiet—rest—removal from the hurry and turmoil in which I live. Yet, duty seems to keep me here, and I live on, gloomy and resigned. This last summer I had a plan laid to come out again and see you. I meant just to make my way straight for your hill, and live there, within the circle of woods, where I could sit and see the West, and the day die over the river, as in the days of old. I failed; but, if I live, another summer will not pass with this desire ungratified.

Poetry, with me, is dead and buried, beyond the reach of resurrection. I have not composed a line for nearly a year. I rejoice that the same damnable fact is not true of you. *The Gift*, which I publish to-mor-row morning, and of which I send you some copies, is a proof of that. Davie, you are a poet. . . . Why, there is more of the genuine, deep, passionate spirit of poesy in these lines, than you will find in volumes that pass current for poetry, now . . . If *I* had the inspi-ration that God has given you, I should be the greatest poet in America—*so recognized*, in less than two years. I used to think that I was to be the chosen instrument, the medium by which you would be brought into con-tact with the public; but I give that up, now. I have been watching, with a sort of passive curiosity, to see whether the poet in you would actually live, and sing, and die, utterly unheard. Perhaps it will be so; and, if so, then 't is best so. What is the use of making a tempest in this tea-pot of a world,—of striving to mingle the irreconcilable element of human effort with the sublime, eternal elements of fate, or providence, or whatever you choose to call it? Submission is wisdom. Whither the mighty current tends, I cannot guess; but I do know that to stem it is madness, to cross it is misery. God help us!

TO DAVID TAYLOR.

BUFFALO; January 27, 1863.

Five minutes since, I received at the post-office a letter draped in the second-mourning drab of the dead-letter office, and, opening the envelope with curious expectation, I discovered your letter of November 25, 1862. It and its contents had passed under the scrutiny of the Eye at Washington—wherefore, I know not. Have you rebellious tendencies, or have I? At any rate, your letter has just arrived, and I read it with a strange choking in the gullet. Oh, Davie! out of my inward misery I look back to you, through the golden picture you hold up to my eyes, and you stand, far, far away, associated with all that is dearest in my life,—chief in the realm of memory,—one with the blessed sinless past that can return no more! Oh, if I could only weep out at my eyes the fever that is in my heart,—the restless, throbbing disquietude,—the sinking, dull pain of regret and remorse that consume me! But I am here, forced to run in the preordained grooves, and my only refuge from mental torture is in the culture of a damned, sneering, icy indifference. Why should a man be thus unhappy; what have I done? I have but drifted onward, in obedience to a tide that seemed resistless. I did not bring myself here; I did not want to come here; I did not make myself the wretch, sinful and demoralized, that I am. Madman or slave, must man be one? . . .

Let me look, with you, Davie, back to the past of which you are still a part. Could we not build it up, again,—that temple in ruins, in which we made merry, in the golden light of poesy and youth? If I came back, could we not rebuild it?—or would I bring my cursed Buffalo heart back with me, only to find that the vision could never be recalled, and to be more wretched in consequence?

I propose you a problem, at which you and I shall work, as if it had come up for the first time, and did not look at us with the gray-browed, ancient, blearing eyes of the Sphinx—oldest of things. Let us seek 'how to be happy—how to make the best and most of life.' Let us be earnest, candid, free of prejudices and educational bias,—as if we entered earth, now, and confronted the main question but newly. It may be we shall touch the 'Fortunate Isles' and see God, whom we knew in childhood.

TO HIS BROTHER.

BUFFALO, *February* 27, 1863.

I am inaugurating an attempt to square myself off with one or two of my few correspondents, and, though it is pretty late to begin (2½ A. M.), I hope to get out a little budget, in the first place, for Detroit. . . . Buffalo has had the gayest winter known for a dozen years, and I have been in the thickest of it. . . . If you have read the recent *Courier*, you would see that I have been in verse, again, a little.* I am also engaged to deliver another paper or poem before the Buffalo Historical Society, two weeks from to-day.† You will

* Poem read at the celebration of Washington's Birthday by the Buffalo Central School.

† 'The Last of the Kah-Kwahs.'

see that, when it comes. I have also several invites to
lecture, which I can't accept, as I haven't any lecture.
I am steadying down to work, again, and hauling off
as much as possible from the gaieties. I hope to do
some good business this coming season.

TO HIS BROTHER.

May 7, 1863.

. . . How happy a man must be whose work is done
at six o'clock. Here I am, at two A. M.—and it's a
regular thing. Still, I manage to weave in so much
recreation as is needed for the comfort of the outer
man, and so keep my health.

TO HIS MOTHER.

BUFFALO, *August* 24, 1863.

. . . I think of you all, and of your quiet lives, and,
like the May Queen, am 'often, often with you when
you think I'm far away.'

John's visit, by the bye, was a very pleasant episode;
but it was sadly marred by my lack, at the time, of all
leisure. . . . He would tell you, doubtless, of how I
got through the draft, nicely, and was entirely pacific
in my intentions, even had I been drafted. I feel,
now, that I have something to work for, and really get
up quite an appearance of ambition to myself. Everything in a business way is going very well. It is quite
wonderful, indeed, that a citizen should be so well off,
when his country is engaged in a desperate effort to
cut its own throat. . . .

How is the work on the farm? Are harvesting and
haying well advanced? Does Walter want an extra
hand? I wonder how I could rake and bind, now, on
a pinch! But poorly, I suspect. Still, it must be the
muscle and vitality I acquired in the days of my cap-

tivity which subsist me now. Consequently, I do not regret that part of the past.

John would, of course, tell you lots of things about my way of living, here. He may have given you rather a doleful account of my late hours, hard work, etc.; for I noticed he was not prepossessed in favor of the newspaper business. You must remember, should this have been the case, that that time was an exceptional one; moreover that the n. b. aforesaid is the only business I am fitted for; that I like it and could like no other, and that I am being tolerably successful in it.

TO HIS BROTHER.

BUFFALO, *November* 10, 1863.

. . . My matters are flourishing as well as I can expect. . . . I feel- sure, if the country holds together and does not bleed and batter itself to death, that I shall work through, all right. Of the country, however, I am by no means sure. It looks to me, now, as if we were entered upon a real revolution, which may last the life-time of any of us and result, algebraically speaking, in X. Such things have been in the world's history, before, and why not again? Man is not a whit a wiser or better animal than he was when Greece and Rome, successively, crumbled away in blood.

TO DAVID TAYLOR.

BUFFALO. *February* —, 1864.

. . . I have come strangely out of my blues of late, Davie, and am driving ahead, whither I know not, in a queer sort of energetic way, with teeth clenched, as it were, and eyes fixed on vacancy. I am growing, and I know it. Worse, perhaps,—stronger, I *know.* Men have not power to cast me down, or up. . . . Out of the ashes of what you and I once knew in common,—

up from the desolate hearth where we fed together that strange fire of truest love for poesy,—has sprung up, for me, a something which is going to make my life. . . . The fact is, that old life has become only a memory; for long, it was much—very much—more. I doubt whether the time has not passed, forever, in which I can be thrown back into the phases of feeling which were once to me the best. I am sentimental— if that is the word—no longer. . I think fancy remains; she has a stronger wing than ever, if I am not much mistaken. A sort of business-like, practical imagination remains, also, if you will allow the contradiction of terms. But, long since, the longings, the yearnings, the exaltations which filled me when I knew poetry first, have died of sheer starvation and hard usage. I look back, now, with strange interest, Davie, on our common stock of experience; but the interest is practical, withal. That was what made me what I am and am to be. Can you not see how what I have attempted to describe for you is going to come out of that age of the happy ideal, and the other age of the miserable real, which succeeded it? And you will walk through the valley, and emerge from it, too,—oh, friend of my heart! Davie, I must and shall try to see you, the coming summer. It would be worth gold to us, both, to compare notes and try a sounding again, together, in the new seas we have got into. It must be done.

TO HIS BROTHER.

BUFFALO, *March* 10, 1864.

. . . I send you the copy of verses you ask. It was published in a little Central Fair pamphlet, from which I cut it. Here is also another copy of the Golden Wedding piece, and of the *Ministry of Art*, which some of you may like to have. These things won me lots of good words and, what is worth more, served to relight all my old fires of ambition, in that

line. It is probable that I shall follow up the verse
writing.

TO CHARLES W. FAIRRINGTON.

BUFFALO, *March* 10, 1864.

. . . I have been scribbling a good deal lately,—
always, however, because I am cornered into it. I
have no time to work my own fancies into verse. The
best I can do is to write under pressure of a necessity,
begotten by some occasion. I send you two or three
of my latest. Remember, each one of them was the
work of the night and day preceding the hour of their
recitation. Pardon this burst of egotism. It is only
the foretaste of what you will have to stand if I get
along-side of you.

TO HIS BROTHER.

BUFFALO, *June* 29, 1864.

Yours of the 25th was, of course, as you may imagine, read by me with more than ordinary interest. I
think I may safely congratulate, as I most heartily
God bless you! . . . I hope, by the time I come
round to see you next summer, I shall stay at the
Hotel de Gray at Detroit. It will be jolly. I would
not be precipitate about that, however; for you are
both young, or else I am deuced old. I can afford to
wait till there is a clear sky, wherein may soar, serene
and cloudless, the Moon of Honey. Give A—— my
best love. Aside from the folks yonder, over the river,
who else should have it?

TO HIS MOTHER.

BUFFALO, *April* 17, 1865.

. . . There is a possibility that I may be in Europe,
before long. Within a few days, I have had a proposition made to me by Mr. Fargo* to take his son,

---

* The late William G. Fargo, President of the American Express Co.

a lad of nineteen, to Europe, and there travel and reside for one, two, or three years, at my discretion. My business would be, simply, to direct the boy's studies, and see that he did not get into mischief. Mr. F. pays all expenses, handsomely, including tutors for myself, as well as his son, if I want them, and a salary, besides. . . . Mr. Warren offers to take care of my interest, here, and, if everything goes on as at present, have it all paid for, by the time I come back. The chance, you will agree, is a splendid one. It would realize what has been my dream, for years past, and would give me a fair opportunity to test whether I have got anything in me worth cultivating, in a literary way. I should write and read and study, as well as travel, and could choose a residence just in the places, of all the world, best adapted for these purposes. I have not, by any means, made up my mind that I am going, yet, and there are many things which may interfere to prevent; still, I think it probable that the thing, wildly unreal as it seems, will become an actuality. I want you to write me and tell me what you think. Of course, I shall see you before I go, which, at the earliest, will be six weeks from now.

TO HIS BROTHER.

BUFFALO, *May* 8, 1865.

Your good letter came to-day. I blame myself for not having written you before, but my mind has really been much distracted. As you will see by my note to Isabella, the European idea is nearly *un fait accompli.* I wish you were going, too; but it may be some consolation to you, when I say, that I would rather stay here and be married, if everything were right for that, than, even, go to Europe. But my usual luck pursues me in that regard, and I am, apparently, as far from forming any matrimonial attachment as I ever was. Consequently, the next best thing for me is to travel, and fit myself for some kind of useful single life.

TO DAVID TAYLOR.

DETROIT, *May* 25, 1865.

Dear and Unforgotten Friend: I felt the dew in my eyes as I re-read your letter, yesterday, coming here on the cars; with my face towards you and my heart in a very tempest of sad and painful emotion. For what you say in reproach, or worse, I blame myself, not you, David; but, with a confidence born of our ancient love, I call upon you, as you read this, to forget the darksome latter years that have risen between us, and think of me, again, as you were wont of old. . . . Know thou, oh, brother of my heart and soul, that my love for you can never change. Time may intervene, space may intervene, and so, for years, I become hidden from you; but you are, to me, now and ever, what you were once. There are but two others on the wide earth to whom, beside yourself, I am kindred. Life has been all a dark, troubled dream to me, except as it stands associated with you and these. It passes before me, now, all unreal and phantasmal, except as to the sorrow and the torture of it; and there is left to me, of light and reality, only what I owe to you and two others. . . .

I have several unfinished letters to you in my desk. They were each smitten with the palsy, in the act of talking with you. Two years ago, this month, I likewise got out as far as Chicago, on my way to see you. I was recalled and prevented. I shall not see you for years to come, now. On the seventh of next month I sail for Europe, to be gone, probably, three years. Every line of *Childe Harold* that we used to read and rant together is burning truth to me now. I leave Buffalo under bright external auspices, but with a heart of gall.

Howsoever these things be, a long farewell to Locksley Hall!
Now for me the woods may wither, now for me the roof-tree fall.
Comes a vapour from the margin, blackening over heath and holt,
Cramming all the blast before it, in its breast a thunderbolt.
Let it fall on Locksley Hall, with rain or hail or fire or snow;
For the mighty wind arises, roaring seaward, and I go.

Oh, David! we knew it not then, but those were the
halcyon and enchanted days and nights! They can
never return to us any more. I need not tell you that
my life, for six years past, has been very unhappy.
Were it not for the dread of something after death,—
a consciousness that the capacity to be tortured out-
lasts the grave,—I would gladly, gladly, be under the
grass, with the one word, 'Infelix,' pointing to my
place of rest. You, too, have been unhappy. Is it
not strange? What does it mean? Is Love or Hate
the god of this wretched earth? . . . My faith and
opinions are all at sea. My conscience is more sensitive than a whipped back, pickled, and gives me un-
told agonies. This, alone, I have: I can endure, with
a face which tells no tales. I have not hope, but something which, perhaps, answers the same purpose,—a
sort of intellectual perception that a change must come,
before long, and that it cannot be for the worse. . . .

I was looking, the other day, over some of your old
pieces, and the conviction came back to me that the
lyrical element exists in your mind as it does in no
other mind in America. I think I could sing myself
happy if I had your gift. I wish I could stir you up
to try it for yourself. I shall try my hand, again, when
I get out of this country. I shall, perhaps, be happy
then, and when I am happy, if only for a minute, my
ears still fill with unutterable music.

Here is a photograph which I want you to look at,
and know that its eyes are the eyes of one who will
never cease to see you in memory. The gold of perpetual sunlight and the silver of moons that were mag-
ical surround you, in my mind, forever, Davy!

I have not seen —— for a long time. He is an

honest man and a true friend ;• but I cannot make myself agreeable to everybody, as I once could. Men do not interest me, as once, and they discern the fact, and I go on my way alone, or among those who are content with only the plating of friendship. David, it is my opinion there are many more women in the world whom a man might love and marry, than men whom a man can take as the twin and brother of his heart. As I said, I found but you and two others. They know you, and, sometime, we shall all meet and see what the spiritual kindred means.

I have to break off here. Good-by, Davy, dear friend of my youth. Write, if this reaches you in time to allow you to answer me before the seventh. I will write to you from some nook wherefrom I shall look forth and see the purple of the heather.

CHAPTER V.

YEARS OF TRAVEL. 1865–1868.

WHEN the letters given last, in the preceding chapter, were written, Gray saw himself near to a happy turn in his life, which was reached, as he expected it, a few days afterwards. Early in June, 1865, he sailed for Liverpool, with the young gentleman who had been confided to his care. He left behind him the strain and the drudgery of an exhausting profession—the fret of bondage to a mode of life which was disappointing his best desires. He left them, with a prospect before him of years of lingering travel in Europe and the farther East, of leisurely observation, of ripening study,—of a calm, slow absorption of the art, the history, the civilization of the older world. It was a promise so beautifully in keeping with the dreams and hopes of his life that it could not fail to charm away the saddened moods which had grown upon him, and to recall the healthier spirits of his youth. The very winds of the Atlantic, on his outward voyage, appear to have blown the melancholy vapors out of his brain, and he landed on the other shore well prepared for the best enjoyment of his great opportunity.

Beginning on ship-board, June 15, 1865, and ending, likewise, in mid-Atlantic, April 14, 1868, he wrote, during his travels, for publication in the *Buffalo*

Courier, a series of letters, fifty-eight in number, which will now form the contents of the second volume of this memorial collection of his writings. Not many who look into that volume will leave the letters unread; probably no one who reads them will ask why they have been reprinted. They are, most of them, from ground that has been traveled over and written about until the world is tired of it, in books, and yet their charm is wholly fresh. They have a quality which is quite their own,—a pervading, unobtrusive poetry, touched with a humor akin to poetry,—for the delicate vein of which it will not be easy to find any just comparison in the literature of travel.

It is not the intention to repeat at all, in this place, the narrative of travel and life that is given in the letters referred to. But something will be drawn from the private letters which Gray wrote to his friends, while abroad, to trace the movements of his feeling and thinking, and to follow the effect upon him of the powerful new influences under which he was brought.

TO WILLIAM P. LETCHWORTH.

On Board the S. S. 'China,'
Near Queenstown, *June* 15, 1865.

It was a bitter disappointment to me to be obliged to leave Buffalo, without having felt the friendly grasp of your hand in farewell. . . . I wanted to talk to you, as to the way in which I might make the very most of this European pilgrimage of mine. I tremble lest I shall not be able to do the best with such a golden opportunity. My general idea is, to absorb as much as possible of literary culture, and to settle, if I can, before I come back, the question, whether I am to be justified in making of literature a life. Believe me, I shrink from the assumption involved in this intention; and yet I will try to do the best I can. If my friends have misjudged the character or degree of my ability, I shall be sorry—very sorry—but it will not have been my fault. . . . I conjure you to keep me in your remembrance, and, also, to guard with added jealousy, for my sake, the gates of the 'Happy Valley.' When I come back, I hope to be worthier of it and you, and we shall talk of beautiful things together, yet, with the waterfall sounding a symphony for us.

TO HIS MOTHER.

On Board the ' China,'
In St. George's Channel, *June* 16, 1865.

I wrote you, I think, from Boston, and on Monday of last week, the day after I sailed, I sent a note, to John, ashore at Halifax. Since then, we have been steadily pursuing our voyage,—the sea, for the most part, having been as calm as a mill-pond. . . . Of course, I do not fail to think, every other minute, now-a-days, of the first voyage of us all, across the Atlantic. There is much difference, to be sure, between the steamer *China* and the ship *Constitution*. We are lodged comfortably, and fed better than one would be at most first-class hotels. The passengers are mostly of the kid-glove variety, and everything is arranged with reference to the elegant habits of the kid-glove animal. Yet, I question whether there are so many strong, cheery, brave hearts, crossing for pleasure or sentiment, on the *China*, as there crossed on the *Constitution*, to the tune of 'Cheer, Boys, Cheer,'—the emigrant's song. . . . It seems very strange to be going back, over the track which we traveled sixteen years ago, and I can scarcely convince myself that one or the other of the experiences—that or the present— is not a dream. . . .

My young companion greatly improves upon acquaintance, and I have far higher hopes now, than before, of doing him and his father a good service. I think I have his confidence and respect, fully.

TO HIS MOTHER.

LONDON, *July* 9, 1865.

. . . You cannot imagine how jolly it is to be absolute master of one's movements,—to go or stay just wherever taste leads, in this paradise of the student or observer. . . . My young friend, F——, is turning out a hundred per cent. better than my most sanguine expectation of him foretold. I am really getting fond of him, and earnestly ambitious to be of service to him. . . . As for myself, this experience is just what I needed. It has, even now, put more life and energy into my mind than I have felt in five years at Buffalo. I am sure I shall be richly paid for the time I am absent. Even to have seen London and breathed its atmosphere, seems to have given me a mental leverage that I never could have obtained at home. . . . Our lodgings are very plain, but pleasant. They are situated within a stone's throw, almost, of the Thames, near Waterloo Bridge.

While at London, David received from his friend, Mr. Letchworth, a gift which, then and always, was very precious to him. This was Edgar A. Poe's watch, —the watch which the poet had carried for many years before his death, and which, preserved by his mother-in-law, Mrs. Clemm, at Baltimore, had lately come, well authenticated, into Mr. Letchworth's possession. Regarding David Gray as fitly the heir to such a relic and memento of the most original genius among American poets, he transmitted the watch to him.* The following are passages from a letter which David wrote to Mr. L., on meeting Mr. Josiah Letchworth in London and receiving the watch from his hands:

LONDON, *July* 22, 1865.

. . . I know that friendship does not, like justice, flourish a pair of scales, and I accept and have accepted your friendship as one of God's choice gifts to me. And, now, of this, its latest and crowning manifestation, I need scarcely say that I receive the treasure you commit to me; that it will be sacredly kept and guarded, and that the stipulation you make will be religiously respected. Furthermore, permit me, though it may seem conceited, to say that you have not misjudged, in choosing a repository for this precious relic. I do not think Edgar Allen Poe has had a more loving and reverent student than, for ten years past, I have been. With the first money I ever earned I bought his works, and, deep in the Wisconsin backwoods, I devoured every word of them, over and over and over, and literally lived under the spell of his weird and magnificent genius. . . . As I look upon this golden souvenir of his brief life, I thrill with a recollection of times when the intensity of my sympathy with his writings had almost seemed to call his spirit to my side, and when I would gladly have spent my years in labor to have taken him by the hand and gazed into his eyes, but for a moment. When I think of these things, and remember, as well, that I have often met him (almost alone of the authors I love) in dreams, and held dim converse with him, thus, I do not wonder much that I am so strangely chosen to keep this

---

*Since the death of David Gray, this watch has been given by Mrs. Gray (with Mr. Letchworth's approval) to the Buffalo Library, and added to the very valuable and interesting collection of literary souvenirs which that institution exhibits.

last relic of him. It seems, rather, to be fit and proper that you have done as you have. . . .

The effect already produced upon me by the change of continents has been gratifying beyond my most sanguine expectations. I am renewing my youth and freshness; my mind has not been so happy and wide awake, as it is now, for ten years. I almost hope that I am, at last, making up for opportunities lacked or wasted in my past life, and that something like a regular process of culture has begun for me. All my old ambition, and more than that, seems to have revived in me, and, therefore, it is superfluous for me to say, that whatever my capacity and these golden opportunities, taken as factors in the sum, may be able to work out, will be wrought to the last figure. I have always told you my incredulity as to the estimate you and others place upon my abilities; and I cannot say that my faith in this respect has at all increased. But this I can assure you, and all others who love me: what God has enabled me to do, by His help *will be done*. . . . You know how I was haunted and dogged by 'evil things in robes of sorrow' while I remained in Buffalo. All these have ceased to hound my steps. I think the ghosts are laid for good and all. I am very happy, and I want to refine and climax that happiness by having you with me, next winter. Is it asking too much?

Leaving London, the day on which the above was written, Gray and his companion traveled slowly into Scotland and reached Edinburgh at the end of July. The long, full letter which he wrote, then, from his native city—revisiting it after sixteen years—has been liberally quoted from in the first chapter of these memoirs (page 6). Before quitting Edinburgh and Scotland, where they stayed some weeks, he wrote to his partner and friend, Joseph Warren:

EDINBURGH, *September* 1, 1865.

... I cannot quite justify to myself the fact that
I am *here* while you are *there ;* and I tell you gravely,
although I know full well what I should lose, I would
start for the *Courier* office to-morrow if I thought you
would be less displeased than gratified by the move. ...
I know so well what you have to struggle under, at the
office, that I am scarcely less unhappy, thinking of
you. I repeat it in all seriousness,—you have but to
say half a word, and I am home. I have already
reaped a vast benefit from my trip, and I would not
consider that I had achieved an abortion, coming back
now. But I want to be guided by you, in my coming
back as I was in my going out; and I hope you will
give the subject your best consideration, allowing no
sort of romantic regard for my interests to swerve you
unduly, in deciding what is the best practical, matter-
of-fact course for me to pursue. ...

Except my letters, I have written nothing since I
came over here; but I venture to hope that, when the
subject I am trying to think out shall form itself, I
shall be able to go at it with good heart. The faith
which you and other good friends so strangely have in
me almost serves me, instead of the faith in myself
which I wish I possessed.

TO JOSEPH WARREN.

LONDON, *October* 5, 1865.

... You speak of the possibility of my voluntary
divorcement from its [the *Courier's*] ancient service.
For myself, I do not see the slightest chance of that. I
trust, in the past three or four months I have gained a
good deal of mental strength and capital; but I certainly have not grown greatly in my estimate of my
own powers. I have contracted, as yet, no higher
ambition than that of returning to Buffalo, with my
liabilities in part cleared off, and of settling down to

be a first-class editor—if I can ever be that individual. I believe that life, with some little modifications, would give all the chance for the working out of whatever ability may be in me that any other would; and I am almost ready, *now*, to come home and go to work with an earnestness I have not felt for years. So, please never to think of me except as your traveling associate, who is soon to return, a much more valuable man than he went away.

TO HIS BROTHER.

PARIS, *November* 30, 1865.

. . . We have settled down in quiet, comfortable quarters, here, and are intent on getting a little French picked up. Devoting ourselves almost exclusively to that, we have taken no time for sight-seeing, and I have not even gathered material, since I have been here, for a letter to the *Courier*. French comes rather toughly; but, I think, in a few weeks more I shall have it under the fifth rib. I am sure I shall be repaid for all the labor I am expending, now. We have lots of pleasant acquaintances here.

TO JOSEPH WARREN.

PARIS, *December* 7, 1865.

. . . I have not found my life in Paris at all productive of newspaper letters. I have been trying hard for several weeks to start some natural sort of correspondence out of it; but thus far in vain. It is like this: We came here and settled down in a quiet hotel to study French. We have scarcely begun the round of sight-seeing, and I am not at all *en rapport* with the sources of Parisian news. What I could write, now, would be either of things which everybody knows too much already, or of which I do not know enough. Therefore, have patience for a little.

TO HIS MOTHER.

PARIS, *December* 20, 1865.

. . . We have been living for the past six weeks at a sort of private hotel, kept by a nice old French couple, in which we have a comfortable suite of rooms, along with two other young Buffalonians. We break- fast, commonly, about noon — all France does — and then sally forth to a French lesson; after which, the day is spent in sight-seeing, walking about the city, or study. Dinner, at *table d'hôte*, comes off at six o'clock, when we sit down to a snug little meal of ten courses, the table-talk being a lively melange of English, Ger- man, French and Spanish. In the evening we go to the theater, opera, or some other of the thousand Par- isian shows, or spend the time socially, with some one of the score or two of American families of our ac- quaintance, resident in the city. . . . My general purpose in staying so long in Paris has been to learn something of France and the French language, here, at the very center and source of everything French. About ten days more will probably finish our Parisian experience, for the present, and we will then take up our traps and proceed to Rome. I have got a little start in French, which will suffice for the exigencies of travel, and upon which I hope to build, by and by, a tolerable knowledge of the language.

We are to be met in Rome by Henry Richmond, my true and tried friend. With him, we will explore Italy, this winter, and, in the spring, it is my purpose to find some quiet town or village, in the neighborhood of Switzerland, probably, where we will settle down to study French and German. . . .

I celebrated my twenty-ninth birthday last month. Did you think of it? That makes us all pretty old, does n't it? I only hope and pray we may be all spared to meet, at least once more, in Detroit. As for me, I am ten years younger in feeling and five in appearance than when I left the editorial room.

TO JOSEPH WARREN.

NAPLES, *February* 4, 1866.

. . . I wrote a long letter to the *Courier* from Nice, and another from Genoa. I have another one on the stocks, from Naples. The scow is afloat again, and I dare-say the water deepens. Be merciful and forgive! The fact, simply, was, that I could n't write letters from Paris in the two months I was there. Imagine the consolation administered when I learned, from a letter written to me by a friend in Buffalo, that my silence was generally attributed among my home acquaintances to the fact that I had fallen into dissipated habits! I suppose I allow these things to trouble me more than I ought; but it did make me boil with indignation. I would not go aside a step, myself, to put my heel on the wicked, cruel lie; but, if it should ever find its way where it might work me harm, I think I can rely on you and the true friends I have at home to clear me of an utterly baseless charge.

TO JOSEPH WARREN.

FLORENCE, *April* 15, 1866.

. . . Although I am deriving all the benefit I expected from Europe, and feel myself expanding and strengthening every day, I still yearn to get back to the serious business of life, and grudge every moment which may even seem to be devoted to pleasure, merely. You may think this is a wondrous change over the spirit of my dream; but such as I write the truth is. I am, a thousand times a day, thankful for the chance I have had, and I value it, perhaps, chiefly because it has lifted me out of the dust and bustle in which I was merged, and enabled me to review, long and well, all the outs and ins of my career. Besides all this, I know I am fairly shoveling in general information, at present, and my old poetic tastes and ambitions are stronger upon me than ever before. I have actually written some verse lately, and I have even a scheme for a long poem (!) to be worked out the present summer.

TO JOSEPH WARREN.

GENEVA, *June* 21, 1866.

. . . We have now been three weeks settled; our home is the 'bosom' of a very kind, pleasant family, on the outskirts of this quiet little city, and we get French, and nothing but French, the whole day long. Besides that, we are living very cheaply, simply and virtuously,—getting up at six in the morning, taking walks after tea with madame, and going to church Sundays, like young Christians, as we are. Altogether, we could not have made a better hit; the place is the very one I had been wishing for, while doubting the probability of finding it. I shall soon be a tolerable French scholar, if that will be worth anything to me.

TO HIS BROTHER.

GENEVA, *August* 24, 1866.

. . . Returning to the pension one evening, about five weeks ago, I found a telegram telling me that my old and dear friend Stillson had arrived at London and was seeking me. A few days after, he bounced in on me, and, for a week, we had a glorious time together, here. We went up the lake and among the mountains, and fairly revelled in the joy of our meeting, until he was forced to leave me. Europe used to be a dream with Stillson and me, so hopelessly far away and so ravishingly bright that, you may imagine, the joint fulfillment of it brought some genuine pleasure.

TO COL. JOHN HAY.

BRUSSELS, *November* 29, 1866.

. . . Can't you run up, now, and dip your fist with us into the moss of Flemish antiquity. I find Belgium exceeding rich in interest, historic and other. . . . I am reading what I can and writing a little; but I feel sadly the want of some mental stimulus. Colonel, if you'll come anywhere and meet me, I'll engage we shall do something that shall make the age tremble. It is not often that immortality is thus thrust upon the young. ('Circular sent on receipt of a dollar in postage stamps.')

TO HIS BROTHER-IN-LAW.

BERLIN, *December* 30, 1886.

. . . The fact is, the life of a traveler is a very ordinary and unexciting one, after the first year's harvest of sensations has been gathered in. I have a genuine eagerness to see Jerusalem and the Nile; but, with these exceptions, all places I have not seen are about equally indifferent to me. I shall only visit them as I would read books from which to get needed information. I take a great deal of interest, just now, in European politics, which are in a very attractive state at present, as you are doubtless seeing. My little stay in Berlin has been useful, in giving me some idea of the character of the people, which has suddenly thrown off its disguise and come out as the dominant nation of Europe, and which, moreover, is by no means yet at the summit of its powers.

TO HIS SISTER.

CONSTANTINOPLE, *February* 16, 1867.

. . . Here I am, with my window looking full out on that Bosphorus of which we have all seen pictures since our infancy. Do you remember the little framed

steel engraving of it, which used to hang somewhere in
our little parlor, in the Sciennes? I am not sure but
it is in the house, yet. Well, I recognized every feature of the wondrous scene from my memory of that.
There was the Golden Horn—Seraglio Point—the
lovely shore of either continent. Look at the little
picture, again, for me, and fancy me sailing up and
down in these waters in a Turkish caïque.

TO JOSEPH WARREN.

BEYROUT, *February* 21, 1867.

The date of this letter will show you how badly my
plans epistolary have prospered. I have positively had
no leisure—no leisure unless I stole it from hours
which, to me, have been the most valuable of my
life. Bear with me, therefore, and I will try to do
better. We start, to-day, for Jerusalem, on horseback
and with tents, by way of Baalbec, Damascus, Caper-
naum, Nazareth, etc. We have a fine party with us
and are in splendid trim. In twenty days we shall see
the Holy City.

TO HIS PARENTS.

BEYROUT, *March* 22, 1867.

About ten days ago I dropped you a little note, saying that I was just recovering from an attack of the
small-pox, my headquarters being, then, Damascus.
I improve the opportunity of the very first mail
for the civilized world since that time to write you,
again, and dilate fully on affairs personal, being convinced that your liveliest interest is, by this time,
awakened there anent. To begin, therefore, away at
the beginning: You remember, I wrote you a note
from this very place, about a month and a day ago,
saying that I was about starting, with a nice party, for
Jerusalem, by way of Damascus, etc. We left, the

day I mailed that note, and, that very day, our chapter of mischances began. A terrific storm caught us in the afternoon, on Lebanon, and, before we got housed for the night, we were pretty roughly used and our ladies rather frightened. The weather continued bad for three days, so that our cavalcade could not be started, but was forced to cling for shelter to the mud walls of the house in the little mountain Arab village which we had made in the storm. I got impatient at this waiting, and, with a Russian gentleman of our party, conceived the idea of starting in advance, and gaining sufficient time on the party to permit us to visit the famous Cedars of Solomon, in the mountains. We started, accordingly—we two—and threw ourselves on the country for lodgings and provisions. Four days we lived with the Arabs, in quite a charming way, as I will describe to you, sometime. The fourth day, I, alone, reached the Cedars, the snow being so very deep and the climbing so steep that my friend was obliged to give it up, half-way. That day was a pretty toilsome one, but it was a success, and I got back to Baalbec (look up your map) late at night, tired but victorious. The next day I started out to study the splendid ruins of Baalbec, and I had just daylight enough given me in which to do it. Before I had quite got through, the blood had begun to congest in my head, and my eyes were closed to the faintest ray of light. We started on (the party reassembled by this time) for Damascus,—I with my eyes guardedly bandaged, and suffering intensely from pain in them. This pain and total blindness continued, for the three days during which we were on the way to Damascus, and, finally, I was led in, like Paul of old, and lodged not far from ‘the street called Straight,’ if not quite on it. I thought I should be all right when the inflammation of my eyes was allayed a bit; but I soon discovered that something else was to pay. In short, I was obliged to go, in a very few hours, to bed, and that bed I kept for fifteen days. The third day, to my and my doctor's surprise, the small-pox showed itself in full blaze. My head and face were one mass of pustules, and the attack, in fact, was, though short, very sharp, indeed. As I told you, I was well cared for. My friends stayed by, till I was out of danger, and my friend Fargo, from beginning to end, stuck by me like a brick, despising danger and behaving nobly. I wanted for nothing,—even away out there in the heart of Syria, where an European face is as rare as a Turk's in Detroit, almost. Everybody befriended me, in fact. A week ago to-day, I got the doctor's permission to get up, and, once on my legs, my strength and spirits came back as rapidly as they had fled, before. Each day I gained. I was able to visit all the sights of Damascus, —to take long rides in its glorious vicinity,—to appreciate fully, with eyes both bodily and mental, its world-old associations, and, finally, to make the journey thence hither. We arrived here yesterday evening, safe and sound, having been absent just a month;—not a long time, considering the events crowded into it. I feel myself, now, as well as ever, bating, perhaps, just a little feebleness of legs and eyes. You will ask, next, how has my beauty fared in the visitation? I hasten to inform the entire fair sex, that I have come off so little the worse that it will not be safe for them to calculate on any damage done. I have a few pits on the brow, and one or two on the chin, and my nose is a *leetle* mottled. Seriously, I thank God with my whole heart for the mercy and goodness He has showed me in this unusual providence of His. His ways are wise and good. Praise Him with me, all you whom I love, and whom I dreamed of in my delirium, and prayed for so often, in the long watches of my sick nights.

You may wonder how I caught the disease, especially as, if my memory serves me right, I had it slightly once before. My theory is, that the virus struck me on board the steamer in which we came from Constantinople to Smyrna, which was swarming with Moslem pilgrims, bound for Mecca. They are famous as conductors of disease, and I have no doubt I owe mine to some unfortunate of them. My experience in going to the Cedars, of course, precipitated and intensified the malady.

And, now, as to our future movements: It rejoices me to say that we are not to be defrauded of our journey through the Holy Land to Jerusalem. We start to-morrow morning, again, by way of Tyre, Sidon, Mt. Carmel, Nazareth, Tiberias, Samaria and Bethel, to Jerusalem, and have our old dragoman, who took care of us, before, more like a father than a servant. I believe he verily loves me like one of his own boys. In ten or twelve days, D. V., we shall be at the Holy City, when I shall write you again. Meanwhile, be happy as regards me, for this is the crowning part of my travels, and I am to be regarded with envy, but with no graver sentiment.

The journey to Jerusalem was made as it had been arranged for, and it is certain that David found more in it to interest him than in any other part of his travels. His note-book gives evidence of the fact, in the minuteness and uncommon fullness of the memoranda which he entered. But he wrote nothing of it to the *Courier*, and there is a singular break at this period in his private correspondence. In a later letter he attributes the delinquency to days of hard travel and sight-seeing and nights of weak eyes. It was known, afterwards, to some of his friends, that he had planned a book, in which the fruits of his visit to the Holy Land would be used; but nothing is known definitely of the plan, nor why it was given up.

By a passing glance, only, as it were, he saw Egypt and the Nile, sailing from Alexandria to Brindisi, and arriving in Rome, for a second visit, on the 23d of April. At Rome he found his artist friends, Coleman and Vedder, with others, and passed some delightful days; after which he journeyed northwards, and his letters are resumed:

TO JOSEPH WARREN.

VENICE, *May* 5, 1867.

. . . I have been working hard and earnestly of late, as often as I have been able to do so, and I am sure I have written some better poems than any of mine you have yet seen; albeit I begin to see, as I never did before, how perfectly mottled with imperfection they are, and how altogether puny is my grasp of any subject. But, perhaps, in the year that is coming, I shall do better and will bring or send home a little ' volume.' I would like to start with a little v. of poems, and, after that, I have several ideas for books in mingled prose and verse, which I think would work up well.

TO DAVID TAYLOR.

MILAN, ITALY, *May* —, 1867.

It is nearly eleven years since the strange and close communion of long ago was broken up; it is, at least, half-a-dozen since I last saw your face; but, as I read your letter over again,—as I look on its familiar hand-writing,—it seems to me that I have parted with you and lost your figure among the brush of the Wisconsin openings, yonder, only a moment since. Oh, this mystery of life!—what does it all mean? That we were brought together in that strange way; that we lived together, as we did, and that we were so divided,

—you to remain as a sort of landmark to me of my
lost years,—I to enter and wander in such a labyrinth
of circumstances as I have found this world to be!
Always, when I think of it, David, it appears to me
that our discovery of each other was an extraordinary
thing. I have met thousands of men, since, of taste,
education and all that; but, in the whole lot, never
have I met but one, except yourself, who has even that
understanding of poetry which was ours in common,—
to speak of nothing more. It is a sort of pastime of
mine,—a sort of necessity with me, rather,—to seek the
acquaintance of man after man, as the stream of new
men sweeps by me, and to sound them, one by one, to
see if I may not find, some time, even some faint
repetition of the experience I used to have when we
were together. It never comes. I doubt if the rest of
the world contains the material for it.

I do not discover much change in you, judging from
your letters. You are a trifle older,—your features
seem to be a little more fixed and sternly set,—but
the old look is in them, still. I fear as much could
not be said of myself. You know my character, the
weakness of which has permitted me to be, all these
years, a kind of shuttlecock, batted about from phase
to phase of change. But that is of little importance,
as affecting our relations, I think. . . . If we should
come together twenty years from now, I know we
should feel the very same, and fall into the very ways
of old, saving that now and then we would miss the
presence of our youth.

I want to imitate your example and begin by writing
something about myself; but what to write on that
subject puzzles me. I feel like saying—Wait a little,
till the smoke clears away, before you ask to know
about the battle. I am traveling on a road, Davie, the
end of which I do not see, yet. I have solved nothing,
thus far. The Sphinx looks at me implacably, with her
riddle still unread. Yet, a hope draws me on, that

sometime I will stop groping and suddenly *see*. As for worldly affairs, they give me very little trouble. There is no danger of my ever being rich, nor of my ever wanting a living, as long as I can work. My philosophy stands me perfectly, as far as all such questions are concerned. Since I have come abroad, traveling through the greater part of Europe and in the East, I have had many experiences, that memory will amuse herself with, sufficiently, and, on the whole, I am glad I came. But, after all, travel is of little use to a man who has any imagination of his own. He sees it all, or something perhaps far better, sitting in front of the sinking fagots of his hearth, or watching the whirl of the snow out of his window. I do not know that I have anything more to say about myself. I shall be home in about a year from now, and then shall try to see you as soon as possible.

Your two poems are the truest bits of yourself in your letters. . . . Send both pieces somewhere. They might as well be in print as not: though it makes but little difference to you or me, I fancy,—the attainment of that dazzling distinction. The days of *Graham's Magazine* are long past, are n't they?

TO HIS MOTHER.

PARIS, *May* 24, 1867.

. . . We stay here two or three weeks, then say good-bye to our friends and move off to some quiet home in Germany for the summer. . . . I am not so much to be 'pitted' as I was, and never felt so well in my life, as now.

TO HIS BROTHER-IN-LAW.

PARIS, *July* 3, 1867.

. . . This Paris is the worst place I ever saw for a letter-writer to be stationed in, or, in fact, for any one who would perform any sort of serious business. One's room, more or less elevated towards the seventh heaven, is a locality which one visits, here, only once in the twenty-four hours, and that for purely animal purposes. As soon as sleep is through with, there is nothing thought of but to dart down into the great eating and drinking, talking and sight-seeing world. And the peculiarity of this world in Paris is, that it is always glad to see you, always entertaining, always exciting, even, and never by any chance a bore.

TO WILLIAM P. LETCHWORTH.

GOTHA, *July* 11, 1867.

. . . Ah, Glen Iris! Shall we ever be there together, again? And if I should be able, some time, to lay down, there, my pilgrim-staff, will we have the youth in our hearts which made us so happy, long ago? God knows; but the place and the days that belong to it seem all to be lifted so far, far away, that I catch myself dreaming of your deeded and titled property as of some lost land,—of faery or fancy, or what not. Well, that is not bad advice which Longfellow's psalm sings to us, in regard to our duty in the time present; and you must not think, because I boo-hoo so easily over by-gones, that I have no heart for what lies under my hand. On the contrary, I think I can say that my European privileges have been most healthily enjoyed and profited by. I am not in the least *blasé*, but preserve as keen an appetite as ever for all that is worth seeing and studying. In the past year, I have acquired a tolerable mastery of French, have traveled a little in ten countries, and have had small-pox. I am now, with my friend Fargo, paying vigorous court to German, and I hope to master that and do some reading therein before I get home. So you see the *dolce far niente* does not enter largely into my plans. I have great literary ambition, too; but the percentage which gets accomplished of what I plan is so dismally small that I will not say much on that score. Suffice it that, if God has given me anything to say to people, I will try and have it decently said before I die. If He has n't, I shall not pretend that He has, but shall rest very content.

At least, I hope to do many things a great deal worthier than *The Bark of Life*, of which your partiality leads you to speak too warmly. It was so thoroughly a forced performance, done to order on a given subject (I think I had filled nine or ten identical orders before)—that I cannot in conscience help you to defend it. . . . As to the last stanza, I think the idea I had, regarded the translation from Life to Immortality, which we suppose to lie in the future of the individual. The *Bark*,—poor, old hackneyed means of conveyance—is conventionally considered as individual property, I think, and so I intended to use it to the end. But I see how these last lines may easily be applied in a general sense; and so they are faulty and highflown and vague, as I feel in my inmost marrow.

I would give a great deal to see and read Amanda Jones' book.* If it contains some of her older pieces, which I know, it is worth its weight in gold. Except Mrs. Browning, I can name no woman, living or dead, who has shown such a mastery of poetic expression and such a grandeur of poetic conception, as are evinced in that piece of Miss Jones' from the Egyptian mythology. It rang in my ears all the while I was in Egypt, and there seemed to be something of mysterious grandeur about it which made it kin to Cheops himself.

TO JOSEPH WARREN.

GOTHA, *August* 20, 1867.

. . . Knowing as much as I do, now, about Germany, I find we are fixed about as well here as we

---

* Poems. By Amanda T. Jones. New York: Hurd & Houghton, 1867.

could expect. It is true, my darling idea of getting into a family rests unachieved; but, in order to succeed there, we would have to go into some large city, or place where more English is spoken, where manners are not so simple, and where, consequently, temptations are more numerous than here. We can live cheaply, quietly and studiously, here, if anywhere in Germany, and I am content for some months to come.

TO HIS FATHER.

GOTHA, *September* 15, 1867.

. . . I am not doing anything like what I expected in the writing line; and, perhaps, my German and a pretty fair knowledge of Germany will be all that I shall have to show for this six months. The fact is, I am a social being, and I do not work well when entirely deprived of the stimulus of the right kind of companionship. Mental solitude, however, is said to be a good master in some branches, and, if so, then I shall reap some advantage of this period of my European life. At all events, we shall remain in Germany till perhaps 1st February, and then, ho! for Petersburg.

TO HIS MOTHER.

GOTHA, *October* 7, 1867.

. . . I cannot describe to you my emotion on reading of your sickness and your recovery therefrom. Somehow, for a month before, I had had a presentiment of something happening to you, and had had times of the deepest anxiety and longing for news. Your letter brought at once a fulfillment to my fears and an answer to my eager hope. God be thanked that you got through it and are up again! For my sake, and all our sakes, do take care of yourself;

don't do anything beyond or even up to your strength, if it should never be done,— and be careful not to expose yourself in the coming winter. I have all along felt an abiding faith that we are all to be spared to meet, next year, at home, and that faith or feeling has sustained me in a good many hours of loneliness. The longer I stay away, and the nearer the period of our reunion approaches, the more my heart yearns towards Detroit, and, above all things, my dearest mother, towards you. I often think, and in my deepest heart realize, that if you should be taken away from earth I should have nothing left to live for. This may seem strong language from one who has *done* so little to testify his filial love; but it is strictly true and a faithful picture of my constant feeling, nevertheless. . . . In the wide world, there is no spot which has a special attraction for me other than that where you are. So, you see, you have a deal to live for and much reason to take care of yourself; for I know that each one of your children feels just as I do. . . .

We live in a very simple community, where there is as much gossip retailed as in any village I ever saw, and in which *die Amerikaner* make somewhat of a sensation, being courted sedulously by some mothers with marriageable daughters, and held in awful dread by others. Upon the whole, I am getting a little tired of the monotony of the thing, and shall be glad to get on the tramp again.

TO DAVID TAYLOR.

GOTHA, *October* 23, 1867.

. . . I cannot explain the reason, but it is a fact, that I need to be in a certain rare mood, in order to write you. When I am in my normal condition, the utterance of my thoughts on paper does not seem to be the thing to send you, at all. The world I have so long lived in is one you could have little patience or sympathy with, and it would appear that a certain amount of cleansing from it is requisite, before I can present myself and be recognizable before you. To-day, a peculiar atmosphere bathes the many-colored trees. It is the October you love, and loved to paint long ago, and I feel my way to you more easily through its hazy air than usual. I *will* write to you.

To show you that I am as much of a fool as ever, I am going to copy various fragments of verse which have lately effused from my sodden brain.* My sober opinion, at the solemn age of 31, Davie, is that both you and I escaped being poets by less than a hair's breadth. A single drop of this chemical or that, more or less,—an atom added on this side or subtracted on that,—and the mass would have been inflammable and blazed in sacred fire. As it is, it is something to have a little of the poet's nature, if not of his faculty. . . . It is strange, Davie, what a long, incurable, chronic ailment is this one of poetry; for disease it certainly is,—inasmuch as no man in an entirely healthy state thinks of writing verses. It has disappeared in me, sometimes, for nearly a year at a stretch, but invariably breaks out again. I have no doubt your experience is the same.

Enough of poetry,—perhaps I will never speak of it again; and now to practical matters. I have no news of myself to tell you. I am much the same as I have been, any time within five years; moodier, perhaps,—for the hypochondria I inherit from my father grows upon me, steadily. Its attacks are longer and more violent, and the reaction proportionally slower and of briefer duration.

* The poems copied were the sonnet entitled, 'The Half-world's Width Divides Us,' 'On Lebanon,' and 'The Soul's Failure,' all of which are printed elsewhere in this volume.

TO CHARLES W. FAIRRINGTON.

GOTHA, *November* 5, 1867.

. . . I saw the announcement of Rarey's death* in a Dutch paper in Rotterdam. How it stunned and shocked me, and how strangely it struck me, when I read in your letter that my message was the last he ever read. And our day is coming, too, surely, surely. Ah! I cannot bear to think of it. It seems as if *we must* be made exceptions to the pitiless general rule. But we will not be.

TO HIS BROTHER.

GOTHA, *November* 6, 1867.

. . . We have made some good, kind friends, here, in Gotha, whom I shall be sorry to leave, and who will be sorry to have me leave ; but, apart from these few, there is nothing here I shall not be glad to get away from. One advantage the place has had for us,—it has been sheerly impossible to speak English in it. Since Bayard Taylor left, I have scarcely exchanged an English word with anyone except Fargo. I got pretty well acquainted with Bayard, here. . . . He is a very clever and remarkably well-informed man.

TO DAVID TAYLOR.

ST. PETERSBURG, *December* 23, 1867.

Your letter reached me to-day, and made all my soul glow with divine warmth. I rushed with it, the first instant I could, under cover, and read it, to the amazement of a huge Russian official, in one of the museums where Russia has piled up specimens of her subterranean and other natural treasures. You remember one of the wonders of our boyhood,—the story of that huge corpse of a mammoth, found by a Tungusian

* John S. Rarey.

fisherman on the shores of the White Sea, to the bones
of which the frozen flesh; with antediluvian hair
thereon, still clung in masses. It was in the shadow
of that identical monster that I devoured your epistle.
. . . Let me tell you, in the first place, that it pleases
me amazingly to find you still so warm on the subject
of our long-ago life and experiences. I believe that,
to this day, I am softer on that point than on any
other. I often spend hours in aimless wandering
through that portion of my past life, and emerge,
dazed and wondering what it all has meant, but,
withal, soothed, if not happy, from the exercise. I
fully agree with you, that our mutual intercourse in
those few years was the crisis,—the deciding circumstance of both our lives. As for myself, I thought,
once, I had outlived the influence of it, or nearly so ;
but, no ! I have only been going round in a circle, and
I verily believe we are liker to each other to-day than
ever before. . . . You have remained in your isolation
and solitude, while I have nearly boxed the compass
of human sights and experiences. It is rather queer,
therefore, that we should stand, to-day, after all these
years of separation, on, as near as may be, the identical
point of space in the realm of mortal feeling and
speculation. . . .

Ink is weak and paper is vain, when a man wants to
empty his soul of the whirlwind which inhabits him.
I would like to have one long summer-night session
with you. We would start from the river-side, about
gloaming, and sit a half-hour on every fence, as we
came up. By that means, the moon would be large
and white ere we reached the weird swamp, where the
mist used to meet us and the tamaracks were wont to
whisper and shudder as they listened. Passing the
Pentherer shanty (is it haunted?—it ought to be ; for
was ever a cleaner bit of domestic tragedy than it
knew, enacted?)—passing that, I say, we would mount
the knoll and look down into those round basins of

mist, which I see often in my dreams; and then we would go back, again, I think, by Davie Mair's fence; and the marsh is about the best place for us,—there, accordingly, we would seat ourselves and have it out. Oh, unutterable mystery of life! No man can help us to unriddle it; and, yet, there is consolation in the act of confronting it, in company with one who also knows that it is. I hope, once again, at least, to have that consolation; and,—who knows?—perhaps, when we meet again, one or other will have made a discovery, and will *know* something. . . .

TO JOSEPH WARREN.

VIENNA, *February* 16, 1868.

. . . I am satisfied to come home, albeit Spain grieveth me sore and plucketh me by the beard in an exasperating wise. I am content, I say, as I ought to be, if I have a conscience. I feel that I am coming home, if I say it myself, well paid for my three years. My mind is rich; my character has settled into something like symmetrical shape; my views on a good many things have become clear; I trust, with God's help, to keep the momentum I have got, and lay myself now to my work in earnestness, honesty and industry. Whether I am going to make a good Democratic editor, I cannot say till I get at it. . . .

I have had, here, in Vienna, nearly four weeks of moneyless waiting for money, and, in that time, thanks to the influence, partly, of my glorious friend John Hay, I have done much toward putting in order the cargo I have been, for nearly three years, picking up. . . . I have a book begun,—had I had three months more it would have been finished. When I do finish it, I think it will be something out of the usual run. . . .

A week or two of my stay here was made pleasant by the presence of Gen. McClellan, my hero, and his wife, whose acquaintance and friendship I enjoyed immensely.

TO HIS SISTER.

VIENNA, *February* 16, 1868.

Perhaps you will pardon the long delay into which I have fallen before answering your good letter, in consideration of the news I have now to tell you. As our good Methodist brethren used to sing, up in the woods, so, now, I :—' I 'm on my journey home!' That is my ditty, at last. Yesterday I received the summons which turns our faces westward. We go from here, in four or five days, to Paris; thence, in two or three days, to London; thence, I will run up, if possible, for a week in Scotland, and then we sail. And I, oh, I am well content to think of this near prospect of taking you all to my heart again. To give up Spain,— the *bonne bouche* of all,—grieveth me sore; but the compensations are too great for me to think of that. Oh, I am glad, glad! . . .

As for myself, I hear always good accounts from Buffalo, and affairs there, and I go back feeling strong and well-furnished for useful and hard work. You see, I did write some Russian letters. The Palestine business I am keeping for some better purpose; but, before that fructifies, I hope to have long spells at yarn-spinning with you, about all the manifold and strange sights and adventures which there and elsewhere me befell. I am, on the whole, well satisfied with the results already gathered in, of my stay abroad. I feel it will probably lengthen and enhance the value of my life, inestimably. I have a memory, now, which I would not sell for all A. T. Stewart's gold; and never did I feel so spirited and strong as now, in the use of my pen. I hope to do something with it, one of these days, which will be creditable.

And now, after all this braggadocia about myself, you have to take this wretched apology of a letter as an answer to yours. Fact is, I feel too good to do anything more than tell you the news and shout over it.

CHAPTER VI.

THE PRIME OF LIFE. 1868–1882.

BEFORE the end of April, 1868, Gray was at home, in Buffalo, settling himself again to his work, after the long fallow-time that he had enjoyed under foreign skies. The change which three years of wide travel and leisurely study had wrought in him was immense. He had been singularly 'cultivated' by his experience, in the best sense of the word. It had ripened him in character, matured him in powers, perfected him in bearing and manners. The old personal charm which he possessed, of voice and speech and look, was all preserved, in its naturalness, with something added to it, of the grace that comes from a full and assuring knowledge of the world. He came back, too, with mind and body in thorough health, with feelings rejuvenated, with ambitions revived, and with a strong desire, often expressed, for the hard work which he saw before him.

He was soon grappling it, and found nothing to disappoint him in the burden that waited for his shoulders. Two months after taking it up, he wrote to his parents —June 28, 1868:

This is really the first hour of leisure I have had for some weeks. Mr. Warren has been a good deal away, and I have been anxious to get the complete run of things in the office. Consequently, I have given my whole mind to details of business, and have taken, temporarily, on my shoulders, much more of a burden than I mean permanently to carry. . . .

You would smile if you knew how far you strike from the mark in speaking of worldly ambition and the desire of human praise and approbation as heading the list of temptations to which I am subject. No more of this, at present, however. Suffice it to say, that my life abroad seems to have crystallized, as regards its results in my character, into an intense desire to do my duty, as far as I can see that. 'Earnest — honest — industrious:' — these three words I brought home with me, and have inscribed on the tablets of my mind. I hope to live them and make progress with them toward greater light than I am now permitted to enjoy.

In September, he wrote to his brother-in-law:

You guess rightly that I am busy these days. Mr. Warren has turned so much of a 'political necessity' in Albany, Utica and elsewhere, that he scarcely does anything in the office, of late, and I am consequently conductor and somewhat of brakesman and stoker, too, of the daily newspaper train. But I like it, for my health is good and my faculties sound; and it seems as if a man ought to feel a little flattered when the world demands and puts a value on even the moments of his time. So I scrub away and keep the blues at a safe distance by incessant industry.

Soon after this was written, David met for the first time the lady who became, afterwards, his wife,—Miss Martha Guthrie, then residing in New Orleans. They were guests, together, for a few days, at 'Glen Iris,' the romantic country-place of Mr. Letchworth, and began their acquaintance in the midst of scenes as lovely as

9

nature and man have ever combined to create. The
wooing followed quickly on the acquaintance, and
David's cup was filled with happiness that autumn,
even while he toiled the hardest. When the secret of
his happiness was ripe for disclosure, he wrote to his
brother :

BUFFALO, *November* 27, 1868.

I think, now, I may speak with a little assurance
of my plans,—premising, however, that there may be
alterations made, even at fifty-nine minutes past the
eleventh hour. Well, then, I am coming to see you
before this old year goes out, God willing. But I am
going somewhere else, first. Not to put too fine a
point upon it, I am going to start next Tuesday for
New Orleans, for the purpose of visiting the young
person who, in the not far distant future is, if all be
well, to be Mrs. David Gray. This thing has been
going on for some time, but, partly because of the
liability of slips between lip and cup, and partly because I would have much preferred to tell you all about
it by word of mouth, I have refrained from making the
tender confession. . . . John, congratulate me, my boy.
I am a fit subject. Far, far better than I deserve has
the beneficent Father dealt with me in this thing.
All my utmost expectations are fulfilled. I am content
and happy, as not before in a decade of years. I want
to leave something to tell, against my coming, and so
refrain from quite unveiling the mystery. Pardon me
for this.

He was married at New Orleans on the 2d of the
next coming June, and the happiness of life began for
him, in the serene, domestic phase of it which he had
coveted most. While the slow-footed days of spring
were still fretting him with their tardiness, he wrote to
his father and mother :

BUFFALO, *April* 4, 1869.

. . . I am wearying very much for the 20th of next month, when I shall start for the south. I look forward to the time, not only because of the happy change it will bring to my way of life, but for the rest I shall have, which I considerably need. I am hoping, now, that I will be able to make my marriage a pretext for a radical change in my hours of work. If I can only shift some of the night work to other shoulders, I shall be much better off. Perhaps I will be able to do so.

He *was* able, perhaps, to relieve himself, for a time, after his marriage, of some part of his wearing editorial labors; to diminish a little the long night-watches of his responsible post, and to gain a little more leisure than he had known before, for the enjoyment of his newly founded home. But it cannot have been for long. Those who remember the pretty cottage home on Niagara street to which David Gray brought his bride, and which she and he made hospitable and delightful to their friends for a decade of years, remember, too, how scanty was the freedom which David, himself, had for 'slippered ease' in his snug library, there. Only one weekly evening he was sure of, for his own, and that was the Saturday night. Hence, that came to be, ere long, a kind of consecrated and privileged night for some of Gray's long-time friends, who grew into the expectation and habit of gathering at his cheerful hearth, to spend the final hours of every week. During several years, those 'Saturday nights at Gray's,' as they came to be called, were seldom interrupted, and they ranked before everything else among the enjoyments of the small number who shared them.

The prime factor in their delightfulness was Gray, himself, with his geniality, his many-sidedness, his imaginativeness, his humor, his rich equipment for conversation, his exquisite reading.   Very often, the evening was spent in listening to the great poems of the master-singers, as David read them, with pauses for comment.   His reading was unlike any other which those who heard it ever knew.   It was a perfect voicing of the music of poetry.   One had the feeling, while he listened, that it gave him the very melody and the very tones that were singing in the imagination of the poet, when his thoughts caught step with the rhythm of his words.   In a letter that has been quoted in a former chapter, he called his way of reading poetry a ' *singing* of verses,' and said that he learned it from his old Wisconsin friend, David Taylor.   But it only suggested *singing* so far as it brought out, with the wonderful effect that it did, the whole melody and musical quality of the verse ; and, whatever hint of it may have come from another, the delicious art of his reading could only have been perfected by Gray himself.   It needed his voice, his face, his manner, his emotional sensitiveness, his quick, sympathetic following of a poet's thought—even Browning's—through all turns and changes, to make David Gray's reading of poetry the exquisite, unique performance it was.   Of elocution, there was nothing in it that could be taught to anybody.

But, if our host was first in the pleasure-making of those ' Saturday nights,' he had a rare auxiliary in one of his guests—the one who resembled him, perhaps, as little as any, but who was most perfectly complementary to him in character and genius.   This was

Dr. William B. Wright, author of *The Brook, and Other Poems;* physician by profession, and teacher of languages in the State Normal School at Buffalo by preference for the avocation that committed him to a studious life. Dr. Wright, who had served in the Union army until the duty of war was wholly done, (he was *Major* Wright, then), lived so quietly thereafter, and so entirely within the round of his school work, his studies, and the few friendships which sufficed him, that not many people knew him for what he was. But when he died, at the prime of life, in 1880, the feeling of his friends was not exaggerated by one of them who said: ' He was the *best* and the *greatest* man I ever knew; I have never come in contact with another who made on me such an impression of great qualities.' There was, in fact, that effect of *greatness* in the superiority of mind and character which those who drew close to him were made to feel, but which was veiled to stranger eyes by the beautiful simplicity of his nature. A grave, meditative, often silent man, but easy and unreserved in talk,—oddly humorous, loving homely, expressive phrases and words, and always seeming to bring out, as it were, the primitive flavors of the language in his conversation! A man of perfect honesty, of profoundly reverent but unshrinking courage in his thinking, with a large-souled tolerance for all faithfulness of belief! A man who fed his mind equally on the old philosophies and the new sciences, but who found the breath of the life of his spirit in the atmosphere of poetry! A man who was so impelled to seek, first, after wisdom, and, beyond wisdom, righteousness, that no lower ambitions were possible to him! There was perfection of companionship in the association of this character with that of Gray,—the large strength of the one with the fine sweetness of the other; and much of the memorable delightfulness of the 'Saturday nights at Gray's' came from the meeting of those two, with other bright and pleasant company around them.

But the house on Niagara street was hospitable on many nights and days, and to many people. Gray found his best enjoyment in agreeable society, and opened wide doors to it whenever he could. His acquaintance at home and abroad had become large, especially among men and women of letters and of art, and no one in Buffalo, during those years, entertained more visitors of distinction than he.

The period now reached in Gray's life was one in which he devoted his energies and his powers most entirely to his newspaper, and permitted himself to do almost no writing outside of it. The result of his devoted labors was a notable elevation in the character and reputation of the *Courier*. He gave it a standing much more independent of partisan relations than is often achieved by any party journal, even among those of the highest rank. But this eminent success for his paper was gained at great cost to himself, as appeared a few years later.

Meantime he wrote little, as has been said, outside of the *Courier* columns. He did prepare a lecture for the closing of the winter course of the Young Men's Association, in February, 1871, of which neither the manuscript nor any full report appears to have been preserved. The better things in literature that he had hoped to do were all put off to an unpromising future. He wrote to his brother, in January, 1870: 'As for the volume you speak of, it will not be forthcoming till I possess more of my own time. I want to give something better than the fag-ends of days to that.' But nothing better than 'the fag-ends of days' ever belonged to him, again, until he had lost the strength to use it.

One poem he wrote, however, in 1872, which is more likely, perhaps, than any other that he left us, to have a lasting place in literature. It was one entitled *The Last Council*, written for an interesting occasion at Glen Iris, when nineteen representatives of the Seneca and the Mohawk tribes of Indians, including descendants of the great chieftains, Red Jacket, Cornplanter and Brant, were assembled, on the invitation of Mr. Letchworth. They came together to re-open the long-abandoned and neglected old Council House of the Seneca nation, which Mr. Letchworth had caused to be removed from Caneadea to Glen Iris (eighteen miles from its original site) and to be carefully re-erected and restored for permanent preservation. The event was afterwards fully recounted by Gray in a fine historical article, published with illustrations in *Scribner's Monthly* of July, 1877.

Naturally, his correspondence during the years of this laborious period was limited, and not much of interest or significance can be gleaned from it. Some passages, however, have been found that will help to carry forward the story of his life.

August 8, 1870, his first child was born, a son, who received his father's name. Writing to his sister, a few days after, David informed her that the 'little rascal begins already to emerge from the state of pulpitude and shows the moulding influence of a dawning soul within.'

Writing November 6, 1870, to his friend, Col. John Hay, he touched what was, no doubt, often wistfully in his mind—the thought of a field in journalism different from that of the political daily newspaper. 'How I wish,' he exclaimed, 'you and I could get hold of some good thing together. I think we could infuse new blood into any carcass of decent promise; leastways, you could, and I could make you do it. But tell me what you are doing and thinking about.'

A couple of months later—January 14, 1871—Col. Hay having joined the staff of the *New York Tribune*, Gray wrote to him:

Ah! my boy; it is my hour of triumph. You are now on the treadmill and *you*, too, are turned into a poor fiend and do not write letters any more. But it is a *triste* victory. I want to hear from you. Almost daily I meet happy people who have seen J. H.; but what is that to me? I want to get your own affidavit that you are alive and occasionally have a thought for those who love you well. You are doing splendidly. Of course, everybody may tell you that, but none have so good means of knowing it and so good a right to say it as I. I am not going to dream any more dreams for you, or make any more plans. You are well enough off as you are, for a while.

In a letter dated May 19, 1872, to his brother, then abroad, traveling in the east, he wrote:

. . . As for me, I keep on in the same unvarying round of unremitting and exhausting employment. I went to Cincinnati and assisted (in the French sense) at the nomination of Horace Greeley for President. . . . I am much interested in seeing the democratic party coming up to the point of supporting him. I fully believe that, by this unexpected turn of affairs, there will be an opportunity for parties to get out of some bad ruts, and that an impulse in the direction of purer and better government will be given to the country. But what do you care,—pilgrim to the ruined shrines of buried empires and civilizations,—for the latest ripple on the surface of American politics? I change the theme.

TO HIS BROTHER.

BUFFALO, *November* 3, 1872.

. . . I write now principally to say that, this long and wearisome political campaign having almost closed, we are looking forward to the near prospect of seeing you all, again. . . . This past summer and fall have been very toilsome and tedious to me, as you may imagine, and I rejoice at the prospect of being able to emerge a little from party politics, soon. . . . I have not been so well in three years as I am now, in spite of politics.

TO COL. JOHN HAY.

BUFFALO, *December* 15, 1872.

I think it must be all along of my not writing to you that the world has been going to rack and ruin in the year past. I am going to re-establish communications and restore the normal order of things.

We *have* seen some curious happenings, since the year began, haven't we? You remember, you and I assisted at the fête of Sedan, and now there are the Cincinnati convention, the liberal campaign and the death of Greeley, added to the roll of strange events.

How many times I have wished to talk with you and rub my rustic views against your cosmopolitan ones. . . .

By the way, in last Thursday's *Tribune* appeared an announcement of a new book of verse, *The Brook, and Other Poems*. That book I have a deep interest in, and its author is one of the grandest men and friends I ever saw. When it comes out, read it through, and see if it does not contain some grand verse. Your critic did n't quite get the idea of it; for, I think, beneath its surface of 'woods and waters' is some of the rarest poetic thinking. Look especially at the last two parts of *The Brook*, and at some of the shorter pieces, such as *Noontide, Coquette*, etc., and I think you will agree with me. . . .

What are you doing or contemplating in a literary way? Or are you working too hard to think of anything outside of newspapers? As for me, I am drudging away, but hoping also that things may open up, so that I can have a little leisure for better thoughts.

And now good-night, and let me hear from you, if you still are John Hay of Vienna.

TO HIS BROTHER.

BUFFALO, *April 6*, 1873.

It makes me more ashamed than I can tell to think that, since I saw you, four months have passed, in which I have not given any of you the scrape of a pen. Well, I have pretty good material out of which to frame excuses, if I chose to. These have been months of hard, constant, absorbing, exhausting work,—work which so nearly uses up my vital energies that the smallest opportunities for absolute relaxation are perforce improved to the utmost. Saturdays, when the strain is partially lifted—and Sunday nights, which I always try to spend at home, usually find me even too languid and lazy for reading, which I so much need; and writing seems out of the question. But, all the more, I think, we keep you all in our minds and talk of you, Mattie and I. Then, too, her pen has done something to bridge the gap of my silence and keep us from altogether slipping out of your minds. Between you and me, I should be a pretty poor stick without her, in many ways.

Further, in this letter, he gave his brother an account of some financial embarrassments that had come upon him, in connection with his newspaper interest, and remarked upon them:

Fortunately, my utter lack of business habits and disposition has its advantages as well as disadvantages; for, as I fail in carefulness, as to getting into trouble, so also I stand the trouble, when it comes, with tolerable equanimity. But, of all this, perhaps, you had better say 'nothing to nobody.' I shall work out, somehow, and be a wiser if a sadder man. The most I regret is, the shutting off of the prospect of future easier times and the opportunity to do some other work than that of the daily editorial drudge.

Three months later, in allusion to the same matters, he wrote: 'I keep up a good heart and have faith that I will come out, all right. My life is one that does not leave a large margin for leisure; but I try to be content and think it is the very thing I need,—*the raal hat*, as Davie Taylor used to say.'

In June of that year he wrote one of his last occasional poems, at the invitation of the Press Association of the State of New York. It was read at a meeting in Lockport, and the following letter, written soon afterwards to his friend, Mr. L. B. Proctor, is inter-

esting as a frank expression of the view which the
writer entertained of his own relations to poetry and
to journalism.

BUFFALO, *June* 19, 1874.

I have passed through the ordeal,—please let me call
it that,—of the editorial convention at Lockport. Although my poem is not all I could wish it to be, in
phrase and in thought, yet I feel, after all, a sort of
consciousness, which I venture to express only to you,
that it was favorably received. The room in which
the convention was held is very large. As it was
crowded, I have thought my voice was not sufficiently
heavy for the room, and audience. I expected, certainly, to meet you at the convention, and your absence,
I confess, affected me somewhat; for, on such occasions, nothing strengthens me so much, nothing gives
me so much courage, as the presence of my more intimate friends. . . .

As I am a journalist, it was expected my theme
would relate to my profession; but to bring such a
subject into the domain of poetry! 'Aye, there's the
rub.' And, yet, specialists of consummate ripeness and
culture, in all departments of knowledge, wait upon
the bidding of journalism. The laureate, with his
chastened measures; the novelists of both hemispheres;
the patient compiler,—even the imperative, sure-sighted
critic,—all are bringing their best tribute to journalism. Why, then, should I not have 'cudgeled my
brain' for a poetic offering to it? For, as I once said
to you, I am a poet by nature, and a journalist by
compulsion? Could I have consulted my own taste in
choosing an occupation, I should have dwelt in those
regions where poetry is born and nourished and plumes
itself for its glorious flight. But, perhaps, my wings,
like those of Icarus, being only fastened to my shoulders with wax, would have melted as I flew, leaving

me to fall, like him, to the ground. I cannot deny the fact that, like Thomas Noon Talfourd and Lord Tenderden, I am more proud of my iambics and hexameters than of any laurels I ever won, or expect to win, in the editorial chair. And yet, by determination, by unremitting toil, I have learned to love journalism. Habit, you know, does everything; and, so, I now come easily to the task of aiding in the great work of furnishing the public that intellectual aliment which, in these days, can be found only in newspapers,—to which, every morning, the people come, eager to break their mental fast. This brings me to say, that fresh and eager minds should alone minister to the newspaper; for there is no other work which consumes vitality so fast as carefully executed newspaper composition. With these views, I sat down to write my poem on journals and journalism, for the late editorial convention.

TO HIS BROTHER.

BUFFALO, *July* 15, 1874.

. . . We sail to-morrow evening on the *Badger State* for a trip up the lakes, probably not farther than Mackinaw, and return. . . . I have been off duty now for a month, skirmishing about the country for the benefit of my nervous system, which had got a little below par, and think that ten days of the lake air will put me in good condition.

After returning from Mackinaw, he made a long-promised visit of a week, with his friend, Dr. Wright, to the home of the latter's father, at Campbell Hall, Orange County, N. Y., and seems to have been greatly the better for it. The visit was repeated a year later, with his family. Monotonous hard work filled the interval, as it filled the succeeding twelve months, until he escaped again for a brief vacation,—this time to Block Island, off the New England coast.

TO DOCTOR WILLIAM B. WRIGHT.

BLOCK ISLAND, R. I., *July* 21, 1876.

We have been islanders, now, just a week, and I can speak confidently. Never before have I been in any place where the facilities were so abundant for making the acquaintance of old Ocean. And I find the old fellow as interesting as I had hoped—quite capable of making up all defects of society, and what not, from which I might otherwise have suffered. Surf-bathing every day . . . ; long walks on bare downs, overlooking the sea, and with its 'break, break,' ever in sight and hearing; cod-fishing in a Block Island boat of two masts, and with an antique mariner or two to sail you and bait your hooks, out on the banks, a half-score miles from the island; a run of twenty minutes, after tea, up to the top of Beacon Hill, whence the sunset is seen,—these are the leading events of my life, here. And are they not enough? The interstices are filled with lazy lounging in the shade and occasional readings (piece-meal) of Emerson, Ruskin and Hawthorne. I am perfectly reconciled to the routine. The place ensures safety, health and enjoyment to the children, and I feel so permeated with the spirit of it, and of my new life, that I have almost lost recollection of a state of hard work and anxiety. My face is as red as the sunset I gaze on, nightly, and I can run, jump, swim and walk like a young savage.

Of course, I have little hope of tempting you out here; but, if it were convenient for you, and you had the inclination, you might do worse than to come. . . . You would at first think the island bare and burned up; it has no trees and the season has been unusually

dry and hot;—but in a day or two the ocean would
embrace you and you would be grandly happy, as I
am;—all the more if you choose to use your legs vig-
orously in tramping, as I do. If you come, bring the
oldest suit of clothes you ever saw. I dress like a
gaberlunzie. . . . I shall be here ten days yet, at any
rate.

This brief rest, taken so much to his liking, in the
lap of the sea, was followed by the strain and labor
of the presidential canvass of 1876. It was followed,
too, in the midst of that canvass, by the sudden death
of Joseph Warren, senior editor of the *Courier* and
long-recognized leader of the democratic party in
Western New York. This death was doubly serious
to Gray. It deprived him of a friend, towards whom
his feeling was very warm, and it threw upon him
responsibilities and duties which were new to his
experience, uncongenial, in every way, and trying to
him, beyond any possible description. Succeeding,
now, to the chief editorship of the *Courier*, he was
brought, directly, into those relationships with practical politics and with practical politicians which he had
known and felt only in an indirect way while Mr.
Warren lived. That he was gravely affected by this
serious change in the conditions of his journalistic
work, is unquestionable.

But, if the political campaign of 1876 was an
extremely trying experience to the new chief-editor of
the *Courier*, the result of it was the bitterest disappointment, no doubt, of his life. He had become
personally acquainted with Mr. Tilden,—even intimately and confidentially so,—while the latter was

Governor of the State of New York, and had acquired
an enthusiastic regard for him.   He looked upon Mr.
Tilden as one of the wisest of statesmen, one of the
purest of patriots, one of the most excellent of gentlemen.   He expected his election to the presidency, and
anticipated from it a great purification of politics and
a notable elevation of the character of our adminis-
trative government.   He fully believed, afterwards,
that Mr. Tilden *had been* elected, and that he and the
nation were defrauded, by dishonest manipulations of
the result in Louisiana and elsewhere.   It was a black
and evil and exasperating outcome, to him,—very hard
to be submissive to.   No doubt he suffered, moreover,
a half-conscious disappointment of personal ambitions
in the matter, which few people knew of.   His relations
with Mr. Tilden were such that, while it is not probable
he would have accepted any political office, he was sure
to have stood among the trusted counselors of the
president, if the democratic candidate had entered the
White House.   The failure to secure what he believed
had been won fairly, at the polls, was an immeasurably
hard blow to him, therefore, in his friendship, in his
patriotism, and in his personal ambition, as well.

But he bore it with equanimity, with dignity, with
the temper of a Christian man.   There is no sign of
passion in his editorial writing during all the discussions of that threatening crisis.   On the contrary, he
exerted the whole influence of his journal to calm the
dangerous excitement of the time, and to inspire trust
in peaceful measures for the settlement of the moment-
ous dispute.   Four days after the election, on the 11th
of November, he wrote, under the caption *Keep Cool:*

In these days of excitement and suspense, the *Courier* has no sympathy with those hot-headed people, whether democrats or republicans, who indulge in loud talk about the terrible things to happen in the case of the happening of such and such other things. It is not necessary or desirable to have the public feeling any more inflamed than it is now. The votes are being counted, of a close election, and all the people can do is to keep quiet and wait for full returns. We have not the slightest doubt of Mr. Tilden's election, and believe that it will soon be triumphantly established. But, in any case, the good sense and moderation of the people will be equal to any crisis that can possibly develop itself. Let us keep cool and good-natured. Let nothing be said or done to irritate political opponents, or sow the seeds of violence in the popular mind. Permit no insult or abuse on the part of republicans, or republican journals, to disturb democratic self-control or poison democratic patriotism. Remember that the country is greater than party. This thing will come out all right if we only have patience. Justice will be done; the right will triumph. Keep cool!

To bring himself to this pacific temper and this spirit of moderation, which he firmly and calmly preserved through all the agitated four months of the undetermined electoral count, required, under the circumstances, a most admirable subjugation of personal feelings, and a thoughtful fidelity to the welfare of the country, which are not too common among the conductors of partisan journals.

But the strain he was under, during all that trying period, from the beginning of the presidential canvass of 1876 to the closing of the 'count' on the 2d of March, 1877,—the unresting labor performed and the excitements gone through,—had done him mortal harm.

He wrote to his brother in April: 'I cannot stand so much work as I once could.' Early in July he went with his family to Block Island for a few weeks of rest, and ended a brief letter, written just before starting, with the remark—not a common one with him—'I am tired to death.' Writing from Block Island to Mr. Letchworth, he said:

BLOCK ISLAND, R. I., *July* 14, 1877.

In my long solitary walks by the ocean, a vision of the Glen rises before me. This is good enough as a place in which to seek health for the body; but health and peace for the spirit are elsewhere, and I do n't think I shall find them till I sit amidst the lights and airs and sweet scents and sounds of our beloved valley. . . . I expect to look down on you in passing home-ward again, sometime about the 25th inst. I will leave my benediction in the upper air.

On the 25th, he was still lingering on the island for another week of its tonic air, and wrote to his brother: 'I am having a gorgeous time, physically; am getting great good from it.'

Early in August, he returned home, summoned abruptly by news of the railroad riots then outbreaking, at Buffalo and elsewhere; and, not many days after-wards, he was smitten with what must have been a genuine *coup de soleil*, though it seemed but a slight touch at the time. He thought lightly of the matter, after he had recovered a little from the first effects of the prostration, and barely mentioned it in a letter to his brother, written August 28th:

I had a little touch—a premonition rather—of a sun-stroke, last week, and my head is not feeling first-rate, yet. But, happily, by prompt measures, I was able to ward off danger and shall be all right, soon. . . . We have safely accomplished our transportation from 192 Niagara street to 77 Park place and enjoy the change very much.

But he had not yet begun to feel the real hurt of the stroke that seemed so light. It was a deeper wound than he knew, and he had received it at a time when his vital energies were seriously impaired. Its mischievous effects on him were wrought with some slowness and in a deceptive way. Going back to his work, after a few days of repose, he soon found that his strength was waning, and his brain refusing to be tasked. Even yet, it was thought that a few weeks of quiet would suffice to restore him, and he went away, to his favorite resting-place—always open to him—at Glen Iris. While there, he wrote the little poem ' Rest,' which is believed to be the last that came from his pen.

But, before September ended, his physician and his friends had become convinced that something more radical was needed to lift him from his prostration, and he crossed the Atlantic, for the benefits of the sea-voyage and for such stay in England and Scotland as might prove to be good. The journey was a lonely one, for his family was necessarily left behind, but it gave him renewed strength and life. From the many letters which he wrote to his wife during this pilgrimage of convalescence, a few passages only will be quoted.

STEAMSHIP 'CITY OF RICHMOND,'
Sunday, October 7, 1877.

. . . My pusillanimous heart looked with devouring
envy, for a little, on a happy father who had his little
ones with him.   It made me think, of course, with
double sharpness of regret, of the dear boys I was
leaving.   But the inspiration of the ocean overcame,
speedily, all painful feelings. . . .   This morning, I
woke about seven, after ten hours of the best sleep I
have had in many weeks; and, when I went on deck,
I almost walked, or ran, on tip-toe,—so light and
strong did I feel.   The weather is superb,—scarcely a
cloud in the sky; and a light breeze which just tips
the waves with a feather-a-piece of foam. . . . A little
land-sparrow has been following us, very wing-weary,
evidently, and I have been wishing it would come on
board and share my room with me.   I would be very
good to it.   But I fear it will fly until it is forced
to drop into the hungry deep.

A few days at Bradford, with his friend Colonel
Shepard, U. S. consul there, a fortnight in Scotland, a
night at Fryston Hall, as the guest of Lord Houghton,
and a week in London, filled his time until near the
end of November.   From London he wrote: 'I certainly keep gaining.   My physical strength is unquestionably greater than it has been at any time since my
stroke.   I go about all day, now, without thinking of
fatigue, till night.'   His few days in London were
busily and agreeably spent, among friends who brought
him into acquaintance with many people of the literary
world whom he found it delightful to meet.   He also
renewed friendship with his old Edinburgh school-
mate, Mr. John Pettie, the artist, whom he had not
seen since they were boys together.   Going, then, to

Paris, for a few days, he found it 'a little too lively' for him, and he returned to England, writing from Folkestone, November 30th:

I am back in Folkestone, where I arrived last evening, and where I have had a thoroughly healthful day, roaming over the Kentish downs. I walked almost to Dover, and am able to testify that 'there's milestones on the Dover road,' in the words of old Aunt Betsey Trotwood. . . . I feel nearer to you, in England, and that is the sweetest feeling Europe has now to give me. . . . My present plan is to go up to London, to-morrow or next day, to get the things I left there; thence to run down to the Isle of Wight, or some place in that neighborhood, and stay there till the day before my ship sails. Yesterday, coming from Paris, I met a very pleasant Englishman and his wife, from whom I learned a deal as to attractive places on the south coast. When we parted we exchanged cards, and my *compagnon de voyage* proved to be Mr. Trevelyan, author of that book you liked so much—the Life of Macaulay.

From Ventnor, Isle of Wight, he wrote, Dec. 6th:

I arrived at two this afternoon, from Southampton, where I stopped last night, and a walk along the coast, from which I have just come in, inclines me to think that the praises of this island have not been tuned in too high a key. In the first place, I have seen the sun for the first time in a week, and the sky is blue when clear, not turnip color. Then the climate, as it appears to-day, is a sort of mild semi-spring. The lanes and hedges are green, many shrubs are in blossom, and I heard the birds singing cheerily, away in the depths of a thicket, surrounding a grand mansion. The shore, too, is superbly picturesque in its conformation,—bold headlands and long reaches of sandy beach ; while, above, tower quite high hills, to the top of which I shall make my way to-morrow. The place, however, has a decidedly high-priced and aristocratic flavor. On all sides, as you walk, you are warned against trespassing, here, and violating the sanctities of something or other, there. But I shall, no doubt, enjoy it for the five or six days I have to spend, and I'm sure I shall enjoy leaving it for the purpose of taking my way homeward.

He sailed from Liverpool for home December 13th, and, in his last letter from Ventnor, before leaving the Isle of Wight, written December 9th, described his state of health, as follows :

I feel confident that, if I take care of myself and arrange my work so as to avoid extra fatigue, I shall be all right, now. I consulted a doctor in Paris and he told me he thought there would be no danger. Of course, I shall not be as strong as I once was ; but I shall be able to resume my place and be at my post, and I feel that it is time that were done. You know, niches that are left empty, even by the most distinguished statues, have a way of filling up. So I shall come, as I have planned.

Reaching home, happily, on Christmas morning, he seemed to be in fairly good health and his hope of being able to resume work was fulfilled. Little more than a month passed, indeed, before he reported to his brother : 'I am again up to the eyes in work.' But he was able to add : 'In the midst of it all, I have been steadily gaining strength and tone. Indeed, my progress, the past month, has been surprising, and a subject to me of devout thankfulness. I can work with as much ease, now, as ever, while I take care not to work late or exhaust myself too much.'

He continued in this state of health for some two years, always working to nearly the limit of his strength, and always feeling that he might pass the breaking-point at any moment. Early in 1880, the line was overstepped, and he was forced to quit his post for several weeks, which he spent with friends at Norfolk, Va. He wrote to his brother at this time:

I do not think that my physical condition is as bad as you seem to fear. A week of rest has had a marked effect, in restoring my nerve-vigor, and I dare say that a month of it will put me in condition to resume work with safety; the more, as I now see my way clear to taking it easy and dropping night-work. If, however, the event should prove otherwise, I will cheerfully accept my physical break-down as an indication from God that I am to leave my present business. No doubt, some other way of making a living will be opened to me.

Recovering, again, from the prostration, he resumed once more the editorial direction of the *Courier*, working prudently, at first, a few hours daily, but being gradually drawn, by the exactions of his post, into the over-work which was so surely fatal to him. He knew the danger and saw no escape from it. An exclamation which appears in one of his letters (July, 1881) —'I keep up remarkably well; but O! I would be glad to get out of this business!'—expressed, no doubt, the continual, sad longing he felt. In the summer of 1882, the inevitable catastrophe occurred. He fell in the galling harness, again, and so had riddance of it, finding no more strength to put it on. He lived afterwards for six years, and with usefulness, but only as a shattered man.

As he was stricken at this time, his brain seemed partly paralyzed for a season,—not producing the slightest derangement of mind, but only a general numbness of its faculties. He had no comprehension of his own state, and was helpless in the hands of ready friends and of a courageous wife. The co-operation of these sent him, once more, over the sea, with his whole family, this time, to care for him and to give him companionship. He was saved by that measure, for the time, and owed entirely to it, no doubt, the precarious strength of body and the perfect clearness of mind which he regained.

CHAPTER VII.

Religious Experience.

THE religious sentiment was a profoundly inherent one in David Gray's nature. It was by that, and by his poetical sensibility, that he was fashioned as a man. These two were elemental in his character and his life; but the strain of natural piety was the more powerful of the two and dominated everything else. Its demands were the need that he always felt to be supreme; his spiritual cravings were the spring of his sorrow and his joy. The time in his life when he lost, for some years, the satisfaction of them, was the period of dark unhappiness which his letters have disclosed.

The parental and home influences which surrounded him in his boyhood were all tenderly but strictly religious. He was bred in an atmosphere of piety, and educated to the considering of questions of religious belief and religious practice as though all other matters were insignificant in the comparison. His parents were members of the Baptist church at Edinburgh, until 1839, when their views underwent some change, which David's brother has described in the following:

The *Christian Baptist*, a religious periodical, published by Alexander Campbell of Bethany, Va., had found its way into father's hands and led him to the belief that 'the Bible and the Bible alone is an all-sufficient guide in faith and practice.' Feeling that this could not be strictly lived up to in the Baptist connection, he, with four others, met for the first time on the last Sunday in 1839, in Roman Eagle Hall, Lawn Market, as a little body of Disciples of Christ. In a year and a half their numbers had swelled to one hundred and fifty. In August, 1847, Alexander Campbell, then traveling in Great Britain, delivered a series of discourses before large audiences in Waterloo Rooms, in the interest of the cause of truth, generally, and to strengthen the little congregation whose views coincided with his own. He was a frequent visitor at our house while in Edinburgh, and I well remember with what enthusiasm both young and old of us turned out to hear the great American orator. David, though young at that time, was well informed on religious subjects and especially intelligent in the Scriptures; so that when, two years later, we were living near Waupun, Wis., and found there a meeting of Disciples, it was with a very competent knowledge of what he was doing that he publicly confessed his faith in Christ, and was 'buried with him in baptism,' in the creek that ran near the school-house, where meetings were held. During all his stay in Wisconsin, he continued faithfully and earnestly devoted to a life consistent with his profession. He took much interest in religious subjects and read a great deal.

It was just before the Crimean war that Dr. John Thomas, of New Jersey, published a book called 'Elpsis Israel,' in which was set forth a complete outline of prophecy to be fulfilled by Russia, the 'King of the North.' David's interest in that book and in passing events was intense. He thought that Dr. Thomas held the key to unfulfilled prophecy, and, for a time, at least, was captivated by his teachings—believing that the European war, then commencing, was the beginning of the fulfillment of prophecy, and that, soon after, the Kingdom of Israel was to be established in Palestine,

their King. Dogmatism took possession
in subsequent writings, and so displeased
. lost, in time, all faith in him; and in
.ters from Edinburgh he alluded to Chris-
teaching as the doctrine of 'corner lots in

David came to Buffalo with religious feelings of the
utmost fervor still animating him, but with opinions
so peculiar that he found none among the Christian
churches of the city that he could join himself to with
a sense of fellowship, or with an approving conscience.
He wrote at that time (September 26, 1856) to his
friend Lindsay:

I feel rather destitute, as far as religious matters go.
Few 'means of grace,' as the Babylonish slang is,
are mine, other than may have fallen to the lot of
Robinson Crusoe on the desolate island. I find that
between me and the generality of religionists there is
a great gulf fixed, and passage on my part is out of
the question. I debated with myself the propriety of
joining the Baptists in the ordinance of the Lord's
Supper; but, as far as I can see, such is not my duty.
My sentiments, if declared to most of them, would be
pronounced monstrous, and I think it would be something of deceit to sit down. . . . And this is supposing
such an act to be perfectly salutary to my own religious
constitution. But, in communing with a body, do I
not, in a manner, identify myself with said body, all
its follies, etc., included? I don't know about that;
perhaps it is this way: A company are found pro-
fessedly following Jesus, and, in pursuance of such
profession, orderly fulfilling one of the Master's re-
quirements; now, can I not take them simply at their
word, as to the reality of their discipleship, and reap
the blessing in thus fulfilling with them, tho' on my

own account, the institution of the Lord ? Give me
your ideas on this matter, my dear Edmond, for I need
all the help I can get. I mentioned Robinson Crusoe
before, and really, when I think of it, I am on a spiritual
Juan Fernandez here.

In a letter to the same friend, November 26, 1856,
he wrote:

I do not mix a great deal with people here, altho' I
have met some real good young men . . . who, if they
could be drawn out of the clutches of error, would
ornament any cause. But this I have little hope of;
for I am not rooted and grounded in the faith enough,
myself, yet, to do any more than creep slowly on to
firmer footing. Oh! how I wish that I were like
Apollos, 'mighty in the Word.' How puny, then,
would the arguments and foils of the enemy seem;
for, it appears to me, there is a direct answer to every
objection to the truth, ready, somewhere in the Word of
Truth, to be read. Till we can in some degree master
this power of applying and using Scripture, we must
be content often to fall and rise,—often to remain
under a cloud when we could wish to be lightning,
almost,—and often to feel the chagrin of knowing that
something might be said to advantage and that we
can't say it. I think I shall, as my convictions go
now—in fact, I have determined to—take the first
opportunity for re-immersion. I am growing more
settled on that point, and I feel it a decided comfort
that I am settling, at last.

The following spring found him still troubled by the
question of ' re-immersion,' which had not been settled
in his mind as he thought it to be, and evidently
acquiring some distrust of the guide whose interpreta-
tions of Scripture he had been faithfully following.
He wrote to Edmond Lindsay, May 27, 1857 :

Respecting the question of re-immersion, I am still in my old position of painful indecision. How it will result with me, I know not. I am sometimes inclined to think that John Thomas has got hold of some technicalities, and is pushing things far beyond where the spirit of revelation will sustain him. It certainly weighs against him, when he subverts our previous ideas of Scripture, that he substitutes a something which I confess to be hard of comprehension; and that, moreover, a complete re-translation of Holy Writ is necessary to its establishment. However, that is nothing to the point. If J. T. has been simply a fallible man, and has run his theories to the ground, the truth which he has been the means of bringing to light claims attention, still. I, certainly, speaking of the Gospel now, would speak of it as the 'Gospel of the Kingdom,' and not merely as the 'things concerning Jesus.' I am very sorely tried, in not having any intercourse tending to sharpen and strengthen me in these matters.

TO THE SAME.

BUFFALO, *August* 20, 1857.

Touching the subject of re-immersion, . . . I am sorry to say that I have no progress to report. I have been corresponding with Walter, with Mr. Beattie, soliloquizing with myself, growing alternately angry and interested over John Thomas' *Herald*, and now I believe I am in a position which calls for—a continuation of the process. My views, however, are decidedly modified, as well, I perceive, as Walter's, respecting the Gospel, and, if I settle down somewhere into the position my father used to hold, you must not rail on me for retrograding, but rather pity me for having been so long driven about of the winds and tossed. God knows, if I had seen re-immersion to be an end to my perplexities, I should almost have submitted if it had been a baptism of fire.

TO THE SAME.

BUFFALO, *March* 5, 1858.

I think I have extended my vision and learned a little, in the past year or two that I have struggled and striven through. If it amounts to anything, it is that brother John Thomas has *not* gathered up all the truth into the circle of his belief;—a discovery which it took me a long and painful time to make, and which I had to work into from the most fortified state of opposite belief. The fact is, I think, that J. T. has, like many other men, got hold of a valuable idea, and has been so transported with his discovery that he has made it a kind of all-in-all, to the exclusion of every other. Following him closely, I could not see the error in which I was, except by a kind of *reductio ad absurdum;* I saw where his course had led me, and thereby saw its falseness . . . I confess to you, my experience since surmounting this long existent difficulty has been a most pleasant one. Instead of my mind being in a perpetual struggle, in consequence of my faith, I find my faith the one composing and supporting element,—a most salutary change, I assure you.

TO THE SAME.

BUFFALO, *May* 19, 1858.

I desire very much to talk with you, now, on the things of the Kingdom. I think a happy change has come over my mind since you saw me; as I have been able to correct my ideas on almost everything, so it has been with my understanding of Scripture, and with my ideas of the Christian system. The isolated, contracted kind of life which was mine in Wisconsin gave me corresponding ideas. I think intercourse with my fellows has had a corrective influence on me. But on this I will not enlarge. May God in His infinite mercy keep me from trusting in my own strength and wisdom!

The state of feeling expressed in the last of these letters was one in which David continued, probably, for some time longer. If not joined with any church, he was actively engaged in Christian work, not only in his connection with the Young Men's Christian Union, but also, and especially, as one of the teachers of a mission Sunday-school, which he helped to carry on for several years in the worst district of the city,—the 'Five Points of Buffalo,' as it was called in those days. He was greatly interested in the class of waifs whom he had gathered under his teaching in this school, and on whom he exerted an influence—there can be no doubt of it—which affected the lives of some among them, if not all. He kept acquaintance with them, as far as possible, and watched their course in after years, with great satisfaction from the knowledge that several of these 'children of the street' had become successful, trustworthy, useful members of society.

But a chill of some nature came upon David's religious feelings, after a time, and his life for several years was much troubled by it. His brother states that 'he came in contact with men whose influence was against Christianity, and that an effect was produced on his mind, at first imperceptible to himself.' The effect of that influence, whatever it may have been, was undoubtedly helped by the excitements and distractions into which he was led, first by his newspaper associations, and afterwards by the gay life of 'society' into which he plunged. As early as in August, 1861, he wrote: 'In religious matters I seem to suffer a total eclipse.' But, as he said a little later to one who questioned him: 'These things are never out of my

mind.' It was the always present thought of his
spiritual alienation which clouded his life at that
period, and which gave their tone of bitterness to some
of the letters that have been quoted in a former chapter. The following is from a letter which he wrote to
a very near friend, in March, 1865:

I know your loving Christian heart would like to
have me say that I, too, had found that rest and
refuge which are better than any philosophy or experience afford. I cannot say it, H., yet. I only know
that I am wretched, and must be, till a great change
comes. I do not seek to evade the wretchedness, until
I can exchange it—not for pleasure, nor happiness,
even, but for *blessedness*. But how that change is to
be made I know not yet. Anything that anybody,
even you, could say to me, instantly resolves itself into
a theory or system, and then it is assailable; then the
whole pack of doubts and questionings leap on it like
mad and tear it down, and trample it into the undis-
tinguishable mire into which other systems have been
worried to death before it. But just let me wait and
ruminate and suffer. It cannot be wrong, that. While
I feel, more keenly than words can speak, my loathsome
baseness and utter weakness, I still have a forlorn
feeling that God is love, and that love is leading me
even now. Remember, I don't use that feeling as a
justification of my miserable status.

The change which he hoped and waited for was long
in coming to him. He did not find it during the years
of his old-world pilgrimage, although his religious feelings were much touched and wakened, several times.
While traveling in Italy, in 1866, his attention was
first turned, as it seems, to the simple and earnest
communion of the 'Plymouth Brethren,' so called,

which he afterwards joined. The incident that interested him in them was related in a letter to his father and mother, written from Venice, May 9th of that year:

At Bologna, a week or ten days ago, at the hotel there, I got into conversation with an English gentleman, who, from some remarks he let fall, at once seemed to be a Christian, and not of the kind who rely much on churches or ministers. I found he had become converted, as he said, by reading the New Testament and hearing the word preached by an Italian evangelist, and had found himself drawn to sympathy with the Plymouth Brethren, although he had never formally joined their communion. Having owed some of his knowledge of the Gospel to Italy, he had, since, as much as possible, for eight years, been devoting himself to testifying among the Italians his gratitude. He was able to tell me some very interesting things about a religious reformation now in progress through Italy,—that to which he is giving his aid. In most of its leading features, this reformation is exactly such as that of Britain and America. It is an uprising of faith and knowledge, gained simply and solely from the Scriptures, and in which the thraldom of the priesthood is utterly repudiated. The little churches of these believers, scattered throughout Italy, almost altogether composed of the poor in this world's goods, and often subjected to grievous persecutions from the Catholic Church, have struck out a form of church order and government precisely that of the Reformation called Campbellite. They meet once a week to break bread. They likewise recognize the necessity of the believer's baptism, and profess to have no other rule or authority than that of the Bible for their conduct. Their evangelists, men who give their strength to the work for no money remuneration, are now busily spreading what I have no doubt is the very Gospel, in every part of a country which, five years ago, was hermetically sealed against the light. A good proof of the genuineness of the movement is, that the various missionary societies and evangelizing agencies of the orthodox churches in Britain look coldly on the 'Free Christian Church of Italy,' and invite it to declare its creed and take to itself a distinctive name, before they will give it aid,—an invitation, I am glad to say, which the Italian believers courteously but firmly decline. This is interesting, is n't it? My friend, Col. Cartan—like Mr. Symonds, he is a retired officer—seemed to be a devoted and intelligent man, and I enjoyed the two or three days communication I had with him, very much.

The next year he was in the Holy Land, and no other part of his travel interested him so much as the visiting of the scenes of the Gospel history. It was the interest of a Christian believer that he felt, and he was probably never shaken in that belief; but his faith had become spiritually cold, and, even yet, there was no kindling of it anew. Soon after his return from Palestine, while at Gotha, Germany, in July, 1867, he wrote to his friend David Taylor:

The idea struck me suddenly with a thump, the other day, to ask you whereabouts you have arrived nowadays on the religious question. I almost smile when I remember how we arranged that subject between us, long ago; how sore and sensitive I used to feel on it, and how religiously we avoided it. For better or worse, that is all changed with me, now, and I would really like, if you happen to feel interested in this respect, when you next write, that you would speak out whatever you may have to say. As for myself, touching religion, I am almost led to doubt whether some important faculty has not been omitted in my make-up, so utterly have I failed to find foothold in the dark and dubious realm,—so totally barren of results does my life seem to be, so far as the forming of beliefs, or even of opinions, goes. I am altogether a negative, while you are a positive man; and thus I cannot but think that you must be pretty well defined and fixed in your notions. If so, give me the benefit, as you can. Life is too short for discussions and arguments; so you need dread nothing of that sort on my side.

Ten more years were yet to pass before the light which he looked for—the light which had shone upon his spirit in youth and which his manhood had lost—reappeared to him. In 1877 he experienced a change which made him, for all the remainder of his life, a totally different man. Early in the summer of that year, his thoughts became fixed on the questions of religion with more seriousness than he had shown before. Mrs. Gray says:

When we were at Block Island, that year, he carried a copy of the New Testament with him in all his walks. Davy [their young son] was his almost constant companion on these walks, and he used to tell me how his father would lie down on the cliffs near the sea and read his Testament, very often reading aloud to Davy and talking with him about what he had read. From that time until he died, there was no subject that had for him so deep an interest.

Soon after coming home from Block Island, he suffered the prostration which first broke his strength, and he then went abroad, as has been told, for three months. On returning from England, he paid a visit to his parents at Detroit, and while there, at a Sunday morning meeting of the Disciples, he made a public confession of faith which impressed those who heard it very deeply. His brother writes of this: 'He confessed that he had been a wanderer, subject to very great religious aberration; but he thanked the Heavenly Father that he had been spared to see his folly. He desired to humbly acknowledge his wrong, and for the future to live by help from above, as a true and devoted servant of Christ.' On the 30th of August following he was received 'by experience' (the church record states) into the Washington Street Baptist Church, at Buffalo. 'Rev. Dr. Hotchkiss, a man of profound research and knowledge of the Scriptures' (says David's brother), 'was then pastor, and with him David held much in common, enjoying his expositions as well as his spiritual life. But the divided state of the church filled his mind with sadness, and led him often to speak of it, as "the church in ruins;" and at the same time he became gradually convinced that faithful allegiance to Christ required him to take a position of separation from all the confusion prevailing in the religious world.'

In June, 1879, he wrote to his brother:

I do want to have a long talk with you about many subjects. My heart is full. . . . Meantime I am waiting and inquiring as to my duty. But, thank God! although I am undecided on some points of conduct, I have peace and joy and the assurance of forgiveness of sin through the mercy of God in Christ Jesus; and what could a man wish for, more,—save that he might grow in grace and in the knowledge of that Blessed One who has not only died that we might live, but has entered into the heavens to appear for us in the presence of His Father?

He found himself, now, drawn by an increasing attraction towards the people known as the Plymouth Brethren, among whom were already counted some of the friends who were dearest to him. Writing to one of these, on the 2d of April, 1880, he said:

It is grand to see the glories of Christ shining out of every page of Scripture. Everywhere He is 'set forth' as the object of our wonder, adoration and love. O, that my wretched lean and cold heart might be filled with Him. I am conscious of suffering sadly for lack of more intimate and simple communion with His people than I now enjoy, and I long for the time when I shall see my way clear to have fellowship with your brethren. But, for the present, I dare not follow my inclination in this matter. If these Washington Street Baptists are God's people, as I believe they are, what right have I to leave them? Admit that they are uninstructed, and that their order in some things is not that of the New Testament; still, it should be my business, rather to try and set them right than to turn my back on them. And, then, while I feel that the position held by your brethren is the true one, and I intensely desire to be with them in their separation from the world and oneness with Christ, I cannot comprehend how they can stand in resistance to the (to me) plain and unmistakable appointment of Christ, in regard to baptism. Something wrong in both places, I am forced to think; and what right have I to think of making (if I may use the phrase) a choice of evils? There is no such thing tolerated in the Word of God. The logic of my present reasoning would be, come out of both, or all, and stay out till the way be made clear. And yet, and yet,—I shrink from that as a great peril! I pray that, while I am waiting for more light, I may be strengthened and built up in the life of Christ,—that He may dwell in my heart by faith, and

that I may know His love which passeth knowledge.
I know that He alone can keep me, in this state of trial
and transition, and I *do* want to look only to Him.

TO HIS BROTHER.

BUFFALO, *February* 15, 1881.

I read with great interest the articles in the papers
you sent me, and have very little criticism to make on
the editor's presentation of the subject. I would give
baptism just the place and just the importance the
Word gives it; but, at the same time, would be careful
not to let it obscure other and greater truths. See
Luke iii: 16, where a comparison of baptisms is made.
It is the baptism of the Holy Spirit which gives us
our union with Christ (1 Cor. xii: 13), our life and
standing in Him; and it appears (among other passages, see Acts x: 44) that that mighty change sometimes took place before water baptism was administered.
I merely throw these out as suggestions, and not at all
as taking up a controversy with you; for I don't
think you and I would differ on the subject. I do
wish we could often get together for conversation and
communion regarding the things of Christ. I have
but poor opportunities; nevertheless, I have had great
joy and comfort in my recent studies of the Scriptures.
Can't you run down soon and spend a Sunday with us,
again? . . .

TO THE SAME.

BUFFALO, *May* 18, 1881.

I have devoted all the few spare hours I have had
since you kindly sent me Mr. Patton's book to its
perusal, and have been greatly interested in it. He
certainly has a great deal of truth, some of which is
new to me and very valuable. But I fear he goes
farther in some things than the Word, fairly read, will
sustain him. . . .

In fact, we must always be entirely ready to stop and unload the most attractive theory when we collide with a plain statement of the Word. Our theories may easily be wrong; but the Word cannot be. Let us hold ourselves perfectly subject to it, even though that leave us to wait in great confusion and ignorance. More light will come, if our hearts be right before God. It was with his heart (not head) that David set himself to understand the times of his people, and immediately the angel was sent to enlighten him. I would very much enjoy a long talk with you all,—not an argument; I do n't think much good comes of arguing. But it is delightful to go to the Book and question it and bow before its wondrous answers. Patton's book, at any rate, is very suggestive; and he certainly has brought out a new and vivid meaning in many Scriptures that were meaningless to me, before.

TO THE SAME.

BUFFALO, *August* 24, 1881.

. . . By the way, I have chanced to learn a little, lately, of those people in Pittsburgh ('Zion's Watch Tower') with whom Mr. Patton seems to be in sympathy. I think I saw one of their tracts in your possession. I have read a little of Mr. Russell's writing, myself— perhaps the same tract I saw you have. It is very significant that, here and there throughout the country, we are seeing a breaking away of earnest, hungry souls from the corruptions of the professing church. There is a movement of a similar kind just now in Chicago, and it seems to me that Moody's Conference at Northfield is squinting decidedly in the same direction. But, alas! I find the Pittsburgh Watchmen of Zion do not always seem to be content simply with what is written. They want to know more than is revealed, and draw on their imaginations to make up the deficiency. At least, that is what I am bound to think of much of their teaching (and Mr. Patton's) as to the destiny of the unsaved dead, the various 'orders' and classes of saved, and some other subjects. But, with this, they have much of the inspiring truth which has been brought out among our so-called 'Plymouth' friends, and this activity of inquiry is surely better than the spiritual death we find inside the churches. . . .

TO THE SAME.

BUFFALO, *May* 2, 1882.

In this day of ruin and apostacy of what calls itself the Church, there is nothing left for us but the unchangeable Lord Jesus Christ, himself. The day of man's building for God is past. Gathered to His name —to that alone—and waiting for Him in the place of humiliation and rejection, where He once was for us,—that is the Christian's position, as it seems to me. Diligent, fervent in spirit in His service, alert in testimony for Him; but, most of all, watching and yearning for His coming,—having no ties or plans in this world that would keep our hearts here a moment,—that is how He would have us be, for the 'very, very little while' (Heb. x: 37, literal translation) until He come. Ah, John, may He give us grace and strength and love for Himself in our hearts, that we may be thus kept!

The precise time at which David became finally persuaded to join the little company of the Plymouth Brethren in Buffalo does not appear; but his affiliation with them occurred, probably, within the year 1882. His brother, who understood his religious feelings better than any other person, perhaps, has this to say on the subject:

Amongst this people, he felt that he was in a measure answering to the promptings of his mind, as enlightened by careful study of the Scriptures. Though his old friends might often charge him with narrowness and bigotry, still he never shrank from making known his views, believing that his former indifference but obligated him the more to faithfully bear witness for the truth. That his position was often one of severe suffering to his sensitive nature cannot be doubted, in view of what he once said on this subject in connection with his family: 'Do you think it costs me no pain to sever myself from all that is dearest to me? No mere sentiment, nothing but loyalty to Christ, could induce me to take this position.' But, in taking it, there was the result of that deep earnestness which carried his mind to the extreme limit of self-abnegation, and which sought rather the infliction of sacrifice that he might bear witness more faithfully. His principal question to himself was, 'How shall I best declare my gratitude for the unspeakable mercy that has been bestowed upon me?' His thought was, that if he had formerly served the things of time and sense, he had been spared to see the folly of that, and all his care was that he might live no longer to these things, but to Him who died to save the world. Following his sickness in 1882–4, this was especially true; for in his removal from journalism he recognized, again, the wisdom and goodness of a Father's care, and he believed it a direct interposition of that higher will.

His sojourn at that time in Europe was marked by the enjoyment he found in communion with little bodies of those who had heard and followed the teachings of Scripture, as expounded to them by John Darby, years before, on his sojourn in the French and Swiss Alps; and it was his delight to find so many of his own brethren who were faithful and true to what they had learned. In Great Britain, many of those little assemblies were enlivened by his presence and strengthened by his words.

CHAPTER VIII.

LAST YEARS AND DEATH. 1882–1888.

IT was by an act of high courage on the part of his wife that Gray was taken across the Atlantic, in September, 1882. The strange cloud upon his mind had thickened, until he knew nothing of what was done; he was as helpless as the youngest of the three children—a babe of eight months—who went with them. He was so ill on the voyage that the ship's surgeon expressed doubt of his living to the end of it. Mrs. Gray was inexperienced in ocean travel, and a situation more forlorn than her's cannot easily be conceived. But a brave, affectionate heart, with great hopefulness and resolution, carried her through the terrible trial; and she had her reward. Before a week passed, after landing at Liverpool, the darkness in David's brain began to be lighted with gleams of consciousness. He recognized, for the first time since leaving home, the strangeness of his surroundings, and was soon able to understand what had happened to him and whither he had been brought. When he knew that he had his family about him, his joy was very great. His mental recovery was rapid, and his physical improvement so encouraging that he had strength for considerable walks in Liverpool, before his stay of a fortnight in that city was ended.

From Liverpool, the family went, first, under advice, to Clifton, a beautiful suburb of the old city of Bristol; but unfavorable weather, there, drove them further south, and they settled themselves at Ventnor, in the Isle of Wight. It was a place which David had found pleasant on his visit in 1877, and he now came back to it with much delight. He improved visibly, from day to day, during three months at Ventnor, and the time was a happy one for all. His first letter home was written from that place, in November, to his brother. He touched in it, a little, on some questions as to the future, and remarked: 'It is a subject on which I think little, knowing as I do that the way will be opened for us as we proceed. But this much I may say: It does seem as if I had done my last newspaper work, and as if my connection with politics were definitely closed.'

On the 1st of January following, he wrote again:

A happy New Year to you and yours! And please extend the fervent wish and prayer to Randolph street, as well as to the dear ones on Adams avenue. How blessed it is for us that we know where the highest—the only true—happiness is unfailingly to be found, and that it is not for a paltry year, but for eternity! Rejoice in the Lord always; again I say, rejoice! In Him is happiness—reasonable, unfailing, infinite. To Him be praise! . . .

That I am doing well and gaining strength, this letter will in itself show you. As it is *the biggest thing* yet out from my hand, I regard it with some pride and amazement.

The beginning of the new year brought fog and damp weather to the Isle of Wight, and it was thought best to proceed to the south of France for the remainder of the winter.   At Paris, the party halted for some time, waiting the arrival of David's brother, who joined them there early in February, with his wife. While at Paris, David wrote to his father and mother:

Paris is, by long odds, the most magnificent and brilliant city in the world; but the Christian is continually made to feel that the god of this world is supreme in it, and that it is, for God's people, an enemy's country.   Yet, even here, I have found a few who meet together every first day in the week, to remember the death of the Lord Jesus Christ; and, in breaking bread with them and joining in their simple, warm-hearted worship, I have had unspeakable joy and blessing.   There are about fifty or sixty of them, I should think. . . .   How wonderful have been the grace and loving-kindness that have kept us as a family!   Even in the stroke that has laid me aside, I cannot fail to feel a Father's hand, and that in love.   It assures me that *I am a son*, and the object of His tender, watchful care.   And, though it seems as if I shall have to begin life all over again when I get through with this vacation, yet I know He will prepare my path.   Infinite power, infinite wisdom, infinite love, —all these are ours in our Blessed Lord.   'All things are your's, and ye are Christ's, and Christ is God's.' What a chain is that!

The two brothers, with their families, traveled south, together, in February, as far as the little town of St. Raphael, on the Mediterranean, between Marseilles and Cannes, where David, and his, were advised to remain through the spring.   'Here,' writes Mrs. Gray, ' our invalid was by the sea, once more, and we could see him grow strong. His spirits rose and he reveled in the beauties of sea and land. We saw the spring come, and many long tramps the family took, together, by the ocean and inland among the Esterelle mountains, no one standing the fatigue better or getting more enjoyment from the lovely scenes about us than he.'

The improved state of David's health while at St. Raphael, and afterwards at Cannes, was shown by the industry of his pen in correspondence. A few passages only can be culled out of many letters that he wrote to his father and mother, to his brother, then traveling in Italy, and to other friends.

TO JAMES N. JOHNSTON.

St. Raphael, *March* 9, 1883.

. . . Let me suggest and urge that you come over in May and join us in Switzerland. There, on the high, tonic summits of God's mountains, you and I could perchance breathe fresh, vigorous health. For myself, as you know, I have everything to be thankful for. The first stages of my convalescence were simply marvelous. Afterward, however, the pace slowed down a little, and, for six weeks past, I have been reminded not to expect too much. This is the first day since we left Ventnor, two months ago, that I have felt equal to a letter, and even now my right side admonishes me to hasten to a close. It was a pretty hard knock-over, James, and deep wounds need time to heal. That we have made no mistake in coming here, my improved sleep and recovered strength happily assure me.

TO HIS PARENTS, ON THEIR GOLDEN WEDDING ANNIVERSARY.

St. Raphael, *March* 15, 1883.

You may imagine that you have been much in our thoughts and in our talks and prayers these days, and especially are we all with you in spirit to-day. It seems a little hard that neither of your sons should be with you on so memorable an occasion; but, that, I feel well assured, has all been wisely and lovingly ordered, and so we bow to it thankfully. I wish I could send you a wedding present worthy of the occasion, and which would in some small measure express the love that is in my heart for you both; but, that being impossible—'silver and gold have I none'—I do the next best thing,—a better thing, perhaps, after all: I invoke for you the best blessings that can flow from the source of Divine Love. If God will that we shall all be spared to meet again in the body, I am sure it will be to praise Him together for all His goodness.

TO HIS SISTER.

St. Raphael, *March* 31, 1883.

. . . I have just learned of a little meeting of brethren at Cannes, about twenty miles from here, and hope to break bread with them to-morrow. Wherever we have been, I have been rejoiced by sweet fellowship with the Lord's people. It is especially pleasant in this God-less country to find such simple-hearted lovers of the Lord Jesus and such intelligent students of His Word as I have lately met. Truly our way has been wonderfully prepared for us, and we should be faithless and ungrateful, indeed, if we did not trust in the Father's continued love and care of us for the days to come.

TO JAMES N. JOHNSTON.

. . . Your ideas as to the future of the Gray family, I am glad to see, are ours. Sometimes I am tempted to an anxious thought, when I look forward to beginning business life again; but when I remember how lovingly, graciously and tenderly I have been dealt with by my Father, my heart well may murmurings cease. The 37th Psalm has been a useful scripture to me; likewise a verse or two in the 13th of Hebrews.

TO HIS FATHER.

CANNES, *April* 25, 1883.

We have been tenderly and lovingly guided in every step of our journeyings; but in none has the wise care of our Father been more strikingly displayed than in our choice of this place as a waiting-station. It is a lovely spot, with a superb winter and spring climate, and the air of the ocean and the mountains, both of which distil their aërial chemicals for our benefit, is good for us all and is doing me especial good. Then, the resources of the place are so varied as to be almost inexhaustible; I mean in the way of walks and excursions. Every morning, Guthrie* and I discover some new ramble among the hills or among the nooks of the sea-shore, which fairly inspires us by its rich and brilliant beauty. But, best of all, I have, also, company, as much as I want, and of the best. I had the address of a brother in the Lord here at Cannes, but I somehow got the idea that there was no meeting, and so I did not make haste to put myself in communication with him. When, finally, I did write him, however, the second day after brought him and another brother, an evangelist, to St. Raphael, to see me, and I have had

* His younger son.

the privilege of remembering the Lord's death at His table every Lord's day since; for they told me of the meeting, here, which has been to me a great blessing and joy. It was through the friend to whom I wrote, Mr. Gounet, that we came to Cannes, and secured delightful quarters at a less rate than we had been paying at St. Raphael. . . . Indeed, wherever I turn, I am made to realize what a wondrous bond that is which binds together members of Christ's body. In company with Mr. Gounet, I have visited a number of the brethren at their houses, and you ought to see me, some time, talking with them about the things of God, in my bad French, and enjoying a fellowship as intimate as if I had known them all my life. . . .

I note with interest what you say about getting on to a piece of land, after I get back, if I am spared to see America again. I may say that I have often had similar plans in my mind, and in most respects, perhaps, yours is feasible. It is best, however, I think, that I should let my way open up before me as I go along. I certainly have no fear but that I shall be able to find some way of getting an honest and quiet living. The promises are too numerous and positive to admit of doubt on this head. My constant prayer is that I may be guided absolutely by the Word of God; that I may have no will of my own in the matter, and that, whatever I do, whether in word or deed, I may be enabled to do all in the name of the Lord Jesus. It certainly looks to me as if the Lord had meant, in His recent dealings with me, to take me out of the business I was in. He knows I waited for Him to do that in His own time and way; but, if I am mistaken in this, I will know the fact in due time.

Leaving Cannes about the middle of May, Gray went next to Geneva, with his family, and was received into the same household in which, eighteen years before, he had lived and studied French for six months. From Geneva he wrote to his brother, June 10th:

During our sojourn here, I have made numerous inquiries and one or two excursions with a view to decide where we had best move to. I have some thought of starting . to-morrow into the Canton de Vaud, to see what I can find. There are meetings of brethren in almost all the villages of that country, which would make it preferable, if I can find other essential conditions fulfilled. The gathering here is a large and very happy one, and I have profited by that not a little.

Two weeks later he was at the opposite end of Lake Leman, at Clarens, which he described to his father as an 'earthly paradise.' 'There is no water in the world,' he added, ' so deeply blue as that of Lake Leman, and the superb mountains that tower from its shores, all round, make it look still more mirror-like. In some places, the mountains are vine-clad or wooded far up their sides, while in other directions the glittering, snow-clad peaks of the Alps look down at us, and fairly *peek* in at our windows.' Writing, also, to his friend Johnston, from Clarens, he said:

Please overhaul your Byron (*Childe Harold*, third canto, I think) and read what he says of Clarens. You might also glance over the once familiar screed about *The Prisoner of Chillon;* for I rowed the family up the lake from our hotel door to the prison of Bonnivard this forenoon. It was a couple of hours of good rowing, there and back, and I was not a bit tired; so you may imagine, as a skilled oarsman, that I am not in a very feeble physical condition. Indeed, James, I am happy to say that I feel myself unmistakably gaining in health and strength. Progress has been slow and symptoms often discouraging, but, though the scars are still fresh, I feel that a cure has been made. For this I humbly thank my God and Father. I take it from His hand as signifying that He wills I should re-enter, by and by, the struggle of this earthly life. I should have been quite content, I trust, had He willed otherwise; but, as it is, trusting to His strength, to be manifested in my weakness, His wisdom in my folly, I shall come back thankfully and renew the fight. And I can add in truth and verity, that my main, if not my only, anxiety is, that I may be kept faithful to Him whose I am and whom I serve. But enough of that. Talk is cheap; the rough event will show. . . .

Before we came here I had spent over a week in the mountains, studying up the question of high places of resort. My Paris doctor strongly recommends a month or two at an elevation of not less than 4,000 or 5,000 feet, and I have been testing a few such stations. Where we shall mount to is not yet decided, nor will it be for a week, yet; for the season continues cold and the high altitudes are not habitable till the heat begins. Probably you will next hear of me as a chamois hunter, or a member of the Alpine Club.

The mountain station finally chosen was at Morgins, Canton de Valais, which David described in his first letter, written from it (July 6th), as 'a valley, about 4,600 feet above sea-level, high, green hills around it, densely wooded with hemlock and pine on one side; a mountain torrent rushing down the center and the high Alps peeping over at us.' 'The air,' he added, 'is very bracing and I feel sure it is going to do me good. Moreover, it is not very expensive.' A week later he wrote to his father:

When I go out in the mornings and smell the smells of the woods and take in the atmospheric champagne, I feel like walking on my tip-toes. . . . The green hill-sides are dotted with *chalets* of the natives, whose sole industry and occupation is the keeping of cows. The dairy people drive them up, as soon as the snow leaves the lower hills, and they (the cows) keep grazing on the fresh young herbage, higher and higher up, as the season advances, till you meet them, sometimes, 7,000 or 8,000 feet up. The weather has been rather unsettled since we came; but I have managed, nevertheless, to have a long ramble over the hills nearly every day, and I find that even a five 'hours vigorous excursion of this sort does not tire me unduly.

Those 'vigorous excursions,' however, were a sad mistake, as would seem to be proved by the result. The bracing mountain-air tempted him beyond his strength, to a measure of bodily exercise which harmed rather than healed his disordered nerves. His need was still the same that it had been—rest—and he misunderstood it. Mrs. Gray writes: 'I cannot but believe that his strength was greatly overtaxed and the chance for his recovery lost by that summer in the mountains. Each day, he used up his vitality in exercise, and when, the latter part of August, we went down into the plain again, a great depression fell upon him, from which he never really rallied.'

On coming down from the mountains, the family stayed ten days at Lucerne, from which place David, feeling badly affected by the change, wrote: 'It occurs to me that perhaps I am not to recover my former health and strength entirely; but will always be a sort of barometrically-affected being and "lame duck." If so, why, so be it. I surely have enough already to be thankful for.' While at Lucerne, he had an oppor- tunity to consult his Paris physician, and was advised by him to go to Badenweiler, a charming little spa on the edge of the Black Forest, and to try the effect of its baths. 'The doctor,' says Mrs. Gray, 'saw that David had lost ground, and when I told him how he had gone mad on the subject of exercise, he shook his head and forbade long walks or anything that would, in the least, fatigue.' The baths were tried, but did not prove to be beneficial. After a fortnight at Baden- weiler, the patient invalid was forced to say: 'I 'm not exactly where I would like to be, physically, yet.' A week afterwards, he had become convinced that he must not hope to return home for any kind of work or busi- ness until another year. His physician, he wrote, found 'a condition of weakness of the involuntary nerve system (and, by consequence, of the digestive and other organs and functions), which looks to a still longer time for recovery than I had hoped.' 'The doctor inti- mates,' he continued, 'that I have been overdoing all summer, and that I must now come down to a regimen of rest and no end of coddling.' In another letter to his brother, he reported a still more emphatic expression from the doctor,—that it would be madness for him to think of any kind of business in his present state; and 'I am admonished,' he added, 'in various ways, from within, that he is right.' Hence the decision to remain in Europe through another winter. 'This side the ocean,' he remarked, 'is better than the other for an idle man. There is no place in the United States for an invalid who is able to be out of the hospital. So, if the Lord will, we leave here for winter-quarters at Montreux, on Thursday morning.'

From October until the following March, the family was settled quietly in 'pension' at Montreux, on Lake Leman, or the Lake of Geneva, with the boys attending school. 'A beautiful spot,' was David's account of it, 'with delightful surroundings; and the air agrees with us all.' Whether, on the whole, he made any clear progress towards health through the winter, seemed doubtful; but his letters were all contented and hopeful:

TO HIS BROTHER.

PENSION MOOSER,
MONTREUX, *November* 6, 1883.

. . . Time is wearing on with us, here, so quietly and stealthily that the winter is like to get past without notice, almost. I have subsided so completely into the laziness of my life that the little routine of eating, sleeping, walking, etc., quite fills it up, and leaves me no leisure to get weary or dull in. My commonest thought is one of lively thankfulness, as often as I realize how wonderfully I am being blessed, in getting this opportunity for rest and recuperation. Indeed, John, from the moment I ceased to be able to do for myself, I seem to have been lying on a bed of down; perfectly cared for, and with the strength of the Almighty arms supporting my weakness. I feel quite confident that I am to be a well man again, and I hope, even, that in some way the last bit of my life may be of some use in the Blessed Master's service; but, surely, after what has befallen me, I should have no misgiving, whatever His will may be concerning me. In fine, what a discovery it is, when one finds out, actually and really, that 'He careth for us'!

And you may be sure, dear John, that I count among the choicest of God's gifts the brother's love of which I am having such an experience these days. You have fairly got my burden on your back, and I am getting so I do not worry about it. . . .

There is a little meeting here, in Montreux, where the loaf is broken, every first day of the week, in remembrance of the Lord's death.

TO HIS FATHER AND MOTHER.

MONTREUX, *December* 1, 1883.

. . . The routine of my life is uneventful enough, and the large amount of time-killing it includes would surely lie heavy on my conscience, were it not that, on the authority of the doctors, it is just the kind of thing that I am to make a business of for the time being. And so I fill my empty days with sunshine and meditation, and praise the grace that sends them to me in my need.

TO JAMES N. JOHNSTON.

MONTREUX, *December* 18, 1883.

. . . Ah! James, I wish you could drop over here, one of these fine, sunny, southern winter mornings! This morning, I sauntered down the hill from high Montreux and struck the lake-shore in its northwestward trend. Half or three-quarters of an hour brought me under the walls of Chillon, and I gazed off, on each side of the castle, at the blue expanse of the lake, and the Alps beyond. Half an hour further, still along the lake, and there were the Hotel Byron and Villeneuve, the former place, with its beautiful grounds and view, redolent to me of Stillson. You can imagine, perhaps, what thoughts accompanied me. . . . If you could come over, what walks and talks we *would* have, around the poetic lake!

TO HIS FATHER.

MONTREUX, *February* 12, 1884.

. . . I feel myself of late improving, although but slowly, and not in all respects, yet. My sleep continues more or less unreliable, but, in spite of that, there is a decrease in nervous irritability,—which is a great comfort, both to me and to the good folks I live with. In short, my belief is confirmed, that it is the gracious purpose of our loving Father to restore me, in His own good time, to physical health. . . .

Our meeting here is very small, and has no highly-gifted brethren; besides, we speak divers tongues and do not always perfectly understand each other. But, all the same, each Lord's day morning we do marvelously realize the presence and blessing of a loving, living Lord; and what could we ask for more? Every Monday afternoon, too, we have an English meeting, to which friends gather from various towns along the lake-shore, for the study of the Word. We have had a very interesting time in this meeting over the Epistle to the Romans.

TO HIS BROTHER.

MONTREUX, *March* 26, 1884.

. . . I am very well, except that my sleep continues defective, which prevents me from gaining nervous strength, as I am sure I otherwise should. But I feel confident that when I get away from here, and snuff the salt of the ocean once more, there will be a marked improvement. For that reason, I am not sorry that our days in Montreux are numbered. The Lord willing, we expect now to leave for London, Wednesday or Thursday of next week. . . .

You ask me what I think I had best turn my hand to, when I get through with my long holiday, and I am forced to reply that I have not an idea. I believe I am spoiled for literary work, unless it be of some purely hack kind, in a newspaper or elsewhere, which would be as legitimate a way of earning a living as breaking stones. What I mean is, that if I undertook to 'look into my heart and write,' as Longfellow enjoins upon authors, the product would certainly not be such as could have any cash value. For mercantile business, I never have developed any talent; but no saying what I may yet do! All the same, I had to smile at your amiable suggestion, that I could be useful to you as a sort of counselor. But, John, I do have the firmest confidence that something honest will turn up for me when the time comes. When I look back and see how our way has been opened for us, I cannot doubt nor feel anxious.

Leaving Montreux at the beginning of April, the party traveled, without stoppage, to London, and made a stay of some weeks in the great city, having excellent lodgings in Horbury Crescent, Nottinghill Gate. The change into 'the bracing air of England,' as he described it, was of notable benefit to Gray. 'Almost from the first night,' he wrote, 'I have been sleeping better—I might almost say luxuriously—and in every other respect I am feeling better, as a consequence. It really seems as if my old frame were, at last, getting satisfactorily tinkered and put together again.' Among the letters which he wrote from London was one to his father, containing the following passage:

I do indeed feel the kindness of God to you, my dear parents, as among the choicest of His blessings and mercies to myself. When I think of the way in which He has spared you to us all so long, in quietness, comfort and happiness,—independent of all men and dependent only on Himself,—my eyes fill with sweet waters and my heart melts in gratitude. And if it should be His will that we should all be in the body for a little while longer, and thus permitted to meet again here below, will we not rejoice in praising and exalting together His blessed and holy name? For, surely, He *is* good. My life, both physically and spiritually,—both for time and eternity,—He surely has 'redeemed from destruction;' while of a truth, as a family, we can all say that 'He crowneth us with loving-kindness and tender mercies.' And, above all, when I think of 'the exceeding riches of His grace' that He has made ours in His Son,—the unspeakable revelation of His love to us, that we have in that Blessed and Holy One,—I feel constrained to that 'continual offering' of praise of which the apostle speaks (Hebrews xiii: 15); which is assuredly the fitting service of those who have gone forth to Jesus, without the camp, bearing His reproach, and who have in this world no continuing city, but are seeking one to come. May the Lord keep us all, while we praise Him for His goodness to us, with true pilgrim hearts in our breasts! If His grace can thus make us sing with joy on the road, what will it be to be with Him—to see Him as He is?

The stay at London was prolonged into May; then Edinburgh and the friends there were visited, and, on the 7th of June, the family sailed from Liverpool for home. Twelve days later, David wrote to his brother from Buffalo, to announce their arrival, to say for himself that he was 'feeling first-rate,' and to promise a speedy visit to Detroit.

He came home quite undetermined as to plans for the future. His interest in the *Buffalo Courier* had been sold before his return, through the agency of his brother, and he regarded his connection with journalism as wholly severed. It was an unspeakable relief to him to feel free from what had been, for many years, a most wearing yoke of bondage, to his spirit and his body alike. The proceeds of the sale of his stock in the Courier Company had been profitably invested at Detroit, in the business of his brother, and whether that city or Buffalo should be made his future residence was the question now uppermost in his mind. His father, mother, sister and brother were in one; the friendships and acquaintanceships of his life were chiefly in the other. For his own part, he rather feared the strong attractions of the latter character which drew him towards Buffalo. His past life in that city, with its ambitions, its social activities, its political agitations, had been a life of worldliness, in his present view of it, which he looked back upon with a certain loathing, and the possibly surviving influences from which he dreaded to place himself under. He foresaw, moreover, an incongruity between his old relations to Buffalo and the new relations that he would need to form, which might make itself unpleasantly felt. He expressed himself partly on the subject in his letter to his brother, written the day of his arrival in Buffalo:

Friends, many, devoted and affectionate, crowd round us here, and already I have assurances that employment of some suitable kind will be forthcoming, soon, if we will but stay in Buffalo. But these good people do not yet realize that I am no longer the David Gray they knew, and that as soon as they find out what a different world I am now in, they must lose interest in me. Thanks be to the Lord Jesus, I do feel myself a stranger in these scenes, in which I was once a familiar dweller; and I look to Him to keep me, amidst all seductions and attractions they may present, in some measure faithful to Him. And I am quite content to wait till His mind and will are made apparent, as to our future.

The considerations which favored a continued residence at Buffalo, having reference more especially to his own employment, and to the future prospects of his family, prevailed in the end, and a new home was settled in the autumn of 1885, on West Utica street, exchanged later for one on Summer street. Of the quiet life which he led after this settlement, even in the midst of the presidential canvass which placed his friend, Grover Cleveland, at the head of the national government, he wrote October 13th:

As yet this easy, vegetable existence does not worry me, though I foresee that some occupation will ere long become a necessity for me. For the nonce, as to this there are no new developments. Pretty nearly all my friends are plunged over head in politics, and little else will be thought of till after election. Whenever I want to realize a truly luxurious sensation, I only need to recollect how I should be feeling and perspiring, about now, had I not been delivered from that sort of thing. Thanks be to God!

After the election he wrote: 'I feel satisfied that a good thing has happened to the country in Cleveland's election. . . . Depend upon it, he will disappoint the spoilsmen, but not those who want better government.' For the sake of the country, and as a friend of Mr. Cleveland, the result of the election pleased him; but of personal interest in it, as a party success, he had none whatever. 'Strange,' he wrote, 'that the result I fought so hard to bring about for twenty years should now, when realized, be a matter of not the slightest consequence to me. When a man has been taken into the Vanderbilt family he does n't set much store by a ticket for soup.' There was talk among some of his friends of an official place for him, under the new administration at Washington, and it was well understood that President Cleveland felt cordially inclined to encourage the proposal. Indeed, there is extant a personal letter from the President to Gray, which left no doubt of his disposition. But David had reached a state of feeling which he expressed in writing to his brother on the subject: 'I could touch no office that carried with it any political obligation;' and so he declined, gratefully, all suggestions of that nature.

At the same time, he had a great longing for some continuous and regular employment. He tired of idling, and his income was narrow, without personal earnings to reinforce it. But such employments as he could venture to undertake were not easily found. He was able to put very little strain upon himself, either in labor or in excitement, without breaking under it. Thus two years and more passed, after his return from abroad, before the occupation that would fit his strength and fill his time was discovered. Meantime, he undertook some occasional tasks, like that of preparing editorial matter for a monthly trade journal—the *Real Estate and Builders' Monthly*—which he did for a time and very happily.

At one time he wrote to his brother—May 22, 1885:

I have thought, if other things fail, of establishing myself in an accessible office, and advertising to do any and all sorts of literary job-work,—writing business pamphlets, advertising matter, revising and correcting manuscripts, translations, etc. Do you think I could make it go? I need not say it is rather dreary business, waiting as I have to do; but I feel assured that He who took me out of journalism will see that I do n't have to go back into it again. I suppose I could get an editorial place any day; but I shudder at the thought.

At length, in November, 1886, an appointment came to him which met his wishes in an admirable way. He was chosen Secretary to the Board of Commissioners of the State Reservation at Niagara—a board entrusted with the care and management of the lands lately taken by the State of New York for the preservation of the scenery of Niagara Falls. The commissioners were most of them his personal friends; the duties of the office were light and pleasant, and it was detached from partisan politics by the nature and constitution of the board. David accepted the appointment with great pleasure and was happy in it, until the following October, when the secretaryship of the Park Commission of the City of Buffalo became vacant and was tendered to him. This latter appeared, for several reasons, to be the preferable place, and he resigned from the Niagara board to enter it. But the commissioners of the Niagara Reservation requested a continuation of his service with them until the end of the year, and the labors of both secretaryships were thus laid upon him for two months. It was a fatal over-taxing of his strength. A man in health might easily, perhaps, have gone through the double task, and it is probable that David himself had no thought, at the first, that he was putting an overstrain upon his weakened powers. He had made a great gain of strength, apparently, during the preceding summer. Having spent some weeks with his brother and friends at Oak Camp, in Michigan, they thought him better than he had been for years,—more interested in things,—more capable of enjoyment,—more like his younger self. But the terms on which nature gave him this better state of feeling were evidently very rigorous, and unwittingly he violated them when the duties of the two offices came upon him. There were two annual reports to prepare; there were journeys to New York and Albany to make; there was the slight friction of adjustment to new duties and the little anxiety of a quittance from older ones—and, altogether, they proved too much. After the strain had mostly ended and the mischief had been done, writing in January, he told how it had affected him.

In getting through the double work devolved on me for a month past, and not yet completed, I have been obliged to practice the most rigid economy of my physical and mental strength. For I soon found, to my alarm, that my old nervous and cerebral symptoms were recurring under the pressure, and I have been just feeling my way along, like a blind man, not knowing the moment I should strike something hard. Thank God for His mercy! I have been kept up through the worst of it and I feel quite confident as to what remains. I went to New York, the last days of December; but even then did not get rid of the Niagara end of my load, since I was requested to stay on another month. . . . Remember, the work I am making such a fuss about would n't ruffle a hair of an ordinary busi-- ness man; but there are times when even the grass-hopper is a burden, and that has been my plight.

But he had not yet felt the worst of the effects of his overwork. They came later, after another journey to New York and a final clearing away of the duties of his Niagara secretaryship. Then the signs of break-ing began to show themselves in him, very rapidly. Early in March it became apparent that he must give up his work entirely, for a time, and he received a leave of absence from the Park Commission. For some days he remained at home, weak and shaken, and apprehensive of a more helpless prostration, but always cheerful and unrepining. He had never, from the beginning of his invalidism, made any complaint. Mrs. Gray has written: 'I never heard a murmur escape his lips; no matter what came, it was all right. "God knows best "—" His will be done." The last Monday morning, after he had eaten his breakfast, propped up with pillows in bed, as I took away the tray and arranged his pillows, he looked up at me and said: "It 's all mercy and goodness, Mums,—mercy and goodness." He had complained to me during the pre-vious week that he could not pray; but this morning he told me joyfully that he had *thawed out morally*— he could pray again.'

His mind was clouded, somewhat as it had been in the first stages of his illness in 1882; and yet he kept a curious mastery of himself. Attempting one day to tell something, he lost the thread, and, after hesitating a moment, being unable to finish, he laughingly said : ' Well, Gray, why do n't you go on ? '

Something more than rest being evidently needed for his recuperation, and the ocean having been always his best physician, a voyage to Cuba was determined on, and his faithful brother came from Detroit to be his companion in it.   The following, from the pen of the brother, Mr. John S. Gray, tells what remains .of the sorrowful story :

We were ready to start just when the great 'blizzard' of March 12th blocked the eastern roads and stopped all travel.   This delayed us until Thursday, the 15th.   David was thankful for the storm that gave him a reprieve, and kept him longer at home. We were assured that the Delaware, Lackawanna and Western Railway Co. would send a train through, leaving Buffalo at 5 P. M., with a sleeper attached ; but, on arrival at the depot, we found they were unable to get a sleeper ready until the 9 P. M. train.   So we were obliged to take the long drive back to the house. Calling another hack, we were surprised to find it had just returned from a funeral, well furnished with the signs of mourning.   David asserted that, if we were superstitious, we might conjure some meaning out of these unexpected fittings, but finally agreed to the conviction that if we heard of the 5 P. M. train running off the track, we would know why there was no sleeper on it, and we not permitted to go by it.

At the house he passed two hours in a sleep by the fireside.   When the time came to be off we roused him against his inclination, and said, ' Do n't you want to go to the depot ? '   ' Show me the man,' he said, ' that wants to go to the depot.'   ' Yes, but you are going to take a sea-voyage, which has always done you so much good in like circumstances, and you surely want to do what is to improve your health.' 'Yes, I suppose so,' he said, and rose with some effort to take the painful farewell from each of the home circle.

We were soon in the sleeper, and the fatal journey began. We talked pleasantly together until it was proposed to retire. 'John,' he said, as he was helped to his bed, for he was tired and weak and needed a good deal of help, 'you are a perfect brick—a p. b.' He dropped asleep immediately in his berth, No. 4, opposite to mine. Sleep was out of the question with me, and I often looked to find him resting quietly. Hour after hour passed, and he did not move. Stopping at a station, shortly after midnight, I heard railroad hands under the car testing the wheels, and one said, 'These trucks are not fit for a freight car.' The words were not at all soporific, and, when we started up again, the train flew round curves at a high rate of speed, and the car pitched from one side to another more violently than a ship in a rough sea. An extra lurch came, a crash of broken glass and timbers, darkness, shrieks and screams—all in an instant,—and the car lay on its side in the bed of an old canal. Being on the under side, I was covered with débris, and unable to move for some time. As I began to work myself loose and climb up, to where I thought to find David, I called him again and again, then groped in the darkness for him, all to no avail. An alarm was given that the car was on fire, and, from a lamp that had not been extinguished, the flame was spreading; but, fortunately, some one managed to put it out. An open window overhead was the only means of exit, and through that the passengers made their escape. Perched by the side of the window, I sat calling for help to rescue my brother, but none came for a long time, nearly every one being disabled. Efforts were being made, with snow, to put out a fire that was spreading in the wreck of the day-coach ahead of us. When it was seen to be impossible to stop the spread of the

13

flames, the most active of the workers came running
back, and asked if every one was out of the sleepers.
I called to him that my brother was in the wreck, and
immediately our rescuer, who was Dr. P. L. Graham,
of Lobo, Ont., entered the car and found him, but was
unable to move him till more help came. Farmers
from the neighborhood began to arrive, and, with their
help, David was borne out on a mattress and laid upon
the snow. But his pulse was so low that Dr. Graham
pronounced him dying. A little spirits strengthened
the pulse, and we were assured that there was little
probability of immediate death. The flames spread
rapidly, and, in a few minutes after David was out of
the wreck, the entire three cars were in a sheet of flame.
The telegraph wires overhead were melted by the heat,
and, as they began dropping about us, we hurriedly
moved him away.

The time of the accident was about 2.45 A. M. of
the 16th inst., and it must have been 6 A. M. before
the rescuing train came up from Binghamton. We
quickly got him up the twenty-five foot embankment
and into the car. The physicians who came with the
train could find no outward signs of injury, but were
so busy doing what they could for those whose wounds
could be helped, that no critical examination was made
till we reached the hospital in Binghamton; then it
was decided that his injury was concussion of the
brain. No word, look or sign of consciousness ever
came from him, and, though no outward injury was
manifest, it was easy to see that he was beyond the
hope of recovery.

At midnight of the 16th, his wife and Mr. John G.
Milburn arrived from Buffalo. In addition to them
was Dr. Graham, who had proved an invaluable friend
from the first and who remained with us to the last.
The hours of watching at the bedside were only varied
by frequent changes in his respiration or temperature,
which all too surely foretold the fatal end.

Warm-hearted citizens of Binghamton came often, to offer their services and sympathies, and we cannot forget their kind words. Sunday evening, while hospital physician Dr. W. A. Moore was making his regular visit, we noticed a sudden change. The sun was setting in a clear sky, for the first time since the great storm. The asylum to the east of Binghamton, and the hills about it, were lighted up in golden tints, making a scene from the window, near which David lay, of rare and radiant beauty. His eyes were closed to all earthly scenes; but we thought, when the last faint glimmer of daylight disappeared, as he quietly passed away, that they were but opening to the more radiant scenes of a brighter and better world of immortality.

It was 8.37 P. M. when he breathed his last, and on Monday we returned to Buffalo with his remains, arriving at the home on Summer street exactly one short and eventful week from the time he was watching at the window for my coming.

CHAPTER IX.

Estimates.

DAVID GRAY died in the faith that God had ordered his life and ordered it wholly for the best. He believed, with no doubting, that the gracious hand of a Divine Father had led him, with wise and loving purposes, through all the turnings of the way, from his cradle to his grave. Is there one of us who will question that faith? And yet—David Gray was worn to death by a yoke which his neck was never fitted to bear. He spent his life in a calling which did not exercise the best of his gifts and did not satisfy the highest of his aspirations. How inexplicable it is! Judging humanly, one would say that he belonged to Religion or to Letters, or to both, and that the affairs of the forum, of the market-place and of the street, which daily journalism has to deal with, were alien, altogether, to the ends for which his temper and his genius were shaped. He lifted journalism, it is true, to a higher plane, so far as one example might do it. He kept one newspaper clean, while springs of filthiness were breaking open in so many; he gave it a quality and a tone which have not been common enough in our press to pass without note. That was the worthy outcome of a laborious life; but it does not seem to be an adequate remainder from David Gray. It was

impossible to know him and not want more,—more of
a lasting product from the brain and heart that he
wore out on things of the hour and the day.

Of course, it is worse than futile to mar the memory of
a life that has been well lived and of work that has been
nobly done with 'ifs' and idle guesses of what might
have been. But how can one put away the thought of
some different career, that *will* rise in a case like this?
The thought of David Gray as a religious teacher, for
example! Not as a preacher, in the common sense—
for his fine gift of speech had little oratory in it—but
as a teacher of religion,—as a teacher of the primitive
truth and practical life of Christianity, apart from all
ecclesiasticism and all theology, which came to be, for
him, the one, only worthy object of human knowledge.
His fervor and fineness of spirit, his moral delicacy,
his fullness of sympathy, his many-sided openness of
nature, his clearness of thought, his pictorial speech,
and the exquisite coloring that it took from a dozen
coöperative faculties and qualities of his mind,—they
could not have failed to be a powerful influence in the
religious world, if he had employed them at his prime
as he strove to employ them in his feeble later years.

Or, if we think of David Gray as living the life
which invited him most in his youth,—the life of a man
of letters, simply and wholly so,—it seems to be certain
that the world would have been something richer than
it is, by reason of the work he would have done in it.
As a poet, it is not to be expected that he would have
found a place in the choir of the supreme singers. He
produced nothing which would seem to promise so
much as that. Yet nothing that he did produce can

fairly be held to denote the limitations of his genius; for, after his powers matured, there was no year of his life when the poet-soul in him was not under fetters, forged and riveted upon it by inexorable circumstances. If there is one avocation in life more deadly to poetical inspiration than another, it is the avocation of political daily journalism; and David Gray was delivered to the slavery of the political press for more than twenty years. It was only as a fugitive, so to speak, that he ever ran for an hour into the fair fields where visions may be seen and songs may be sung; and it is amazing that he was always able to bring back from those stolen flights so much melody and beauty as he did.

Of spontaneous poetry—of poetry that is a natural blossoming of moods and thoughts—he wrote almost none after his twenty-third year. Nearly all that we have from him, except the earlier verse, was written, as he said in one of his letters, ' under pressure of a necessity, begotten by some occasion,' and because he was 'cornered into it!' It is useless to say that he could not write otherwise while treading the inexorable mill of the daily newspaper; and the few years of his respite from it, when abroad, were scarcely more favorable. Those years of travel were the years of his liberal education. He was an itinerant student, with the old world at large for his university,—having matriculated at no other. It was a time of his life which he gave, purposely, to an hungry absorption of ideas and emotions, as well as to a diligent study of languages, of literatures, of countries and of people. It was not a time for productive work.

Yet he did produce in that time a body of writing

which is the one adequate and satisfying performance
of his pen. The series of letters that he wrote as a
traveling correspondent, for current publication in the
Buffalo Courier, and which fill the volume appended
to this, are really unique of their kind. For the most
part, they relate to the very commonplaces of European
travel,—to scenes and things which are pointed at in
all the guide-books, and which have been ink-spattered
by the tourists of many generations. But one reads
them as if they told the story of a new world, first-
visited and freshly described. The landscapes, the
cities, the monuments, the legend- and history-haunted
places of Europe, are set before us like new discoveries.
It is as though one had visited them who was able, with
the strong breath of his enthusiasm and imagination,
to blow away the dust of commonplace sentiment which
settles so easily on the highways, and to uncover freshly,
again, the whole beauty and venerableness and poetry
that are underneath it.

There is no conscious fine-writing in these letters,—
no working of emotions for display,—no elaborated
description for description's sake. But the perfect
word in unfailing perfect use; the epithet which is a
picture rolled small; the phrase that moves one's feelings as though it had struck a secret spring; the glint
of humor that is like a smile on an eloquent face,—can
we find in English literature another composition of
their kind that is so jeweled with these exquisite
things? Twenty years ago, the *Letters of Travel* had
their ephemeral publication in newspaper print, were
read in a circle comparatively small and outside of the
critical world,—were admired and remembered by a

few. If their quality were common, that would naturally have been their end. But, being what they are, they could not rest in such burial. Literature was wronged by it; the economy of letters was violated in their loss. The twenty years and more which have aged all the incidents of their story take nothing whatever from the abiding charm that is in them; and so, without apology or hesitation, they are reproduced, now, and given publication in a more permanent form. To those who read them they will justify themselves quickly enough. Taken as a whole, they represent the best of David Gray as a literary artist,—as a poet constrained to prose,—and indicate what, under circumstances more favorable, he might have done.

But, after all, it was David Gray as a man, among his fellow-men, in his conversation and daily walk, as we saw his face, as we listened to his voice, as we caught the benediction of his smile, who was loved and mourned by those who knew him. His death was the going out of a candle which God had not chosen to set on any high place, but which shone on many lives, nevertheless, in the community to which he belonged. It drew more tears than often fall on even good men's graves. The common grief and the sense of private and public loss were tenderly expressed by many voices and many pens. This memoir may fitly be closed by repeating a few of the affectionate tributes that were publicly paid to the memory of David Gray when he died.

The death of David Gray, as other men die, would have occasioned profound regret. That death met him so unexpectedly and so cruelly, awakes, even in stranger hearts, the tenderest sympathy. But for those who knew David Gray, and loved him as few men are ever loved, his death brings a sorrow for 'the man they held as half divine,' beyond the reach of words.

As I recall the personal associations of twenty-five years, and remember the offices of his friendship, his ever suggestive thought, his fine genius, which in a less material age had ranked him with the builders of loftiest song, I realize that as beautifully equipped a soul has passed away as ever adorns and inspires.

His journalistic career will be sketched by his associates of the press ; yet I will say that, while Mr. Gray was ever loyal to his party, and heartily accepted its economic theories, his sympathies seemed to me broader than any partisan creed. I well remember the first time I ever saw him. It was in Paris, when he was on his first visit abroad. It was just after the close of our war, and that struggle, its causes and its issue, were the subject of a long talk at our first interview. I shall never forget with what earnest words he held slavery responsible for the war, and his rejoicing at its overthrow. We spoke of the heroisms which overleap the restraints of law in revolutions, for we were on suggestive revolutionary ground, and I was much impressed by his broad philosophy and humanity.

This sentiment, 'I am a man, and whatever interests humanity interests me,' underlay all his political and personal character. It entered into his daily life, gave tone to his professional work, and, when most intense in his partisan devotion, the heart of David Gray was his Mentor and guide. This is high eulogium, but it will be justified by his contemporary journalists of every shade of political opinion. Political journalism, which owes so much to our friend, was not the most congenial sphere for his gifts. His nature craved 'the still air of delightful studies.' Literature was his natural sphere. He had genius, a philosophic mind, and a style pure and melodious. He was a born poet, and his verse easily rose to the plane of the highest themes. But what words can give even shadowy intimation of that social charm which delighted and captivated? His simplicity, his geniality, his glowing friendship, and that loyalty which was his manhood's crown, made of David Gray the prince of friends and of hosts. Several years ago, a few friends used to meet him on Saturday evenings in his little home on Niagara street,—a home which seemed more regal than the most pretentious palace, for 'David,' as his friends loved to call him, was its master. One of the group, a kindred soul, and most royally endowed, preceded him to the shadowy land. Their common friends will ever associate Wright with Gray, in their heart of hearts.

I have said our friend was a philosopher, but he subordinated his philosophy to a simple Christian faith. Instead of the grandeur of churchly ritual and priestly ceremonial, he sought a service simple, meditative, without intervention of priest in stately temple, and found it among the Plymouth Brethren. Here he was teacher and scholar. Here, and in his daily communings, his spirit was brought in closest sympathy with his Master. If there was an element of mysticism in his religious life, it was proof of his kinship with those rare souls who, in all the Christian ages, have sought to unify their spirits with the Divine.

David Gray's home! How profound and universal the sympathy with that loving and heroic wife, in all her sad errand, to the end, to the end!

David Gray was as a son to Buffalo. He gave to her service the vigor of his manhood, and in that service he lost it. He interwove 'sweetness and light' with her noisy commerce. He, in large degree, wedded her to the humanities. She will gratefully remember her son.—*James O. Putnam.*

DAVID GRAY.

While, on the anvil of his life,
    The daily blows rang full and strong,
        Forging the hot iron of his thought
Into the plowshare or the knife,
        Whate'er his busy hammer wrought,
His wearying toil, or short or long,
    He lightened with a song.

Men say the toiler's task is done,
    And soon his work they may forget—
        A rusted share, a broken blade,
Cast to one side at set of sun,
        All that is left of what he made:
But, now the sun is fully set,
His singing lingers with us yet.
            —*Allen G. Bigelow.*

With genius of a high order, keen intellect, tender sensibility, fine moral sense, high ambition, untiring industry, conscientious devotion to duty, all consecrated and subordinated to enlightened religious convictions —a 'pure and radiant' soul was David Gray. . . . Amid the record of even the selected spirits who are continually 'falling from us,' Memory must look very far back to find one who was 'loved with such love, and with such sorrow mourned.'—*Jabez Loton, in the Bulletin of the Young Men's Christian Association.*

Mr. Gray's editorial style was perfect. With him, the composition of a leader was a fine art. The infinite pains he gave to the minutest details of this work, together with the other responsibilities of the position, while it made many of his productions sufficiently finished for a magazine article or an essay for a review, kept him at his desk at hours when he should have been at rest, and seriously impaired his health. As a reader of exchanges he was unequaled. Mr. Gray could go through a pile of newspapers and find in them interesting matter that everyone else had overlooked. One of his most marked characteristics as a newspaper man was his infinite patience. To those who worked by his side it was a constant marvel. Illegible manuscripts, which proved too much for the tempers of his subordinates, would go to him and be put into shape for the printer with painful care, but without the slightest indication of disturbed serenity. A constant stream of visitors, with and without errands, poured into his office, and were always graciously received. Even after the most tedious of them all had gone, he never showed to his associates the slightest shade of annoyance over the loss of time which they caused him. His disinclination to discharge a correspondent or other subordinate, who performed his work ill, greatly added to the burden of his own duties. His forbearance in this respect was perhaps carried to an extreme, and his anxiety to avoid hurting the feelings of friends or, in fact, anybody else, was almost a failing. Could he have cultivated, at times, a little asperity, it would doubtless have aided him to escape some of the ills of his later years.—*The Buffalo Courier.*

It was John Hay, we believe, who said playfully of David Gray, that he was 'the loveliest of his sex'; and the phrase, in its best sense, was appropriate to the man; but it must be remembered that the amiability it suggests was allied to sterling principle, the gentleness to courage, the grace to strength, the poetic sensibility to firm purpose.

There is something simple yet noble in the very name of David Gray, that suggests the thought of him that bore it; and in his case nature, who does not always deal in harmonies, took pains to establish a correspondence between a fine, strong spirit and the form in which it was housed.—*The Rochester Post-Express.*

The death of David Gray has drawn from men and newspapers expressions of sympathy and tributes of affection and admiration of an extraordinary character. To those who only knew this 'rare soul' in his later years, some of these expressions will seem extravagant, but they who knew the David Gray of twenty years ago, and who ever felt the spell of his winning and stimulating personality, believe that ordinary language is inadequate to describe his peculiar charm, and that it is not easy to exaggerate the possibilities of a poetic nature and literary taste like his, had they been nurtured and aided by circumstances.—*The Buffalo Commercial Advertiser.*

To do justice to the virtue and talents of our dead friend would tax time and space beyond what these busy hours can grant. Of a lovely and loving disposition, he was, first of all, a poet. Inconsistent with the stern routine of journalism as were his exquisite tastes and delicate fancies, the flowers of Mr. Gray's poesy grew thick along the iron track of duty.—*The Buffalo Express.*

David Gray's was, in every sense, what is called a noble life. His was the sort of spirit to which mankind owes much. He wrote with the grace of Lamb and the humane humor of the English essayist. Invincibly modest of his own fitness, he let slip oppor-

tunities that have made men of half his metal famous
and influential.   Determined, but not dogmatic, he
carried conviction into every incident of daily life.—
The New York Star.

Probably no man living in Buffalo was so widely
beloved as the kindly, upright, able man who, for many
years, made *The Buffalo Courier* one of the great
journals of the country.   No man ever more completely impressed his personality on the newspaper he
edited.   No man ever gave to a newspaper the impress
of a nobler personality.   David Gray was a pure-
minded, generous, kindly man, full of sympathy with
all that is good, full of energy and industry in the
expression of that sympathy, and in support of every
good movement and of the highest ideals of the school
of politics which his judgment favored.— *The Buffalo
Evening News.*

He was so long a part and parcel of Buffalo; his
name and genius were so intimately associated with
her every effort for all that makes a city great, that
she was justly proud of him, as he was loyally devoted
to her; nor could the bonds which had so long bound
them in mutual affection be severed without a poignant
pang piercing the city's heart. . . .   Gentle without
weakness, learned without pedantry, his was a gracious
courtesy and singular modesty which enhanced his rare
worth, while his deeply religious heart was ever bowed
in reverence to Almighty God and the great truths of
eternity.   Cut down like a flower when its fragrance
is sweetest, David Gray goes to the grave sincerely
mourned by all who appreciate those qualities which
ennoble life.— *The Catholic Union.*

A rare and interesting study was the character of David Gray. He was a manly man, if. to possess a scrupulously honorable and sensitively honest nature could make him so. He preferred to avoid the turbulence and strife of an active business career, as he did a literary career that compelled him to dip his pen in the chalice of bitterness, or with the sharpened point of criticism. As an editor he was calm, courteous and polished, and of a school that has been well-nigh driven out in these rushing and aggressive times. There was no pleasure for him in compassing the downfall of a foe; he would go much further in an attempt to persuade such an one to be a friend. If fortune had been more kind to him, he would have been a poetic dreamer, drifting along life's river, only seeing that which would satisfy his poetic longings, turning away from that which would tend to mar or disfigure his dream of beauty and peace.—*The Sunday Times.*

·He was an honor to American journalism, and by his elevated thought, choice diction, and manly, high-toned treatment of all topics that came under his editorial review, made his paper a model for his contemporaries. He was ever the genial, generous, warm and true-hearted friend. His untimely death is a public calamity.—*Buffalo Christian Advocate.*

David Gray is dead; he goes to his grave attended by the sincere grief of all who knew the brightness of his gifts and the gentleness of his character. The press notices of him have been especially appreciative and sympathetic. Rarely has a fuller wealth of eulogy been paid to any man than has been paid to his memory by the journalists of this state. His memory is, indeed, precious, and all who knew and, therefore, loved him will say that in his death ' there cracked a noble heart.' —*The Rochester Democrat and Chronicle.*

Mr. Gray was one of the gentlest of men, one of the most graceful and able writers the press of New York has had, a poet by nature. His friends are legion, and many who never had a personal acquaintance with him loved him for the manliness of his character, the elevating tone of his teaching, the gentleness, sincerity, nobility of his nature. The death of such a man is a loss to humanity.—*The Utica Herald.*

POEMS.

The Fog-Bell at Night.

I.

Out on the dim and desolate lake,
    Chime on chime falls, measured and slow;
Scarce the dull trance of the night they break,
    Sounding so wearily, long and low;
Telling the hour in its voiceless flight—
    Stirring old thoughts of our dear, dead joys:
O, dreary, mysterious night,
    Shadow and fear have at last a voice.

II.

Far in a region of dream-delight,
    Fondly I wandered but moments ago,—
Ah, that knell from the distant night,
    Hanging my dreams with trappings of woe!
Sadly, solemnly tolling—tolling,
    Floating afar on the misty air;
Every bell like a dirge is knolling,
    Every chime is a funeral prayer!

14

III.

'Life!' they cry to the mariner, seaward,—
  What to the slumbering thousands near?
Father above, do they beckon us Thee-ward?
  See! I strain thro' the night to hear!
Sadly, solemnly tolling—tolling,
  Dying away on the ghostly air,—
Every bell for a soul is knolling,
  Every chime is a funeral prayer!

SIR JOHN FRANKLIN AND HIS CREW.

Toll the saintly minster bell,
  For we know they're now at rest;
Where they lie, they sleep as well
  As in kirkyard old and blest.
Let the requiem echo free
  From the shores of England, forth,
Over leagues of angry sea,
  Toward the silence of the North.

Half a score of years or more,
  They were phantoms in our dreams;
Many a night, on many a shore
  Lit by wan Aurora gleams,
We have tracked the ghostly band—
  Seen distressful signals wave—
Till we find dim William's Land
  Holy with the heroes' grave.

Toll the bell! that they may rest,
　　Haunting specters of our brain,—
They for whom her tireless quest
　　Love pursued so long in vain.
Nevermore let fancy feign
　　That the wondering Esquimau
Haply sees them toil again,
　　Wild and haggard, through the snow.

From The Erebus they pass'd
　　To a realm of light and balm;
And The Terror sailed at last
　　Into peace and perfect calm.
Toll the bell; but let its voice,
　　Moaning in the minster dome,
Change at times, and half rejoice;
　　For the mariners are home!

———

THE CREW OF THE ADVANCE

They spread their ship's white sails, and like a dream
Fled outward, on the seaward-sighing breeze;
Till soon the *memory* of a dream they grew
To us, who gazed afar on vacant sea.
But night by night, to them, and star by star,
The skies of the great North-land opened and shone,
And brighter flashed the icy-jeweled gates
Of the dim regions, as they neared and entered;
And Solitude, who sat there, heavy-eyed,
A moment stirred, and rose, and shut them in.

They were the guests of Death, yet feared him not.
They knew him in his deepest cavern-haunts,
Touching his marble hand, as if in sport,
And drawing difficult breath beneath the spell
Of his most stony eye.   Ah! never came
Into those drear dominions whisper of Spring,
Or far-off echoed voice of those who dwell
Down in the land of Summer, which, to them,
Was even as heaven.   The very thoughts they sent,
White messenger-birds, to southward, failed in flight
Winging that deathful bar of frost and darkness.
Nor more to us came token that 't was well
With this our venture in the realm of Night;
Save haply to some sleepless, listening hearts,
When Norland winds came wailing down the night,
A sign was borne, that Love would start to hear—
A sigh, mayhap, she well would understand,
And with quick, tremulous fingers would detach
From the wild, floating woof of midnight's music.

They roamed the chambers of God's mysteries,
And in their wondering sight He rallied forth
The Aurora-armies, flashing, till they seemed
A dance of angels on the slopes of heaven!
The unsetting moon lit up with myriad gems
Valley and berg fantastic; and the ear
That ached with depth of silence, caught at times
Strange consciousness of music from the air.
It was a night of wildering dreams, till, lo!
Above an icy cliff the timid Dawn
Stood, draped in white, unearthly robes, and smiled
Wan pity o'er them!

They were guests of Death;
But at his very fireless hearth they planted
The banner of Life—the banner of more than Life—
Of Life's crowned monarch—glorious, conquering
    Manhood!
And he, of all that band so brave—so true—
Our mouths are mute as his when we go seeking
For words that would not wrong his nobleness.
He wavered not where giants might have wavered;
He wrested from the thrice-clenched hand of Danger
The jewel Victory.

We thank Thee, God,
That Thou hast given our hero back. His grave
Is ours, whereon to weep; nor shall the summers
Heap moss enough to hide him from our grief.

To Glen Iris.

To thee, sweetest valley, Glen Iris, to thee,—
More fair than the vision of poet may be,
And beyond what the artist may dream, when his eyes
Are dim with the hues of the loveliest skies;
To thee and thy forest, whose foliage forever
Is fresh with the mists of thy light-flashing river;
Thy flowers that are swayed in the softest of airs;
Thy birds in the greenest and deepest of lairs;
Thy lights and thy shadows, thy sweet river's fall,
That sings into slumber or reverie,—all,

To thee, though our lips cannot utter a word,
Our spirits are singing in rapture unheard!
For 't is part of thy magic—thy beauty-wrought spell—
What thou whisperest to us we never can tell.
Sweet Glen of the Rainbow, to thee there are given,
As fresh as the day when they sprung into birth,
All the joys and the graces we love most of earth;
And the sunlight flings o'er thee the glories of heaven!
So, The Nameless now drink from thy pleasure-brimmed
    chalice,
And pledge thee the rainbow-ideal of valleys,—
A Beulah where thrice-happy mortals that see thee
Forget all their cares, for thy waters are Lethe.
And we shout and rejoice that thou art what thou art—
The beautiful home of a beautiful heart.

OUTRIVALLED.

No tale of days divine with love, or starry eves, is
    mine;
I only know that One was once who made all life
    divine;
Whose presence circled to my soul its all of earth or
    skies,—
Who drew my glamoured sight from heaven, to dwell
    upon her eyes;
And Hope (that fell from heaven to hell) up-soared on
    wings of light,
Till that sweet vision darkly changed, and melted into
    night.

It came, a whisper—low at first—that she was false to
me;
And louder grew the words accurst, 'Another, and not
thee!'
They bade me see the signs she wore, howe'er she sighed
or smiled,
That told the Eden of my love a paradise defiled.
And by his spell upon her eyes, his spell on heart and
breath,
His bridal sign upon her cheek, I knew the Rival,
Death!

I did not rail of broken vows;—O God! so white and
shriven;—
I watched her life, my star of life, set in its dream of
heaven;
And all the haunted nights my prayer was wild, the
while I ween
She could' not see my heart at hers, for a shade that
dwelt between;
But gazing past me thro' the gloom, the light in her
eyes renewed,
For ghostly in the dark, without, he stood—the King
who wooed.

He gave her brow the palest pearl, and wildly with her
hair
Inwove a thread of heavenly gold, that made her brow
more fair;
The rose of love she wore for him blushed with a crimson flame,
And in her eyes the fire of life upflickered as he came.

Then over all there fell a veil, pale, chill, like winter
    breath,
And forth they went, my love and he, the kingly Rival,
    Death.

THE LAKE.

At the night's most solemn hour,
  When the stars are lost o'erhead,
And the silence hath a power
  Deeper, thus to darkness wed;—
When the lighthouse-lantern keeps
Vigil, while the city sleeps,
Circling slowly in the night,
With its bursts of meteor-light;—

Then, although the wind be dead,
  Miles upon the glooming lake,
Deep within its mystic bed
  Life and motion seem to wake.
Hour by hour a stir—a sound—
Rises on the stillness 'round;
O'er and o'er, on the shore,
Breaks that deep and haunting roar.

Nightly thus my thoughts, as well,
  Sink to motionless repose,
And the murmur that may dwell
In the heart (as in a shell),
  Ebbing faint, no longer flows.

Shadows of approaching sleep
Fall around me, dense and deep,
Save whene'er the fitful gleam
Flashes, of some meteor-dream.

Half-awake and half a-dream
  Then, in that dim border-land,
I can watch a stranger stream
  Break on a more haunted strand.
In my mind, as o'er the lake,
Life and motion seem to wake,
As if in the sea-caves of Thought
Still the tidal SPIRIT wrought.

So must ever be, I ween,
  In the Mind's mysterious sea,
Mystic tides, unruled, unseen,
  Palpitating ceaselessly.
And when Death shall work his will
In that wave (made strangely chill),
Will the roar on the shore,
Ceasing then, be heard no more?

ELIHU BURRITT.

They know, who wander in o'erarching woods,
How spreads the whisper of a coming storm
From leaf to leaf—from eager bough to bough,
Till answering miles of forest swing and sway,
And mock the gathering clouds, and with wild voices
Call to the hollow Thunder in his lair.

So ran the tremor of a coming storm
Thro' the old realms of Europe, when he came
Across the misty sea, to the Queen-Isle,—
This mild, but dauntless, eager, large-souled Quixote.

The doves of peace were fluttering in their nests,
The gentle olive flung affrighted arms,
And threw mad leaves, despairing, on the blast—
All this, when first I saw him.   I remember ,
He stilled us, gathered troops of boy-Bedouins,
And thrilled us into silence with his eyes,
And drew ours into his, with a quaint story
Of children, brothers in America.
Then, sounding the deep wells of Truth and Feeling,
(These lie in Boyhood's heart so deep, serene,
Unruffled, and so clear, they seem not there)—
He threw great words upon us—spake of Right—
Right, broken, bleeding—Right, upraised and victor!
Truth never seemed so noble as when there
It fell in living vigor from his lips;
Peace never seemed a goddess, till she sat
Throned on the high, white calmness of his brow.

The dust of Time scarce falls on such an one.
The eye as clear, the brain as clear, the soul
More sharply obvious in its more-worn robes—
In else, my Boyhood's memory 's true to night.

There is a means whereby a soul, unbowed
By years, may grow with years but more sublime.
If one hath placed his feet upon the heights
Of universal Love, and Truth, and Virtue,
The envious waves may break themselves upon him;

They do but toss new conquests to his feet,
Whereon he rises higher.   Storms of Hate
May rend the angry skies; they only serve
To bleach the sea-assaulted cliff to marble,
That it may gleam, and be, afar, a beacon!

JEANNIE LORIMER.

Oh, bonny Jeannie Lorimer, what glamour has come
    owre ye?
What sudden wae is this that swims sae watery in
    your ee?
Your braw white gown came hame yestreen, your bridal
    is before ye,
Oh, bonny Jeannie Lorimer, what ill have you to
    dree?

The birds sing cheery in the wood aboon the Elder's
    How;
The flowers are fairest on its brae, the berries biggest
    grow;
But eerie, aye, it seems, to pass the cot sae bleak and
    bare,
And think on sic a warm fireside as anee was keepit
    there.
'Tis twelve gude years and mair sin syne—'twas at the
    Martinmas term—
The neebors a' plad sair; but, no—the laird maun hae
    the farm;

Sae, gatherin' up his sma' estate, the Elder turned his
    face,
And took his ae bit callant's hand, sad-hearted frae the
    place.
And soon the hares cam' loupin wild owre a' the
    garden knowe,
And cock and pheasant o' the laird's ran thick about
    the How.
A fine bit lad, the Elder's was — sae blue and gleg
    his ee;
And weel baith he and Jeannie lo'ed thegither aye
    to be.
How mony a ploy they had their lanes, what warlds o'
    nests they kenned,
What dams they biggit in the burn, and houses with-
    out end;
Their lives were like the burn's twa banks, as fairly
    matched and green,
While childhood, like the burnie's sel', ran singin'
    down between.
Sair heart had Jeannie Lorimer that day they gaed
    awa',
And mony a day, beside, her een were wat when na
    ane saw;
For na ane kenned how big a load sae young a heart
    could keep,
Or how ilk gloaming, at the How, she grat her grief to
    sleep.
But years draw by, the lass grew fair, in spite the
    bairnie's woes;
The bud cast off the secret worm and bonny bloomed
    the rose.

Some said that aye the Elder's lad was upmost in her
 thocht;
Her mither scoffed: 'Wad Jeannie wait, and waste
 her days for nocht?'
For only anee across the seas some word had wandered
 hame.
That tauld them in some far-off part, wi' fearsome
 outra name;
And though they say that some do well, and keep their
 fathers' faith,
So far, wi' black and barbarous folk is maist the same
 as death.
So folk forgot; and in the kirk, at last, the stated
 prayer
That bore the exiles' name on high, shook Jeannie's
 heart nae mair;
And, woman grown, on a' the Strath, the lads wi' love
 gaed wild,
And still she put their offers by; alike on a' she
 smiled.
'There's mony anither lass,' folk said, 'has rued sic
 reckless play;'
But Jeannie didna wait owre lang to tine her market
 day.
The favored wooer came, at last; she named the bridal
 hour;
And surely love amang the dew ne'er found a fairer
 flower.
Oh, bonny Jeannie Lorimer, your lover comes to
 own ye,
The morrow is your bridal morn, and blithe it ought
 to be;

Then wae for some uncanny thing that surely has
 befa'n ye,
Oh, wae for something in your face your lover mauna
 see!
The licht was fadin' yester-e'en, the birds to sleep had
 gane,
When Jeannie slippit frae the house, and took the road
 her lane—
Mayhap it was some pensive thocht that led her ower
 the knowe,
And, cross the stile and down the path that skirts the
 Elder's How;
Some thocht o' by-gone days, perchance, for, oh, what
 wrang were thine
If ae last nicht the morrow's bride be lassie o' lang
 syne!
Here stands the Elder's cot, its door leans broken on
 the stair,
And a' the smiling shapes it kenned gang in and out
 nae mair.
The summer-house is yonder, yet,—the tree that held
 the swing;
But, oh, the waesomeness that clings like mould to
 every thing!
Gae hame then, Jeannie Lorimer, the dew is on your
 track,
Nor risk the sweets o' life ye hae for them that come
 na back!
'Come back!' the word was on her tongue, when quick,
 wi' breast on flame,
She heard a foot come round the house,—a stranger
 spak' her name;

She ran, but, oh, nor far she fled, nor long her heart's
    alarms,
For a' he looked sae big and braw, she sprang into his
    arms!
He spak' her name, 't was no' the voice, though saft and
    sweet it seemed,
But something when it ceased reca'ed the music she
    had dreamed;
And when she met his saft blue een, their fond licht
    aye the same,
She kenned, through a' the change o' years, the Elder's
    lad, come hame!
But wae for them that only ken the joy their lives
    have lost,
And, oh, for love that only gies its blossom to the
    frost!
' And would ye sooth ha' lo'ed?' he said; 'and was your
    heart sae true?'
'The years were lang,' she sobbed him back, 'I never
    lo'ed but you!'
Then from the How he turned his face, and nane but
    Jeannie saw;
Oh, waesome tryst, for Love was there, but Hope
    stayed far awa'!

Oh, bonny Jeannie Lorimer, your wedded years be-
    tide ye;
Ye'll gang yon road again, mayhap, wi' bairns about
    your knee;
But nane will see the wraith to walk wi' waesome een
    beside ye,
Oh, bonny Jeannie Lorimer, forever, till ye dee!

COMING.

She said she 'd come in May, but it seemed so far away
    That our hearts grew sick at first to think of waiting
        her so long;
And the months were counted o'er, to the day that
        should restore
    In one rich gift the Spring to earth, to us our light
        and song.

And Autumn shed its leaves on the wind that comes
        and grieves
    In the wood and 'round the houses, like a ghost that
        died of woe;
And the dull, cold clouds, at last, drooped and whitened
        in the blast,
    Till all the earth lay still as death, in one long dream
        of snow.

But long ere Spring had filled the earth with sap, or
        thrilled
    The subtle nerves of flowers, or called to swallows
        o'er the main,
Our hearts had felt the stir of the Spring to come with
        her,
    And yearned with joyous thoughts to greet our dar-
        ling back again.

And the snowdrop floated up from the snow its fragile
    cup;
  And the violets stole the blue of heaven, one morning
    after rain;
And the wild anemone met us trembling on the lea,—
  All with the sole sweet words to tell: 'She is com-
    ing back again.'

Fast, fast, O March, fleet past, on thy winter-battling
    blast,
  And, gentle April, linger not beneath thy skies of
    rain;
But strew thy scanty flowers, and speed the happy
    hours
  That bring sweet May to earth, to us our darling
    back again!

A March Scene.

—The time, eleven at night. The scene is this:
I followed the long glimmer of city lights,
Now loitering on, a lonesome space in gloom.
Now, as I neared and passed a shining lamp,
Starting to note my shadow black and large
Sweep 'round and forward, far into the night.
The straggling files of city sentinels
I followed thus, in a deserted street,
Whence I could dimly see where lay the lake,
With its low mutter and moan of restless ice;
And farther on could hear the quicker crush
And plash, as mass on mass in dark disorder
Slid downward in the current. Wildly rose
Midnight and storm, together, o'er the lake;

15

The very spirit of desolation seemed,
Up from that long, low stretch of lifeless night,
To rise on wings of gloom, and darken earth.
And, oh! the maniac voices of the wind!
It must be such a wild, wild wail as this
Goes up to God from his sin-blighted world!
With thoughts of these, I walked,—when quick there
    came
A patter of childish feet along the pavement,
And underneath my very eyes there grew
A little thing of rags—a little face,
That showed a moment like a dream before me,
Then slid from the pale glimmer of the lamp—
Rags, pitiable face and all—into deep night!

    The wind is wild and cold now—
      Poor, shepherdless lamb and shorn,
    Why wander from the fold now
      Thy tiny feet forlorn?
Hath Squalor cast adrift, to-night, her sorrow-born?

    The deep of utter joylessness
      Thy darkling life hath trod—
    Thy Life! poor blighted boylessness,
      A dead flower in the sod!
Will blessed dew or spring avail for such, O God?

    And heaven is dark and boonless
      Above thy clouded brow,
    Midnight is wild and moonless—
      Will't ever be as now?
I marvel if my God hath ken of such as thou!

Oh ! if the heavenly roses
 E'er blossom beneath thee sweet,
Among the leaves and posies
 (Soft even to angel feet),
What thoughts of these cold stones across thy dreams
 will fleet !

The Bark of Life.

'T is the mid-watch of Time, on a mystical sea,
 With the wind of the night in motion ;
Deep sunk is the shadowy land on the lee,
 And the ship is alone on the ocean.

O pilot, who watchest the boreal star,
 What ship, and where seek ye to moor her?
' 'T is the Bark of Life that is bearing afar,
 With a port that none knoweth, before her.'

And why do ye leave the delight of the land
 For the wild sea's realm of wonder?
' By the strong wind of fate all her canvas is fanned,
 And its secret tide rolls under.'

And, the bright shore lost, is it long ere again
 To its haven the bark shall be drifted?
' No more shall its blue hills rise from the main,
 Nor an oar, in its calm, be lifted.'

But the green glades of youth and its dreams are there,
 With the rapture of song ringing through them?
' And forever the sea and the barren air ·
 Are met o'er the dim land that knew them.'

And the graves that we loved there, too, where the heart
  O'er its beautiful dead sat moaning?
'No voice of the lover shall mingle its art
  With the billow their dirge intoning.'

There were farewells kissed, and forevermore
  From ours are the pale lips parted?
'Oh, nought, save its dream, may the past restore,
  Or its pang to the sorrowful-hearted!'

Enough; but the mid-watch passes apace,
  And, see, o'er the wave, yon token:
O pilot, a smile is on ocean's face,
  And the trance of the night is broken!

And star telleth star of the glory to be,
  And the billow is flushed with its warning,
And, white on the verge of the eastern sea,
  Lo! the feet of the world's new morning!

And away where the skirt of her bright robe streams,
  And the shadows have parted asunder,
Not the faded shore of our vanished dreams,
  But a fairer, is shining yonder!

The orient's quivering deeps lie bare,
  And the gleam of the stars has fainted,
Where its glimmering emerald swims in air
  And its wavering lines are painted.

Then speed where its waiting port shall ope,
  O pilot, thy sure bark steering,
For, over its far-away hills of hope
  The train of the years is nearing!

All radiant the Future's fields outspread,
   And closes the Past's dim portal,
'Till the sea of Time shall give up its dead,
   And the beautiful be the immortal.

———

I heard the Rose make tender moan
For the quick waning season's wrong
That stole the soul of odor from her.

Then said I: Let it, Sweet, atone,
That, changed to music of my song,
Thy fragrance breathes in endless summer!
            —*From the German of Bodenstedt.*

———

ON LEBANON.

Those days we spent on Lebanon,
   Held captive by the sieging snow—
What bright things are forgot and gone,
   While these have kept their after-glow!
It seemed but monotone, in truth,
   That morning gaze o'er mountain mass,
Our council with the hamlet's youth,
   The daily sortie up the pass,—
And, last, your father's fire o' nights,
Sweet Maiden of the Maronites!

Sometimes the battling clouds would break,
   And from the rifted azure, fair,
We saw an eagle slant, and take,
   Broad-winged, the stormy slopes of air.

And once, when winter's stubborn heart
　　Half broke in sunshine o'er the place,
We held our bridles to depart,
　　Eager and gleeful—but your face,
It did not mirror our delights,
O Maiden of the Maronites!

Bright face! how Arab-wild would glow,
　　Through shifting mood of storm or calm,
Its beauty, born of sun and snow,
　　Between the cedar and the palm.
Nor, as I watched its changing thought
　　Could alien speech be long disguise;
For ere one English phrase *she* caught
　　I learned the Arabic of her eyes—
The love-lore of their dusks and lights,
My Maiden of the Maronites!

We parted soon, and upward fared,
　　Snow-fettered, till the pass was ours,
And all beneath us, golden-aired,
　　Lay Syria, in a dream of flowers.
Then spurred we, for before us burned
　　White Baalbec's signal in the noon,
And, ere to way-side camp we turned,
　　'Twixt us and you and far Bhâmdun
All Lebanon raised his icy heights,
My Maiden of the Maronites!

Yet, still, those days on Lebanon
　　As steadfast keep their after-glow
As if they owned a summer sun,
　　And roses blossomed in the snow;

And when, with fire of heart and brain,
   And the quick pulse's speed increased,
And wordless longings, come again
   Vision and passion of the East,
I dream —— ah! wild are Fancy's flights,
O Maiden of the Maronites!

A GOLDEN WEDDING POEM.

Read at the Golden Wedding anniversary of Mr. and Mrs. James
Goold, of Albany, N. Y.

I.

O Love, whose patient pilgrim feet
   Life's longest path have trod;
Whose ministry hath symbolled sweet
   The dearer love of God,—
The sacred myrtle wreathes again
   Thine altar, as of old;
And what was green with summer, then,
   Is mellowed, now, to gold.

II.

Not now, as then, the Future's face
   Is flushed with fancy's light,
But Memory, with a milder grace,
   Shall rule the feast, to-night.
Blest was the sun of joy that shone,
   Nor less the blinding shower,—
The bud of fifty years agone
   Is love's perfected flower!

III.

O Memory, ope thy mystic door;
    O dream of youth, return;
And let the lights that gleamed of yore
    Beside this altar burn!
The past is plain; 't was love designed
    E'en sorrow's iron chain,
And mercy's shining thread has twined
    With the dark warp of pain.

IV.

So be it, still. O Thou who hast
    That younger bridal blest,
Till the May-morn of love has passed
    To evening's golden west,—
Come to this later Cana, Lord,
    And, at Thy touch divine,
The water of that earlier board
    To-night shall turn to wine.

THE SOUL'S FAILURE.

Is the day dead in yonder blood-stained west?
    And is the summer fled beyond recalling?
Idle we sat all day, and were unblest,
    Vain hopes and evil dreams our souls enthralling;
Till all is come to nought—the worst and best
    Are even as one—the night is falling—falling;
Our hearts have found no thing of what they craved:
      "The harvest is past,
      The summer is ended,
      And we are not saved."

Was hemlock in the golden cup of youth?
That now we sit and mark the cold Death creeping
Over our lives, while yet we feel, in sooth,
No sleepfulness of Death, but only, weeping,
Suffer his wrong and vainly pray his ruth,
And rest and shelter from the night-wind's sweeping;
And from its voice 'round us forever raved:
  "The harvest is past,
  The summer is ended,
  And we are not saved."

———

I.

When I see those little feet of thine,
Lost am I to know, O sweetest maiden,
How such beauty's burden bear they ever!

II.

When I touch that little hand of thine,
Lost am I to know, O sweetest maiden,
How of wound so deep it can be giver!

III.

When I see those ripe rose lips of thine,
Lost am I to know, O sweetest maiden,
Why their fruit of kisses yield they never!

IV.

When I gaze in those deep eyes of thine,
Lost am I to know, O sweetest maiden,
Why they yearn for love, yet never, never

V.

Look on mine!—O, let this heart be thine,
Which for thee more truly, sweetest maiden,
Beats, than other heart shall beat forever!

VI.

List what love has sung for ear of thine;
List, for lover lips, O sweetest maiden,
Softer plaints of love shall sing thee never!

—From the German of Bodenstedt.

DEDICATION IN A LADY'S ALBUM.

I think, now, of some knight in fairy times,
Whose footstep falters on the charméd limits
Of some enchanted place, where, in the hush
Of vacant halls, white Silence is uprisen,
Her finger high uplifted to forbid
The impending foot; for, Mary, so my pen
Hath faltered at the white, untrodden threshold
Of this, thy Book of Beauty.   I would fain
Some worthier hand than mine had broke the spell
Which sat till now about its golden rim.
But, as it is, the spell is broken; and these pages—
May their unwritten vacancy become
A beauteous garden, where sweet thoughts shall blos-
　　　som;—
A place where dear desires and hopes shall nestle;—
A fount, where Memory, mayhap worn and weary,
In after years shall, bending, drink, and rise
Thrilled with the wild, wild life of long ago!

To Miss Clara Louise Kellogg.

Rare-gifted child of Song, whose tongue has learned
  The magic language of that sunnier land
  Where passion speaks in music—'neath thy wand
Of Art our hearts have melted, thrilled and yearned!
    Deeper we drink of that enchanted wine,
    Because the rich Italian draught divine
Is poured out to us by no alien hand.
    Sing on, fair girl; for other lands than thine
Shall hail thy coming; and we say 'Farewell'
To thee, but not to that sweet Voice, whose spell
Has peopled memory with such singing throngs
  Of fairy echoes. Sing, and we shall tell,
    With rising pride the more thy fame shall shine,
That thou art still Columbia's child—and Song's.

Murillo's 'Immaculate Conception.'

Whence is the spell—O, fair and free from guile,
  Thou with the young moon shod!—that binds my
    brain?
Is thine that orb of fable which did wane,

Darkening o'er sad Ortygia's templed isle,—
Beautiful Artemis, hid from earth awhile,
　　And on the pale monk's vigil risen again,
　　A wonder in the starry sky of Spain?
Comes the Myth back, Madonna, in thy smile?
　　Yea! thou dost teach that the Divine may be
The same, to passing creeds and ages given;
And how the Greek hath dreamed, or churchman
　　　　striven,
　　What reck we, who with eyes tear-blinded see
Thee standing loveliest in the open heaven?—
　　Ave Maria! only heaven and thee!

New Year Greetings.

1860.

Toll for the dying Year, O midnight bells!
　　Twelve times amid the darkness, deep and slow;
The winds are whispering their low farewells,
　　The earth is draped, a bier of funeral snow,—
Toll for the dead Old Year!　On many a hearth
　　To-night the fires of household joy are lit;
And many a home is filled with laughing mirth,
　　While happy shadows past the windows flit.

But, in the night without, the last peal dies;
　　The startled air throbs fainter, far abroad,
And up the silence of the winter skies
　　The dead Year wings its solemn way to God.

Forever, with its round of eve and morn,
  Forever, with its life on land and sea—
With all its fleeting shapes and shadows, borne
  From Time, into the past Eternity.

O Memory! watcher by the bed of death,
  Who treasurest up last words and parting sighs,
In whom the Past has life and form and breath—
  Who ever walk'st with backward-gazing eyes—
Tell us what gleanings of the year are thine?
  What hast thou gathered that our eyes may see?
Thou art sole heir of vanished Fifty-Nine,
  What has he left,—bequeathed and willed to thee?

He scattered flowers beneath the feet of Joy,
  The flush of hope,—the thrill of love divine;
Sunlight of heart and bliss without alloy,
  We had them all with thee, Old Fifty-Nine!
Nor less to some the old, old ache of grief,
  And tears that all thy sunlight has not dried;
And we have seen, although the time was brief,
  How in it men have sorrowed, sinned, and died.

Much thou hast given, but much is also gone.
  Spring, as of yore, re-clothed the empty bowers;
Glad Summer failed not, golden Autumn shone,
  And Winter swept us bare of all our flowers.
To many a heart the dower of love was brought;
  To many a heart there is a grave, instead;
And so the pictured woof of Time was wrought,
  And the old story of our life re-read.

But there is more; the scroll of all thy deeds
  Thine other daughter, thoughtful History, took,
And he shall thrill who some time comes and reads
  Thy storied wonders in her deathless book.
For no inert, dull life was thine, Old Year;
  Thy parting footsteps are not echoless;
And, up from thy dim charnel, we can hear
  The living issues of the future press.

The clash of arms awoke thee at thy birth;
  The clarion, echoing in wild Alpine vales,
And noise of meeting hosts that shook the earth,
  Came Westward, borne on all thy Summer gales.
Thy flowers of Spring were fed with battle's rain;
  The harvests of long years were reaped in thee;
And Destiny has set in thy domain
  The germ of mightier changes yet to be.

Thou shalt not be forgotten; in the line
  Of years and centuries thy name shall stand
Illustrious and immortal, Fifty-nine!
  And coming peoples yet shall point the hand
And say: In such a year, when Freedom pined,
  Prostrate and bleeding with the Austrian chains,
Once more her flag was flung upon the wind,
  And the free blood of heroes gushed again!

Nor less in our own annals, though alarms
  Of gathering ill beset the nation's way,
Men shall look back, and see amid thy storms
  The crescent morning of a better day.

For brave words said, for good deeds nobly done
  In Freedom's holy war, that grows sublime
With its long list of battles, lost and won,—
  Thou shalt not be forgotten in all time.

Toll for the dead Old Year, O midnight bells!
  But long ere dawn's returning hours begin,
Speak from yon towers in longer, louder swells,
  And ring the New Year with its promise in.
Ring forth a welcome on the frosty air,
  For Hope leads foremost in the New Year's track;
Time's youngest morn comes flushed with life, and fair,
  And night with all its clouds rolls swiftly back.

No stain, as yet, of earthly foot is cast
  Upon the future's pure untrodden snow;
Would that no shadow of the evil Past
  Across this threshold of the year might go,—
But Love and Justice, entering hand in hand,
  To dwell in heavenly temples with us here!
And so, as ne'er before, from land to land
  Should speed this message of a Glad New Year.

1861.

'60.

The blue-eyed gentian shone with April's tear,
  The face of June with roses was a-glow,
And Autumn led us onward through the sere
And fallen leaves, till, lo! we stand, Old Year,
  Beside thy grave of snow!

Under the shroud that wraps the world in rest,
    We lay, with thee, the Past that once was ours;
Thy bloom returns not at the heart's behest,
But in the book of memory shall be pressed
        Only thy faded flowers.

Farewell to thee—to thine, and ours, Old Year;
    To days that passed in toil or passed in vain,
To bright-eyed dreams entombed beside thee here,
To hopes that left us when they seemed most dear,
        To loves whose fruit was pain.

'61.

The bells have rung a requiem; yet once more
    They wake, and flood the air with music's mirth;
And joyful echoes peal it o'er and o'er,
And the great heart of nature at its core
        Throbs with the New Year's birth!

A starrier sky of promise bends serene
    Over the future, pathless and untrod;
And life, re-clothed with Hope's own evergreen,
Stands like the Christmas-tree we reared yestreen,
        Hung with the gifts of God.

O stately daughter—latest born of Time—
    Heiress of good or evil yet to be,
Go bravely forth, though ill may cloud thy prime;
For History, pausing in her task sublime,
        Expectant waits for thee.

1862.

Grasp the kindly hand of friendship; bid each dark-
    some thought, away;
Let the heart speak forth its fullness in the greeting of
    to-day;
Beautiful with youth and promise, hope and radiance
    in her train,
Face to face the New Year meets us, and the world is
    young again!

Take us back, O wizard Memory, to that way-mark of
    the past,
Where we stood and, gazing forward, gave this friendly
    greeting last;
Show again the rising tempest, how it broke the land's
    repose,—
How the south-wind, soft with summer, to a dread
    sirocco rose;
Make us pale with battle tidings; take our hearts and
    let them beat
To the wild and throbbing music of the war-drum in
    the street;
Take us back—but, ah! it needs not, while the drama
    of the year,
Moving still to solemn climax, holds us tranced in hope
    or fear—
While the flag that drooped at Sumter, flings its eager
    colors forth,
Beckoning on the looming thunders of the dark and
    wrathful North.

16

Hark! the din is hushed a moment; night and winter
    fold the earth,—
Many a face is bent to listen, by the camp-fire and the
    hearth,—
Now the dead Year's dirge has sounded o'er the white
    and sleeping lands,
And, with folded scroll of history held aloft in shadowy
    hands,
While the bells' low vibrant murmur quivers faint and
    .far abroad,
Through the Nation's stormy midnight, the Old Year
    goes up to God!

Grasp the friendly hand, O people! pass the olden
    word of cheer;
Close the door *one* day to trouble, while ye greet the
    new-born Year.
Mute she stands, and holds the secret of a good or evil
    fate,
But the sibyl Hope is whispering at the Future's open
    gate:
'Haply joy will come with Summer, and the Winter-
    night will wane,
And the New Year's light may smile us back to happy
    peace again!'

1863.

'62.

As, when a people throng the Monarch's bier
Whose evil reign has filled the land with gloom,
The dirge they chant speaks more of joy than woe,—
So, at thy grave, dark Year, we say farewell;

But not as when we part with aught beloved.
Thy face has not been fair, to win our hearts;
Fleeting and soon forgot were all thy smiles;
Thy shadows stay, to lengthen o'er our lives.
Thy birth was 'mid the din and storm of war;
The glare of battle lit thee on the path
Where wild-eyed terrors chased thy flying feet.
Sin's bitter fruit, the broken dream of love,
Dead garlands from the wintry hills of life,
And echoes of a music hushed for aye,—
These are the gathered trophies at thy tomb,
Where Memory sits, enamored of the Past,
With steadfast eyes upon the folded scroll
Whereon thy name, Dead Year, is writ in blood.

'63.

But, when the dead king's infant heir is brought
And set amid the purple of the throne,
The people read a promise in his eyes,
And all the land rings musical with joy.
So, robed in winter's ermine, crowned with light,
We give thee welcome, youngest of the years!
The Future's awful portals move ajar—
Enter: we send the angel Hope before;
And where she may not walk, our prayers shall lead.
Dark-folded is the nation's Flower of Fate,—
Touch with thy light and warmth the mystic bud,
And make it bloom, a glory in all lands.
Hide with thy snow's white calm the stain of blood;
Heal with thy Spring's soft balm the wounds of war;

Bring Summer, in whose glow the nation's tears
Shall pass in rainbow-gleaming mists away ;
And, greeting thee, our eyes are turned to Heaven,
O glad New Year, for thou dost come from God !

1864.

Over lands that mutely lie
   Wrapped in snow's white slumber,
Under deeps of midnight sky,
   Peals the fateful number.

Voices of the steeple's height,
   Tolling joy and sorrow,
To the Old ye bid good-night,
   To the New, good-morrow !

Pass, Old Year,—we shed no tear
   At thy darksome leaving !
Much is taken that was dear,
   Much is left for grieving.

Wreath and garland were not rife
   Where thy pathway brought us ;
Mingled is the woof of life
   Hands of thine have wrought us.

Deeps of trouble, heights of rest,
   Broke the year's long level ;
With us, all the road abreast,
   Angel walked and devil.

Pass the Old and come the New !
   Let the bells ring bolder !
All things hopeful, young and true,
   Press the New Year's shoulder !

Underneath her happier star—
  Skies serene and stilly—
Close the crimson rose of war,
  Blossom forth the lily!

Come the New and pass the Old!
  Asphodel and laurel,
Summer's green and autumn's gold,
  Be her brave apparel!

Come! for through her open gate
  History stoops to enter;
And with new-born hopes elate
  Throbs the heart of winter.

THE CROSS OF GOLD.

I.

The fifth from the north wall;
Row innermost; and the pall
Plain black—all black—except
The cross on which she wept,
Ere she lay down and slept.

II.

This one is hers, and this—
The marble next it—his.
So lie in brave accord
The lady and her lord,
Her cross and his red sword.

III.

And, now, what seek'st thou here;
Having nor care nor fear
To vex with thy hot tread
These halls of the long dead,—
To flash the torch's light
Upon their utter night?—
What word hast thou to thrust
Into her ear of dust?

IV.

Spake then the haggard priest:
' In lands of the far East
I dreamed of finding rest—
What time my lips had prest
The cross on this dead breast.

V.

' And if my sin be shriven,
And mercy live in heaven,
Surely this hour, and here,
My long woe's end is near—
Is near—and I am brought
To peace, and painless thought
Of her who lies at rest,
This cross upon her breast,

VI.

' Whose passionate heart is cold
Beneath this cross of gold;
Who lieth, still and mute,
In sleep so absolute.

Yea, by this precious sign
Shall sleep most sweet be mine ;
And I, at last, am blest,
Knowing she went to rest
This cross upon her breast.'

To J. H.*

The happy time when dreams have power to cheat
Is past, dear friend, for me.   As in old days,
So, still, at times, they throng their ancient ways
And trail their shining robes before my feet,
Or stand, half-lifted to their native skies
By the soft oval of white arms, with eyes
Closing on looks unutterably sweet.
Then the grim Truth beside me will arise
And slay them, and their beauty is no more,—
No more their beauty—saving such as dies
Into the marble of mute lips, or flies
With the swift light of dying smiles, before
The eye that strains to watch can tell, for tears,
How passing fair it shone—how dusk have grown the
    years.

DIVIDED.

The half-world's width divides us ; where she sits
Noonday has broadened o'er the prairied West ; '
For me, beneath an alien sky, unblest,
The day dies and the bird of evening flits.

* This poem is printed from a copy which has the following note
appended : 'Written by David Gray in 1867, at the Legation in
Vienna.   JOHN HAY.'

Nor do I dream that in her happier breast
Stirs thought of me.   Untroubled beams the star,
And reeks not of the drifting mariner's quest,
Who, for dear life, may seek it on mid-sea.
The half-world's width divides us ; yet, from far—
And though I know that nearer may not be
In all the years—yet, O beloved, to thee
Goes out my heart, and, past the crimson bar
Of Sunset, westward yearns away—away—
And dieth towards thee with the dying day !

The Last Indian Council on the Genesee.

The fire sinks low; the drifting smoke
    Dies softly in the autumn haze ;
And silent are the tongues that woke
    In speech of other days.
Gone, too, the dusky ghosts whose feet
    But now yon listening thicket stirred ;
Unscared within its covert meet,
    The squirrel and the bird.

The story of the past is told ;
    But thou, O Valley, sweet and lone—
Glen of the rainbow—thou shalt hold
    Its romance as thine own !
Thoughts of thine ancient forest prime
    Shall sometimes tinge thy summer dreams,
And shape to low poetic rhyme
    The music of thy streams.

When Indian Summer flings her cloak
  Of brooding azure on the woods,
The pathos of a vanished folk
  Shall haunt thy solitudes.
The blue smoke of their fires, once more,
  Far o'er the hills shall seem to rise,
And sunset's golden clouds restore
  The red man's paradise.

Strange sounds of a forgotten tongue
  Shall cling to many a crag and cave,
In wash of falling waters sung,
  Or murmur of the wave.
And, oft, in midmost hush of night,
  Still, o'er the deep-mouthed cataract's roar,
Shall ring the war-cry, from the height,
  That woke the wilds of yore.

Sweet Vale, more peaceful bend thy skies,
  Thy airs be fraught with rarer balm!
A people's busy tumult lies
  Hushed in thy sylvan calm.
Deep be thy peace! while fancy frames
  Soft idyls of thy dwellers fled;—
They loved thee, called thee gentle names,
  In the long summers dead.

Quenched is the fire; the drifting smoke
  Has vanished in the autumn haze;
Gone too, O Vale, the simple folk
  Who loved thee in old days.

But, for their sakes—their lives serene—
Their loves, perchance as sweet as ours—
Oh, be thy woods for aye more green,
And fairer bloom thy flowers!

COMMUNION.

I.

When the great South-wind, loud,
Leaps from his lair of cloud,
And treads the darkness of the sea to foam;
When wild awake is night,
And, not too full nor bright,
The moon sheds stormy light
From heaven's high dome;

II.

Then, while I only keep
Watch of the sounding deep,
And midnight, and the white shore's curving form,
Wakeful, I let the din
Of their shrill voices in,
And feel my spirit win
Strength from the storm.

III.

Strength from the wrestling air
It wins, till I can bear
To beckon him who waits for me, apart—
Him, the long dead, whom love,
Deathless, hath set above
All other Lares of
My hearth and heart.

IV.

The house is still, and swept,
Save where the wind has crept,
And utters at the door its cry of fear.
While the weak moonbeams swim
Down from the casement dim,
I wait for sign of him :
Hush! he is here ;

V.

Betwixt the light and gloom
He fronts me, in mid-room ;
I stir not, nor a greeting hand extend ;
But the loud-throbbing breast
And silence greet him best,
Beloved, yet awful, guest—
Spirit, yet friend !

VI.

He speaks not, but I brook
In his calm eyes to look,
And dare an utterance of my dread delight :
Oh, as in midnights flown,
Bide with me, thou long-gone ;
Are we not here alone—
We and the night?

VII.

Then, gliding on a space,
He takes the ancient place,
Vacant so long, a sorrow's desolate shrine.

Night shuts us in, yet seems
Lit, as in festal dreams,
And the storm past us streams
    In song divine.

VIII.

Slips, then, from my sick heart
Its covering of sad art ;
Joy rushes back in speech as sweet as tears ;
    Tell me, I cry, O friend,
    Whose calm eyes see the end,
    Unto what issues bend
        The awful years?

IX.

Tell me what view is won,
From mountains of the sun,
Over this earth's unstarred and blackened sphere.
    This life of weary breath
    Vainly one questioneth—
    Oh! from the halls of death
        What cheer?   What cheer?

A FRAGMENT.

Our home is in the city's dust and strife ;
From its too feverish air we breathe our life ;
Ours is no soft commune with field and sky ;—
Not ours in depth of summer wood to lie,
And take from Nature's ever lavish hand
The stores of pleasure there at our command—

That bread of soul her hallowed teaching gives;
That wine of heart, which whoso drinketh lives.
From all her life and bloom we dwell apart,
With news of her, alone, to glad the heart.
To us, her every beauty, pomp and grace,
The ever new divineness of her face,
The year's sweet fall, the coming of her springs—
All have the strange, sad feel of distant things.
We cannot watch the flying woof of green
First fastening on the aspen's silvery sheen,
Then deepening where the buds are late and coy,
Till all the woods are waving, wild with joy!
Or, when the summer's deep crescendo tune
Has grown the full-voiced harmony of June,
We only hear its far-off echo swell,
And heart-sick, in the dinful street, can tell
By the quick pulse, the weary, yearning brain,
That life and bliss are flooding earth again!
Even now, when, stealing from the autumn woods,
A mist of dream-land fills the solitudes,
Only the wind without, that sinks and swells,
Sings songs of harvest-home to us, and tells
How Autumn came and gathered up his sheaves,
And walks, a gleaner, through the withered leaves.

Soft Falls the Gentlest of the Hours.

Soft falls the gentlest of the hours,
    Whose star is in the blue,
And comes, across the grass and flowers,
    The angel of the dew.

So let us forth, dear wife, and walk
While earth is still and love may talk;
For love is of the stars, and gains
Its luster as the daylight wanes;
And earth is sweetest when it lies
'Neath curtains of the evening skies,
To such first happy sleep beguiled
As comes to the day-weary child.
The west grows pale, but like the dream
That brightens the young eyelid soon,
See, over earth's calm slumber, beam
Yon silver vision of the moon!
On the far Highlands' crest of woods
Its mellow light divinely broods,
And where the river, calm and deep,
Spreads like a mountain-lake asleep,
By dreamy sail and drifting boat,
A bridge of silver seems to float.

With what sweet discontent the breeze
Stirs the warm darkness of the trees!
And yonder, through their parted gloom,
How bright, like very marble, loom
The walls, the roof that seems to dome
The little temple of our home!
'Our home!' Ah, wife, a word like this
Upbears so deep a freight of bliss,
I tremble as it floats from reach
Even on the current of calm speech!
For, when I brought you home to-day,
Bride of this morn, true wife for aye—
When I had brought you, unaware,
Here, where your father lived, and where
Your childhood dwelt in fairy bowers,
And told you the old home was ours,
I felt my life so touch the sky
It scarcely had been changed to die.
And now, when all love sought to win
Is safe in love's dear realm shut in,—
In this soft day the moonlight makes,—
My heart is like the bird that wakes
(The full orb beaming on his nest)
And cannot sleep for glad unrest
And sense of music in his breast,
Nor wait, that to the dawn be flung
The song of morning on his tongue.
So let us rest a moment yet,
Till yonder star of eve be set:
This open bower, where best of all
We list the river's lapsing tune,
Sit here—and closer fold the shawl—

The dew is in this breath of June;
And I, my blissful heart to ease,
Shall be your bard, to-night, and sing
A song of true love triumphing.
And if my lady's heart it please,
'T will be that long the silent string
Has guarded it, a sacred thing,
For her and for these garden trees.

POEM

Read at the celebration of the Twenty-fifth Anniversary of the
Young Men's Association of Buffalo, March 22, 1861.*

The hearts of men throb faster than of yore;
We measure time by centuries no more;
Life, that but loitered, in the ages gone,
Now, winged with haste and eager-eyed, speeds on.

Our sires can count the summers that have passed
Since she, the city of our homes, was cast
A baby-hamlet on the forest-floor
Of Erie's savage and untraveled shore.
They know how Nature nursed her, standing nigh,
While lonely waters sang her lullaby;
And how the desert blossomed for her sake,
Wild daughter of the forest and the lake!
The years passed on, and Spring, from southern bowers,
Threw in her lap the wild-wood's buds and flowers;

* The circumstances of the composition of this and two other poems
written for the same Association are related on pages 74–75.

The lake's cool breath, in summer, gave her health,
Or brought her dreams when Autumn came by stealth,
In robes of gold and crimson, through the woods
Of Canada's far-stretching solitudes.
And thus it was, wild Nature nurtured her;
And, even when all her borders were astir
With tumult and the sound of frontier strife,
She rose from ashes into statelier life.
Then came a time, when, o'er the waiting land,
Some wizard surely raised his magic wand:
Forth from the wave sprang Commerce to the light,
And spread its myriad glittering wings for flight;
The very wind was wealth, and in our streets
Was poured the treasure of a hundred fleets;
Far empires, that had scarce received a name,
Paid tribute to our city's rising fame;
Till the young West, on many a prairie wold,
Wove her at last a crown of harvest gold,
And all the lakes, upon their shores of green,
Sang 'Coronation' as they made her 'Queen'!

What marvel if we think of her with pride,
'Queen of the Lakes,' nor less the river's bride,—
Enthroned above the wave, from out whose strife
Niagara leaps majestic into life!
Gaze o'er her borders, still the vision sees
That slow-receding wall of ancient trees;
But where, of old, the wild-bird sought the pool,
Now dart the laughing children forth from school;
And now, when stream the sunset's level fires,
Like lighted altars gleam her churches' spires.
Nor, only, has her outward life been fair;

17

Look in her annals, for 't is written there
How to the brotherhood and zeal of youth
Was wed the love of knowledge and of truth.
A blessing rested on the genial rite;
And, lo, the 'Silver Wedding' is to-night!

The night is festive; soul and song divine
Have filled us, thrilled us, more than flashing wine.
But, in our joy, one thought—the first of all—
To those whose long past labor we recall;
One thought to them—the band who met of yore—
But who will meet, as then they met, no more:
We pledge them in our hearts, though festal din
May never summon *all* the wanderers in,—
A toast to them! the youth of other years!
With thoughtful skill, with hope, perchance and fears,
They laid for us the goodly corner-stone
Of the fair fabric time has made our own,
And on whose half-reared pillars we may set
A dome that haply shall be classic yet!
No storied temple Art hath made sublime—
No fane is ours, rich with the spoils of time—
But year by year we build, and slowly rise
The pillars of our temple toward the skies.
Even now we fan a spark within its shrine
Of the same fire that rendered Greece divine:
Already History seeks a refuge here
To trace her record of the pictured year;
Anon has Science found congenial home,
To dream her dreams, beneath our lowly dome;
And Art, the bright-eyed pilgrim from afar,
Has come and found our portal wide ajar.

But, look within our temple's inner hall,
Where books in serried legions line the wall!
They little dream, who lightly enter here,
To what enshrinèd mysteries they draw near.
Listen! a stir is in the haunted air;
Low, echoed voices start and tremble there;
Dim shapes are forming in the yielding gloom,
And muffled foot-falls rustle o'er the room.
A moment since, the dead lay here in state:
Now, from their tombs up-starting, and elate,
Rises the living army of the great!
They stand—the bard who sang, the sage who taught—
Clothed in the immortality of thought!
Yonder is Shakespeare's calm and kingly face,
Still radiant with serene, immortal grace,
As when, by Avon's borders, dew-impearled,
He sang, unconscious of the listening world.
Here Milton speaks, and lifts his sightless eyes,
Blind with too dazzling dreams of Paradise.
Beside him, Bacon smiles upon the shame
That envy vented on a deathless name;
And Scott, the wizard Minstrel of the North,
Waves, in our sight, his bright creations forth.
Yonder, to 'Nature's Bard' the vision turns,
And on us beams the lustrous soul of Burns,
Whose song, that mid the woods of Ayr had birth,
Has carried music's joy through air—and earth.
Nor such as these, alone; for, thronging fast,
Up from dim vistas of the farthest past,
Come poets. heroes of the classic time
When Rome was young, and Athens still sublime.
Here, too, apart, amid the shadows, stand

Statesmen and sages of our native land,
In the deep magic mirror of whose eyes
We almost read our nation's destinies.
But who may rightly name each noble guest
Within this new Valhalla of the West?
Or tell how thought of every clime and age
Is centered here, the people's heritage?

So, each goodly arch and pillar wreathed and fair with
    festive light,
Full before us stands the temple we re-dedicate to-night.
On its front we grave the record of the unreturning
    past,—
Shade and sheen of many summers o'er the tablet
    strangely cast;
And prophetic Hopes stand smiling at the portal, as
    they hold
In our sight the brighter story of the future, half
    unrolled.
Who may tell how, in that future, shall the columned
    fabric rise,
Shining fairer in the sunlight, towering statelier to the
    skies?
Who shall tell what power may issue, swayed by spoken
    word or pen,
From its midst to bless the people, and to rule the
    hearts of men?
Hark! without, the wind is moaning, and the clouds of
    March droop low;
O'er the hills the lingering Winter trails his ermine
    skirts of snow;

Yet the wraith of tearful April walks already in the
    bowers,
And the far-off sun, in secret, thrills the subtle nerves
    of flowers ;
Birds are flying from the southward, buds are shaping
    in the sod,
And the Spring is hasting hither, young and beauti-
    ful, from God.
So, beneath the night of error, with its winter scarce
    away,
All the world is waiting, yearning for a brighter, better
    day,—
For a spring when love and mercy on the highways
    shall be rife,
And in earth's unhappy places bloom the asphodels of
    life.
It is ours to wait and labor—God's to bring that
    morning in ;
Ours to build, with high endeavor—hope and aim to
    heaven akin ;
And our temple's noble summit, stretching upward,
    firm and high,
Shall be dipt in hues of sunrise when the day breaks,
    up the sky.

Brothers, met in festive council, surely, forth from
    yonder shrine,
I can hear a message, whispered, like the Delphic voice
    divine :
'Strong,' it tells us, 'strong for blessing, mighty for
    the help of truth,
Is the fervid soul of Manhood—is the throbbing heart
    of Youth.'

We have read how fierce in battle shone the eagle's
    conquering glance,
When Napoleon filled his legions with the fiery youth
    of France:
So, victorious and glorious the issue of the fight,
When young Manhood flings the gauntlet for the good,
    the true, the right!
Triumphs, more than flushed the legions of the emperor,
    evil-starred,
Wait, when Youth shall bear the banner, in the world's
    'Imperial Guard'!
Forth, my brothers, we are summoned, wheresoe'er the
    field may be—
Where the Wrong is to be vanquished, or the shackled
    Right set free!
Nor, in duty's earnest battles, where the spirit burns
    and strives,
Come the only times for proving the heroic in our lives!
When Columbia counts her heroes, think you she can
    e'er forget
Him—her bravest, though his falchion may not flash
    in battle yet—
Who, while sounds of gathering tumult float around
    him, from afar,
By the mute-mouthed guns of Sumter guards the sleep-
    ing fiend of War?
So, perchance, more great than Valor marching grandly
    to the strife,
Is the godlike might of Patience, in the silent tasks of
    life.

Youth's unselfish, pure devotion, manhood's high and
    conscious power,—
When, to these, did duty's summons sound so urgent
    as this hour?
O'er the land our evil angels, Strife and Faction, wan-
    der free,
And men point the atheist finger, O my country, unto
    thee!
Troubled, trembling, stands the nation, even as Israel
    stood of old,
When the foe pressed darkly round them, and the sea
    before them rolled.
Stars have fallen from out our heaven; night and tem-
    pest are abroad;
Dimly burns the guiding pillar of the nation's covenant
    God:—
But 'tis darkest just ere morning, and the day has lit
    the skies
When the younger, purer spirit of the people shall
    arise;
Wide the wave shall roll asunder, and the nation God
    once blest,
Through the Red Sea of its troubles, shall re-enter
    into rest!

A NINETEENTH CENTURY SAINT.

Beautiful is my darling's face;
    And, yet, I know her heart so well
That, thinking always of the pearl,
    I have not time to praise the shell.

I care not that with words of mine
   Her eyes' deep splendor be extolled,
Nor any wreath of speech would twine
   Within her tresses' wavy gold.
Not mine to praise the Saxon hue
   That on her cheek the rose outstrips,
   Nor see in curvings of her lips
Some Greek ideal born anew.
Ah, no; far other court is due,
   From such as near her heart may dwell,
   My darling, whom I know so well.

I think (while softer fancies sleep)
   Of those old altar-pictures, quaint,
   Which pure-souled Memling loved to paint,
Or those that in fair Florence keep
   His fame, as limner and as saint,
Who, kneeling, painted heaven, and so
Was named of men Angelico.
     All shut, such reliquaries stand,
   Rich paintings on each folded lid
   That keeps the inner beauty hid,*
And almost one is stopped to gaze,
     And half—before the doors expand—
Would lift the censer of his praise.
   But, open! and there straightway beam
   Such glories of the fairer dream,
All other light is quenched than its.

---

* Some of the most beautiful paintings by the old masters are covered by folding lids, on which pictures have been painted by an inferior hand.

Unclouded glows the golden air,
And ringed with heaven's own aureole,
The very deep of Beauty's soul
Throbs visible where The Virgin sits.

So, curtained from the vulgar eye,
Abides the vision, chaste and fair;
And though the world may pass it by,
Or laud its covering unaware,
O soul of love! O heart of prayer!
Look inward; for the shrine is there!

THE CHIMES.

"That fatal bellman!"—Macbeth.

I.

A moment, O Niagara of sound!—
Tremendous torrent, but a moment hush,
For this frail city's sake, and I will crush
My sonnet in the bud!
    The prayer is drowned
In sudden seas of din, that burst unbound
And flood the air to mad distraction full,
Till night—calm night—is like a turbid pool
Stirred up from all its inky depths. Confound
The bellman,—bird of storm, whose perch and bower
Is in the thickest tempest,—him I hold
Even as some Mexique idol, gashed and old,
That dwells in the high horror of his tower,
Among the shrieks of victims; a grim wonder,
Shrined in perpetual heights of blood and thunder.

II.

Sweet bellman, grace! I did thee wrong, up there;
For in thy stormiest clangor dwells a charm
To stir the drowsy soul with grand alarm—
To wake in battle thrills the heart's despair.
Methinks if one should die amid the tear
Of these mad bells, the ghost, tho' all unshriven,
Would quiver, wild-eyed, on the surging air
And ride exultant into open heaven!

III.

Then, oh, to list the peal that drifts afar
Upon the mute and moveless deep of night,
When lullaby winds have sung the toil and jar
Of day asleep, and scarce we know aright
Whether those sounds we list descend or rise,
There is so strange commune of earth and skies!

POEM

Read at the Annual Meeting of the Young Men's Association of Buffalo, February 17, 1862.

To-day, one mighty master-thought rules in all hearts
　　supreme;
It leaps to every parted lip; it gives no choice of theme.
We sit, home-circled, as of yore; we throng in festive
　　halls;
But, strangely, o'er the glare of mirth, a nameless
　　shadow falls.
If phantom-fingers of the wind but touch the door ajar,
We start, and hark, through storm and dark, for tid-
　　ings of the war.

No petty, passing strife, to-day,—no feud of court nor
    king,—
Thus grandly shapes to epic form what future bards
    shall sing.
Not lightly sprang the sword unsheathed, to urge a
    paltry cause ;—
Pale Freedom stood in tears and plead her wrongs and
    broken laws.
Her banner, stained with martyr-blood, and dust of
    many lands,
Up through the troublous past she bore, and gave into
    our hands.
No trivial strife, in sooth ; this cloud that veils our
    heaven, sublime,
Rolled hither, thundering in its course, o'er far-off hills
    of time.
It wrapped dim centuries in gloom ; it broke in wast-
    ing showers— ;
The fateful day of bursting storm and rainbow hope is
    ours !
Annus mirabilis ! The heart of coming time shall
    thrill
To read the rife historic page these passing moments
    fill ;—
To read how Spring came, laughing, up, to glad the
    land anew,
And, lo, the southern flowers she brought were streaked
    with crimson dew !—
And how, of all the birds that come, when winds of
    winter cease,
Through air of balm, from lands of palm, there came
    no dove of peace.

Then shot the signal light of war, a meteor, up the skies :
What sudden frenzy filled our veins, and flashed in
    patriot eyes!
The giant hand that won the land from Nature dropped
    the plough,
And, lo, the steel that broke the soil glitters to guard
    it, now !
And they that sowed reaped other grain than waved
    on Western lea
When o'er the prairie rose the tides of Harvest's gol-
    den sea.

Brave souls, that went, 'mid cheers and tears, on
    Glory's perilous track,
Our hearts stay with you at the wars, till ye come
    proudly back !
Your blood has dyed with richer hue our banner's
    glorious red ;
Ye bring the old chivalric Past back, trooping, from
    the dead !
Not lost shall be the tide that flowed when gallant
    Baker fell,
Or Winthrop's wingèd soul went up to heaven from
    battle's hell !
Nor soon forgot what years it seemed, while, flushed
    with noble ire,
We caught the tidings of your deeds hot from the
    tremulous wire :
How wild Zagonyi, battle-mad, with Valor's breath of
    flame,
Charged, like a mountain-torrent, down the slope of
    death and fame ;

Or how, through all that week of doom, a hero stood
    at bay,
The fiend of thirst within his lines,—without, the roar-
    ing fray,—
Till victor, though in victor's chains, he saw his labor
    done,
And History wrote thy name again, twice-sacred Lex-
    ington!
And is there heart but leaped, to-day, just for one hour
    to be
Where gladly broke through battle-smoke that blaze of
    victory? *
Thank God! the wounded dragon writhes beneath the
    Nation's heel;
The eye of Treason cannot bide the glance of Northern
    steel.
Thank God, and you, so leal and true, whose votive
    blood has dyed,
O softly-flowing Cumberland, thy dusk and silent
    tide!
Thank God! the trampled flag is washed in this wild
    three-days' rain;
It waves in victory's jubilant wind; it shall not droop
    again.

To-night, upon a myriad tents, the snow's white silence
    lies,
And over day's dark tumult falls the calm of winter
    skies,—

* This poem was delivered on the evening of the day which brought
the news of the capture of Fort Donelson.

Grim Battle's sternly sleeping face, touched with the
    moon's soft kiss,—
Another century shall not look on scene so weird as
    this!
To-night, upon its burnished arms, the waiting Nation
    sleeps,—
To-morrow, and its gathered might on faithless treason
    sweeps.
God give us heart for that stern task the morrow has
    to do!—
Stand back, false England, frowning France, and let
    us fight it through!

So, by the Nation's temple gate,
Beside fair Freedom's shrine we wait,
Till, by the lightning from the cloud,
We read the oracle of Fate.
O Temple, 'neath that awful shroud
Of tempest and Tartarean gloom,
More proudly all thy pillars loom!
On the dark background of that sky,
We see how grand thou art, and high.
Not this young hemisphere, alone,
Whose beauteous center is thy throne,
Has hewn the marbles, one by one,
That, lifted to the sky, have shone
A wonder in the setting sun!
Dead centuries bequeathed thee state;
The toiling ages made thee great.
Whenever struggling thought, divine,
Has sprung to birth of noble words,
A gem was wrought to light thy shrine.

Whenever hero hands and swords
Have struck a down-trod people free,
The valor of the sword was thine—
   The hero wrought for thee.
The flinty strength of Scottish hills,
For thee, by blood and toil, was bought :
And long-enduring hearts and wills
For thee, in Alpine quarries, wrought.
And what Titanic blows, of yore,
Woke echoes by Ægean shore,
That in thy massive walls might be
The granite of Thermopylæ !
Then, by what loving art and care
The glorious fabric rose in air !
' Life, fortune, sacred honor' given,
It towered and took the smile of heaven ;
Till, on each gilded spire and cope,
Glittered a starry beam of hope,
And, in far lands of lingering night,
A million tearful eyes, upturned,
Saw how its pinnacles of light
With signals of the morning burned.

O Temple, not this driving gale
Shall 'gainst thy pillared front prevail !
Within thy sacred ark are shrined
The future's folded destinies ;
The garland of our hopes entwined
   Upon thy altar lies ;
And spirits of our sainted sires
Are hovering guardians o'er thy spires.
They hung thy walls with triple zone

Of hues that, now, are Freedom's own:
Red—of the hero hearts that perished;
White—of the stainless faith they cherished:
Blue—of the heaven that bends to bless.
And, while upon their graves shall press
The weight of Freedom's sacred sod,
Sublime thy sacred walls shall stand—
A Home of Hope for every land,
    A Fane of Truth and God.

POEM

Read at the opening of the new Library Building of the Young Men's
Association of Buffalo, January 10, 1865.

'T is written in the Hebrew's sacred story,
When foes beset the mount of Zion's glory,
That Judah's city rose, with valiant hand,
To build, at once, and shield her ancient land.
The ring of hammer from the rising wall
Blent with the sudden trumpet's wakening call;
Peace wore the mail of warfare as she wrought;
Trowel and sword together built and fought;
Till, 'mid the din of their alternate blows,
The gleaming fabric of the temple rose!

All honor to our city, stately ' Queen ' !
A kindred task, methinks, her own has been;
For, while the storm of war around her raged,
A gentler labor, too, her mind engaged.
Her heart was with her country at the wars;
Her steady hand upbore the nation's stars;

And where was poured the loyal hero-blood,
Her votive breast gave forth a mingling flood:
But still, though War's wild tumult did not cease,
Beneath her touch uprose the walls of Peace;
Her art was busy while her sword was bare;
She built, though battle shook the troubled air:
All honor to her generous mind and might!
We sit beneath the temple's dome to-night!

The fires are lit, the waiting portal turns;
At every pane the light of welcome burns,
And, with the host's proud pleasure in our breasts,
We stand expectant of the nearing guests.
Nor start if, soft, in silent stair and hall,
A viewless foot shall seem to glide and fall,
And, rustling past, we feel the garments move
Of her whose birth-place was the brain of Jove;
For, 'round us, here, with double luster, shine
The household fire, the temple's flame, divine,
And the fair goddess of the sage's vow
Stands in our midst, a stately hostess, now!
O ye, thrice-honored, more than guests, to come,
Here at her shrine we wait to greet you HOME!
Come, fervid Science, young and Argus-eyed,
Take thou the place of honor at her side!
Thee Nature beckons to her broad domain,
And craves the sickle for her bending grain!
Here trim thy weird Aladdin-lamp, to shine
And light the mirk of mystery's haunted mine!
Truth, still half-shackled, lifts her cry of pain,—
Come thou and rend her last Promethean chain!
Thou, too, grave History, clad in sober vest,

18

Thrice welcome to thy temple of the West!
Here shall thy thoughtful vision, backward cast,
Recall the pageant of the fleeting past;
And on thy magic mirror, lifted here,
Shall live the image of the pictured year!
'T is thine to stand and vigil keep, sublime,
By the dim death-bed of departing Time;
To walk, anon, in battle's track of flame,
And trace, in lettered light, the roll of fame!
The flags that, bright through battle-smoke, revealed
The path of death on many a trampled field,—
That waved o'er dark Virginia's crimson mire,
Or flapped in wild Antietam's wind of fire,—
The deathless relic of that stormy van
That turned, and rode to fame with Sheridan,—
The starry emblem of the true and free,
That marched with dauntless Sherman to the sea,—
These, won by valor to thy waiting shrine,
(Oh, priceless offering!) History, these are thine!
Come, then, and keep undimmed to farthest age
The Nation's jewels—the Future's heritage!
But, once again, the yielding door is prest:—
A greeting to our temple's fairest guest!
All rarest flowers of fancy and the heart
Kiss welcome to thy coming footsteps, Art!
The light of summer, in far orient isles,
Beams on thy brow and sparkles in thy smiles!
Around thy path the birds of Eden sing,
And blossoming beauty has eternal spring!
Come, for the temple, else, were dark and dull,—
O pilgrim-priestess of the Beautiful!
Come! and, beside thee, in our hearts shall rise

Dim memories of forgotten Paradise;
And, lit with hope, thy pencil's magic dye
Shall paint a rainbow on life's darkest sky!

These are the guests, and Mercy, too, divine,
Shall sit with cloistered Learning at our shrine.
So may they dwell, and Time's advancing scheme
Affirm their welfare and perfect our dream.
With kindred aims, beneath a single dome—
Oh, blest be each,—thrice-blest the common Home!

As one who, o'er a desert's sultry soil,
    A bower's sweet shadow raises,
And dreams what fainting souls may bless his toil,
    What birds may chant his praises;

So, to the sun we lift this kindly shade,
    So, trustful, we bequeath it;—
Deep in the soil of faith its roots are laid,
    Our hearts' best hopes enwreathe it.

Not hither, yet, the summer's minstrels rove,
    To fill the air with singing;
Not yet, on branches of our sacred grove,
    The golden fruit is clinging;

But white, o'erhead, the buds of promise teem,
    And, softly, ere we know it,
Forth from us, here, shall float the deathless dream
    Of artist, sage, or poet!

Here, too, shall Labor, from the dusty street,
    Come, and forget his toiling,
As if the grass grew green beneath his feet,
    And heaven were o'er him smiling.

Hither shall Youth, with bounding heart, repair
  To turn the page of story,
Till life, transfigured, to his eyes shall wear
  Romance's robe of glory.

And Song, to lead his fancy's airiest train,
  Shall send her lithest fairies ;—
To thrill his heart with love's delicious pain,
  Her sad-eyed Highland Marys !

And here are nooks, where, in the shadowy calms,
  Swing open magic portals,
And, walking, we may feel within our palms
  The hands of the immortals !

The poorest life may come, and, haply, yearn
  With hopes new-sprung to blossom,
And, songful, to its lightened task return,—
  A flower upon its bosom !

But not alone for dreams and calm delight
These festal halls are dedicate to-night.
Here shall the soul, at Learning's sacred pyre,
Kindle with grand resolve and high desire ;
And, borne within, stern duty's clarion-call
Shall echo from each ringing arch and wall.
Beneath this dome shall walk in solemn state
The mighty ghosts of earth's departed great ;
Hero and statesman, warrior, bard and sage,
Enshrined, shall hover o'er the pictured page,
And, with their subtle presence, shall inspire
An equal genius and an equal fire.
What need to show that, strong with trust and truth,
Hence, at the call, will spring full-statured youth ?

Or tell how, from these peaceful walks of life,
Already have our heroes sought the strife?
Unguessed till then, we know them heroes, now,
With valor's light a halo on each brow.
What need? Ah! friends, it were enough to tell
That Chapin died and gallant Bidwell fell;
That, while our thought thus wanders to the brave,
The snow is drifting o'er a nameless grave,
And hearts that were the brother-hearts of ours
Are mouldering upward into southern flowers.
Or would you more of proof, I might recite
The tale a veteran told me, yesternight.
Of one you know, and whom I loved, he spoke,
And thus, in simple phrase, his passion broke:

HOW THE YOUNG COLONEL DIED.

You want to hear me tell you, how the young Colonel
    died?
God help me, memory will not fail on that, nor tongue
    be tied.
Aye, write it down and print it, in your biggest type
    of gold,
For, sure, a braver heart than his no mortal breast
    could hold.
'T was the second weary night of that hot and bloody
    June;
Through the brush, along the picket, we walked beneath
    the moon;
Behind us, sixty miles of death, Virginia's thickets lay;
Before us was Cold Harbor,—the hell to come next day!

We talked about old Buffalo, and how the girls we knew,
At the door-steps, with their sweethearts, sat in the
    silver dew ;
And, looking at the fields below, where the mist lay,
    like a pond,
We seemed to see the long dark streets and the white
    lake, far beyond.
Then, turning sudden : 'George,' he said, 'I'm glad a
    moon so bright
Will hold her face to mine, when I lie dead, to-morrow
    night ! '

We charged, at noon, the Colonel led green Erin's old
    brigade ;
'T was Longstreet's blazing cannon behind their breast-
    works played.
We charged, till, full in front, we felt that fiery breaker
    swell—
A sea of rattling muskets, in a storm of grape and
    shell !—
The Colonel led, in fire and smoke his sword would
    wave and shine,
And still the brave sound of his voice drew on the
    straggling line.
Then, all at once, our colors sank ; I saw them reel and
    nod ;
The Colonel jumped and took them, before they touched
    the sod ;
Another spring, and, with a shout—the rebs will mind
    it well—
He stood alone upon their works, waved the old flag,—
    and fell !

As o'er the surf at Wicklow I've seen the sea-gull fly,
His voice had sailed above the storm, and sounded clear
    and high;
It seemed, I swear, I had not heard the hellish rack
    and din,
Till then, all sudden, on my ears, the thunder-crash
    rushed in.
'T was vain to stand up longer; what could they do but
    yield?
Our broken remnant melted back, across the bloody
    field.
I stayed to help the Colonel, and crept to where he
    lay.
A smile came, tender, o'er his face, but he motioned
    me away.
I bent to watch his parting lips and shade him from
    the light—
'I 'm torn to pieces, George,' he said; 'go, save your-
    self—good-night!'
As tender as my mother's, that smile came up and
    shone
Once more upon his marble face, and the gallant soul
    was gone!
Three times the same full moon arose and looked him
    face to face,
Before the rebels flung a truce above the cursed place.

We laid him near Cold Harbor, but the spot is bleak
    and bare,—
I hate to think how I 'm at home, and he still lying
    there.

I doubt his sleep will not be sweet, nor his loving spirit
    still,
Till he lies among the friendly dust of yonder slanting
    hill,
Where, from the streets he loved so well, might float
    their daily hum,
And the lake's low roar upon the beach, in quiet
    nights, would come.
Ah! well, the town might plant his tomb, with marble
    words to tell
How the bravest of her blood was poured when young
    McMahon fell! *

As o'er the homes of Athens towered and shone
The sun-smit marbles of the Parthenon,
So let these walls, with noble purpose crowned,
Tower, till their shade shall fall on classic ground,—
Till something of the Grecian's vanished dream,
A glory on their tinted spires, shall gleam.
All beauteous shapes shall haunt their hushed retreats,
And mingle, viewless, in the hurrying streets,
Or glide, in happy warmth of household domes,
The white-winged angels of a thousand homes.
With nobler life the City's heart shall beat;
A grander rhythm shall time her marching feet;
And History, pausing at these temple gates,
Shall view the widening of her fair estates.
Nor, though the sacred mountains loom afar
That caught the light of Wisdom's rising star,
Shall, o'er thy fane, less lustrous heaven be bent,
O young Minerva of the Occident!

* Colonel James P. McMahon, of the 164th Reg't, N. Y. S. Vols.

Far off, against the evening's purple breast,
Dim, mute, a giant specter, stands The West :
Yonder, the rays of dying sunset tinge
His slow-receding garments' forest-fringe ;
He lingers still, but, lo, I see him turn
To where these templed fires unwonted burn,—
Over his ancient haunts of wood and fell
Dark waves a hand of wonder and farewell:—
His shadowy wings are spread and plumed for flight,
The glimmering phantom fades—and all is night !—
Night, but prophetic ; on these lifted spires
Shall burn a fairer morning's signal-fires.
Fresh in its light, the land shall rise, arrayed,
And softest gales waft in the fleets of trade.
Freedom shall watch her ancient faith increase,
And Right sit, smiling, in the lap of Peace.

So stand, O Temple, by the muses blest,
High o'er the empire of the opening West,
A beacon and a promise, seen afar,
Till, through the future's portals, swung ajar,
With spheral music shall advance, sublime,
The happier era of millennial time !

The Last of the Kah-Kwahs.

Read before the Buffalo Historical Society, March 13, 1863.

For the thread of story upon which a part of these verses is strung,
the writer is mainly indebted to O. H. Marshall, Esq., whose contri-
butions to the Buffalo press, some fifteen or twenty years ago, over
the signature of 'Q,' comprise nearly all that is known of the early
Indian history of this locality. The Kah-Kwah, or, as it was termed
by the French missionaries, the Neutral Nation of Indians, is shown,

we think conclusively, by Mr. Marshall, to have been the tribe which
inhabited the site of this city previous to the conquest and occupation
of the territory by the Seneca tribe of the Iroquois confederacy. The
Neutral Nation was so called from the fact that it was observed by
the Jesuit travelers to be at peace with the neighboring peoples. The
date of the destruction of this remarkable tribe is fixed at about the
year 1647, and various legends survive as to the circumstances which
occasioned the Iroquois invasion. The most dramatic of these was
transferred to paper by Wm. Ketchum, Esq., in the *Commercial Advertiser* of July 12, 1845. This is related as a tradition of the Erie or
Cat Nation; but we believe ' Q' has proved satisfactorily that that
tribe inhabited a region to the westward, and that the tragedy embodied in the legend really refers to the Kah-Kwahs. According to
the narrative of Mr. Ketchum, the fatal quarrel with the Iroquois
arose out of a sort of barbaric tournament, which took place at Tu-
shu-way ('the place of the linden or bass-wood trees,') as the Indian
village formerly located here was called, and in which the young
men of the Iroquois and of the resident tribe participated. A relentless war followed this scene of savage revelry, which ended, only, in
the almost total annihilation of the Neutral Nation. It is said that the
last battle was fought near the old Indian mission-house, a few miles
from here.

Muse of the storied scroll, whose thoughtful eye
Watched the long pageant of the years gone by;
Whose patient art has touched and kept sublime
All that is deathless of departed time;—
Historic muse, whose pilgrim feet have stood
Where many a nation's star has set in blood,
Or followed where the sacred dawn of Right
Crept over Europe's late and lingering night,
Shedding on Roman hills its passing smile,
And brightening on the 'silver-coasted isle';—
Forth from thy home, amid the graves of kings
And brooding gloom of half-forgotten things,
Come where thy broader path, O History, waits,
And walk with empire through her western gates!

Come where a fairer day to earth is born
(The Old World's evening is the New World's morn),
And, in the luster of that larger sun,
Look forth and see thy grandest task begun!
No pomp or kingly glory here has birth,
Nor crumbling temple sinks to classic earth;
But, young and fair, beneath these western skies,
The emblems of a hundred empires rise.
And here are fields, amid whose thunderous strife
The Future's hope, embattled, strikes for life.
Even now the wind is warm with war's red rain,
And Truth and Treason cross the sword again.
Hither, O History, come, and, breathless, wait
While Freedom trembles in the scale of Fate!
Here bring the mirror of thy magic page,
And catch the features of this grander age!
Come, for the path that seeks the West is thine,
And, lo, we build thee, here, this way-side shrine!

And, sooth, its site, that wooes the pilgrim's stay,
Might lure the muse, herself, to brief delay:
Yonder, the lake, with heaven upon its breast,
Sleeps at the open portals of the West;
And the strong river, like a god in wrath,
Leaps from the calm upon his fateful path.
From yon gray ruin's shade the forms are fled
That came, but now, up-thronging from the dead;
But the great heart of Commerce, full and strong,
Throbs to the music of swart Labor's song.
Here, in the coming years, the muse shall rest,
And here, to-night, we hail her as our guest;
And, sleeping by the sounding river's stream,

Her slumber with its visioned past shall gleam;—
Hark, while I strive to read from History's dream:—

The city sleeps: its changing features fade
In the green depths of many a rustling glade;
The wind of summer whispers, sweet and low,
'Mong trees that waved three hundred years ago;
The streamlet seeks the path it knew of yore,
And Erie murmurs to a lonely shore;
The birds are busy in their leafy towers;
The trampled earth is wild again with flowers;
And the same river rolls, in changeless state,
Eternal, solemn, deep and strong as fate.

It is the time when, still, the forest made
For its dusk children a protecting shade,
And by these else untrodden shores they stood,
Embodied spirits of the solitude;—
When, still, at dawn, or day's serener close,
The smoke-wreaths of the Kah-Kwah lodges rose.

No hoary legend of their past declares
Through what uncounted years our home was theirs,—
How oft they hailed, new-glittering in the west,
The moon, a phantom-white canoe, at rest
In deeps of purple twilight.   This, alone,
Of all their vanished story, has not flown:
That, through unnumbered summers' long increase,
The Neutral Nation was the home of peace.
Far to the north the Huron war-whoop rang,
And, eastward, on the stealthy war-path, sprang
The wary Iroquois; but, like the isle

That, locked in wild Niagara's fierce embrace,
Still wears the smile of summer on its face
(Love in the clasp of Madness), so, the while,
With peace the Kah-Kwah villages were filled.
And, as the lake's dark heart of storm is stilled—
The fury of its surge constrained to calm—
Beneath the touch of winter's marble palm,
So, when the braves of warring nations met,
They changed the hatchet for the calumet,
And hid, with stolid face, their mounting ire
From the bright glimmer of the Kah-Kwah fire.

Year followed year, and peaceful Time had cast
A misty autumn-sunshine o'er the past,
And, to the hearts that calmly summered there,
The forehead of the future shone as fair;
Save that, perchance, some wise and wakeful ear
In the great river's ceaseless song could hear,
Through the mirk midnight, when the wind was still,
The murmured presage of approaching ill.

It came, at last—the nation's evil day,
Whose rayless night should never pass away.
A calm foreran the tempest, and, a space,
Fate wore the mask of joy upon his face.
It was a day of revel, feast, and game,
When, from the far-off Iroquois, there came
A hundred plumed and painted warriors, sent
To meet the Kah-Kwah youth in tournament.
And legend tells how sped the mimic fight;
And how the festal fire blazed high at night,
And laugh and shout through all the greenwood rang;
Till, at the last, a deadly quarrel sprang,

Whose shadow, as the frowning guests withdrew,
Deepened, and to a boding war-cloud grew.

And not for long the sudden storm was stayed;
It burst in battle, and in many a glade
Were leaves of green with fearful crimson crossed,
As if by finger of untimely frost.
Fighting, they held the stubborn pathway back,
The foe relentless on their homeward track,
Till the thinned remnant of the Kah-Kwah braves
Chose, where their homes had been, to make their
            graves;
And rallied for the last and hopeless fight,
With the blue ripples of the lake in sight.

Could wand of magic bring that scene, again,
Back, with its terrors, to the battle-plain,
Into these silent streets the wind would bear
Its mingled cry of triumph and despair;
And all the nameless horror of the strife,
That only ended with a nation's life,
Would pass before our startled eyes, and seem
The feverish fancy of an evil dream.
For, in the tumult of that fearful rout,
The watch-light of the Kah-Kwah camp went out;
And, thenceforth, in the pleasant linden shade,
Seneca children, only, laughed and played.
And still the river rolled, in changeless state,
Eternal, solemn, deep and strong as fate.

A few strange words of a forgotten tongue,
That still by lake and river's marge have clung,

Are all that linger, of the past, to tell,
With their weird-sounding music, how it fell
That here the people of that elder day
Sinned, suffered, loved, hoped, hated, passed away.

So, History's dream is told; and, fading, fleet
The shadows of the forest from the street.
But is it much to ask, if it were sought,
That it return, at times, to tinge our thought?—
To tell us, when the winter-fires are lit,
And in the happy heart of home we sit,
That other fires were here, ere ours had shone,
And sank to ashes, years and years agone?—
That where we stand, and, watching, see the West
Ebb, till the stars lie stranded on its breast,
Or homeward ships, more blest than they of Greece,
Returning with the prairie's Golden Fleece,
To other eyes, long since, perchance was given,
Through the same sapphire arch, a glimpse of heaven?
And, haply, not in vain the thought shall rise,
To sadden, it may be, our reveries,
That here have throbbed, with all the bliss of ours,
Hearts that have mouldered upward into flowers!

THE MINISTRY OF ART.

**Read at the opening of the Buffalo Fine Arts Academy,
February 13, 1864.**

The winter night is dark; the wild wind falls
    Asleep in snow, and, sleeping, moans the while;
But Art is mistress here, and, lo, her halls
    Are lit with summer's smile!

And darker night has draped the land in gloom,
   And wilder wind, that will not sleep nor cease,
Beats over broken homes; but here, in bloom,
   Droop only wreaths of peace.

No shadows enter here; and, Art, divine,
   We greet thee, though the iron hand of war
Knocks at our gates; to-night is ours and thine,
   Bright pilgrim from afar!

The bark was blest that bore thee o'er the sea,
   From sunny Italy, from golden Spain,—
From many a temple builded brave to thee
   By Arno, Thames, or Seine.

The time had come, and thou didst take thy way
   Through portals that the sunset left ajar,
And all thy new-found empire, waiting, lay
   Beneath the Western Star.

So, here, thy broadest canvas be unfurled,—
   Thy fairest dreams, O magic Art, be born,—
To limn the features of the younger world,
   Ruddy with hope and morn!

We greet thee, here, we crave thy kindly powers;
   For, as the olden forest's green retreats
Have sunk, with all their freshness and their flowers,
   Beneath the city's streets,—

So is the freshness of our life down-trod;
   So its sweet nooks a dusty highway made;
And, reckless, over Memory's greenest sod,
   Hurry the feet of Trade.

Gone is the hush wherein our spirits gave
  Memnonian music to the stars and sun;
Over our thought's serenest, clearest wave
  The wheels of traffic run.

'T is thine, O Priestess of the Beautiful,
  To bring again the joys our hearts have lost,
And even the windows of life's winter paint
  With pictures of the frost!

Thy spells are potent; these are magic halls;
  Enchantress, thou, whose pencil is thy wand!
Radiant, and far from all these pictured walls,
  Opens a faery land.

As through the gate of some enchanted palace,
  We wander forth, beneath divinest skies;
And there are windless woods and silent valleys,
  Where summer never dies.

Away, away, where soundless streams are falling,
  Where Fancy's sweet will, only, points the track,
Until, at last, her vagrant steps recalling,
  The soul comes singing back!

Or, haply, to some Alpine summit scaling,
  We see the vale beneath us, blue and blest,
As he who spies, o'er heights of pain prevailing,
  His Italy of rest.

Or, in a barque of dreams the soul is drifted
  Athwart a sea where summer sleeps and smiles;
Above whose verge the purple mists are lifted
  That fringe the Golden Isles.

19

There may we meet our vanished Youth's romances ;
    There pluck the lotos, in its fruit or bloom,
By Lethean streams, where never face but Fancy's
    Has bent above their gloom.

Or, haply yet, we walk with hushed October,
    Where the year fades, and, queenly, as she lies,
Stills the mute winds that tarry to disrobe her,
    And smiles before she dies.

Anon, it is a scene in human story,
    Where Freedom's sons uphold her ancient faith ;
Or some immortal face is lit with glory,
    Even as it looks on death ;

Or the calm eyes of some fair saint are looking
    Down, through the gloom of centuries, into ours,
With the white patience of her brow rebuking
    Our puny griefs and powers.

These are thy spells; and thus, O subtle Art,
    Thy magic colors, like the mystic seven,
Melt into one pure ray, that points the heart
    To beauty,—thence to heaven !

So, still, to men reveal the Beautiful,—
    The Beautiful, sole angel whom our eyes
Have held the gift to see, since, dimmed and dull,
    They turned from Paradise.

For, when the gates of Eden closed in wrath,
    She, only, of the angel host, had leave
To pity man, and on his barren path
    Glide forth, a fairer Eve !

So, ever, in the loveliest spots of earth,
   He caught the glitter of her silver wing;
And when his sweetest music chanced to birth,
   Her finger touched the string.

And, still, with glimpses of her heavenly face,
   With dreams, whereof the waking is sweet tears,
With thoughts that never on the lips have place,
   Nor còme, save once, in years,—

With these—with all that makes us thrill or burn,—
   Still does she haunt the heart and light the eyes,
Till, with a longing, wild desire, we yearn
   For the lost Paradise.

So, still, O Art, we follow where thy wand
   Points to the path the Beautiful hath trod;
For Art joins hands with Beauty,—Beauty's hand
   Touches the throne of God!

HUSHED IS THE LONG ROLL'S ANGRY THREAT.

*Read at the opening of the Central Fair, held for the benefit of the
United States Sanitary Commission, February 22, 1864.*

  · Hushed is the long-roll's angry threat,
     The squadron's echoing tramp;
  And Night, her starry pickets set,
     Is guardian of the camp.
  The soldier sleeps; and sleep has spread
     Her tent of dreams above him,—
  One white wall slanting o'er his head,
     And one o'er those that love him!

He sleeps; a thousand wintry miles
    Keep parted, with their gloom,
His bed in battle's slumbering files,—
    This bower of light and bloom.
Oh, would these fairy halls for him
    Might ope, to-night, Elysian;
Or, wafted southward, far and dim,
    Flash o'er him in a vision!

Hush! for methinks the winter wind
    Has swept the camp-fire's place,
And yet, a radiance soft and kind
    Steals o'er the veteran's face.
Oh, surely, gleaming from afar,
    It lights those stains of powder;
And, surely, in his dream of war
    These flowers are shedding odor!

He sleeps; but o'er him, in the skies,
    The milder stars have met;
The heaven of home is o'er his eyes,
    The ruddy Mars has set;
And from his bearded lips, the while,
    A smile has passed, elated.
O Woman, by that soldier's smile
    Your work is consecrated!

Ay! sacred are the magic charms
    That set the night a-glow,
Till Summer into Winter's arms
    Sprang, laughing, from the snow!

The blended skill of hand and heart
　　Wrought in these halls of faery—
With Martha's careful, tireless art,
　　The love and faith of Mary!

Not mirth nor thoughtless revel glides,
　　With Flora, in these bowers;
'T is Mercy's tearful face that hides
　　Behind this mask of flowers.
'T is Woman's constant, fadeless faith
　　This evergreen discloses,—
Her heart of love, outlasting death,
　　That throbs beneath these roses.

O Soldier, fearless be your mien,
　　While the grim work endures!
For her white hand is stretched, unseen,
　　And grasps the Flag with yours.
And God fail us if we fail you,
　　Our debt of love forgetting,
Or cease to keep your glory new
　　In memory's golden setting!

O Woman, angels aid your toil!
　　So weary not, nor cease.
Where battle sternly breaks the soil,
　　You plant the seeds of peace.
And, lo, beyond the war-cloud's frown,
　　Comes clearer sky, and starrier;
And History holds an equal crown
　　For you and for the Warrior!

THE TENTH MUSE.

Read before the New York State Press Association, June, 1874.

I.

How shall the poet sing, or bard be heard,
　　To-day, beside the Babel-stream of time?
　　Tides of the world's wide tumult drown his rhyme :
　　　The clanging air is stirred
With wings of rumor; in his ear
　The lightning's myriad clicking voices pour
The ceaseless babble of the articulate sphere ;
　While, 'round him, o'er and o'er,
With wash of wave, from farthest clime to clime,
　The human ocean, audible, beats its shore.

II.

For, evermore, our earth is clamorous grown,
　And full of tongues.　Her ancient silences
Are broken in their places and o'erthrown.
　The Past sleeps, mute amid its mysteries;
But, on its awful sepulcher of stone,
　　The iron hammer of the Present rings.
　　Gone is the stillness that, with brooding wings,

Folded the midnight of the early world.
    Flown, too,—forever flown—
The hush of history's charmèd dawn,
With the first flag of morning just unfurled,
    When, clear and strong,
    Some single bird of song,
High in the heaven of his own thought withdrawn,
Poured all his soul in melody,
And woke the tongueless earth to vocal ecstacy!

III.

It is a tropic blossoming-time of Speech,—
    A summer, when the bloom of words is rife
    On every growth of life;
And, to its farthest branches' reach,
    Foliage of print is wov'n and wrought
    About the tree of thought.
    The rapid foot of action presses
    Through tangled literary wildernesses.
    So thick, in sooth, the lush papyrus grows,
    Our later Nilus hardly flows.
    No subtle chance nor darkling hint
    But leaps to leaf and flower of print.

    The very secret soul of things,
      That, erst, in brooding dusk, lay hid
      Within its waiting chrysalid,
    Now hatches instant paper wings
And flutters forth to consciousness,
The blithe and swift ephemeron of the Press!

IV.

Well may the bard forego his song,—
   The seer from mountain-top descend!
The Man of News—to him the times belong,
   And to his mastery bend!
   The modern epic, to its unguessed end,
Grows under his prosaic pen.
What shall escape his sweeping ken?
   The hamlet's gossip, the great town's uproar,
And all the loud report of men,
The light tick of his dropping type re-sounds, again!
     His to explore
   And flash the torch in darkest nooks of earth.
Through the great groaning lazar-house of life,
   Or dens of sweltering death, he goes,
   And their black secret shows.
   The ceaseless, armèd tramp of human woes,
Fantastic masques of crime, the strife
   Of vulture passion, honor's dearth
And virtue's sad decay,
   Council of friends and plot of foes,
With all that courts or shuns the day,—
   These must his merciless lens expose,
His portrait of the time display.
   His, open-spread and bare,
   Full in the public light and air,
The good and ill alike to lay;
   That, haply, in the day's broad eye,
   The social rose may flourish fair,
   The deadly nightshade die.
A wizard, he; his sheet a magic glass
   Wherein the mirrored world doth shine,

And all its diverse energies
In hurrying throngs approach and pass,
  Appear and disappear,
 Weaving a web of texture fine
From verge to verge of farthest alien skies;
  Till far and foreign are brought near,
 And myriad threads of destiny intertwine.
  And ever to the ear,
From the same wizard concave, rise,
 In gusts up-blown from every shore and clime,
  The multitudinous voices, blent, yet clear,
 Of the vast surging earth, the din
Of traffic, the low sough of sighs,
The laughter and the cries
 Of many peoples, and the roar of time.
And, lo, Humanity, dismembered, marred
 Of visage, comes, looks wondering in,
 And sees, despite the stain of sin,
And features battle-searred,
 And cruel woes endured beneath the sun,
Her face still bears the mould of the divine,—
 Her mighty many-nationed heart is ONE!

v.

The plastic time takes ever-changing forms.
 The age is past when one compelling mind
 Could sway the armies of mankind,
And lead their dumb, obedient swarms
 To conquest of ideal lands.
The mighty captains of the race
 Sleep in their storied tombs, nor rule again—
 Heroes of sword, or word, or pen—
 With power to loose and bind.

But, in a broader, freer space
　　The circle of the world expands;
　　And, breaking immemorial bands,
The conscious peoples rush apace
　　To blend in one vast commonweal of men!
In the new order thus to be,
　　No priestly power, supreme to blight or bless,
No despot leader, she—
　　The Tenth, our modern, Muse—the Press!
Hers, not, in her own thinking, to be great,
　　But rather to keep free
The channels of the people's thought,
And be the voice and conscience of the State;
　　Setting a gauge whereby the State may see
How, in their seething caverns, palpitate
The pent volcanic forces of its fate.
But not the less her service shall be fraught
　　With active use and blessing, and confer
　　A sacred office on her minister.
His, where the springs of public virtue run,
　　To watch, and keep their current pure and strong;
　　With hand alert, to scourge the wrong
And give the good deed to the sun;
　　The saving word, the larger creed,
　　To speak, and, in the speaking, speed;
　　To preach, with pen of fire,
Men's 'politics' and God's justice shall be one;
　　And so this fallen word redeem,
To heights of its old meaning, from the mire.
　　Not his the prophet's dream,
Or spell of power, the nations to inspire;
　　But, watcher of the seasons, to proclaim

What signs, portentous of the future, flame,
And, in the orient of the world's desire,
   What new-born stars arise.
Or, like some workman, he, who plies
   The chisel with swift patient hands,
And shapes the plan a greater hath designed.
   The rugged marble fronts him, and, behind,
      The invisible Master stands,
         To whom alone
      The secret of the block is known.
The time is long, the watcher's eyes wax blind,
   And weary is the worker, toiling, dumb;
But, at the last, before him there is grown
   A figure of the fairer Age to come!
   The image of the Master's mind,
Girt with Beauty's perfect zone,
Looms, living, from the stone!

MARY LENOX.

A NEW YEAR'S ITEM IN VERSE.

Soften to airs of balm, O winter wind!
Melt soft to summer dew, O snow! and let
A vision of sweet June be in our eyes;
For, like some vernal brook, my story springs
All among happy things, and takes its course
'Mid flowers and sunshine and the birth of love.

You know the place I write of, and, perhaps,
Three hours out from the city, when the train
Has torn in thunder past, you may have marked
The very farm, far on an edge of woods,

And facing an Arcadia of calm fields,
Where Mary Lenox lived.   Her father's house
Was motherless, and so she grew to wield,
In love, and in an eldest daughter's right,
The scepter of the little realm, and blend
The matron and the maiden.   Grace of each
Was in her mien, and steadfast in her eyes
Shone forethought, and a care for others' weal,
And duty, like a star.   Lowly her life,
Bowed with its useful fruit, as autumn bent
Her father's orchard trees; nor less, like these,
It had its due of blossoms, and a crown
Of beauty.

       So she lived, and might have lived;
But rumor of her graces, widely sown,
Came up a crop of wooers.   First, they say,
It was a farmer-lad who touched her heart;
But Edward Maxwell, lawyer, city-bred,
Stormed at the half-made breach, and took the prize,
And one sweet day of summer they were wed.
Then, from the old stone door-step, forth they went,
And down the garden-walk, while all the flowers,
That knew her feet, turned wistful on their stems
And breathed farewells of odor.   And away
On the high road they drove, bridegroom and bride,
And many eyes looked after them through tears,—
Until the great world's gates of distance oped
And took them in.

       The city was their home;
To Mary an enchanted land, where Love
Was chief magician, weaving in her life

Such radiant colors as she had not dreamed.
She seemed to breathe a charmèd air of light
And music. On her pure and plastic mind
Culture began to set its noble seal,
And mould her beauty into shining form.
And she was happy in her husband's love,—
Happy in each day's birth of joyous power
And aspiration,—happy in her home,
Where many a pleasant guest of the heart made stay,
And on whose windows ever seemed to glow
The orient of a future calm and fair.

But trouble came. Whether by slow approach,
Or suddenly and fierce, to Mary's heart
It came, I cannot tell. The adverse fates
Give warning, sometimes, and the straggling gun
Tells of the far attack, that, gathering on,
Rolls near and louder o'er the distant hills;
Anon, on Sabbath mornings of the soul,
The battle bursts in fire. It may have been
That, often, while she sat in light and warmth,
She heard her sorrow, like the outcast wind,
Utter its boding cry, or guessed its face
At the dark pane—God only knows the whole:
But this is certain, that there came a night
(Her babe lay smiling in its sleep the while)
When she had waked from her long dream of bliss,
And, face to face, stood with her mortal woe.
In that dread hour she read her husband's heart
As if by light of hell;—saw the pure love
That filled it once corroded by disease;—
Saw that already he lay bound—heart, mind,

Soul, honor, all—as on a funeral pyre,
Lit by a drunkard's passion, and must burn,—
Unless God's love and hers might quench the fire,—
Burn evermore, down, down to death and doom!

She quailed awhile before her evil fate,
Then, brave and calm, confronted it, and scanned
Its cruel features till she knew them, each.
Then, on her knees, she asked for strength of love
And woman's faith to last in her till death.
Lightly had love upborne her life, thereto,
And, now, love's burden lay on her.   The road
Was weary, but she would be true to love.
For love's sake she would walk it to the end.
And so she rose and took her cross.

                                    From this,
It was not long before the social ground
Began to give to Edward's heavy tread.
The grades are steep on that familiar path
By which he sank.   Yet, sometimes, he would seem
To fix a foot in some precarious ledge,
And nerve himself once more to climb, her hand
Clutching at his with desperate strength, the twain
For dear life straining up the dread ascent,
Then clinging, poised, a moment, till the gulf
Drew them again to deeper deeps.   And yet,
Not wholly died his love; for there were days
That seemed to bring his gentle manhood back;
And Mary half forgot her wasted life,
Forgiving all, and trimmed the lamp of love
Anew, to light her through the dark, to come,
Of heart-break, and neglect, and brutal wrong.

At poverty's grim gates they stood at last,
And took the host's chill welcome, and passed in.
And bravely Mary toiled, with hand and brain,
Throwing her young life, piecemeal, to the wolf
That waited, hungry, for her babe and her;
Nor made complaint, but ever nursed a spark
Of woman's faith in him who madly tried
To tread it in the mire.

               It chanced, I think,
Before her trouble, that her father sold
The pleasant farm, and moved with all his house
Far to the west, whence news infrequent came,
Not cheerful, of hard struggle and hard luck.
So Mary hid her sorrow from her kin,
Sending brave words, though blotted oft with tears;
Striving to think that all was for the best;
That, haply, had her father's door stood near
And open still, pleading for her return,
Weak, and too sorely tried, she might have fled
Her duty, and thrown down her grievous cross.
Poor Mary! trial such as this, I ween,
Might e'en have overborne her, and her guilt
Had not been quite beyond the range of grace.
But there were other trials stored for her,
More grim of shape. One night of woe she sat,
Holding her babe upon her knee, and watched
Her light of life die out on its white face;
And held it, motionless, till morning came,—
Morning, that only seemed another night,
And she the sole sad thing that could not die,
In a great world of death and weltering dark.

Henceforth she was alone, but still held on
In her rough road, and did what woman could.
Within their poor abode she plied the arts
That even give a gentler face to Want.
The squalor of its walls her cunning veiled,
As if with viewless arras, woven of love,
And rarer than the weft of Gobelin, hung
In rooms of kings, and rich with pictured lives
Of saint and martyr. For, although her love
Promised no harvest of an earthly hope,
Methinks it was a secret faith of hers
That, one day, *he*, recalling all, would note
The prints of blood her duteous feet had left,
And would retrace them, back to better life.

Her bright face faded, but her soul was strong.
Sometimes she listened, as if in a dream,
To those who blamed her that she flung her life
Into a bottomless slough, and showed her doors,
Open, wherethrough she yet might pass and find
Freedom, and bread, and honorable place.
Then, if she answered, it was still in dream;
For, on the old stone step, she sat again
With Edward, and looked forth on evening fields,
And heard with him the low of kine, and bells
That tinkled on the hill-side; and she said,
Musing, 'I shall not leave him till I die!'

It fell, at last, that Mary's toil should end.
A dull, cold winter-night possessed the earth;
Wind shuddered in the streets. Weary and faint,
She had lain down, and fallen in feverish sleep,

But woke, betimes (or thought she woke), and looked,
Wondering that, in her fireless room, she felt
No cold, nor pain, nor deadly languor more.
Glad, therefore, she rose up, and, lo, the place
Was filled with summer warmth and light of day,
And at her feet bloomed flowers! Then she saw
It was that garden-ground of long ago!
All things were as of old, and naught seemed strange;
Not even strange that, coming to a bower,
She found her babe, and hid it in her breast.
There, evermore, she had been fain to rest,
But that a hungering impulse led her forth
To seek for something precious she had lost,—
Something, she knew not what, that in her soul
Begat vague yearning and a sense of loss.
By many a path familiar, many a spot
Sacred in lore of her lost youth, she sought,—
But always vainly, till, with anguish pressed,
And woe of that vain quest upon her soul,
She sat her down beside the door, and cried
That she might die. Sudden, her cry was hushed;
For, in an instant, all that garden place
Blossomed to awful radiance, and was stirred
As with a throng, shining, innumerable,
That moved about her, or did seem to move,
And be the border of a mighty host
Whose legions flooded the near fields, the while
The far surge of its camps crested the hills.
She sank with fear; but One came near, and stooped,
And raised her with a hand of human love,
And took her tender babe, that smiled content.
So, she stood still and worshiped, full of peace.

20

Then He (she knew Him, though none told His name),
He who had raised her, turned and cried aloud:
' Restore to her what she hath lost; restore
An hundred-fold of all her wasted love.
Lo, I am Love, and she hath borne my cross!
Her broken heart hath spilled its wealth for me!'

Then they who heard caught up the words, and sent
Their sound far outward, in a wave of song,
That swelled and broadened to a choral sea.
And, ' Give her back whate'er she lost!' they sang;
' Give back an hundred-fold!' the anthem pealed;
' An hundred-fold!' until the heaven was rent,
And took the song from earth, its myriad waves
Gathered and drawn to one melodious tide,
That ebbed, far upward, through the heavenly gates,
And filled the courts unseen. But earth was still.

The noon of night had struck, the clangor ceased
Of bells that told the New Year born; but she
Had passed where years are never born, nor die.
It was that song of Time whose chorus broke
Upon her vision of eternity;
But none the less the beauteous dream came true,
And what she saw but mirrored that which was.
For, surely, angels came to her, and feet
Moved round her, in the hush of that low room,
Of them that waited with the martyr's crown
To place upon her brow. Oh, chiefest prize!
The martyr's crown—whose radiant gold is set
With garnered diamonds of the martyr's tears,
And, in the midst (redeemed from mire of earth

And men's despite), star-like, the jewel Love!
Not many they who choose the proffered cross,
Or, choosing, can endure to such a crown.
But, in the rank of those nearest the throne,
By fagot come, or scaffold, it must be
The silent martyrs of the household sit,
And wear an equal glory,—in whose light
The diadems of angels are made dim.

THANKSGIVING IN WAR TIME.

But the Nation's sky is darkened; can we keep the
    holy day,
While the pillared State is shaken with the storm's
    uprising fray?
Not the less, O people, gather to your fireside altars
    in,—
Ring the louder, turret wardens, o'er the thunder's
    nearing din!
And, as once upon the waters of the wind-tossed
    Galilee,
To a crew whose prayer was mingled with the clamor
    of the sea,
Came the form of One whose presence drove the shud-
    dering tempest back,—
So, perchance, amid the tumult, in the storm's destroy-
    ing track,
While the rage of human hatred rises wilder than
    the seas,
In this holy time of worship, to the nation on its
    knees,

Shall the Power divine, that trod the heaving surges,
    come again,
Walking grandly o'er the passions and the angry
    hearts of men ;
And the sea shall own his presence—all its billows
    sink and cease,
And the Ship of State lie cradled in the happy Port
    of Peace !

THANKSGIVING DAY.

Still thy winds, O wild November, let their angry
    music sleep !
Give us Sabbath o'er the city; hush thy tempest on the
    deep !
With the golden sheaf of Autumn lifted in its stalwart
    hands,
At the threshold of the Winter, lo, a grateful nation
    stands !
Up the year's long path of blessing, heedless, thankless,
    we have trod ;
But, to-day, the people's altar sends its incense up to
    God.
Ring aloud, in spire and turret—in your windy prison
    cells—
Ring the morning in with anthems of Thanksgiving,
    O ye bells !
Gather, O ye people, gather, where the ruddy hearths
    are bright,
And the shades of care and sorrow vanish, backward,
    from the light !

Link anew the charmèd circle of the household's broken
    chain,

Let the land be full of worship, and the heart, of love,
    again ;

Homeward to the festal service call the wandering
    child that roams ;

For, to-day, the nation's altars are its firesides and its
    homes.

Moon by moon the year has circled, and before us is
    unrolled

All the seasons' perfect drama, as in countless years of
    old :

In the valley sank the snow-drift, and the snow-drop
    sprang anew,

And, anon, Earth woke in flowers from a summer-dream
    of dew.

Winter, Spring and Summer failed not, and she drank
    the light and rain.

Till the sun-lit heaven lay mirrored in her waving fields
    of grain.

O'er the wave, the white-winged vessels *came*, as *went*
    the ships of Greece—

Happy Argonauts, returning with the prairies' golden
    fleece.

O'er the land, the song of Labor, in the workshop and
    the field,

Forth, from ocean unto ocean, in a choral wave has
    pealed.

Therefore, wake, in all your turrets—in your windy
    prison-cells—

Ring the morning in with anthems of Thanksgiving,
    O ye bells !

REST.

Once more, blessed valley, I seek and have found thee:
  Tired, hunted, I ran, with the mad world hallooing;
  I slipped to thy shade—I am safe from pursuing—
No care climbeth over the green walls that bound thee.
In the hush of thy woodlands that draw me and woo me,
By the rush of thy waters whose thunders thrill thro' me,
  In deep hemlock cover, in vine-trellised arbor,
  My heart finds once more a blest haven and harbor.
But the summers are many, the years have flown fleetly,
  Since first we came hither, with revel and laughter.
  Ah! how easy the jest, then, the mirth following after,
The poem to praise thee, the song that ran sweetly.

   .   .   .   .

It was joy, then, that met us, by greenwood and meadow;
It is rest, now, rest only, we crave in thy shadow.
  GLEN IRIS, 1887.

LECTURES AND MISCELLANY.

ROBERT BURNS AND HIS POETRY.

From an address delivered on the One Hundred and Sixth Anniversary of the Poet's birth—January 25, 1865.

. . . The poet was as fully identified with his class as the man. His singing robes were no holiday garments, but an every-day suit, familiar with the wind and weather, with the rain and the sun of heaven. He sought no high-sounding titles or pompous themes for his verse. A very coarse and unsuggestive condition of things surrounded him; he lived in a world of commonplace; but he made no frantic effort to get out of it when he wrote. He stayed in it, and sang of it, and men wondered to see springs of music gush where there had been only barren desert, before. The ground he stood upon was good enough and high enough for him; he wanted no artificial Parnassus from which to descry objects worthy of his muse. His was the true touch of Midas, transmuting whatever came to his hand to poetic gold. When his dramatic mind ranged outward, seeking exercise of its strength, it was content to endow the ' Twa Brigs ' of Ayr with intelligence, or to draw from the mouths of the faithful dogs that trotted at his heels wisdom, pathos and exquisite humor. The daisy, ' wee, modest, crimson-tippèd flower,' to which his plow

gave burial, was not too insignificant a subject for his
pen. It fell, indeed, into its shallow sepulcher; but
Burns was there, to sing it up, again, into deathless
bloom. Its fragrance is eternal, and the tear that
Burns shed upon its fringed eye-lid sparkles, still, in
our sight, 'an immortal drop of dew.' A poet less
great than Burns would scarcely dare, like him, to
choose a pet sheep and an 'Auld mare, Maggie,' as
subjects for plaintive elegy and manly apostrophe.
The lesser bard, too, would start, aghast, were his
poetic vision directed to the spectacle of a certain
familiar but detested insect climbing to 'the vera
topmost towering height' of a lady's bonnet in church.
But it was in his address to a creature no more poetic
than a louse, that Burns gave voice to his unsurpass-
able exclamation:

> O wad some Power the giftie gie us
> To see oursels as others see us !
> It wad frae mony a blunder free us
> And foolish notion :
> What airs in dress an' gait wad lea'e us
> And even Devotion !

The trunk of the elephant is so fashioned that it
may rend great boughs from the forest trees, or, with
a subtle movement, pick from the ground the smallest
needle. So is it with the mind of the great poet.

With equal faithfulness and straightforward, single-
hearted simplicity, Burns treated the human material
that came to his hand. He sang what was in his own
heart—the good and the bad of it—with such truth-
fulness that his song goes straight to all other hearts.
His is a heart-language, which does not need to be

interpreted to be understood. His very frankness gave him enemies; for Burns made an open breast of his sins and failings,—while some wore Pharisaical waist-coats over theirs. The confessions of the poet to these people sounded like accusation of themselves. They pronounced over him bans of bitter excommunication; he retorted in wicked and savage satire.

And here, in parenthesis, let me say all that I deem it necessary for me to say of the dark side of Burns' character. Almost before the world was told that he had genius, it was published that he had vices. It is true. But his sins lay on the surface of his nature. They were born, not from that great, deep, true heart of his, but out of the storm and fury of the passions that swept over it. Great, too, may have been his fault, but greater still was his repentance. Let him that is without sin cast the first stone. . . . Let the bard speak for himself,—while at the same time he weaves for all his kind a shining vail of charity, beneath which the whitest of us may not scorn to shelter :

> Then gently scan your brother Man,
>   Still gentler sister Woman ;
> Tho' they may gang a kennin' wrang,
>   To step aside is human :
> One point must still be greatly dark,
>   The moving *why* they do it ;
> And just as lamely can ye mark
>   How far perhaps they rue it.
>
> Who made the heart, 't is *He* alone
>   Decidedly can try us,
> He knows each chord—its various tone,
>   Each spring—its various bias:

> Then at the balance let's be mute,
>   We never can adjust it ;
> What's *done* we partly may compute,
>   But know not what's *resisted!*

Poetry is a vague word. Philosophers and critics have not been very successful in defining it; and, in most minds where the school-girl's definition—that poetry means just long lines and short ones—is rejected as unsatisfactory, there exists but a dim and shifting idea of what poetry is and is not. There is a great distance, for instance, between the sublime periods of Milton, which appeal to the imagination, and some of the formal couplets of Pope, which do little more than tickle the ear. I think an approach may be made towards establishing for the subject manageable conditions, if we gather up the great mass of poetry into the form of a pyramid. At the base of the figure, I should place the works of those poets who have sounded the widest scale of song—whose poetry is built most broadly upon the hearts and minds of mankind. Ranging upward towards the apex should come the minstrelsy of narrower scope, and the pyramid would be crowned with that which is, perhaps, the highest order of poetry, while it certainly has the narrowest basis in human nature,—I mean that which is the offspring of pure imagination. If Shakespeare were not a pyramid in himself, broader than the broadest and as high as the highest, he should be the far-stretching foundation of the poetic pile. Just second to him, among all the poets of Anglo-Saxon speech, I would place Robert Burns. I have shown that he stood with his feet down upon the lower stratum of society, and that he sought and found his poetic work right where he stood, and did it without airs or affectation. Thus, speaking truly what was in his own heart, he gave speech to the heart of humanity. Painting with conscientious fidelity the human nature around him, his pictures are true of men everywhere. Because he loved deeply and sang truly, it was given to him to sing the love-songs of the world. The fiery words he spoke in denunciation of the false, the mean, and the tyrannical, burn into the carcasses of tyranny, falsehood and meanness forever. His brave words of cheer to the down-hearted, of counsel to the doubting, of brotherly love to all, are like branches from the sacred tree cast into the Marah of human life. They sink into its bitter waters, and, beneath the spell of their virtue, the stream runs, sweetening in the sun, away to the ocean of eternity. Nor less potent was he, when he lifted his voice for trampled freedom,—for human equality and human rights,—for the precious doctrine of honest independence. His words are the texts of a gospel that is to be preached to all the world; which echo from generation to generation—from clime to clime.

I wish to speak of but one other characteristic of Burns, namely, the intense love of and sympathy with all nature, animate and inanimate, which burned in his soul and pervades his poetry. Better than any man I know of, he answers to Tennyson's description of the poet, dowered as he was

> With the hate of hate,
> The scorn of scorn, the love of love.

But love was the ruling passion. It went out in a warm tide from his heart,—towards the poor among

whom his lot was cast, first,—towards his country, next,
—towards his race and nature, last.   He did his best
to help the misery that came within his reach; he wept
over the sorrow he could not heal.   The spirit of his
song has entrance, alike, into palace and hovel; but its
peculiar home is at the poor man's hearth.   There it
sits, now, and will sit, while Love is mistress of the
human heart.   In its presence, Care will sometimes
spread her dingy wings and take flight; Grief, herself,
will melt to music and tears; Penury will stand transfigured in her rags.   Look, how the poet-magician entered, once, and made a temple of the peasant's home,
—a very Sabbath of sacredness and light and heavenly
peace of 'the cotter's Saturday night'!   Look, how
he even took the coarse and homely fare of his peasant
countrymen and seasoned it with his cheerful, kindly
genius, so that the poor man thereafter might sit down
contented—yea, proud—to his table, knowing that his
'haggis' had been ennobled, his oat-meal porridge
blessed, by the muse,—his kail spiced with Burns'
benediction;—that kings do not sit to a banquet so
enlivened by poetic wine!

Speaking of the love with which Burns regarded
mankind, I scarcely need say that womankind was not
excluded from his heart, as they are from Mahomet's
paradise.   'The lasses,' he was accustomed to say, 'I
love them a'.'   For it was a part of his poetic creed
that Nature—

> Her 'prentice hand she tried on man,
> And then she made the lasses, O.

He might, on just occasion, be rough and rude to men;
but his whole being softened in the presence of the

gentler sex. Poesy knows no sweeter, tenderer voice than that in which he addressed his 'Mary in heaven.' Woman never inspired more melting melody than that in which he bade eternal farewell to his sweet 'Highland Mary.'

Love of country was interwoven with every fiber of Burns' frame. Scotland may well be proud of her son, for her fair fame was dearer to him than life. No painter, limning the face of his beloved, could dwell more devotedly upon his task than did Burns, when he turned his pen to speak of 'Scotland, his auld respectit mither.' Upon the canvas of his verse she lives, with all her features of mountain, river, field, wood, burn and brae, forever glorious and beautiful. But his patriotism was no blind, undiscriminating passion. While he loved Scotland—*because* he loved her—he was no slavish partisan of the corrupt and capricious power that ruled her. He gloried in her constitution and her charter of rights; but his muse administered most unpalatable advice to the king, and took still more improper liberties with the king's ministers. His love of freedom led him to sympathize keenly with the French in their revolutionary struggle, and to oppose most warmly the war that Britain waged to maintain the stability of the rotten old thrones of Europe. How he regarded the infant republic that sprang into existence on our own soil, during his young manhood, may be guessed from an incident of his career as an exciseman. It occurred at a dinner in Dumfries, attended, for the most part, by government officials, like himself. After the Scottish drink had circulated freely, some one proposed the health of William Pitt, the prime minister at that time. 'I give you the health of George Washington,—a greater and better man,' cried Burns. The company demurred, and the poet left the room in disgust.

How the heart of Burns went out in tenderness to all created things is better illustrated in his own *Address to a Mouse* than another writer could do it in volumes. Like the mountain daisy of which I have spoken, the nest of the little animal had been turned under by Burns' plough. . . . Could anything more be said to prove the all-embracing sympathy of Burns' nature? Yes; and Burns has said it. It is in his *Address to the Deil*, wherein, after recounting the mischiefs for which his Satanic Majesty is held responsible, the poet first anathematizes, then scolds, and at last fairly pities, in this fashion:

> But, fare you weel, auld Nickie-ben!
> O wad ye tak a thought and men'!
> Ye aiblins might—I dinna ken—
>   Still hae a stake—
> I'm wae to think upo' yon den,
>   Even for your sake!

Milton paints Satan a desperate yet valiant and almost chivalric warrior; Goethe makes his Mephistopheles a cunning, malicious, yet gentlemanly fiend; Burns, too, calls up the Devil to sit for his portrait, but dismisses him with a pitying wish for his reformation!

I wish to glance, now, for a few moments, at the influence exerted by Burns and his works upon the literature and the life of the age. It is almost superfluous to say that he is, to Scotland, even more than a Shakespeare. The tongue in which he wrote is a language, not a mere dialect. The direct outgrowth of the Saxon invasion, it, or something like it, pervaded England and Scotland, alike, as late as the thirteenth century. The English under Edward and the Scotch under Bruce, when they clashed on the field of Bannockburn, spoke a common tongue. Scotland, isolated and unvisited by further invasion, kept it with little change, until Burns made it classic. In England, on the other hand, the mingling of the Norman element cut down its grotesque syllables, added new words and softened the terminations of old ones, until it came, through the filter of Chaucer, Spenser and Shakespeare, to be the English of the present day. But, though thus noble and ancient in its origin, around the Scottish language no rich or copious literature has crystallized. A stream of purest song has, indeed, trickled down from the mountains and out of unexplorable recesses of the past,—now murmuring madrigals of the softest beauty,—now dashing over rocks in cataracts of wildest passion,—anon, spreading in pellucid deeps of rarest melody; but deduct this, with the writings of half-a-dozen minor poets, and Scottish literature, until Burns, is almost a nullity. He it is who has deepened and widened and filled full the rivulet of Scottish minstrelsy. He has made the rugged Doric of his fathers to be read in all lands, from the backwoods of this continent to the sultry plains of the Orient. And, should his mother tongue, at last, be lost in the broader, stronger current of English speech, he will have built the beautiful monument of the departed language. Long may its death be delayed; for in its rough but expressive syllables are embalmed ideas of beauty which will die with it! Its grave would cover the last fragments of a nationality which has been the brave nurse of heroes and which is still glorious with the deeds of Wallace and Bruce. The flow of its music, now tender, now wild, is caught from the winds and the woods, from the burns and the birds of auld Scotland; and, if it should die, the memory of its sweetness would haunt the Scottish heart, like the voice of a mother who has been years and years in heaven.

I think it may be shown that, to no insignificant extent, *English* literature has been vitalized and enriched by the writings of Robert Burns. He was born in the barrenest, forlornest period of that literature. The golden sun of the Elizabethan era had set in a murky vapor of conventionality. The star of Milton, too, had gone down; and such will-o'-the-wisps as Prior, Pope, Gay and Parnell had flashed abroad, only to make darkness visible. Not even Thomson and Goldsmith and Gray, with their contemporaries, who followed, had been able to break the dense shell of artificiality which encrusted poetry. With the restoration of the monarchy, the art of verse-making had fallen into the hands of court-fools and laureates equally foolish. To write poetry was to string stilted couplets into fulsome eulogy of some influential person, or in malignant satire of some harmless one. The heart of the land seemed to be in the process of ossification. Form took the place of soul; licentiousness served for imagination; falsehood wore the mask and did the duty of feeling. In a word, at the beginning of the latter half of the eighteenth century the body of

English poetry had shrunk to a mere skeleton; breath it seemed to have none. Whence came that marvelous infusion of new life with which, in the half century following, it was suddenly thrilled? . . . I do not seek to point the paternity of the last great period in English literature; but this I assert, without fear: that the first star which rose in that splendid heaven of genius,—which led up the shining constellations,—was Robert Burns. The sky of poesy was lonely when he moved to his post in the van of the starry march. But, quick, came Wordsworth, and beamed with a calm planetary light. Coleridge arose and set the east ablaze with splendor. Byron flashed, a glorious meteor, among the celestial train. Scott, another Mars of song, stood suddenly in the northern heaven. The ray of Shelley's star shot, trembling and delicate, from the highest regions of the blue; while the wan, yet beautiful, orb of Keats made its brief circuit near the horizon,—and, heaven upon heaven, rose the hosts of other and scarcely lesser lights. But all these found their pathway made bright and easy; for Burns had traversed it before them. Even into the hands of Cowper, who is the first poet of the revival, had fallen the shabby little Kilmarnock book of the Scottish ploughman's songs. Not one of the others but revered him as a master. Byron declared him the greatest poet, next to Shakespeare, of the language; Keats made a pilgrimage of love to his grave. Fresh and brimming from the fountain of Nature was the cup of poesy which he had brought, and men, thirsty with an age of drought, quaffed eagerly and drank deeply of its crystal contents. . . .

21

All this might have happened, even if the voice of Burns had never been heard beyond his native meadows; but none the less truly did all this follow, in logical sequence, the event of his poet-birth. The new dawn of British poesy reddened upon the shores of morning when he stood beside the Scottish lassie, in the field of the reapers, and the dream of love, born of her blue eyes, rose upon him in the light of beauty and melted into rhyme.

SCIENCE AND POETRY.

From a lecture delivered before the Buffalo Society of Natural
Sciences, 1876.

How is it to fare with Poetry in a world transformed
by Science? Coleridge defined poetry as the antithesis
of science. It is certain that the clear, dry sky of
scientific knowledge is utterly unlike that vague atmosphere of dream and phantasy in which the Muse has
been wont to move and have her being. Her ancient
haunts of tradition and sweet illusion are fast breaking
up. Is there danger that Poetry will be driven to emi-
grate, like wild game when settlers come and clear
away the forests? It is certain that the poets have
not been free from apprehension on this score. Edgar
Allan Poe, from whose *Sonnet to Science*, I have
already quoted a couplet, puts the case thus passion-
ately to the innovator: ' Hast thou not,' he says—

> Hast thou not dragged Diana from her car?
>   And driven the Hamadryad from the wood
> To seek a shelter in some happier star?
>   Hast thou not torn the Naiad from her flood,
> The Elfin from the green grass, and from me
> The summer dream beneath the tamarind tree?

And the same complaint and protest Schiller utters in the person of his Max Piccolomini, in *Wallenstein:*

> The intelligible forms of ancient poets,
> The fair humanities of old religion,
> The power, the beauty, and the majesty,
> That had their haunts in dale or piny mountain,
> Or forest by slow stream, or pebbly spring,
> Or chasms and watery depths ; all these have vanish'd.
> *They live no longer in the faith of reason!*
>
> .   .   .   .
>
> And to you starry world they now are gone,
> Spirits or gods, that used to share this earth
> With man as with their friend.

Leaving the poets, if we should question that respectable oracle, the ' reading public,' I think we should find further ground for alarm as to the prosperity of the Muse. For is it not true that, within a few years, the men of science have furnished most of the reading matter of the people? Moreover, does not the mind, fed with the solid acquisitions of science, or stimulated by its splendid discoveries, grow less and less tolerant of imaginings which add nothing to stock of knowledge, and melodies which convey no information? Our poets ransack the universe for fresh themes, and vie with the india-rubber man of the circus in the agilities of their art; but, at best, the interest they arouse is languid and brief. ' The truth is,' says the admirable author of *The Victorian Poets,* ' our school-girls and spinsters wander down the lanes with Darwin, Huxley and Spencer under their arms ; or, if they carry Tennyson, Longfellow and Morris, read them in the light of spectrum analysis, or test them by the economics of Mill and Bain.'

These things we might regard as the flying scud and spray of tendency which announce a coming wave. And, indeed, there is an impending breaker, dark and threatening enough of aspect, which men already discern and have named.

The scientific hypothesis which finds in matter 'the promise and potency of every form and quality of life'; which announces mind as but an effluence of matter, and man as differing in degree but not in kind from Nature's lowest form; which discovers the genesis of man's loftiest and sacredest ideas in blind movements of the brute, and which, in thus bounding our past, denies our future;—this hypothesis, I say, has already, with various modifications, become a creed. The ablest expounders of the Evolution theory, I believe, are careful to explain that, even if it shall some time pass into the domain of demonstrated knowledge, it will not say all that is to be said of man, his nature and his destiny. But the disciple is generally less cautious than the master, and, accordingly, there is a large and growing class of intellectual men for whom the high-water mark of modern knowledge is a scientific materialism that tolerates no qualification or supplement. I am not here to discuss the merits of the philosophy of Spencer and Darwin; I do not know enough, and, were I a thousand times equipped for the task, I should say, Let it pass to the test of time, which tries all! But, gentlemen, my whole being rises in me when I assert that, if the tremendous assumption of these men shall ever in its entirety become accepted, evident truth, with that time there will come, also, a counter-statement of science which will conserve the spiritual oxygen of our world, and save the souls of men from death by asphyxiation.

It seems to me that a natural history of the poetic faculty and emotion, such as has yet to be compiled, will contribute largely to the affirmation of that other side of truth from which the face of the absorbed observer of material phenomena is necessarily turned. Poetry has its basis in that portion of our nature which is capable of transcending, in its cognitions, the objects of observation and reason. Call this the emotional part of us, or the spiritual, or what you will, or insist that it is but a function, or form of activity, of the invisible mind, and the fact still remains that thereby every man that lives, or with whom history acquaints us, has sustained some sort of relations to that transmaterial sphere which scientists agree to name the Unknowable. This fact, alone, should offer, I think, at least, strong presumptive evidence that man is something more than the merely material animal of whom the naturalist gives his account. But let us see in what manner poetry attests the spiritual nature of man and bears witness of truths beyond the reach of science. And here I am fortunate in being able to quote the words of a writer who represents, perhaps, better than any other American, the scientific school of which Herbert Spencer is the greatest teacher. I refer to John Fiske, author of *Outlines of Cosmic Philosophy*, who, in a recently published essay, sums up the latest dicta of Science as to the universe and its destiny. 'A senseless bubble-play of Titan forces, with life, love and aspiration brought forth only to be extinguished,' is 'the awful picture,' he says, 'which

science shows us,' and before this picture he thus
meditates : 'The human mind, however "scientific" in
its training, must often recoil from the conclusion that
this is all; and there are moments when one passion-
ately feels that this cannot be all. On warm June
mornings, in green country lanes, with sweet pine-odors
wafted in the breeze which sighs through the branches,
and cloud-shadows flitting over far-off blue mountains,
while little birds sing their love songs, and golden-
haired children weave garlands of wild roses ; or when,
in the solemn twilight, we listen to wondrous harmonies
of Beethoven and Chopin, that stir the heart like
voices from an unknown world ; at such times one
feels that the profoundest answer which science can
give to our questionings is but a superficial answer
after all. At these moments, when the world seems
fullest of beauty, one feels most strongly that it is but
the harbinger of something else,—that the ceaseless
play of phenomena is no mere sport of Titans, but an
orderly scene, with its reason for existing, its

> One divine far-off event
> To which the whole creation moves. '

No better illustration could be desired of the mode
in which the poetic sentiment or emotion hints to our
minds the transcendent verities of existence. Gazing
at a lovely landscape, or at some weird after-sunset
play of clouds in the western sky, we are cognizant,
through this emotion, of elements in the scene which
have no record in the books of the scientist. He can
tell us the geology of the distant hills over which our
eyes strain and our hearts yearn; he will easily explain

the laws of light and of atmospheric action in accordance with which the cloud-curtain is hung for a moment between our eyes and immeasurable space; but the vision which has meanwhile been ours remains a secret between the seeing soul and the infinite beyond of which it has had tidings.

The poetic emotion, then, as I must call it, for lack of a better phrase, is that endowment of our nature—possessed in a greater or less degree by universal mankind—by which you and I are enabled to take cognizance of a spiritual side of things,—by force of which come our higher yearnings, ardors, aspirations. The poetic *faculty*, again, is that gift of the poet whereby, entering into the ideal world, he is able to give us report of its eternal facts. And, such is the inherent quality of the poet's high themes, that language must take wings of music in order to meet it and bring it from the heaven of his vision down to men. Measure and melody are the conditions upon which poetic thought consents to be wedded to words.

This emotion, therefore, to which the poet, with his vision and faculty divine, gives voice or makes appeal, is at once an evidence of our higher nature and an impulse to its development. This it is which sometimes causes a flower to bloom at the dusty way-side of life, or fresh fountains to spring in the crossings of the desert. It is the fire of the fly; the glow of the poor earth-born worm. To it, in tones of his own, each of a thousand poets has spoken. In the vision of Homer, we behold human conflict haloed with a heroic light, while gods and mortals meet in middle sky. The world-embracing stage behind which he stands whose poet's eye glanced 'from heaven to earth, from earth to heaven,' and whose pen gave

> To airy nothing
> A local habitation and a name,

shows us the common world of matter and men, indeed, but transfigured and lifted into true spiritual relations. The song of Tennyson equally repeats, above the din of modern life, its part of the immortal harmonies of the 'choir invisible.'

'Beauty,' says Ruskin, 'is the signature of God upon all His works.' This beauty it is the office of Poetry to discover and reproduce in art. The visible heaven and earth are everywhere stamped with this divine seal. But it is not merely, nor chiefly, the earthly beautiful which Poetry sees and celebrates. With the æsthetic sentiment, which takes pleasure in Beauty as she is perceived by the senses, is joined in the human soul an unquenchable thirst for a supernal loveliness. 'This thirst,' said Poe, in his definition of what he named 'the poetic principle,' 'belongs to the immortality of man. It is at once a consequence and an indication of his perennial existence. It is the desire of the moth for the star. It is no mere appreciation of the Beauty before us, but a wild effort to reach the Beauty above. Inspired by an ecstatic prescience of the glories beyond the grave, we struggle, by multiform combinations among the things and thoughts of time, to attain a portion of that loveliness whose very elements, perhaps, appertain to eternity alone.' To Poetry, accordingly, the whole material creation is but a garment of the eternal and infinite Beautiful.

Through the thin and perishable vail of matter she catches glimpses of an inner glory. Stand with her when the out-streaming radiance smites her on the face, and your feet tread almost on holy ground. Not far off passes Religion, and enters in within the vail.

It follows, I think, if poetry be thus rooted in an essential part of our nature, that it is in no real danger of becoming obsolete. Science and poetry will continue to co-exist, and may even become good friends. The dauntless and tireless scientist will not cease to question nature and push outward the lines of physical knowledge; but, on the other hand, he can scarcely make any serious invasion of Poetry's spiritual domain. The tide of materialism, of which we spoke before, will do no harm by driving her to higher ground. And, here, let me forestall possible misapprehension by recording, once for all, my sincere though humble and unintelligent homage to the modern scientific worker, whose arrival among us is a bright omen of our time. Who, before him, has shown a more unselfish, unwearied devotion to appointed duty; a more ready loyalty to truth? If that truth be sometimes a fragment rather than a rounded whole; if, in his rapt contemplation of the material facts of the universe, he fails to do justice to its spiritual realities, let us remember that his very disability is a measure of his self-sacrifice, and that rarely without the payment of such penalties can special study be successfully pursued. That he is willing thus to immolate himself on the altar of his specialty; that his capital of tireless patience and varied intellectual resource are freely spent, if thereby he may ransom a new fact from the unknown, surely entitles him to

the world's gratitude. There is no money in his business, nor much of popular applause. He works for his
work's sake, and only in the consciousness that it will
add something to the common stock of knowledge does
he find or seek reward. We who, without sharing his
toil, are permitted to enjoy its results, should at least
be ready to own our debt. The air is vexed, just now,
with talk of the conflict of science with this and that;
but who needs to be told that, while the theories and
speculations of scientists may well be heretical, the
facts and demonstrations of science can be at war with
no truth? The book of Nature is God's book, and
men cannot study it too diligently nor draw too copi-
ously from its stores of wisdom. Nor do I know how
a man can be honest with himself and towards his
Maker unless he stands ready to prove all things,
holding fast that which is good. The things that can
be shaken, let them fall—the quicker the better—that
'those things which cannot be shaken may remain.'

What is true of truth is equally true of poetry. No
extension of scientific knowledge can ever make the
universe less full of wonder. That knowledge, when
it shall have drawn its widest circle, will still be but a
tiniest islet in the infinite ocean of the unknown.
Around its shores will brood a mystery denser than
that which shrouded the fabled Hesperides. Whatever,
therefore, has been wont to stir the human heart to
poetic emotion is likely still to remain in undiminished
quantity. Nor will the need of poetry grow permanently less. Intellectual concentration demands its
counterpoise in enlargement of the imagination. An
abundance of the bread of prose calls for liberal

draughts of the poetic wine. The world will still need
its knowledge transmuted to wisdom—its facts divinely
set on fire of the muse.

Having succeeded in lodging our Lady of the Lyre
in a place of safety, we may proceed to inquire what
relations Science and Poetry have sustained to and are
likely to establish with each other, and what may be
the prospect of ultimate alliance between the pair.
And, first, we note that the history of scientific progress discloses the scientist frequently in debt, if not to
the poet, to that important element of the poetic faculty
named the imagination. This is, indeed, implied in
what has been already said of scientific speculation
and hypothesis, which result from the effort of the
mind to project its guess, or intuition of truth, in
advance of known facts. 'Science does not know its
debt to imagination,' says Emerson in his last volume.
'Goethe did not believe that a great naturalist could
exist without this faculty. He was himself conscious
of its help, which made him a prophet among the doctors. From this vision he gave brave hints to the
zoologist, the botanist, and the optician.' 'Have I not
sufficient reason to feel proud,' exclaims the great German, himself, 'when, for twenty years, I have been
forced to own to myself that the great Newton, and
all mathematicians and august calculators with him,
have fallen into a decided error respecting the theory
of colors; and that I, amongst millions, am the only
one who knows the truth on this important subject?'
In like manner, as the astronomer Kepler exultingly
confessed, it was a divine guess which gave to the
world his famous laws of planetary movement. 'I care

not whether my work be read now or by posterity,' he
cried.   'I can afford to wait a century for readers,
when God himself has waited six thousand years for
an observer.   I triumph.   I have stolen the golden
secret of the Egyptians.   I will indulge my sacred
fury.'   Manifestly here again we have a poet as well
as discoverer ; who, indeed, discovered by virtue of his
poetic faculty.

But, I think, Emerson to the contrary notwithstanding, the scientists are now ready enough to concede the
extent of their obligations to the imagination.   'The
instrument of discovery in science,' Sir Benjamin
Brodie has termed it, 'without the aid of which Newton would never have invented fluxions, nor Davy have
decomposed the earths and alkalies, nor would Columbus have found out another continent.'   And, 'in fact,'
adds Tyndall, 'without this power our knowledge of
nature would be a mere tabulation of coexistencies and
sequences.   We should still believe in the succession
of day and night, of summer and winter, but the soul of
force would be dislodged from our universe; casual relations would disappear, and with them that science which
is now binding the parts of nature to an organic whole.'

But, even more interesting than the achievements of
the imagination in science, are the anticipations of
scientific thought and discovery to be met with in
poetry.   It is one of the remarkable facts in the history of the human mind that the theory of the constitution of matter now accepted by scientific men is
found projected with wonderful detail in the rolling
hexameters of a Roman poet, who lived a century before
the Christian era.   The 'atom' of modern chemistry,

hunted long and found, at last, in these latter days, in
the dark of its own invisibility, is identical with the
ultimate, indivisible, indestructible 'seed,' or 'shape,'
or 'first-beginning' of Lucretius. From its combinations all forms of matter proceed. 'The whole nature
of these "first-beginnings,"' he says, 'lies far beneath
the ken of sense. Strong in their solid singleness,'
they cannot be worn away, 'though stricken by countless blows through eternity.'   It is true, the atomic
theory is two centuries older than Lucretius, but it is
in his poem on 'Nature' that we find its elaboration,
every leading feature of which science has either veri-
fied, or found to be a foreshadowing of the fact.   Even
the modern doctrines of the nature of force and the
conservation of energy are predicted in this poet's marvelous apocalypse of the mysteries of the cosmic order.

It would be easy to glean from Shakespeare a sheaf of
scientific auguries.   Puck's 'girdle round the earth in
forty minutes' has become a familiar citation in these
days of electric telegraph cables; but here is a less
noticed passage, which is quite as striking as a forecast
of the development theory—natural selection, survival
of the fittest, origin of species, and all:

> Nature is made better by no mean,
> But nature makes that mean : so, over that art
> Which you say adds to nature, is an art
> That nature makes. . . .
>   We marry
> A gentler scion to the wildest stock,
> And make conceive a bark of baser kind
> By bud of nobler race: This is an art
> Which does mend nature,—change it rather; but
> The art itself is nature.—*Winter's Tale.*

In the works of a little known English poet, who died some years before Darwin published, we find a still bolder statement of the latter's theory as it refers to the origin of man. It is Thomas Lovell Beddoes, a man of undoubted genius, though of posthumous fame, who, through a character in one of his tragedies, thus speaks:

> I have a bit of *Fiat* in my soul,
> And can myself create my little world;
> Had I been born a four-legged child, methinks
> I might have found the steps from dog to man,
> And crept into his nature.

So much for the obligations of Science to the poets, and to their peculiar weapon, the imagination. Has Poetry been able to draw from Science her payment of the debt? Thus far, I think, the question must be given a negative answer. The poets do not yet seem able to assimilate with ease the strong food cooked for them in the crucible and retort of the physicist. True, the spread of scientific knowledge has had its influence on recent poetry. The votary of the muse, in dealing with natural objects, is instinctively more truthful in his descriptions than of yore. The flowers with which he decks his verse betray a knowledge of botany that was not always his, and he is careful to refer to the naturalist before committing himself to any statement of zoological fact. Numerous words, phrases, and figures of speech have also found their way out of the laboratory and museum to enrich the bard's vocabulary. Nay, we even see in the newspapers, now and then, a violent attempt to smuggle science, wholesale, through the lines of poetry, as when the enamored scientist calls on his adored 'highest of vertebrates' to alleviate the disturbed condition of his nerve-centers, and in woful numbers tells the chemical analysis of the wasted tissue her unkindness has cost him. But this sort of thing, it will be admitted, does not promise much for the ultimate harmony of Science and Poetry. The truth is, the poets up to this time, as a friend of mine recently remarked, 'have gone to science with the aims of milliners. They have borrowed from her a little finery to ornament their stanzas. To point a comparison, to gild their style, to color their mysticism, are the only tax they have laid upon her.'

From this criticism, two living poets must be cordially exempted, to wit, Emerson and Tennyson. The poems of the former are distinctly imbued with the modern scientific knowledge, albeit the whole mass of it seems to have fallen and melted, as easily as a snowflake, in the all-embracing ocean of the poet's idealism. We need not look for any trace of materialism, at any rate, in a writer who declares that ' the higher use of the material world is but to furnish types to express the thoughts of the mind,' and to whom ' nature itself is only a vast trope.' Yet Emerson tells us how—

> The gentler deities
> Showed me the lore of colors and of sounds,
> The innumerable tenements of beauty,
> The miracle of generative force,
> Far-reaching concords of astronomy
> Felt in the plants, and in the punctual birds;
> Better, the linkèd purpose of the whole.

Here, too, is a strain which an English scientist has taken as a fit motto for one of his profoundest discourses on material nature:

Hearken ! hearken !
If thou wouldst know the mystic song
Chanted when the sphere was young.
Aloft, abroad, the pæan swells ;

.   .   .   .

To the open ear it sings
Sweet the genesis of things,
Of tendency through endless ages,
Of star-dust, and star-pilgrimages,
Of rounded worlds, of space and time,
Of the old flood's subsiding slime,
Of chemic matter, force and form,
Of poles and powers, cold, wet, and warm ;
The rushing metamorphosis,
Dissolving all that fixture is,
Melts things that be to things that seem,
And solid nature to a dream.

If Emerson shows us modern materialism taken up and held, so to speak, in complete solution in his larger spiritualism, no less clearly does Tennyson reflect the turmoil of the two still unharmonized elements. In his early poem of *Locksley Hall* we find him exulting in the scientific conquests of his age :

Mother-Age (for mine I knew not) help me as when life begun ;
Rift the hills, and roll the waters, flash the lightnings, weigh
    the sun;—

.

and later, in the *In Memoriam*, acknowledging the same strong inspiration, he asks himself :

Is this an hour—

.   .   .   .

A time to sicken and to swoon,
  When Science reaches forth her arms
  To feel from world to world, and charms
Her secret from the latest moon ?

But the grand debate of the *In Memoriam* is that carried on between the suggestions of this Science on the one hand and the poet's own spiritual intuitions on the other. Remember how he confronts the idea on which Science would have us place such gloomy stress, of the pitilessness of Nature:

> Are God and Nature then at strife,
>   That Nature lends such evil dreams?
>   So careful of the type she seems,
> So careless of the single life.

But this is not the worst. He has appealed to Nature, and she makes answer:

> ' So careful of the type?' But no.
>   From scarpèd cliff and quarried stone
>   She cries, 'A thousand types are gone:
> I care for nothing, all shall go.
>
> Thou makest thine appeal to me:
>   I bring to life, I bring to death:
>   The spirit does but mean the breath:
> I know no more.' And he, shall he,
>
> Man, her last work, who seemed so fair,
>   Such splendid purpose in his eyes,
>   Who roll'd the psalm to wintry skies,
> Who built him fanes of fruitless prayer,
>
> Who trusted God was love indeed
>   And love Creation's final law—
>   Tho' Nature, red in tooth and claw
> With ravine, shrieked against his creed—
>
> Who loved, who suffer'd countless ills,
>   Who battled for the True, the Just,
>   Be blown about the desert dust,
> Or seal'd within the iron hills?

No more? A monster then, a dream,
   A discord. Dragons of the prime,
   That tear each other in their slime
Were mellow music match'd with him.

Thus far the negations of Science: the replication
is that of an older authority:

I trust I have not wasted breath ;
   I think we are not wholly brain,
   Magnetic mockeries ; not in vain
Like Paul with beasts, I fought with Death;

Not only cunning casts in clay :
   Let Science prove we are, and then
   What matters Science unto men,
At least, to me? I would not stay.

Let him, the wiser man who springs
   Hereafter, up from childhood shape
   His action like the greater ape,
But I was born to other things.

     .   .   .   .   .   .

That which we dare invoke to bless ;
   Our dearest faith ; our ghastliest doubt ;
   He, They, One, All ; within, without ;
The Power in darkness whom we guess :

I found Him not in world or sun,
   Or eagle's wing, or insect's eye ;
   Nor thro' the questions men may try,
The petty cobwebs we have spun ;

If e'er, when faith had fall'n asleep,
   I heard a voice, ' Believe no more,'
   And heard an ever-breaking shore
That tumbled in the Godless deep ;

A warmth within the breast would melt
   The freezing reason's colder part,
   And like a man in wrath the heart
Stood up and answer'd, ' I have felt.'

No, like a child in doubt and fear ;
  But that blind clamor made me wise ;
  Then was I as a child that cries,
But, crying, knows his father near ;

And what I am beheld again
  What is, and no man understands ;
  And out of darkness came the hands
That reach thro' Nature, moulding men.

I have read you so much of this, not alone to illus-
trate the impress of science on the song of the great
poet of our time, but also to exemplify what we have
already asserted as a perennial office of poetry, viz.,
to affirm the spiritual nature of man and give expression to its inextinguishable intuitions. It is plain, I
think, from the brief review we have given, that here,
as at other points of contact, the reciprocal attitude of
Science and Poetry is not yet all that could be desired.
Science, thus far, is aggressive. Poetry struggles to
assert herself among unfamiliar surroundings. For
her it is a period of transition. What prospect, if
any, is discernible of a better understanding between
the twain ?

As we have already allowed two of the poets to
utter their apprehensions of war, I am rejoiced to be
able at this point to introduce two authoritative voices
which prophesy peace. Luckily, too, one is that of a
great poet, and the other that of an eminent living
scientist. It is Wordsworth who has left on record
the words following : 'The objects of the poet's
thoughts are everywhere ; though the eyes and senses
of men are, it is true, his favorite guides, yet he will
follow wherever he can find an atmosphere of sensation

in which to move his wings. Poetry is the first and last of all knowledge,—it is immortal as the heart of man. If the labors of the men of science should ever create any material revolution, direct or indirect, in our condition and in the impressions which we habitually receive, the poet will sleep then no more than at present; he will be ready to follow the steps of the man of science, not only in those general indirect effects, but he will be at his side, carrying sensation into the midst of the objects of science itself. The remotest discoveries of the chemist, the botanist, or the mineralogist will be as proper objects of the poet's art as any upon which it can be employed, if the time should ever come when these things shall be familiar to us, and the relations under which they are contemplated by the followers of the respective sciences shall be manifestly and palpably material to us, as enjoying and suffering beings. If the time should ever come when what is now called science, thus familiarized to men, shall be ready to put on, as it were, a form of flesh and blood, the poet will lend his divine spirit to aid the transfiguration, and will welcome the being thus produced, as a dear and genuine inmate of the household of man.'

So far, the poet, who little dreamed, we imagine, that the time for testing the truth of his remarkable premonition would come, as it has, so soon. And now I quote from Professor Tyndall, one of the broadest and noblest in spirit, as he is intellectually one of the ablest of contemporary men of science. He says: 'The position of science is already assured; but I think the poet, also, will have a great part to play in the future of the world. To him it will be given for a long time to come to fill those shores which the recession of the theologic tide has left exposed; to him, when he rightly understands his mission, and does not flinch from the tonic discipline which it assuredly demands, we have a right to look for that heightening and brightening of life which so many of us need. He ought to be the interpreter of that power which has hitherto filled and strengthened the human heart.'

It is certain that the conditions imagined by Wordsworth are soon to become actual. The vast field of scientific knowledge, with its wealth of new and inspiring facts, its marvelous discoveries, its sublime generalizations, is rapidly becoming the familiar possession of mankind. Into it, as Wordsworth foretold, poetry must straightway enter. The poet formulates and even anticipates his epoch, but cannot stay outside of it. He must ever be the most modern among his contemporaries. The new material of science, therefore, will be woven into the fabric of his loom. 'The milk of science will go to make the blood of the muse.' What novel forms or hues may thus be introduced into poetry, we shall not know till the poet of the future tells us; but some of the influences hereafter to be felt in his art we may perhaps conjecture. That 'tonic discipline,' for example, of which Prof. Tyndall speaks, and which science is so apt to afford, may give us ground for hope. The intellectual sanity which comes from a broad study and clear views of nature must effectually rid the poet of whatever morbid humors now taint his verse. A corresponding enlightenment of his audience, moreover, will compel him to the rejection of whatever is spurious in feeling and thought. He will not, indeed, cease to speak of nature as she reflects herself in his own soul, but he will realize for himself and his race nobler, juster relations to all external things. 'The splendor of meaning that plays over the visible world,' and which it is his to interpret, must increase with the enlargement of his intellectual vision. He will not slight the dire lesson of human littleness which science teaches, as it never was taught before. 'Lord, what is man that Thou art mindful of him,' sang the bard of ancient Israel, and modern discovery gives fresh and awful significance to the strain. But now, even as then, there must await a larger truth to be pealed forth in joyous, sublime antiphony. 'Thou hast made him,' breaks forth, again, the psalmist, 'a little lower than the angels, and hast crowned him with glory and honor.' It will surely be for the coming bard to lift, above the noise of the world's intellectual activity, a new song of spiritual cheer for humanity. To him, as to none of his predecessors, will be given glimpses of the divine wisdom that orders the universe —readings of the eternal runes of nature. Think you that science has exhausted, or can exhaust, the sense of these sacred texts? For myself, I prefer to think of knowledge—of the acquisitions of the intellect— rather as a means to high ends than as an end in themselves. Better than to comprehend the mathematics, is to know the music, of the spheres.

In a word, it remains for Poetry to extend the amplest hospitality to the results of science; to feed her insight with its revelations; to accept gratefully its stimulus, its correction, its inspirations. Science, on the other hand, will recognize a higher knowledge, and learn the reverence that beseems her august office. The sacred vessels of the temple wherein she serves she will handle as priestess, not scullion. Already the signs abound of the advent of this better scientific spirit.

> Who loves not Knowledge? Who shall rail
>   Against her beauty? May she mix
>   With men and prosper! Who shall fix
> Her pillars? Let her work prevail.

But let her know well her limitations:

> Half-grown as yet, a child, and vain,—
>   She cannot fight the fear of death.
>   What is she, cut from love and faith,
> But some wild Pallas from the brain
>
> Of demons? fiery-hot to burst
>   All barriers in her onward race
>   For power. Let her know her place;
> She is the second, not the first.
>
> A higher hand must make her mild,
>   If all be not in vain; and guide
>   Her footsteps, moving side by side
> With Wisdom, like the younger child.

This should be the lesson and end of my discourse, but, if you will allow me to reverse the usual order, having drawn my moral, I will close with a story. It shall be very short:

A few years ago I ascended the famous Mount Etna, in Sicily. Twelve miles of rugged, up-hill driving brought us from the sea-shore to the point on the mountain-side where the serious work of the ascent begins. A little hamlet, named Nicolosi, built of lava, stands here, marking the line where cultivation ends, and above which the devastation of the volcano is perpetual. We arrived late in the afternoon and were to rest till midnight, when the start for the summit would be made. I strolled from the single little inn and sought the house of the venerable savant of the village, Dr. Gemmelaro. He might well be called 'the old man of the mountain.' An accomplished scientist, for fifty years, I think he informed me, he had lived up there, his hand always on Etna's pulse, the watcher of its uneasy slumbers, the historian of its eruptions. He told me much of the volcano and his life-long vigil on its side. At last, leaving the genial old gentleman, I sauntered, full of scientific information, up through the village, and took a view of the region towards the summit. I was visibly on the slope of the mountain, the surface of which in my vicinity was composed of soft ashes, utterly barren and black. Looking upwards, I could see half-a-dozen or more volcanic cones which had been craters in their day, and which rose like little warts on the vast side of Etna himself. The whole scene was one of unspeakable desolation. It realized, somewhat, the dream of science of the ultimate doom of things. Eight or nine thousand feet above, towered Etna, and, while his form was wrapped in clouds and mystery, his seemed a palpable and awful, though invisible, presence. As I stood in the gathering dusk a girl came tripping up from the village and passed me, a lighted lantern in her hand. Curious to learn her errand, I watched her pick her way among the cinder, up the mountain. She stopped at a rude

shrine of lava, which I had not noticed before, and
which rose from a black hillock overlooking the village.
The shrine contained a lamp, which she carefully lit.
She hurried down again and homeward; but the seed
of light she had planted in the dark sprang up and
gleamed like a star. Soon the blackness of the night
came down on the blackness of the mountain; Nicolosi
and a score of villages far below went to sleep, and still
I watched the cheerful glimmer of the maiden's light.
Set at the edge of the awful waste, a simple spark of
human faith and aspiration, it seemed to defy the
horror of the great darkness around it. I remembered
that, in the hidden cloud above, slept the fires of
Etna—that mighty smithy where Hæphestus and
his Cyclopean helpers forged the forces of nature.
But a power higher than nature and stronger than its
merciless forces was that of which the light in the lava
shrine sent its glimmering message. Above the mystery of material nature—yea, out of matter's very
wreck and death—it surely hinted of infinite Life and
Love.

The incident came back to my mind as I sat down
to write of Science and Poetry. I wonder if you will
see in my Sicilian girl any similitude, however faint, of
the poetic Muse, or be willing to concede to Poetry
some spiritual use, such as I have tried to typify by
the lamp in the lava?

Niagara Falls by Winter Moonlight.

From the Buffalo Courier, March 6, 1861.

Nobody chooses the February moon to visit the Falls by; not one in five hundred, we are persuaded, knows anything about the apocalypse which is vouchsafed to him who, in these glorious winter nights, seeks the isle, not of Patmos, but of the Goat.

At least, not a solitary foot but ours creaked in the crisp snow of the island, when we made the familiar tour a few midnights ago. What gloomy grandeur dwelt in that forest fastness, then! What savage music the wind made, moaning through the forsaken wood, and shaking the crystal castanets that dangled from the icy fingers of the trees! How the full moon seemed molten in its brightness, filling all heaven with radiance, and doing with the snow what Shakespeare said could never be done with the lily—that is, painting it with a whiter whiteness. No toll to pay at the gateway; no importunate Jehu to cry, 'Kerridge, sir?' none of the thousand and one devices and traps to catch your loose change; no peddlers and venders, runners and loafers, to wage war upon you, till you cry for quarter, and get it by paying quarters;—nothing of all these—which are the summer complaint of vis-

itors at the Falls—is to be endured, now.   Winter,
with its whip of frost, has scourged the money-chang-
ers from the place, and, in the temple of Nature, built
around Nature's grandest altar, there is loneliness and
Sabbath quiet.

You break the crust of the glittering, crisp snow,
passing through the wood that bars the moon with its
bare maple boughs, or hides it with masses of dark
hemlock foliage, and, at last, you stop and listen.   The
everlasting song of Niagara rises in the night.   It is
high in mid-air when you hear it first,—a column of
sound, as it were, stretching massive and unchangeable
into heaven.   But, standing at the brink, it is the
depth of the din which strikes you.   The thunder of
the cataract seems to boom up out of the earth's very
center, as if from some tremendous, unfathomable fountain of sound.

The earth was quiet with snow, and the heaven was
serene and bright with stars; and wilder, by contrast,
in that dim, uncertain light, seemed to rage the battle
of the waters.   That is the first impression of the
scene—a battle.   Away in the dark arc of the Horse-
shoe is the center of the conflict; above, is a Balaklava,
across which there are wild charges and skirmishings
and retreats,—and in every direction there is tumult
and the mad zeal of battle.   Up from this stormy
chaos, and out of the bewilderment of soul and sense,
rises at last the true conception of Niagara in its might
and unity.   One might think that Nature had ordained
the cataract to be the perpetual embodiment of the
spirit which dwelt of old in the continent, while it was
yet undiscovered by civilization.   The tide of progress

and human empire gradually oversweeps the land, from east to west, but Niagara still breasts the current and is untamed by it.   The solitude of the primeval woods, the wilderness and the savage glory of nature, which have passed away elsewhere, still find a fitting voice and expression in Niagara.

But the moonlight showed us, also, that there is a power which has the audacity to stand in warlike attitude, even against Niagara.   It has built its great mounds of defense at the base of the cataract, and, night by night, has stretched white ramparts around the waters, and reared its gleaming towers, amid the very fury of the assaulting wave.   The moon shone on the icy fortifications, and changed fantastic pinnacles and ridges and cornices of marvelous device to glittering silver, and the feats of oriental magic paled in glory before the work of the enchantment of the frost.

There was another wonder.   It was long before we discovered it,—the spectral child of Mist and Moonlight;   but when we had watched and waited and almost despaired, suddenly the chasm beneath was spanned by the faery arch of the Lunar Bow.   It held its perfect arc of lambent light between two rugged bergs that rose, like piers of the magic bridge, out of the darkness.   So soft, so tender were its half-tinted hues, with such a wan, phantom-like beauty it hung above the war of waters, it was as if Love hovered over the couch of Madness.   They do not yet know all about the cataract who have not seen this strange and gentle offspring of Niagara, bending over the foam and radiant 'with moon-tints of purple and pearl.'

THE GREAT STORM.

From the Buffalo Courier, January, 1864.

Our exchanges for the past few days have come
to us crowded with freezing recitals relative to the
great storm which officiated at the birth of the New
Year.   The cruelest convulsions of nature are more
merciful than those which owe their origin to human
sources, and thus the ravages of frost and tempest over
half a continent will soon be forgotten in the raging of
that more pitiless and protracted storm which sweeps
the national heaven.   Yet the war of the elements
which has just ceased is certainly a phenomenon of
more than ordinary character.   We have not heard,
as yet, from the terrific snow-hurricane while it was
still in its boisterous infancy, but, days before it strode,
colossal, into this longitude, we know that it was stalk-
ing over the prairies, and gathering giant strength in
its gymnastic exercises beyond the Mississippi.

Nursed, probably, among the snows and cliffs of the
Rocky Mountains, it started, about Wednesday of last
week, eastward on its mysterious errand.   Its path was
at least five hundred miles—perhaps a thousand—
wide, and Green Bay and Memphis simultaneously

shivered under its icy breath. Eastward it came,—not so fast as might have been expected, but rather with a sort of stately deliberation, which beseemed its resistless and imperial might. In its stormy march upon Buffalo, the telegraph was nearly two days its herald. Nor was the worst over when all shuddering humanity had recoiled before the furious assault of its vanguard. One, two, three days, and as many nights, came up the howling, shrieking, whirling, rushing and dashing reinforcements of the hurricane. And when one line of tempestuous battle had charged and broken itself on opposing matter, and had passed, not to the rear, but away, wildly again as ever, to the front, the next, bristling with bayonets of frost, and white with banners of snow, was already upon the swift heels of its predecessor. Thus, for three days, as we have said, passed the rushing, impetuous procession of the great storm, and in like manner it seems to have hurled itself still eastward, until its passion was cooled off, most likely, in the Atlantic.

In sooth, the year has had a stormy birth. It came to us out of the very lap of the tempest. But, inasmuch as soothsayers differ as to the interpretation of auguries, we choose to take for a good omen the storm which celebrated the entry upon the stage of time of the young year 1864.

www.ingramcontent.com/pod-product-compliance
Lightning Source LLC
Chambersburg PA
CBHW051123120726
47905CB00005B/1403